# LUCKY no. 5

A NOVEL

## MONICA MICHELLE

NOVELISTA PUBLISHING * NEW YORK

www.novelistapublishing.com

Library of Congress Cataloging-in-Publication Data
2013952653

Michelle, Monica
Lucky No. 5:  a novel/ Monica Michelle. – 1st ed.
ISBN 978-0-9860536-2-7

Printed in the United States of America.
Paperback Edition

*My father. My lion. My friend.*
*My corner has never been lonely and for that my love is unbounded!*
*My Mother. My treasure. My friend.*
*Our laughs are immeasurable, our bond is impermeable and for that*
*my love is incalculable!*

*Thank you!*

# Prologue

**BLASE** felt foolish sitting at the bar in The Living Room on the seventh floor of the W Hotel in Times Square. As usual, Randy was over an hour late for their date. His repeated text messages telling her he should be there shortly added even more insult to injury; especially considering she knew they weren't true. This time, however, the good part about waiting was the handsome young bartender who was mixing her drinks. Noticing her empty martini glass, he flashed his breathtaking smile and asked her if she wanted another French martini. Blase thought for a moment and relented.

"Yes, I'll have another, but this time can you make it a Lychee martini with a splash of Chambord, please?"

The young bartender smiled again and said, "Of course. Would you like one Lychee or two?"

Noticing he was flirting, she rendered a blushed smile and replied, "Two please!"

At that moment, Blase's phone buzzed again. She picked it up and punched in the pass code to unlock. She saw she had another text message from Randy that read: *Baby, I'll be right there, order me a Jack and Coke. :)*

She thought, *Is there really something to smile about? You're an hour and ten minutes late.* Blase sighed as she put the phone back on the bar and decided not to order the Jack and Coke as requested.

The bartender set her new chilled martini glass with two Lychees at the bottom on top of a napkin in front of her. He stood shaking the contents of the martini shaker and asked, "So what's your name, beautiful?"

Blase smiled back and said, "My name is Blase."

"Blaze, like a fire?"

"No. Blase pronounced like lace with a B in front of it, Blase!"

The handsome bartender smiled again and as he poured her martini, he added, "That's a beautiful and fitting name." He began to pour the splash of Chambord into her glass to give the martini a beautiful two-toned color of deep purple on the bottom and a misty white at the top.

Blase nodded with a seductive smirk. "Thank you, it looks yummy!"

He smiled back and stood to wait until she took her first sip.

Noticing his anticipation, she obliged and took a sip. "Mmm, you make a great martini." He winked and extended his hand for a handshake. Blase extended hers back.

"I'm Rafael. It's a pleasure to meet you, Blase," he said with what Blase thought was an unfamiliar accent.

"Likewise, Rafael." Just as they were finishing their handshake, Blase's Blackberry buzzed again; this time with an incoming call. Rafael acknowledged the call with a nod and walked to the other side of the bar to give her some privacy.

Blase answered the phone with a pensive, "Hello."

"Baby, please don't be upset with me, but I have to go home to check on something at my house. Can we meet tomorrow night instead?" Randy asked.

"Are you kidding me, Randolph? I've been waiting here for you for an hour and twenty-three minutes now. I canceled my massage appointment to accommodate your schedule today and you're pulling this crap again?"

"Come on, babe. Don't do this. When we met, you knew my situation and sometimes, unfortunately things like this happen. I have to take care of home first."

Blase calmed herself and thought, *Yes, the Mrs. comes first, of course.* She took a sip of her martini. "You're right, take care of home and I'll take care of Blase."

Randy was quiet for a few seconds because he couldn't figure out if she was being sarcastic or humorous. Either way, he didn't like her tone.

"Blase, baby, I promise we'll see each other all day tomorrow. I miss you, baby."

Blase hung up.

**BLASE** and Randy had been dating just over a year. She met him in one of the Bar Lounges he owned. She was there for a birthday party for one of her Howard University Alumni friends. Randy noticed Blase's smile as she sat and laughed with her friends. He sent drinks over to her and her friend via one of the waitresses. When the ladies looked over to find out who sent the drink and thank him, Blase couldn't help but be knocked back by not only his arresting features, but also his faultless style. Randy was dressed in a breezy cream suit and a cream button down shirt. His monochromatic style was interrupted by his brown leather driving loafers with white contrast stitching and a brown matching belt. He was well manicured and crisp.

Randy made his way over to the sofa where she and her best friend from Howard University, Fallon, were sitting. He stopped and asserted, "I don't think I've seen two women this fine-looking in here, ever." He flashed his brilliant smile.

Blase and Fallon smiled back and Blase replied, "Thank you, and thank you for our drinks."

"You're more than welcome. It was my pleasure. My name is Randolph Bell, but most people call me Randy. And you lovely ladies are?"

Fallon spoke first as she extended her hand. "Hi. I'm Fallon Flynn, nice to meet you."

Randy shook Fallon's hand, but bordered on being rude by continuing his prolonged gaze in Blase's direction. He smiled in acknowledgment, turned to Blase, extended his hand, and said, "And you Miss, what is your name?"

She extended her hand. "Hello, I'm Blase Morgan. Nice to meet you, Randy." As they shook hands, Randy repeated slowly, "Blaze."

"While I have moments where I am a raging inferno, my name is pronounced Blase, like lace with a B in front of it."

Randy held his look of intrigue and said, "That's a beautiful and interesting name. Are you from New York?"

"Yes, I am from New York, but my mother is Ethiopian. In her younger years, she was a very popular model in Europe and she often traveled to Paris for work, so my name is of both African and French origin."

Randy's curiosity was emergent with each word. They were both preoccupied in conversation forgetting Fallon was also sitting next to them. Fallon, noticing the evident chemistry, decided to go and talk with another one of their college friends.

Randy and Blase continued to talk into the wee hours of the morning, despite a few interruptions by his staff members. By 2:00 a.m. Blase decided it was time to head home. She and Randy exchanged phone numbers and he walked her and Fallon to her car. Randy kissed Blase's hand, said a mannerly good night to Fallon, and watched as the ladies slinked into Blase's white BMW 650i and drove off.

**BLASE'S** phone rung again. She knew it was Randy calling back. She pressed talk and held the phone to her ear. Before she could say anything, Randy began speaking.

"Babe, don't hang up. Come on now, you know I want to see you. Let's spend the day together tomorrow."

Blase did a mental overview of her schedule for the next day. "Randy tomorrow is not good for me. I have to see patients in my White Plains office, so I'll call you to reschedule." She took a long sip of her martini and thought, *I'm glad I didn't order his damn Jack and Coke.*

"Ah, come on, babe. We can meet after your patients. I will come up to your place and we can order in. I'm fully staffed tomorrow, so I don't need to be at any of my spots."

Frustrated with the audacity of his insistence, Blase responded, "I'll text you tomorrow if I can make it. You keep your evening free until you hear from me. How about that?"

Randy agreed and they hung up.

The bartender walked over to Blase and told her the gentleman at the other end of the bar was sending her a drink. She looked in that direction and saw a man so dark he almost blended in to the black décor if not for his grey suit. She smiled at him, and he raised his glass at her. She told the bartender she wanted another martini. As he was pulling another glass out of the refrigerator, he held up two fingers and silently mouthed, "Two Lychees?" The volume of the music had amplified in preparation for the influx of Wednesday night city dwellers. She nodded back in agreement and silently mouthed, "And a bottle of water."

While Blase was sipping her final martini for the night, the shadow colored gentleman walked over and said a kindly hello. They exchanged a few words and business cards and he was on his way. Blase went on to watch as the men and women in the bar mingled. The music was a great mix of R&B and Pop. As she eavesdropped on a conversation two women were having next to her, Blase overheard one tell the other she'd just gotten engaged. Her friend hugged and congratulated her. As the engaged young woman pulled away from the hug she told her friend how she basically had to give her boyfriend an ultimatum to get him to propose.

Their conversation continued, but Blase's mind cruised to memories of past loves. At some point in her life, she was told by one of her Psychologist friends that she was what they call a Serial Monogamist. She always had a hassle-free and unintentional approach to her relationships and she had never cared about or given much thought to marriage or children. She lived in the moments of those connections and delighted in them. Though, at thirty-nine, Blase couldn't help but wonder where the years had gone, and if she really wanted to be married with a family. Blase dated some acutely notable men in her life, and she wondered if she'd ever passed up "the one" while she was pursuing her career goals and didn't even realize it.

Blase decided to order one more bottle of water before she left. Opening the bottle, she took a sip and started thinking again. She thought of her two thriving skin care and wellness spas, Melesse Wellness Spa, she'd worked so hard to build and turn into both profitable and highly recommended businesses. She thought of her fetching new three bedroom condominium in Harlem that she was still in the process of decorating. And lastly she thought about how aside from Sugar, her caramel colored Pomeranian, it was twenty-two hundred square feet of bareness. Blase realized she did want a family, but given her bleak relationship status, the only place she could think of beginning was by revisiting her bygones.

# BRAINCHILD

# What If?

**BLASE** woke up at 5:30 a.m. the next morning with a slight headache. Despite her best efforts, she still had a bit of a hangover. Not much of a drinker, she believed the third martini put her over the top. She pulled her butter yellow down comforter and sheets away from her body, sat up, and placed one foot on the brown and white area rug that sat on top of her mahogany hardwood floors. With the other leg still in the bed, she instinctually picked up her cell phone to check for new messages. Blase's dog was still asleep at the foot of the bed. She decided not to read her emails, but checked the two new text messages. The first was from Randy that was sent at 2:00 a.m.: *Please make time for me today. I really miss you babe. Xoxo*

Blase sucked her teeth and moved on to the next message. It was from her childhood best friend Brielle: *The early bird gets the worm. I'm on mile #2, where are you?*

Blase sighed. She forgot she was supposed to meet Brielle at the gym that morning. She touched her screen to reply: *The bird has a broken wing this a.m. Meet u @ Starbucks on 8th for cup #1 @ 7am. Sorry girl!*

She pressed Send and put her phone back on her nightstand.

With both feet now on the floor, she rose, schlepped to the kitchen, opened the refrigerator door, and pulled out a bottle of water. As Blase opened the bottle, she walked to her bathroom, opened the cabinet, and took out a bottle of pain relievers. She twisted off the top of the bottle, poured two pills out and into her hand, and popped them in her mouth. She washed them down with the water and went about her morning.

Since Blase was meeting Brielle for coffee, she decided to check her emails and voicemails before she went to her offices. *Nothing out of the norm in my correspondences this morning,* she thought. Her assistant had virtually updated her calendar of appointments, and she saw that her 9:00 a.m. had been pushed to 1:00 p.m. This was great because it would give her a little more time to tell Brielle about her plan.

When Blase arrived at Starbucks, Brielle was set up at a table in the corner with her laptop open and a bottle of water. She could tell she was busy typing something and having a conversation on her Bluetooth headset. Blase walked to the counter and ordered two grande skinny cinnamon dolce lattes. She brought the coffees over to the table, sat one next to Brielle's water, and one in front of herself. Brielle put one finger up and whispered, "Give me one minute." Blase nodded, took a sip of her coffee, and listened to Brielle's conversation.

"Tony, if you want to be successful in this business, you're going to have to put the work in. Clients won't just come to you, you have to put yourself out there and go and find new clients. In this economy, people are thirsting for financial advice. People are scared about their retirement, how they'll pay their children's tuition, and I don't even want to talk about healthcare. Use your resources and that tremendous personality of yours and go out there and get that business. I believe in you, which is why you are still a part of my team. Listen, my client just walked in, so I've gotta run. I'll call you later to discuss any of your other concerns. In the meantime, stop second guessing yourself and just use your instincts. Good luck at your nine o'clock appointment. Talk soon!"

Blase chuckled. "Damn girl, did you give the poor man a word in edgewise?"

Brielle laughed. "Listen, these young guys come in to this business thinking it is going to be fast money, not realizing as a Financial Advisor, you are asking people to trust you with their money, life savings, and livelihood. It's not a fast food or drive-thru kind of business. Its quality verses quantity sometimes. They start doubting themselves if they don't close certain types of clients. They start bottom feeding just for numbers. Don't get me wrong, numbers matter, but good clients who trust you and provide for a great source of referrals, this means longevity in this business. It's my job as their team leader to be their cheerleader. Heck, I'll even put on a damn uniform and shake some pom-poms if it meant they would meet my financial quotas. Your girl likes to be number one and I will settle for nothing less."

She winked at Blase and picked up her coffee. "Non-fat milk, right?"

Blase gave her a disapproving smirk. "Of course."

After Brielle took a sip of her coffee, she closed her laptop.

"Okay, so what the hell prevented you from coming to the gym this morning? I thought you were on this new mind and body improvement kick. I did drive down from New Rochelle you know."

Blase took another sip. "I went to meet Randy for what was supposed to be dinner and drinks and of course—"

"Let me guess, he had to be with the Mrs.?"

Blase was ashamed. "Yeah, girl. I mean you would think after a year of Brady and a year of Frank, I'd be used to the married man thing by now," Blase whined as she picked up her coffee to sip it again.

Brielle gave her an outright glower. "Blase Morgan, there is nothing about a married man you should ever get used too. Girl, you know I don't judge you, I just don't understand why you put yourself through all of that drama when there are plenty of single men out here. It's not like you only date brothers, so you have options. I mean…"

As Brielle continued on her anticipated sermon, Blase thought of how she secretly knew most people disapproved of her choices in men over the past three years. She hadn't planned to meet any of them. Randy admitted to her on their first date that he had recently married, but he'd only married his wife because they dated for fifteen years and he just felt it was the right thing to do. Blase enjoyed Randy's company on the first few dates, and the next thing she knew it was a year later. Brady, on the other hand, was different from any man she'd ever dated, in that he was the oldest. Brady Cohen was a 53-year-old Jewish CEO of his own private equities firm. She'd met him in a hotel bar while she was at a medical convention. They ran into each other two nights in a row and had unlimited conversation each night. He was an attractive six-foot tall man with dark salt and pepper hair, blue eyes, and chiseled features. He kept himself tangibly fit, but smoked too many cigars for Blase's liking. He had been married to his college sweetheart for thirty years. Brady lived in Colorado so Blase didn't really consider their relationship a real relationship since it was long distance, but it did last a year. The end came when Brady's wife started to notice a difference in his conduct and his trips to New York became stretched with each visit. She decided to have the eldest of their five children surprise him in New York on one of his visits since she lived in Pennsylvania. When Brady's 26-year-old daughter knocked on his hotel room door while Blase was showering, he decided that day he couldn't do it anymore. Fortunately, he was dressed when she knocked, so he answered as if he was walking out the door. He told his daughter to walk with him and then offered to take her to lunch. While they were walking to a nearby

Bistro, he texted Blase and told her what happened. Brady still emails Blase regularly and sends flowers once a month to her office in Harlem.

Brielle continued talking. "….and men on a whole just don't seem to be the way our daddies were, girl…"

Blase thought about the first married man she dated. Frank McKenzie was a banker whom she met at a Black MBA networking event with Brielle. He was an outstandingly handsome man. Everyone at the event seemed to have been drawn to him. He was modishly meticulous and seeped of new wealth. He stood four inches taller than Blase with oatmeal colored skin, dark-rimmed hazel eyes, short curly hair, and a high-pitched nose. Frank asked Blase out that very evening. He complimented her to no end on her wealthy dark complexion and long wavy hair. He'd asked her where she was from because he thought she had such attention-grabbing features. She explained that her mother was Ethiopian and her father was from North Carolina. With her maternal grandmother's soft definite features and her father's profound cherry espresso skin tone and hair texture, Blase was always questioned about her heritage. Most people assumed she had some foreign lineage, but when guessed outright, most people guessed wrong. Her 5'9" height made her an anomaly amongst her peers, but adding to that her complexion and natural black, silky, wavy hair dangling down to her mid back made her look exotic and curious. Her eyes were the color of Brazil nutshells, and her frame svelte but rounded. She was most often asked if she was of West Indian descent.

Frank was awestruck by Blase's beauty. He didn't think black women came in exotic decadent varieties. He grew up in Portland, Maine where his mother was a dainty blonde haired blue eyed woman, and his father was just a shade darker than he. They lived very quiet, reclusive, and secluded lives. His father was a product of a mixed marriage as well. Frank's friends were white and his girlfriends had been snowy women. His wife of 10 years was a frail and bland Australian woman. Frank was unhappy in his marriage, but he didn't want to leave his wife because he believed she'd take all of his money and his children and move back to Australia. Though he lived in New York and lavished Blase with beautiful and extravagant gifts, Blase couldn't get passed his preoccupation with her looks. She believed in the year they dated, he never really liked her for who she was, but rather for being his first African-American dating experience.

As Brielle finished her last thought, she took a sip of her coffee.

"So, I guess I say all of that to say, I think you can meet a good single man, don't you think?"

Blase sipped some more of her coffee. "Yes, I do, Brie. You are so right, but I was thinking, what if I've already met mister right and let him slip right through my fingers. What if I didn't see a good thing while I had him in the past?"

Brielle looked perplexed.

"What I'm saying is I've had five boyfriends in my life, from college until I met Frank. I never really thought about a family with any of them because I was either in school or trying to build my practice. So, what if I missed out on my Mr. Right? What if I let him walk right out of my life because I had tunnel vision?"

Brielle placed one elbow on the table and rested her chin in her palm, completely enthralled with Blase's comments.

Blase went on. "So after Randy basically stood me up again last night, I started thinking, the only way for me to really find the answer is to revisit my past."

"What the hell are you talking about, B?" Brielle responded while shaking her head back and forth.

"What I'm talking about is an idea. Well actually, I have a plan—"

"Which is?" Brielle interrupted as she sipped her coffee.

"Which is…to call my ex-boyfriends and invite them on a vacation with me!"

"Excuse me?" Brielle squealed while putting her cup back on the table. "You mean like the movie Mamma Mia?" She laughed not taking her friend seriously.

Blase laughed also. "No girl. Not all at the same time and same place. I'm talking my five exes, five different vacations in five months to make sure there is nothing that I missed." She winced as she waited for Brielle's response.

Brielle sat in tangled silence. She squinted as if her thoughts would get more progressive with the gesture. Finally, drinking the last of her coffee Brielle responded, "Umm, B they are your exes for a reason, you know I don't believe in—"

Blase shook her head in disapproval and spoke over Brielle. "Yes, but I broke up with all of them. Well, except for Cup I guess, but short of the married men, I've never been broken up with. I still feel like there are loose ends."

"With all of them, girl?" Brielle's response was dry.

"Yes, with all of them, Brie. Keep in mind all is only five for crying out loud. The marrieds don't count. Oh my God, I just realized the whole five thing. You know five is my lucky number! Plus I need a vacation. I haven't taken one since Puerto Rico all of those years ago."

Brielle smiled. "Well overdose on the damn vacations, why don't you! Go big or go home as they say."

They both laughed.

"Lucky number five, huh?" Brielle asked indecisively.

"Lucky number five," Blase responded absolutely.

"Well, have you told anyone else about this ingenious plan of yours?"

"No!"

"Not even Fallon or Sheridan?"

"Not even. No one but you so far, honey. Don't you just feel privileged?"

Brielle smiled and grabbed Blase's hand. "Yes, because you know I'm the only one who would try and talk you out of this Ghost of Christmases past adventure, so I'm surprised, sweetie. But listen, if it will provide you with some resolve or closure—although, won't a damn thing be closed if you are spending time in various tropical locales with them—then whatever makes you happy, girl. I don't have the energy to go Brielle on you this morning. I just used it all up on Tony!" She chuckled while putting her laptop back in her designer laptop bag, and then she looked at her watch.

"Okay, Dr. Morgan. It's time to make this money. I have an 11:30 meeting in midtown."

Blase decided she wanted to stop in her Harlem practice before she met her first client at her new White Plains location. "Okay, Ms. Campbell, let's move. And sorry again about this morning." Blase rose from her seat and leaned in to give Brielle a hug.

They both walked out to the street together.

"Listen don't fly off into the sun without reaching out to me first. I want to know the agenda in case any one of them is bitter and decides to try and off you or something," Brielle said half joking, half serious. She reached in for a cheek-to-cheek kiss.

"Sure thing," Blase responded with a concerned look.

They walked to their respective cars. All that was left for Blase to do was to do it.

# Sister Circle

**AFTER** her last appointment, Blase sat at her desk in her office in White Plains and stared at her laptop screen. She was deep in thought about her plan when her Blackberry buzzed. As usual, Randy didn't give Blase a chance to call him to decide whether they were going to see one another that evening. She looked at the clock and saw that it was 6:30 p.m. She let the call go to voicemail and picked up her office phone to call her Harlem Spa.

"Melesse Wellness Spa," Beth answered in a jovial tone.

"Hi, Beth. It's Blase. Is Sheridan still there?"

"Oh. Hi, Blase. Yes, she is still here. Hold on, I'll transfer you to her. She's in the kitchen." Beth used the intercom feature to announce that Blase was on the phone before she transferred her to the extension.

Sheridan picked up immediately. "Hi, B. How are you?"

"I'm good. We are all set up here. How is it going down there?"

"All is well so far. Juliette has one more appointment scheduled for 6:45. It's a thirty minute reflexology massage. Fumiko left about an hour ago, and Darshana is finishing with her last Botox client now," she responded.

"Okay great. So it looks like you'll be out of there by 7:30 or so?" Blase asked.

"Sure does," Sheridan crooned.

"Okay, well Marta is going to be in with me in the morning, right?"

"Yes. You guys have two clients at nine and 9:30 before the interviews begin at ten," Sheridan confirmed.

"How many interviews do we have scheduled for tomorrow?"

Sheridan checked her computer. "We have two for the masseuse position and three for the esthetician position."

"Okay, are the interview forms, applications, and our company packets prepared?"

"Yes. I've got them sitting on my desk ready."

"Great. I can't think of anything else. Oh, wait; don't forget to tell Maria to wipe down the paintings in the patient lounge. Also wash and refill the glasses at the water station in the lounge and clean out the refrigerator if necessary in the kitchen," Blase reminded her.

"No problem," Sheridan agreed.

Blase admitted to herself recently that with opening a new location, she probably needed to take on a partner who was also a licensed Dermatologist like her or she would soon be overwhelmed. She was getting a lot more new business as a result of a recent article in a popular women's interest magazine. She also wanted to broaden the practice to include plastic surgery.

Sheridan asked, "Do you want me to stop by your place and take Sugar for a walk before I head home?"

"No, I have her with me today. I'm about to pick her up from the groomer and doggy day care."

Sheridan snickered. She thought paying high prices for dogs to sit around in a room with other dogs was a complete waste of money.

"Don't laugh. Actually the day care I found up here is a lot better. They have an agenda of two hours of doggy aerobics and a doggy and owner meet and greet for a half hour. They also have outside recess and play time for two hours, weather permitting, and obedience training for an hour. So the entire day Sugar is active and will be good and sleepy when I pick her up. She is getting her hair and nails done at the end of the day."

Sheridan sat aghast. She shook her head in disapproval of what she insisted was a complete waste of money, but said, "Oh that sounds nifty. Can I go the next time? I need some grooming myself."

Blase chuckled. "Don't be a smart ass. I might just send you to get that red frizzy thing sitting on top of your skull tamed."

Sheridan forced out, "Very funny. Hey can I be one of your children in my next life?"

"You're practically one now. Speaking of children, what are you doing tonight?" Blase asked.

"Well, I'm not making any babies if that's what you want to know." Sheridan changed her tone from cheery to serious. "Why? What's up?"

"Okay, good. Stay where you are. I'm coming to pick you up, and we are going to dinner, on me!"

"Nice," Sheridan said. "I'll see you soon."


**AS BLASE** drove down the New York State Thruway headed for the Major Deegan Expressway to 138th street in Harlem, she dialed Fallon's number from her hands-free device in her car.

*Hi, you've reached Fallon Flynn of Flynn Destinations. Please leave a detailed message and I will return your call within two hours. Remember, before you travel, begin with Flynn.*

After the auto-recording told her to, Blase left a message. "Fal, it's B. If you aren't busy tonight, meet me and Sheridan at Haru Sushi on Amsterdam Avenue between 80th and 81st streets. We'll be there by 8:30.

I've got big news, and it includes you." She left the cliffhanger to evoke some intrigue.

Blase arrived at her Harlem Spa at 7:45 p.m. after having a brief conversation with the sitters at her doggy day care. She noticed the lights on and figured Maria was still inside cleaning. Sheridan jumped in the car and gave Blase a cheek-to-cheek kiss and started petting Sugar. "Hi, Sugar, don't you look pretty this evening," Sheridan said in her baby voice.

The groomer had put a white bow in the top of Sugar's fluffy hair to match her white rhinestone collar.

"I'm ready for a night out on the town," Blase responded for Sugar.

"Is she coming with us to eat?"

"Oh God no." Blase laughed. "I love her but this little bitch is going home."

Sheridan managed a small sigh of relief.

"Plus I just want to change my jacket. I'm going to run up, and I'll be back in a flash," Blase replied. "Was Maria still cleaning when you left?" she asked.

"Yes, she was vacuuming."

Blase pulled up in front of her building and told Sheridan to watch the car until she came back. As soon as Blase and Sugar got out of the car, Sheridan turned the dial to her favorite radio station and started blasting the music. Blase looked back at the car with a scowl. Sheridan noticed and turned the volume back down. Blase and Sugar were greeted at the lobby door by the building's doorman, Max, a rusty, brass colored, elderly black man with silver grey eyes who smiled greatly and always listened to everyone's problems. More often than not, many of the building's residents could be found standing in the lobby chatting it up with Max about, well, absolutely nothing, and everything at the same time. Without knowing anything about Max's background, you could tell he was a well-read man since he seemed to know a little about everything anyone talked with him about. Max would console you if you needed comfort, motivate you if you needed inspiration, and just be quiet if he couldn't determine what you needed.

"Good evening, Dr. Morgan." Max smiled as he spoke.

"Good evening, Max. How are you today?" she asked.

"I'm doing very well, thank you for asking. And how are you and Miss Sugar doing this beautiful evening?"

Blase looked down at Sugar who was wagging her tail with excitement after seeing Max. "Sugar just came from the beauty parlor, so she's doing a lot better than I am. Makes you wonder who's really in charge here." She grinned.

Max beamed his reassuring smile back and said, "Oh, Dr. Morgan, you have a package here. Let me get it for you." He went behind the contemporary grey lobby guest desk and opened the cloudy tempered glass door to the mailroom. He entered and exited within seconds with a small package for Blase.

She thanked him and dashed to the elevator. While on the elevator, she surveyed the small box. It had her address on it, a bunch of international stamps, and the address of her Sayt Ayat in Ethiopia. When she realized it was a gift from her grandmother, she smiled and got a bit misty eyed. She hadn't visited her grandparents in Addis Ababa, Ethiopia in a few years. It was time to go back as they were getting well on in age. As the elevator doors opened to her floor, she decided she would open the package later when she returned from dinner.

# LUCKY NO. 5

Blase opened the door to her condo, and Sugar set out running in search of her white squeaky bear toy. Sugar grabbed the toy as if her day was too long without it. Blase dropped her bag on the entry table and briskly strode into her bedroom where she hurriedly changed into a lazy dark blue sequenced jacket to top her heather grey jersey dress and black tights. She also changed from her comfortable work shoes into her dark blue patent leather designer pumps. Blase went into the bathroom to check her hair and make-up and misted her signature perfume on as a refresher. She quickly brushed her teeth and was set. She grabbed her wallet clutch out of her workbag and her house keys and made her way back to her car.

When she walked out of the building, she said thank you to Max for holding the door. When she arrived back at her car, Sheridan was sitting in the passenger seat chitchatting on her cell phone. Blase got in the car, turned the radio down even further, and started the car back up. They were parked and standing in Haru at exactly 8:30 p.m.

The hostess seated them and gave them their menus. She asked if they wanted to start with something to drink. They decided to start with a large bottle of hot Sake and some Edamame. They both picked up their menus and browsed for what they wanted to order. Blase took the opportunity to talk with Sheridan about whether she was still happy as a personal assistant. Though they had become close friends, Blase never asked her about her career goals and Sheridan never seemed to talk about any, other than what she was doing.

Blase put her menu down and said, "Okay, so we've been a team for about seven years now, right?"

Sheridan kept surfing her menu and said, "Yep, sure have."

"So, I was wondering—"

Just as Blase was about to ask her, she heard a familiar voice say, "Did you think you were going to leave me that cloak and dagger message and I wouldn't show up?" It was Fallon. She was using a voice that was a bit too loud inside the restaurant as she walked towards them from the door. Both Sheridan and Blase turned and saw Fallon flouncing toward them wearing a silk burnt orange, purple, and cream colored V neck dress, a milk chocolate brown woven belt with milk chocolate platform heels, and an oversized envelope clutch mimicking the color of her belt and shoes underneath a three quarter length cognac colored mink coat.

At 5'5" with wild curly hair, Fallon always dressed as if she stepped right out of a designer fashion show; probably because of her inbred wealth, and because of her petite frame, finding unique designs was uncomplicated.

Fallon sat down in one of the two empty seats at the table after greeting Blase and Sheridan with air kisses. "Hi ladies," she said through an angelic smile.

Blase looked at her and said, "Hi ladies, huh? Where are you sauntering in from, looking like the cat that ate the canary?"

"Oh, I was meeting with a client down the street at the Shark Bar over a cocktail. He's a promoter planning a huge MBA networking cruise and he wants Flynn Destinations to book it and my father's hotel to be one of the sponsors," Fallon answered as she motioned with her eyes for the waitress.

Before anyone could respond, the waitress was there. "Can I help you, miss?" the waitress asked timidly.

"Hi, yes. I'll have a small bottle of chilled Sake please. Did you guys order Edamame?"

They both nodded. The waitress took her order as a table runner brought Blase and Sheridan's hot Sake and Edamame to the table.

Blase said, "Sounds interesting. Do we know this promoter?"

"No," Fallon answered. "I've never met the man before and strangely he knows a ton of people who we went to school with and a few of Sergio's investor friends."

"Hmmm," Blase returned with an inquisitive look on her face.

"But anyway, enough about work. What's with the double-o-seven message?" Fallon questioned.

"Okay, well since you are both here, I'll just get on with it," Blase said. As she was finishing her last word, the waitress came over with Fallon's chilled Sake and asked if they were ready to order. They all nodded and ordered their meals.

After the waitress took their orders and walked away, Blase continued, "Last night I was out waiting on Randy…" the ladies sighed in chorus.

Blase gave them a jaded look in return and continued "….and of course he had to go home and take care of his family."

"What a surprise," Sheridan wisecracked while picking up one of the Edamame pods.

Blase shot her a bothered look, ignored her remark, and said, "So I took the time that I had at the bar to think about my future. Meaning what I really want in my romantic life."

This peaked their interest. They both sat listening keenly.

"Fallon, you've been around throughout all of my relationships, and Sheridan I know you've heard about the ones you weren't around for. Well, I think I've had some great relationships. I think me not being ready for the next step is the reason why most didn't work out. It made me wonder what if. What if I would've put forth a better effort in my relationships? Would I be married now with children as opposed to spending my energy with the married men that I've dated in the past three years?

"You both know I've been very busy working on the Melesse Spas and as a result, have been meeting men in the strangest places, but I don't know why over the past few years I've only been meeting and attracting married men."

Fallon interjected, "Maybe it is the energy you are giving off."

Sheridan shook her head in agreement and said, "Better an idle house then a bad tenant."

Blase and Fallon looked at Sheridan with confusion. Sheridan was known to rattle off random sayings her Irish grandmother used to say. She looked back at them as if her proverb should have made perfect sense to them.

Blase picked up some sushi with her chopsticks as she continued. "Well, that could be it, but I am really wondering if one of my exes was the one. I was telling Brielle what my thoughts and plans were this morning. She thinks I'm crazy, but c'est la vie."

"Of course she does," both ladies said at Brielle's judgment.

Fallon stared at her friend with complete astonishment when she was explaining to her what she was going to do. Sheridan looked equally as baffled.

"But do you even have any feelings for any of these men anymore?" Sheridan inquired.

"Also, do they have any feelings for you?" Fallon added. "Okay, so explain this to me again. You're calling all of your ex-boyfriends and

28

inviting them away on separate vacations to see if there are any coals that were left smoldering you may have overlooked? Have you contacted any of them yet?" Fallon questioned.

Blase knew this news would come as a surprise and she was fully prepared for the rainstorm of questions. "Well no actually. None of the relationships ended on bad terms though. Well, maybe Miller, but they are all single as far as I know. I did hear Adrian may be in a relationship, but I will soon find out either way," Blase answered back.

"So, which ex-boyfriends are we talking about here?" Sheridan inquired.

"I've only had five boyfriends in my life, Sher, so all of them. Five vacations over a five month period. I have no idea where it will lead me, but spiritually this is the direction I want to go in right now," Blase contended.

They all continued to eat their sushi from the enormous decorative boat it was served in. Blase picked up a piece of crunchy spicy salmon roll and dipped it into soy sauce while Sheridan and Fallon did the same. They were all silent for a few moments eating and pondering Blase's decision.

Fallon broke the silence. "Well, girl, you have done so many amazing things in your life so far, it's time for you to think of you. I don't know how you're going to pull this off, but I'm looking forward to the stories and emails about it."

Blase sincerely smiled at Fallon feeling happy she didn't offer resistance or judgment about her idea.

"Me too," Sheridan added. "But what about your practice and your patients? And, well me?"

Blase touched Sheridan on her arm and said, "Don't worry. You will still have your job, Sher. I actually was going to talk to you about that before Fallon walked in. How would you feel about a promotion?"

Sheridan's eyes lit up and she stopped putting the kamikaze roll in her mouth as she was intending. "A promotion? Like as in more money?" she delightedly questioned.

Blase chuckled. "Well yes. We can discuss that, but it would also mean more responsibilities. I would need you to manage both locations, overseeing all of the staff and the daily operations of the business short of seeing clients."

Sheridan was excited at the thought of being the manager of a medical practice. "Nice," she responded.

"I will, however, have to find a Dermatology partner to take on new clients while I am away."

"That is a process that is going to take you a while, I'd imagine," Fallon alleged.

"Actually, do you remember Tracey Steele who went to college with us?" Blase asked Fallon.

"Vaguely. Was she a Business major?"

"No, she was a Biology major with me. After we graduated, she moved to California and started working with a Cosmetic Surgeon and she went on to become a Dermatologist and Cosmetic Surgeon herself," Blase informed them.

"Oh wow. Have you guys kept in touch all of this time?" Sheridan asked.

"No, actually not all of this time. She was in New York about a month ago and she had lunch with a mutual HU alum and she told her I have the practices. She looked me up and we've been talking via email since. She just got a divorce and she and her two daughters are looking for a change," Blase informed as she continued to eat.

Sheridan spoke, "So will I like this Tracey woman? I mean ultimately she will be my boss while you're gone, right?"

Blase shook her head. "I'm only going away for 10 days out of each month, so I'll still be your boss. She is going to hire her own assistant to keep her schedule. I plan on continuing to see patients, but Sheridan I'll need you to be iron clad with my scheduling to make sure there are no mistakes with booking while I'm away. Do you think you can handle managing and being my assistant until June or so? Then I can hire and you can train another assistant."

Sheridan nodded.

"Tracey will be doing cosmetic surgeries in the White Plains practice so essentially it will be an expansion and ideally an enhancement of the practices," Blase confirmed. "Beth will still manage the front desk of the Harlem Spa and we will hire someone part time for the front desk of the White Plains Spa," Blase added.

"Oh," Fallon released. "My niece is looking for some part-time work. She's very professional."

Blase said, "She's hired."

They all laughed.


**BLASE** felt breaking the news to the ladies was far less complicated then she thought it would be. They all knew who her ex-boyfriends were, so it wasn't like she had to introduce the idea plus the men to them.

The waitress came over to ask if the ladies were okay. They all nodded and Blase asked, "We are great, but may we have more hot and cold Sake please?" The waitress bowed and quickly walked away to retrieve their drinks. When she arrived back, she poured Sake into all of their cups and walked away again.

Fallon lifted her cup and told the other ladies to do the same. "Here's to my darling friend Blase whose ideas never cease to amaze me. Get your groove back girl!"

They all clinked their cups and laughed in unison.

"But Fallon, I still need to discuss the vacation packages with you. I will call you in a few days to set up a meeting to put it all together."

Blase drove home pleased she didn't get any negativity or judgment from her friends. As she pulled into her garage, she remembered her grandmother's package. She thought maybe she could incorporate one of her trips with a visit to her mother's country in Africa. The question is which one would she take on that trip? When she arrived at her apartment, Sugar ran to the door when she heard the keys jingle in the lock. Blase immediately picked her up and started petting and nose kissing her. She put Sugar back down and kicked her shoes off underneath her entry foyer table.

While heading for her bedroom, Blase listened to her cell phone messages. There was a message from Randy. *Hey babe, I was hoping we could get together tonight, but I guess you had to work late. Call me back when you get this message. I can always try and stop by for a late night dinner or an after dinner night cap.* Blase immediately erased the message and went to the next. *Blase this is Tracey Steele. Please call me. I want to discuss the partnership opportunity you mentioned via email. Let's schedule a dinner meeting. I'm available this week Thursday or Tuesday or Wednesday of next week. 415-555-2121.*

Blase replayed the message and jotted down the number for safe measure. She also saved the message. The next message was from her mother telling her, she and Blase's Aunt Bernice wanted to see a Broadway show on Saturday of that week and they wanted her to join them. Blase thought it was a great idea. She'd been meaning to see FELA on Broadway for a week or two, but Blase and her friends hadn't been able to coordinate their schedules with the opening of her new spa location.

She scribbled a note to herself to go online later and buy three tickets to the show. The next few messages were from different business associates, another from Randy, and finally one from Brady asking her if she'd received the flower delivery that month and telling her he missed her kisses. She smiled and erased all of the messages. Blase decided to run herself a bubble bath. While her bath was running, she sat down at her computer in her home office and shot Fallon a quick email with budgets for each vacation, and then she ordered the tickets for the Saturday afternoon showing of FELA. Blase sent a quick email to Brady thanking him for the flowers as well as the voicemail message. She added that she missed his smile and clicked Send.

Blase looked over and noticed the package her grandmother sent to her. She turned off her bath water before grabbing the package to unwrap it. She was surprised to see a CD with a photo of her grandfather on the front. The note accompanied was an invitation written in Amharic, which read that her grandmother and aunts were throwing her grandfather a 95th birthday party in June and she must attend. Blase opened the disc holder and realized it was a DVD. She popped it into her computer and saw it was a video montage of her grandfather. Immediately upon seeing photos of her Wund Ayat, Blase began to tear up. She couldn't stop smiling as she put the note next to the other notes she'd scribbled.

Before Blase got into her bubble bath, she poured herself a glass of Pinot Noir so she could sip while she settled her mind on how she was going to contact her exes and whom she was taking where. She put one of her Jazz discs in the CD player to play throughout her home's surround speaker system. As the sounds of Fourplay floated through the air, Blase lit a few of her lavender scented candles and slid into her garden style Jacuzzi tub. She let out a long and much needed sigh. She rested her head on her terrycloth pillow, picked up her glass, closed her eyes, and removed everything else from her thoughts as she began to hark back in time.

# BYGONES

# College Bound

## 1988

**BLASE** walked on the campus of Howard University sporting an asymmetrical hairstyle like her favorite female rapper Salt from the popular rap group Salt-N-Pepa. She donned a pair of blue acid washed jean shorts, a white t-shirt, and white high top Reebok sneakers. Her parents followed behind her carrying some of her luggage and concerned smiles. Blase, however, was enchanted. Growing up in the New York suburb of New Rochelle was fun, but having gone to private school for the majority of her life, she wasn't used to seeing so many people of her own skin color in one place. Her eyes were fixed on all of the different shades and fashions. The music shouted from the car stereos, and it was then she knew for sure she was ready to be on her own and live like a young adult.

Her parents took her to her freshman dorm and dropped her bags in her room. Her roommate hadn't arrived yet, so she took the liberty of choosing her bed and claiming her side of the room. After making a few trips to her parent's SUV, they managed to unload all of Blase's things in her room. Her mother attempted to get her settled while her father roamed the campus double checking to make sure it was properly secure. Given most Historically Black Colleges and Universities are located in low income neighborhoods, security was marginal at best, but some of her father's relatives had graduated from Howard so he was comfortable with leaving his baby there for what would be the beginning of the rest of her life.

As Blase tearfully watched her parents drive away, she couldn't help but start to feel a bit apprehensive about it all. She hadn't met her roommate. Would she like her? Would she be successful as a Biology major? Would she make her parents proud? Her older brother had successfully graduated from college and was on to getting his Juris Doctorate degree. She certainly wasn't the first in her family to go to college and vowed right then she wouldn't be the one to disappoint anyone in her family, most of all, herself.

Deep in thought, Blase didn't even notice the guy standing next to her watching her stand there with her hand resting on top of her head after she'd stopped waving to her parents. Adrian Goodwin watched Blase thinking she was the most beautiful girl he'd ever seen. It said a lot because he was from New Orleans, Louisiana which bred some of the most beautiful sisters in the country. But Adrian thought Blase's dark complexion complimented his toast colored skin perfectly. Adrian stood 5'11", a mere two inches taller than Blase. His ocean blue eyes made him look like he was from some other country or of Creole extraction.

Once Blase came out of her muse induced trance, she turned to her side and looked flustered. She asked, "Why are you staring at me like that?"

After hearing her voice, Adrian lost his words.

She repeated with aggression, "Hello? Why are you standing there staring at me like that?"

Adrian found his voice. "Oh dang, well I just think you are a pretty little lady!"

Blase looked deeper into his eyes and heard his southern drip and was herself at a loss for words. She was so used to men with hip-hop vernacular and cantankerous New York accents that hearing someone whose voice was so dissimilar was an allure in and of itself. She raised her hand. "Hi, my name is Blase. What's yours?"

He extended his hand and took hers to kiss it. "Adrian Goodwin. I'm from Nawlins. Where are you from, Blase?"

She giggled. "Nawlins? Where is that? Is that in this country?"

He chuckled with her. "Yeah, baby, it's in Louisiana. It is properly pronounced New Orleans, but we natives say Nawlins."

She giggled nervously again. "That's cute. I like your accent and your eyes. I'm from New York."

"Yeah I can kinda tell the way you said York with the emphasis on the r and the k."

"Well you're good then, because most people can't figure out where I'm from because I was raised speaking English, Amharic, and Swahili."

He looked her up and down. "Amharic and Swahili? Where yo people from?"

She laughed at his southern accent again.

He held, "Ah'ight, I ain't gone have too much ah yo laughin' at my accent now." He grabbed her hand to hold it.

She peered down, but didn't pull away and looked him right in his eyes. "I think it's real cute. My mom is from Addis Ababa, in Ethiopia, so she taught me Amharic which is a language they speak there, and while she traveled the world, she learned French and Swahili and taught me that too. Actually she taught me and my dad."

"So ya peoples are from the motherland, huh? That's where you get that beautiful complexion of yours, huh?"

She blushed and replied, "No, actually my mom is like the color of, hmmm, I guess cinnamon and my dad is like the sky just after winter's midnight."

"Wow! Well I don't care who you get it from, girl you fine as hell. Can I walk around with you for a while or will I cramp your sty—"

Before he could finish she agreed, "Sure you can walk with me!"

They walked around campus checking out all of the buildings and talking until it was dark outside. Adrian walked Blase back to her dorm and kissed her on the cheek. She smiled and her heart blinked. He asked her if he could meet her for lunch the next day at the Punch Out and with a wide eyed grin, she agreed.

By the second month of their freshman year in college, Adrian and Blase were an item and everyone knew it. The guys were a bit different than they were back in the suburbs of New York. They were from all over the country, so they weren't as color struck about her complexion. Blase got a lot more attention than she was used too because of her silky, dark, long hair and her lithe shape. Adrian made it clear to everyone that Blase was his lady with public displays of affection everywhere they went. He would show up at her dorm with flowers and dedicate songs on the campus radio station. They were pretty much inseparable unless they were in class.

During the summer break after their freshman year, they visited one another as often as possible, but Blase was doing an internship at a local hospital and Adrian was working for his eldest brother at his law firm. Both seemed to have their eyes on the prize. She was considering becoming a doctor and he would follow the other Goodwin men and become a lawyer. When they returned to school to begin their sophomore year, they both were just a little different. She was back to being immersed in her New York hip-hop culture and he in his New Orleans Jazz and Blues. But again, they melted right back into one another's worlds. They spent the better part of their first semester telling the details of the summer they'd missed out on. While their school curriculums grew tougher, their time together seemed to grow more and more effortless and enjoyable, until right before the Christmas holiday.

Blase woke up one morning feeling a pain she'd never felt before. She leaned forward in her bed until she felt the pain again. When she felt it a third time, she couldn't help but let out a thin whimper. It was loud enough, however, to wake her new roommate, Fallon.

Fallon raised her head from her pillow and with her eyes squinted she asked, "Hey, girl. Are you okay?"

Blase looked over at Fallon and couldn't speak.

Noticing the discomfort in Blase's face, Fallon pulled back the covers, got out of bed, walked over to her friend's bed, and sat on the edge.

Blase finally answered with another, more expressed moan. She grabbed Fallon's hand. "I don't know what is going on with me," she whined. But secretly she had a feeling she did know. She asked Fallon to call Adrian as she worked on getting out of the bed. When she pulled the covers back, both she and Fallon looked horrified at what they saw. A plash of blood had formed under and around Blase's shorts. Both girls didn't know how to react at first until Fallon came out of her disbelief and told Blase to lay back down. Blase was terrified. She calmly asked Fallon to call Adrian again and ask him to meet them at Howard University's Hospital.

Even though Blase was in pain, the girls walked to the hospital arm in arm with swiftness. Blase could hardly see through her river of tears, but managed to pull herself together once they entered the emergency room. Blase checked in, was immediately ushered onto a gurney, and to the first available emergency room cubicle.

Adrian was in a deep sleep when the phone rang. He quickly answered it so as not to wake his roommates, and when he heard the news and the tremors in Fallon's voice he was frozen with fear. After he heard Fallon yell for him to hurry, he jumped out of bed and threw on sweats and sneakers to meet them at the hospital.

The ER doctor entered at the same time Adrian did. The doctor looked at him and said, "Can I help you, young man?"

Adrian was panting and sweating from his run to the hospital. He replied, "Yes sir, this is my girlfriend. Is she okay?"

The doctor responded, "I don't know yet but you should go wait in the waiting area until after I talk with your girlfriend."

Adrian asked, "Can I stay here with her, sir?"

"Not right now. I will send someone to get you."

Adrian walked over to Blase and kissed her on the lips and consoled, "I love you, and I'll be right outside. Okay, Lace?"

She nodded, kissed him back, and whined, "I love you. Thank you for coming."

As Fallon was walking out, she thought for a minute of all of the guys she'd met at Howard who seemed to be the complete opposite of Adrian and was happy for her friend.

The ER doctor confirmed what Blase suspected. She was having a miscarriage. He told her they were going to run some diagnostic tests including blood tests and an ultrasound. Once the tests were done, the doctor told Blase, "You will need a D and C, which is a Dilation and Curettage of your cervix to remove any remaining tissue from your uterus."

"Will I still be able to have a baby someday?"

"You shouldn't have any problems with that because you are young, but you will want to talk with your regular OB/GYN about it."

"Okay, thank you. Can my friend come back in now?"

"Yes. I'll tell her to come in."

Fallon walked back into the room just as Blase silently began to cry. Blase cursed herself for slipping and not using condoms at times and for messing up her birth control pills.

Adrian sat in the waiting area anxious and worried. He had no idea what was going on, so he feared the worst. *I can't lose her right now. That's my baby. She's going to be my wife as soon as we graduate.*

Blase looked at Fallon and asked her to go tell Adrian what was going on so he wouldn't worry. When Fallon reached the waiting room, she saw Adrian sitting with his right leg bouncing up and down with his head in his hands. She sat down next to him and offered, "Hey, B is okay, Adrian." She grabbed his hand to calm him down.

He looked at Fallon. "Well, what's wrong with her?"

"I would prefer her to tell you, but she wanted me to come out here and tell you that she is fine and it isn't life threatening."

He breathed a slight sigh of relief. "Can I go in there yet?"

"Not yet. They just have to give her one more procedure and then I'm sure the doctor will let you go be with her. I'm going to go back in, but she's going to be fine, okay?" She gave him an encouraging look.

He shook his head and sat back in his chair. As he grasped the sides of the chair, he looked up at Fallon and said, "Come back and get me as soon as I can go in, ah'ight?"

She nodded and walked back to Blase's room.

After the D and C was performed, the doctor told Blase, "After you leave you may experience some cramping and still a little bit of bleeding, so wear a sanitary pad until the bleeding ceases. You may also experience some nausea and/or vomiting. Each case is different. Do not under any circumstances use a tampon and do not have sexual intercourse. I would advise you to go on some type of birth control, young lady."

Blase nodded shamefully.

"You can stay here until you feel up to walking back to your dorm, but since school is letting out next week, you will need to go see your doctor back home for a follow up visit," he advised.

She nodded again.

"The nurse will be in to issue you your discharge papers, but again you don't have to leave until you feel up to it." With that he walked out.

Blase immediately asked Fallon to get Adrian.

Adrian walked in looking panicky.

Fallon decided to leave to give them some privacy. "I'll be outside waiting when you're ready, girl," she said.

"Thank you, Fallon." Blase blew her a kiss. She reached out for Adrian and he came in for her requested hug. He hugged her so tightly he forced her tears to savagely stream down her face. "Baby, what's going on? What happened?"

"I had a miscarriage, A. I was pregnant," she mumbled.

He pulled back from her and started whipping the tears from her eyes. "Oh baby, I'm so sorry." He hugged Blase again as he started to cry.

Blase was a bit shocked because she'd never seen him so emotional, but the fact that he shared in her hurt and angst was reassuring and welcomed at the same time. They sat there holding each other until they both stopped crying. Then they held each other in silence. It was then that she realized she wanted to spend the rest of her life with Adrian. To her he showed conviction by not only standing by her, but allowing himself to trust her with his vulnerability. They continued their embrace, but he broke the silence. "I want to spend the rest of my life with you Lace. I love you, baby."

She whispered, "I do too, A, and I love you."

AFTER that incident, they moved in with one another for the second semester of their sophomore year without their parents knowing it, and they grew even closer and stronger together. They were "the" couple on campus no one could come between. No matter how many men flirted with her, Blase only had eyes for Adrian, and no matter how many women threw themselves at Adrian, he only had eyes for Blase. They both decided to take summer jobs in Washington, D.C. to stay together, while convincing their parents it was to do something different to help with their studies for their junior years. They began living like a married couple.

Fallon had decided to stay in D.C. to be her father's assistant on his first Hotel development project. She rented a two-bedroom apartment in the same building as Adrian and Blase and continued to date one of the football players from the Washington Redskins who'd graduated from HU the year before. Whenever Blase's parents would drive down to visit, she pretended like she was living with Fallon and would stay there until they left. She knew her parents wouldn't approve of her living with a boyfriend at 19-years-old.

They all continued their living situation in to their junior year. Life was love for them. By the beginning of their senior year, Blase and Adrian began to get restless with one another. The intensity of their school curriculums was getting to them. The anticipation of what would happen after graduation started plaguing both of their minds, and they began to bicker. At first they bickered about nonsensical things like what to watch on television and what to eat for dinner that night, but towards the beginning of the last semester of school the bickering started turning into full on arguments. Yelling matches.

"Lace I want to go out with my friends. I am with you all day, every damn day. Why the hell can't I go out with my homeboys without you questioning it?"

Blase was stunned. "Are you serious? You said we were going to the movies, Adrian. Don't act like I stop you from hanging out with your friends. I've never done that to you. What the hell is wrong with you today?"

"You!" he screamed. "You're walking around here acting like we are married. Hey, when we graduate I'm moving back to New Orleans to go to Law School."

Blase stood there in the living room blindsided. They hadn't discussed what they were going to do after they graduated, and she just assumed he'd do the right thing and propose like she thought he would. She hadn't even given any thought to what she was going to do after they graduated because she thought it would be a collaborative decision. She was wrong.

Looking at Blase for a reaction, Adrian stood cemented in his position. He looked in vain. Blase turned, grabbed her jacket, and walked out the door. She knocked on Fallon's door and asked her to take a ride with her. They got in Blase's car and left. They parked in Adam's Morgan and decided to walk and talk. After walking around the Nation's Capital for three hours with her best friend, she'd made up her mind on what she was going to do.

When she returned home, she told Adrian she respected his decision and she wished him luck. She told him she was moving out at the end of the month and moving in with Fallon. She felt like there was no need to prolong the inevitable. If he was that unhappy with her, she certainly wasn't going to force him to live with her for the remainder of the school year.

It was Adrian's turn to stand in stunned silence. He'd spoken in haste but didn't know how to fix it. Their communication drifted so far out to sea there was no reeling it back in.

Blase said she would start packing that weekend. Once she was moved out, Adrian felt alone and foolish. He did love Blase and did still want to be with her, but was just confused.

Adrian and Blase decided to continue to see each other but live in separate residences to give each other their space. After graduation, at her celebratory dinner, however, Blase broke the news to Adrian that she was moving back to New York and had been accepted to New York University's Medical School.

"Adrian, when you made the decision to make a move with your life without including me in it, I realized that I too could be limiting my possibilities by not making any decisions without you. After I moved out I had my mother pick up all of the medical school applications and I retook the MCAT just to be comfortable with my scores. I applied in December and was accepted in the spring. I figured since you were going to law school in New Orleans I'd go home and continue my education there."

Adrian felt silly. He felt silly for blurting out he was going to law school in New Orleans when he not only hadn't taken the LSAT exams yet, but hadn't thoroughly made the decision. Most of all though, he felt silly because in his right pocket was a one carat engagement ring. He did want to marry Blase and spend the rest of his life with her and thought she wanted the same. "Well congratulations, Lace. I'm happy you got accepted. We are still going to see each other, right, or do you have other news for me?" he asked tightly.

She shook her head and went on with her dinner. At that moment, her parents came over to where they were sitting and asked Adrian if he was excited about law school. He said, "Yes Mr. and Mrs. Morgan, but I'm more excited about the news that Blase was accepted to medical school."

Blase's mother looked confused and asked, "Oh, are you just finding that out tonight?" She looked at Blase with a bit of a frown.

"Yes ma'am, I am, but I guess we all have to stay focused if we want to get ahead in life," he said as he politely excused himself from the table while Blase looked on expressionless.

# Medical School

**AFTER** the graduation dinner, Blase and Adrian didn't see each for the entire summer. Adrian finally broke down and called Blase to ask if he could come to see her. She agreed. She met him at LaGuardia airport at his airline's baggage claim and immediately noticed he looked changed. He appeared a bit more mature, she thought. It was because he'd grown out his beard and mustache and cut his hair short. She liked his new look.

Adrian stopped as he approached Blase to give her a once over. He'd missed her, more than he cared to admit. She walked toward him and they embraced as if time hadn't escaped them. He leaned back out of the hug. "I missed you, Lace." His drawl was smothered in gumbo.

Blase laughed. "Wow, you sound more Nawlins now then you did when I met you!"

He smiled back as he picked up his bags. "Oh don't you start on me now. You are looking nice, fit, and refreshed. New York does your body good, baby."

Blase blushed feeling proud of her healthy eating and exercising over the summer.

When they reached Blase' apartment at NYU, Adrian asked, "Are these your school's dorms?"

"No silly. My parents bought an apartment for me so I don't have to deal with any roommate or dorm room distractions while I'm in school. It was one of my graduation gifts."

"Nice! Hell I have to live at home with my parents while I decide what I'm going to do."

"What do you mean, while you decide what you're going to do? Aren't you in law school right now?"

He sat down and realized he had no choice but to admit to his false outburst. "Naw, Lace. Sit down, baby."

She obliged by sitting next to him on her sofa.

Adrian took Blase's hand into hers. "Back when we were living together, I really don't know what was going on with me. I hadn't even taken the LSAT, let alone applied at any law schools. I was feeling nervous and stressed about our future, and I guess, truth be told, I got cold feet about our future so in a moment of I guess temporary insanity, I blurted out what I did. After I did it and I saw the look on your face, I knew I couldn't just take it back without consequence. I figured when you came back from wherever you went you'd want to talk, but when you came in and said what you said, I still couldn't admit it. I guess it was my pride at that point. So I let it go on."

Blase sat in silence.

"At graduation, when you told me you were accepted to medical school, I really didn't know what to do. Do I ask you not to go when I didn't even have a plan? Naw baby, I couldn't do that, so I just kept it quiet and allowed you to finish what I'd started. I still love you with all of my heart, Lace, and I still want to spend the rest of my life with you." Adrian pulled the ring out of his pocket and knelt down on one knee.

Blase jumped up from the sofa with her eyes swelling and her hands frozen at her sides. *Is he really about to do what I think he's about to do?* She couldn't move.

"Blase when I first saw you on campus I thought you were the most beautiful women I'd ever seen in my life. When I saw you at the airport today after not seeing you or speaking to you for four months, I still thought you were the most beautiful women I'd ever seen in my life. Our time together and our bond as far as I'm concerned is still unbreakable and I know now, more than ever that you are the woman I want to be with, to have my kids, and to grow old with. Blase Melesse Morgan, will you marry me?"

Blase was silent but crying. This is what she'd dreamed of, this is what she wanted, and this is what she expected—a year ago. But now, she wasn't sure. During the summer, Blase and Fallon were hanging out and partying to get it out of her system before she started medical school. Fallon's boyfriend had been traded to the New York Jets and Fallon moved to New York to be with him.

Adrian stayed kneeled down waiting for Blase's response, but to his disappointment, he realized she wasn't prepared to say yes. She was still silent and unable to say anything.

After she moved out, she felt like she lost her best friend. Though they remained an intimate couple, her spirit was broken about their relationship and what she deemed as his betrayal and lack of consideration for what they built. For that, she resigned to taking it as a sign to date other people when she returned to New York; which is exactly what she did when she met Mark Rodriguez at a mutual friend's house party two months earlier.

Adrian's face went from joy to pain in an instant. He climbed up off his knee and stood in front of Blase. "Do you love me, Lace?"

"No, I mean yes. I mean, Adrian where is this coming from? We haven't even spoken in four months. Why would you do this right now?"

"What do you mean right now? Hell, I figured now was the best time since I didn't do it when I planned to at the graduation dinner."

She looked even more twisted. She tilted her head to the side. "Graduation dinner. Wait, what are you talking about?"

He turned and walked away from her. "Lace, I was about to ask you to marry me with this very ring at our graduation dinner when you told me you were accepted to medical school. I'd gotten your parents approval and everything."

She was dumbfounded. Neither of her parents had ever mentioned it. "When you dropped the medical school bomb I decided it wasn't the best thing to do because I wasn't sure if it was something you wanted to do considering what you'd planned. I talked with your parents again and told them I would give you time to get settled here and I would ask you at a later date."

"What?" she yelped. "Do my parents know that you are going to ask me to marry you during this trip?"

"Yes, Lace, they do."

Blase started rambling something in Swahili. She turned, looked at him, and said in English, "Adrian I can't marry you. I can't do the boyfriend/girlfriend thing right now, much less the fiancé thing. Right now, I just want to focus on medical school and that's it."

Adrian was wounded. He felt as if Blase had taken a scalpel and stuck it directly into his heart. He picked up his bags and walked out the door...and out of Blase's life.

**BLASE** called her parents the next day after she was able to process everything that happened. She asked them why they hadn't told her about the proposal and they insisted it wasn't their place to interfere in her personal relationships. She was hurt, but she understood their position. Her parents had been married for 25 years and were still going strong, so she trusted their wisdom. Blase hung up with them and called Fallon to tell her what happened.

Fallon couldn't believe it. "Are you sure letting him leave was the right thing to do, B? I mean you've only known Mark for a few months and he's not exactly the most polished guy you know."

Blase responded, "I am sure. I mean you know how I was after I moved out. I was a wreck even though I put on a good front in front of Adrian and everyone. He could never imagine how much he hurt me."

"Well this was your opportunity to tell him how much he'd hurt you. Why didn't you?" she asked.

"I guess I just couldn't. I don't know. I just couldn't." Blase's voice trailed off leaving the air around her reticent.

"Well, airlines always sell tickets, B. If you change your mind, you can always go down there and get on your knee." She jabbed.

"Oh hell no I won't. There will not be a time when Blase Morgan asks a man to marry her. Never!"

"I hear that, girl. Are you alright?" Fallon consoled.

"Yeah I'm good. I'll call you tomorrow."

"Okay."

They hung up.

Blase sat in her living room staring at the ceiling reflecting on the last four years of her life she'd spent with one man. The one man who broke her virginity and she thought she would spend the rest of her life with and now after he'd done exactly what she was expecting, she didn't want it. At that moment, her phone rang, startling her. She answered quickly. "Hello."

"Belleza, ¿cómo estás?"

Blase smiled. A voice she wanted to hear in a language she wanted to hear it in. "Hi, baby. I'm great now. How are you?"

Mark responded, "I'm good. Why did you say now? Qué pasa?"

"Nothing. Just some crazy family stuff. What are you doing right now? I need a hug. Are you in my area?"

Mark said, "I'm always in your area, whenever you need me to be, Belleza. I'll be there in ten minutes."

Blase was excited. When she met Mark Rodriguez at her friend Marie's house, she first noticed his flawless build. He wore a button up shirt that fit his chiseled body so perfectly it almost seemed painted on. His pants were equally as tight and she loved it. Mark stood six feet even with wheat colored skin that had a buttery intensity. He was a Puerto Rican born and Spanish Harlem bread New Yorker who worked for DHL. He often switched between Spanish and English when they were together because he knew how much she liked him to speak Spanish, and he would often ask her to speak Amharic or Swahili to amplify his fascination with her.

When Mark arrived, he held three roses in his hand. "Hola, Belleza. Dame un beso."

She didn't hesitate to kiss him. Mark was so different from Adrian. He was more affectionate, sexual, and completely uninhibited. He was eccentric with a street edge. She enjoyed the difference. He wore his hair curly and just long enough for Blase to run her fingers through it, and he always smelled of an unfamiliar cologne with a hint of Dial soap. Having grown up partially in Puerto Rico and partially in a low income housing community in Harlem, Mark was the complete contrary of Blase. She found his life and childhood intriguing.

Mark, however, was a bit intimidated by Blase's suburban upper-middle class upbringing and education, but he also thought she was the most absorbing and worldly woman he'd met for their age. He was impressed she was going to medical school, but wondered why she would want to be with a broke Puerto Rican from Harlem.

After a long, passionate kiss, she pulled Mark into her apartment and they immediately began peeling each other's clothes off. Blase pulled Mark's t-shirt over his head to expose his confident chest and perfectly defined arms. Mark picked Blase up with one arm and laid her down on her sofa. He unbuttoned her jean dress as she ran her fingers through his silky hair. He kissed her neck and continued kissing her until he reached her bra. He pulled one side down with his teeth and began softly licking her breasts. Mark put one arm behind her body so he could pull her even closer to him. When he did, Blase instinctually arched her back to mend her body with his mouth. He looked down at her and whispered in her ear. "Dame tu cuerpo, Belleza."

She looked at him with a sultry look of confusion.

He said in a thick Spanish accent, "Give me your body, beauty."

Blase whispered, "It's yours, baby."

They made slow, steady, and sensual love for the next hour. When they were finished, Mark kissed Blase on the side of her lips. "I'm starting to think you only like me for my body, Belleza."

Blase chuckled. "Well, I do like that you always deliver my package on time when I need it."

He laughed.

"No, seriously," she said. "I enjoy your company, Mark. You're a breath of fresh air."

"That's a first. I'm a little nervous with you, Belleza. You have everything going for you and I'm just a package delivery guy."

She quieted him with her fingers. "Let's just enjoy each other. Who cares what I do or you do. Plus, right now I'm a struggling medical student. I haven't completed school yet. Don't jinx me, Papi!"

Mark laughed. "Do you want to get something to eat?"

"Sure."

"Okay, I'm going to go get us something to eat. I'll be right back, rápidamente."

She kissed his lips. "I'll be waiting."

When Mark left, Blase felt vivacious. Mark made her feel like she was an exotic sex goddess. He touched her in places she'd never been touched and made her feel ways she'd never felt before. During their first oral sex experience, Blase climaxed instantly. It was something she'd never experienced with Adrian. Adrian would have to be down there forever to make her rapture. She wondered if all Puerto Rican men were as sexually advanced as Mark. He was indeed her best lover. But then again, she'd only been with Adrian in comparison.

When Mark returned, he had Arroz con Pollo, Tostones, and Flan for two, with two large fruit punches. Until she met Mark, Blase hadn't eaten much Puerto Rican food, but her appetite for it and Mark was ever increasing.

Mark and Blase made love and ate Puerto Rican food on a regular basis for the next year and a half. They went to the movies on occasion, but for the most part, they just enjoyed each other's company physically when

Blase had a break from school. Mark wasn't demanding of her time or his position in her life. He just enjoyed being with her and felt honored she'd fallen for someone like him. He would always bring three flowers— different varieties of flowers, but always three. For their one-year anniversary he gave her three of 12 different varieties of flowers, 36 all in one beautifully assembled bouquet. The most gorgeous bouquet she'd ever seen. Mark's photo albums were filled with pictures of Blase, encouraged by what he thought was her unique beauty. With the bouquet of flowers, he presented her with a photo album of their time together for the past year and he also showed her the photo album he dedicated to photos of solely her. Mark had fallen in love with Blase; true love that had covered him like a second skin.

ONE evening Fallon invited Blase to a party her boyfriend was throwing for his teammate at their home in New Jersey. Blase was a little tired and had promised Mark she was going to spend some time with him, but Fallon insisted. She teased that if she didn't hang with her that night she'd never speak to her again. A threat Blase knew was bogus, but she conceded nonetheless. She told Mark she'd forgotten Fallon invited her to a party and she had to attend, but assured him they'd see one another the next night. Mark, always amenable, didn't mind at all.

Fallon told Blase to dress exceptionally cute and to leave the conservative medical digs in the closet and break out one of her sexiest dresses. When Blase arrived at the party she donned a multi-colored Coogi Sweater dress with bare legs, black leather strappy heels, and a black leather bag. Fallon answered the door and looked her friend up and down and gave her the thumbs up. Fallon was dressed in a pewter Versace mini dress with pewter and crystal strappy heels.

"Girl that's what I'm talking about. This is the party for that dress," Fallon sang.

"Oh yeah. How so?"

"This party is for Melvin's teammate Miller who I want to introduce you to."

"Why? Girl, I'm perfectly happy with Mark," Blase opposed.

"Girl, you need to get out of that one man show routine," Fallon said sarcastically.

Blase huffed. "You're one to talk. Haven't you and Melvin been together since the beginning of time?"

"Yeah, but Melvin never worked for DHL. Step your game up, Blase. Enough with the Latino delivery boy. You're about to be a doctor, girl. You need someone who will be on or above your future pay grade."

Blase couldn't believe her friend was being so shallow, but after a few moments of thought she realized Fallon had come from a family of wealth, so she wasn't at all surprised. "Whatever. Well I'm here so let's get this party started, but make no mistake, I will be back doing the Latin hustle tomorrow night!"

Blase and Fallon laughed together and gave each other a high five.

Just as they were clapping hands Melvin walked around the corner with Miller Jones by his side.

"Hey, babe, we were just coming to look for you," Fallon said to Melvin.

"Hey, babe," he responded while kissing Fallon on the cheek.

"Melvin, aren't you going to introduce your friend to my friend?" Fallon suggested.

Melvin smiled. "Oh, of course. Ehy Dawg this is Fal's best friend, Blase. She's of African suburban Westchester royalty and shit." He hollered.

Miller looked confused but looked Blase up and down and exclaimed, "Oh word? How you doing, Blase? Can I be your African king?"

Blase thought the whole scene was quite worn but she played along anyway. "It depends on if you know how to treat a Queen." She was being coy.

As they were exchanging witty banter, one of the servers walked by with a tray of flutes of champagne. Miller grabbed two glasses and offered one to Blase. "How about we start this way; a toast to the new King and Queen of the night!"

Blase couldn't hide her smile. She looked at Miller with a seductive grin and said, "Cheers!"

"Hell yeah! Cheers! Where are y'all's glasses at? Y'all gotta toast the King and Queen too!"

Fallon and Melvin grabbed two more glasses and they all toasted the evening. "Cheers!"

For the rest of the night, Miller monopolized Blase's time. They talked, and she actually did find him to be a captivating gentleman despite his all sportsman facade. Miller was a true southern man from Jackson, Mississippi and much like a lot of athletes she'd met or read about, he was raised by a single mother. He went to school at the University of Pittsburgh on an Academic scholarship and walked on to the football team after playing in High School for fun. He was so good at football that he was drafted into the NFL before his senior year at U of Pitt. He went into the

NFL, but finished school during his off season and received a dual degree in Math and Communications.

Blase listened to Miller easily and without grandiose tell her about himself, and she felt drawn to him. She was indeed attracted to him, but truly she was fascinated with his life story. Miller had younger twin sisters who suffered from depression, but because his mother was an old school southern black woman who didn't believe in addressing and treating depression, she ignored it and told them to focus on something else and made them join their high school's cheerleading team. They both reluctantly joined and in their cheerleading uniforms one afternoon, they committed suicide by getting high and jumping off the Mississippi River Bridge together. Miller welled up with tears when he told the story of his sisters. He turned his head, wiped his tears, and wondered why he felt close enough to Blase to reveal this story so soon after meeting her. He added that he started a foundation in their honor to advocate for the awareness of depression in children and adolescents in the Black community. And during the off season he travels around the country and tells the story of his sisters to high school kids and hopes they will reach out to him so he can point them in the right direction for professional help. He told Blase after he'd searched for his father, he found that his father suffered from depression as well, and it ran in that side of his family, but no one acknowledged it. His father ended up becoming an alcoholic drug addict and was still out on the streets despite his efforts to help him.

Blase was enthralled. She was flabbergasted at how purposeful Miller was when he spoke and how considerate he was when he asked about her life. He kept refilling her glass with her permission. He seemed genuinely interested in her African and Southern ancestry and equally as interested in her pursuit for her medical degree. By the time they realized it, the sun was starting to come up as they sat near the fireplace in Melvin and Fallon's great room.

Miller said, "I hope you're staying. I know there is an empty bedroom for you in this big ass crib of theirs."

That was the first slang she'd heard him use in the past few hours. "Yes, Fallon sets me up in the guest room around the corner. I hope no one has taken it."

"Well if they did, I'll kick their asses out. Or, you can always come and stay at my place. I live about ten minutes from here."

Blase looked at Miller for a few moments in silence, and he looked back reassuringly.

"Do you have a guest bedroom as nice as the one they have set up here for me?"

He smiled at her consideration. "I have four guest bedrooms, so you can take your pick, Chocolate."

She smiled at his reference to her complexion; particularly since he was as chocolate as she was. Miller had the total athlete's body. He was a wide receiver for his team positioned at 6'2" with a lean but muscular build and an ideal derrière. His smile, while handsome, seemed like it wasn't his original. It looked like he had some major dental work. She wondered what he looked like before he bought his Hollywood smile.

Blase took a leap of faith and decided to go to Miller's house. She hoped and prayed that because he was a friend of Melvin's he wasn't a wolf in sheep's clothing. They both got up and walked to say good-bye to Melvin and Fallon who were in the kitchen talking with a few other late lingerers. Fallon looked at Blase when she told them she was going to stay at Miller's house and if her room was available she could offer it to another guest. Melvin smiled at Miller and gave him a handshake goodbye. Fallon hugged and kissed Blase and whispered, "Wear a condom, fast ass!" She smiled at her slyly. Blase grinned back and shook her head.

As they pulled into the driveway of Miller's house, Blase felt a bit apprehensive. She wondered if Miller expected her to have sex with him because she opted to go home with him.

Miller noticed the tension on Blase's face and reached for her hand to comfort her. "Don't worry, Chocolate. I'm not *that* guy. You have a bed and free reign of the house and that's it. I enjoyed talking to you and getting to know you, so I wouldn't ruin it now. I know ball players get a bad rap, but you're safe with me."

Blase breathed a sigh of relief and gripped his hand tighter. All of his chivalrous talk was actually turning her on. She was glad she'd put a few condoms in her bag, just in case. And then, for a split second, she thought of Mark, but was quickly jarred from the thought when Miller opened her passenger door. He reached for her hand and helped Blase out of the car. Miller took the overnight bag that Blase took from her car at Fallon's house, and they walked hand in hand from the garage into the kitchen of Miller's four thousand square foot home. Blase first noticed his gourmet refrigerator with dual glass doors. She thought her fridge would never be neat enough for her to have glass doors. She was impressed at how meticulous Miller's refrigerator was and asked, "Do you have a housekeeper?"

He looked over at her a bit confused. "Yes, I have two women who come twice a week to keep this place in order. Otherwise, it would be a mess in here. Why do you ask?" He put her bag down near the breakfast island in the kitchen.

Blase sat at one of the breakfast island stools, took off her heels, and said, "Because your refrigerator alone makes me feel like a complete slob."

Miller laughed. "Well, I am a bit of an extremist when it comes to keeping this place clean. My mother raised me to be very tidy so I can't live in chaos. But I've earned the right to have someone clean it for me. Are you hungry?" he asked as he took fruit out of the fruit chiller in the fridge and put it on a plate on the breakfast island.

Blase thought about it for a minute and asked in her most seductive voice, "Are you hungry?"

At this, Miller smiled. He walked around to Blase and lowered his voice and asked, "Kiwi?"

She whispered, "I'd love one, if you'll share it with me."

Miller was completely turned on, but knew he didn't want to take it to that level yet. "Girl you are trying to get me in some trouble tonight."

She responded, "No, I'm trying to get us in some trouble tonight."

Miller liked her slight aggression.

"Are you telling me tonight makes any difference from tonight a month from now?"

Miller looked taken aback. He contemplated her comment for a moment and said, "I guess you're right. I just don't want you to think I'm one of those typical guys, because I'm not."

"Well then I'll just take advantage of you and tomorrow, let's hope we'll respect each other when we wake up!" Blase didn't know if it was the two bottles of champagne they shared or his southern appeal, but she was acting completely out of character and had no reservations about it. She felt liberated taking the lead. She walked over to Miller and stood on her tip-toes and asked, "May I kiss you?"

Miller wrapped his arms around Blase's waist and pulled her close to him and kissed her. She draped her arms around his neck and the kiss went from a small fire to a raging inferno. Miller lifted Blase off of her feet and sat her on top of the breakfast island. He pulled away and looked into her eyes. "Do you still want the guest room?"

"I have a feeling your bed will be a lot more comfortable," she whispered with a pale pant.

Miller didn't think twice. He grabbed Blase, wrapped her legs around his waist, and they kissed all the way to his room.

Blase and Miller both woke at 1:00 p.m. that Saturday. They lay in bed and talked until four, and then Miller ordered take-out for them to eat downstairs in the living room. Dressed in the sheet from Miller's bed, Blase sat in her favorite Indian style position on the living room floor with chop sticks eating Udon Noodles while Miller sat across from her with his back leaned against the sofa eating Beef Negimaki. He'd opened another bottle of Champagne and they sat talking for an hour before Miller moved all of the food aside, untied Blase's sheet, and ate his dessert. Blase was euphoric. She tried not to think of what would happen after she left, but instead, she enjoyed the moment.

By 8:00 p.m., they were both back in bed and fast asleep. Blase woke up at midnight and realized she hadn't maintained contact with anyone in the outside world since 5:00 a.m. that day, most of all Mark. She slithered out of bed and went downstairs to check her two-way pager. She reached into her bag and noticed her condoms, none of which she had used. Fortunately, Miller had a drawer full of his own. She pulled her alpha –

numeric pager out and saw she had ten missed messages. Six of the messages were from Mark and the others were from Fallon and Brielle. She read the message from Mark. The first few were just I miss you messages from Friday evening. Saturday morning his messages showed more unease asking her if she was okay and to send him a message back. His messages ended in panic. He was ready to drive out to New Jersey to Fallon's house to make sure she was okay. Before she sent him a message back, she checked her messages from Fallon. There were two. The first was telling her she was proud of her for living on the edge a little, and the second was to let her know Mark had stopped by around noon to see if she was there. Fallon told the housekeeper to tell him they had gone to the mall because Blase's car was still in the driveway.

Blase cursed and replied to Fallon's message thanking her for covering for her. She told her she was alright and having the time of her life. She then replied to Mark and told him she was sorry she didn't respond to his messages, but in the chaos of the party, she'd temporarily lost her pager. Within seconds of her sending the message, Mark replied and asked her to call him. Blase looked at her pager and knew she couldn't call him from Miller's house. She sent him an alpha message and told him she was driving and would call him when she got back into the city. He told her to call as soon as she got to her apartment and he would come over. Blase cursed again. After responding "*Okay,*" she threw the pager back into her bag and ran back upstairs.

When she reached Miller's room, he was lying with his hands behind his head. "Is everything okay?"

"Yes, everything is fine. I just realized I hadn't communicated with anyone since I laid eyes on you, so I had to go and make sure everyone knew I was okay."

"And would there be a man included in that everyone?" he probed as she climbed back into bed with him.

She was honest. "There is a man that I was seeing casually. Nothing serious at all, so yes, he did send me a message."

Miller didn't look surprised at all. He turned on his side to face Blase. "Well, tell homeboy that he just got cut, and Miller Jones just took his starting position!"

Blase smirked. "How do you know you took the starting position? Suppose you're not finished trying out for the team?"

Miller laughed hard at Blase's flirting. He grabbed her to pull her closer but she stopped him.

"Let's take a shower. I haven't showered since yesterday."

"Ah'ight, but after I put in one more workout, then we'll hit the showers."

Blase giggled as he leaned in for a kiss.

By Sunday afternoon, Blase was exhausted and quite frankly in love. Miller was not only charming and a great lover, but he was educated, gorgeous, and rich. She was a bit afraid of what would happen once she left, but he assured her he took his starting position very seriously and worked hard to stay there.

When they arrived back at Fallon's house, she was sitting on the back patio watching Melvin and a few of his other teammates acting silly and dancing to Snoop Dogg's rap album Doggystyle. Miller and Blase walked to the back and immediately started laughing. Melvin was a massive linebacker, and one of the silliest members of the team so he always kept Fallon amused.

"Hey, girl, glad to see you're still alive," she kidded as she hugged Blase.

"Of course she's alive, and she's glowing. Can't you see it?" Melvin responded for Blase.

Blase couldn't argue, she was beaming. Fallon pulled Blase to the side and asked, "Did you speak to Mark?"

Blase looked over her shoulder and back again. "No, not yet. I was supposed to call him when I got back into the city last night. My pager hasn't stopped going off since two this morning. Miller knew it was him and that my pager was going off. He told me to let it go because that dude is history, but I can't just do him like that. I'll talk with him when I get back to the city."

Fallon looked back at Blase with compassion and they both walked back over to the patio table and sat down to have some Lemonade.

By the time Blase made it back to the city it was almost 9:00 p.m. on Sunday night and she had to prepare for a long week of school. She wasn't really prepared to have a conversation with Mark so she blew him off and told him they would have to talk later in the week, but she preferred the weekend. She also wasn't ready to come down off the Miller cloud she was floating on.

The next Saturday morning, Blase waited for Mark at a local diner. She figured meeting in a neutral place would make it easier on both of them. Mark showed up with three red roses. He was nervous. He knew something happened when she went to that party but was hoping it wasn't what he thought it was. He smiled as he walked in Blase's direction. She stood and they hugged, but his return hug was as if she had just come back from a month long trip. She held on to his embrace until he was ready to release because she genuinely did care for Mark. When he finally eased out of the hug, they both sat down at the same time, and he reached for her hand from across the table to hold.

"Belleza, I missed you, mami. Is everything okay?"

Blase could hardly look Mark in his eyes. "Yes, of course it is. I just had a long week with school, and this weekend I have so much catching up to do. Are you ready to order?"

Mark noticed Blase's inability to look at him and his body descended into the booth. He knew this wasn't going to be a happy reunion. "Belleza, did I do something to upset you? I know I sent you a lot of pages but it was only because I was concerned about you."

"No, Mark, you didn't do anything to upset me. I guess right now my mind is pre-occupied with school work."

Blase looked at him, choked back tears, and abruptly said, "I don't think this is going to work out between us. I need a break."

Mark's heart sprinted. His mouth felt like it was filled with flour, and he couldn't say a word. He was hoping she wouldn't say that. Blase was everything Mark wanted in a woman and more, and in one breath she shattered his heart into pieces. He'd always thought she was out of his league, but he did everything in his power to make her happy, but he estimated he just wasn't good enough.

Mark finally spoke. "I will give you a break. As much space as you need; but please tell me this is really just a break and you're not leaving me for good."

Blase's tears began to fall. She was heartbroken that she was breaking his heart. "No, Mark, this is just a break. I promise I need time to study, and I am not leaving you for good."

Mark got up from his side of the booth, slid into Blase's side of the booth, and hugged her tighter than he did when he greeted her. After he hugged her, he kissed her on the lips. "Te amo la Belleza. Por favor no te olvides de mí." With that, he got up and walked out of the diner. He was too choked up to sit there any longer.

Blase sat in dismay. She couldn't believe what she'd just done. She was hoping she'd made the right decision—Miller.

**MILLER** and Blase became a serious item. Every moment she had outside of medical school, she was with him. They traveled together and he lavished her with expensive gifts. In her second year of medical school, he purchased a new apartment condominium on New York's Upper East Side for her, so she rented out her co-op near the university to another NYU student. Though Blase had some difficulty balancing her personal life with her schooling at times, she believed it was all worth it. She was enjoying her life with Miller and relished in no regrets. After Miller casually mentioned marriage, they decided to look at rings together while they were on a trip to Aruba during the beginning of her summer break before her final year in school.

As Blase and Miller's relationship grew stronger, Fallon and Melvin's relationship finally came to an end. Fallon caught Melvin with another woman and tried to forgive him, but just couldn't recover from it. She moved out, and Melvin bought her a townhouse in Fort Lee, New Jersey. Melvin tried unsuccessfully to win Fallon back, even proposing, but Fallon wouldn't allow herself to live a life with a man she knew could and would cheat on her. Her belief was a leopard doesn't change its spots.

Mark would often call Blase to check on her, and she would assure him she was doing well and she wished him well also. Mark made efforts to see Blase, but she refused, telling him it would be too much of a distraction.

When Blase graduated from medical school, Miller threw her a huge surprise graduation party at the Tavern on the Green in New York City. He told her they were going there for dinner. He arranged a horse and carriage ride to the restaurant and when they arrived, Blase walked in to 60 of her family members and closest friends, including his principal party planning assistants Fallon and Brielle. Blase was moved to tears when she walked in to the restaurant, but stopped in her tracks when she looked to her right and saw Mark walk in with a dozen roses, four different colors, three roses per color and a gift box. Somehow, he'd gotten wind of the party and decided to show up not realizing it was her boyfriend who threw her the party.

When Mark saw Blase standing hand-in-hand with who he knew to be one of NFL's most fêted wide receivers he looked defeated and walked out. He believed her when she told him it wasn't for good. Every single time.

Blase, not being able to show emotion for Mark at the time, continued to smile and hugged Miller for putting the event together. Miller hired a band and even flew in all four of her grandparents. At the end of the evening, Miller and Blase stood side by side with two flutes of champagne in their hands while they watched their family and friends dance and enjoy the party.

Miller leaned in and whispered in Blase's ear. "Marry me, Chocolate." He pulled a black velvet ring box out of his right pocket and opened it to display a substantial pear shaped solitaire ring set in gold. Blase stood in awe of the diamond for a minute until Brielle noticed what was happening and squealed, "Oh my God!"

Blase, startled by the sound, looked up and realized everyone was starting to look at them. She looked at Miller and whispered back, "Absolutely!"

Miller smiled and put the ring on Blase's finger as everyone applauded. Things were perfect and they couldn't get much better. She'd graduated from medical school and was engaged to the love of her life.

# The Residency

**THE NEXT** morning the engagement was in the local newspapers. Blase was so excited, even with the long road ahead of her—completing her residency. When she and Miller woke, she turned to him in the bed and asked, "Mill, are you awake?"

He grinned. "I hope so or else I'd have to face the fact that last night was just a dream. Are you really going to be Mrs. Miller Jones?"

Blase looked happy. "Yes, I am. But I want to talk to you about my residency."

"What is there to talk about? You don't have to do all of that now. I'll take care of you."

Blase sat up in shock. "What do you mean I don't have to do that now? I haven't gotten this far to just stop and be a housewife, Mill. I hope you don't think that."

Miller looked at his love. "Okay, so what do you want to talk about?"

"Well I think I should continue to live here at the condominium until I finish my residency. It will be easier to get to the hospital given the long hours I will be working."

This met Miller's attention. "Stay in the city? What are you talking about, Blase? Our home will be in New Jersey."

"Yes, baby, I know it will, but it will be too demanding for me to travel back and forth from Jersey that often."

"You know I never did ask you. What kind of doctor do you want to be?"

"A Dermatologist."

"Nice. Well if it will make it easier for you, we can try it your way first, but you have to come to New Jersey on your off days."

She smiled. "This is why I can't wait to be your wife. Now what does a fiancée have to do to get some loving from her fiancé?"

"Just keep saying fiancé…say it again, baby!"


THE arrangement was working out very well. Blase would stay at their condominium in New York City while she was on call and stay out in New Jersey when she was off. It worked out so well because from June until the end of the season, Miller was knee deep in football. Practice, spring training, pre-season, and then the regular season and if they make the playoffs, the season is extended well into the beginning of the next year.

As they approached the anniversary of their sixth year together Miller started to act otherwise towards Blase. His patience shifted to frustration because Blase wouldn't set a date for their wedding. She insisted they wait until she finished her residency, when Miller thought they could do it while she was working.

"Chocolate, lots of people get married while they're working. Hell, baby, my schedule is hectic but I want to make time for this. You are acting like you don't want to marry me or something."

Blase observed her man. "Miller, of course I want to marry you, but I really can't focus on planning a wedding right now."

"We can hire someone to plan it. That is just an excuse, Choc." Miller grew more and more agitated with her flimsy excuses.

Honestly, she didn't see them as excuses, but she simply didn't want to get overwhelmed. She wanted to marry Miller, but on her terms. Blase became irked with his persistence. "Miller I'm not giving you an excuse.

You know how hard I've been working. I just don't have the time to stop everything and work with a wedding planner, and despite all that you're saying I know you won't be involved past telling me the people you want to come. It's just a party to you, but it's a one-time spiritual union for me. I want to be focused on that and that only when we have our wedding."

Miller still saw her words as excuses but he decided to let it be. "Ah'ight, well I'm going out. I'll be back later."

She recognized his aggravation and didn't push further. "Okay, baby. I'll see you when you get back."

Miller left and drove from New York City to New Jersey. He called Blase once he reached their home and told her he wasn't coming back because he needed to clear his head. He decided he'd come back in to the city the next day.

THE next day Blase was paged to go to the hospital. While she was there, she eavesdropped on someone saying there was a man in the emergency room who was clinging to life after his delivery truck collided with a fire engine. Immediately, Mark popped in her mind, so she decided to take a stroll down to the ER. When she reached the area, she overheard two nurses mention how handsome the man was and how he had been thrown from his DHL truck into the street on impact. Blase's heart galloped and she picked up speed as she walked toward the operating room. She asked the attending doctor what the patient's name was. He looked on the patient chart and said, "Mark Emilio Rodriguez."

Blase clutched her chest. She walked in to watch the surgery and saw Mark's motionless and bloodied body lying on the operating table and wished she could be in there next to him. Countless thoughts ran through her mind. *What happened? What was he doing that he wasn't paying attention to the fire engine horns? Where was his family?*

Just then another doctor spoke. "Do you know him?"

"Yes," Blase returned without looking at the other doctor.

"Well his sister is in the waiting room. Would you like to go and give her an update?" he asked.

"Sister?"

"Yes, his sister. Her name is Marisol, I believe. Would you like to go and talk with her?"

Blase nodded.

"Okay," he said. "Mark is in critical condition. He has a contusion on the left hemisphere of his brain as a result of the impact. We are trying to determine right now if there is any hemorrhaging. He has three broken ribs on the left side, and his left leg is broken in three places. We will have more information as the surgery progresses but right now we can't give more information until we determine if there is hemorrhaging."

Blase still didn't take her eyes off him as she was given the news. It took everything inside of her to hold back her tears. She finally looked at the doctor, closed her mouth, and repeated what he said. "Contusion to the left hemisphere of his brain, three broken ribs, and his left leg is broken in three places."

The number three kept resonating in her head. *Why three?* she wondered.

Blase walked slowly towards the waiting area. She was still trying to digest the fact that this man who she told she would never leave was lying on an operating table and his fate was dubious. She had to take a moment. She ducked into a bathroom and collapsed in tears. She wept because she never tried to reach out to him after she saw him at her graduation party. She sobbed because she had changed her number a year before so he would stop calling her. She cried because he did nothing but love her and she let him and his love walk out of the diner that morning and didn't look back. After five minutes of non-stop crying, she regained her composure, splashed water on her face, and proceeded to the waiting area where she saw one person who she assumed was Marisol. She was petite with long, curly, black hair and when she turned around her resemblance to Mark was evident.

"Marisol?"

"Yes," she responded.

Blase cleared her throat. "Hello, my name is Dr. Blase Morgan, and I'm not—"

"I know who you are. My brother hasn't stopped talking about you since he met you. Are you the doctor working on him?"

"No, I'm not, but I do have news on his condition."

"And?" she asked through her observable fear.

Blase went on to tell her what she was told and promised she would come back with an update the minute she had one. As Blase was walking away, Marisol grabbed her hand and said,

"Por favor, diga...lo siento, please say something to him. If Emilio hears your voice he will fight. I know he will. He loves you so much, even to this day." She looked at Blase's hand and at her engagement ring.

Blase tried quickly to put it in her pocket, but it was too late.

Marisol said, "I don't care. Just please say something to him. I need Emilio. He is all I have. I don't know if you know it but our parents died eight years ago, and Emilio is all that I have now."

76

Blase grabbed Marisol's hand and said, "I will. I will." As she walked back to Mark's operating room, she was numb. She received a call on her cell phone from Miller and ignored it.

THE surgery lasted four hours and the doctors determined there was no bleeding in his brain, but because of the impact, he had brain edema and had to have fluid drained from his brain. They were able to set his leg with steel rods, and they wrapped his ribs to prevent further damage. They moved Mark to a private room to recover. She went out to the waiting area and delivered the news to Marisol and told her she could go to his room once he's all settled in.

Blase walked into Mark's room and looked at him while he slept. He was discolored and puffed-up and she felt helpless. Tears began to form again and she softly took Mark's hand into hers. When Mark felt Blase's hand he feebly squeezed back. She leaned in and whispered in his ear. "It's Belleza. I'm here."

When Mark squeezed just a bit tighter, she realized he knew it was her. As soon as Marisol walked in the room, she let go of Mark's hand and told her he would be okay. Marisol looked at Blase and asked, "Will you come back to check on him?"

Blase nodded and walked out before she started to cry again. When she reached her floor of the hospital, she called Miller back. "Hi, baby, I'm sorry but an acquaintance of mine has been in surgery for the last few hours so I had to make sure it went well."

"I was wondering what happened to you. I came in to the city and you weren't here. Are you coming home soon?"

"No, I'll probably be here all night."

Miller sighed. "Okay, I'm going to go back to New Jersey. Come back to New Jersey tomorrow after you get some rest."

She agreed, told him she loved him, and terminated the call. After dealing with a few more patients, Blase checked on Mark again before she left the hospital. She decided to take a car service to New Jersey. Seeing Mark made her want to set a date and start planning the wedding. The reality of life being short and precious set in and she didn't want to lose Miller because of being stubborn. As the car approached the driveway, she became overwhelmed with emotions again. She got out of the car, walked into the house, and walked upstairs towards their bedroom. She quickly walked past the home office but stopped and doubled back when she thought she saw a figure in the room. She did. She found Miller naked from the waist down sitting on the leather sofa getting a blowjob from what looked like a whitish yellow woman with a horrible weave. She dropped her bag so they both would hear her and asked, "How long have you been doing this?"

He shot to his feet and pushed the woman off him exposing her bare breasts and full nakedness.

"I said, how long have you been doing this?" she asked him again, calmly.

Miller was wordless. He didn't know what to say, so he didn't say anything at all. As the whitish skin woman gathered her clothes and scurried into the bathroom, Blase dryly repeated, "How long have you been doing this, Miller? I asked you a damn question."

Miller wouldn't answer as he pulled his pants up. He just stood there looking dazed. Blase didn't say another word. She took her engagement ring off, sat it on the small table a sculpture rested on, grabbed her bag, and turned around to walk back downstairs where she called a cab to take her back into the city. Her cab came while she was in the bathroom trying to compose herself. Miller took the opportunity to put the other woman in the cab and sent her on her way. He didn't want Blase to leave.

When Blase came out of the bathroom, Miller was standing there wide eyed and shaky. "Chocolate, it hasn't been going on long. I just met her a few weeks ago at an industry party and one thing led to another."

"One thing led to another, Miller? Is that the most sensible answer you can give me? One thing led to another? Well let me tell you something, whatever the thing was leading you to *that* thing…" she pointed toward the stairs, unaware the woman was gone "…I hope it was worth it because what you did was ruin *this* thing. I mean, Miller if I hadn't have come here tonight…if I hadn't have come here tonight to tell you that we could set a date and get married because I was afraid of losing you, I would've never seen this. You would've never told me about this, and it quite possibly would've continued until God knows when." Her voice ascended into full on rage.

"No, baby, it wouldn't have gone on."

"Oh shut up. Are you seriously going to stand there with your dick wet with this bitch's saliva and try and give me some bullshit excuse? Surely you know me better than that."

Blase calmed to a low lull and said softly, "Well, so much for us." She decided to take the keys to one of the cars and drive home. Because Miller was afraid she would get in to an accident, he got into his Range Rover and followed Blase to the city. He also wanted to try and convince her not to leave him.

During her drive home she worked herself into a full on frenzied wail. Miller became nervous at seeing the Mercedes swerving, so he stayed as close to her as possible. She finally reached the city and pulled the car into the building's parking garage. Miller parked his SUV in a lot up the street and walked to their building. When he arrived at the apartment, he unlocked the door and Blase was standing in the living room drinking a glass of wine. She looked at Miller and coolly said, "Miller. This isn't up for discussion. Our relationship is over." She walked into the bedroom and closed the door. But Miller refused to leave. He stayed in the guest bedroom and fell asleep. When he woke up, Blase was gone. Her clothes, luggage, and everything were gone.

AFTER Blase settled in to her hotel suite, she left and went back to the hospital to check on Mark, although she was off duty. When she got to the hospital, Mark was awake and talking to Marisol. Blase walked in and Mark's eyes lit up with a smile to match. She smiled back at him when she realized he appeared to be feeling better.

"Hello, Mr. Rodriguez. How are you feeling today?" She leaned in and kissed him on the cheek.

Mark's speech was sluggish and drawn out. "I'm feeling okay but I have a terrible headache." He began faintly laughing at his idea of a joke.

Blase and Marisol didn't quite find it funny but Blase managed a grin. "You will feel some pressure because of the trauma to the left side of your head."

Mark nodded his head in acknowledgement. Marisol spoke. "Emilio me voy a la cafeteria. I will bring you back something. I'll be back in about half an hour." She figured she would give them time to talk.

After Marisol left the room, Blase sat down next to Mark and he slowly said, "Te he echado de menos, Belleza." He translated. "I've missed you, beauty."

Blase couldn't believe he cared for her after what she'd done to him. She touched his hand. "I've missed you too. I'm sorry this is the way we have to see one another again."

"At least we are seeing each other again."

She smiled. His spirit was so optimistic and sincere.

"I have my Bachelor's degree now, in Communications. I went to the College of New Rochelle."

Blase again smiled. "I'm very proud of you, Mark."

"I was on my way to an interview when I got into the accident."

"What kind of job were you interviewing for?"

"A job at a radio station. I want to produce radio shows."

Blase was impressed with his ambition. "Well then that is what you shall do. Once you get out of here."

Mark smiled at his first love's confidence in him. "Are you still with that Miller guy?"

Blase responded coldly. "No."

The corners of Mark's mouth turned up swiftly at this news.

Blase received a call on her cell phone and had to excuse herself for a moment. When she walked out of the Mark's room, she saw the call was from Fallon. "Hey, girl. What the hell is going on? I just got a call from Miller. He's looking for you. What happened?"

"The short story is Miller cheated and I left him."

"Holy shit, girl. Are you okay? You are so calm right now."

"Well Mark has been in a terrible accident and I'm in the hospital visiting him now. I'll have to tell you the whole story another time. I'm standing outside of his room right now. I'm staying at the Marriott on the East side."

"A hotel, Blase? Why are you staying at a hotel? Girl bring your stuff to my place."

"No, it's just easier to stay there. I'm only staying for a week, maybe two. But I'm still on call. I'm going to have the locks changed on the condo and go home in a day or so, but Fal I have to go. Meet me at the lobby bar at six o'clock."

Fallon agreed and hung up. Fallon called Brielle to deliver the news and to ask her to meet at the hotel also.

Blase went back in the room and reminisced with Mark for the entire day. Her cell rang incessantly with calls from Miller and a few from her parents. She imagined Miller was calling everyone under the sun to try and find out where she was. No one in the hospital knew she was there because she managed to come in without any other hospital employees who knew her seeing her other than the security.

Mark enjoyed every minute Blase spent with him in the hospital. He was almost wishing he could stay there because once he left, he didn't know if she would allow him to see her again. By the end of the day, Blase reached in to give Mark a hug. She still smelled a little of his cologne and it brought back a flood of memories. She kissed him on the cheek and said she would be back to see him again before he was discharged.

"Hasta Luego, Belleza."

"See you soon."

When she walked out, Mark's doctor was walking in and stopped her. "Hi, you're a doctor here, right?" he asked.

"Yes, but today is my day off. Is everything okay with Mark?"

"Yes. I've just seen you around the hospital and have been meaning to introduce myself. My name is Walter Bailey. I'm one of the Neurology physicians here."

Blase noticed his strong British accent. "Well it's a pleasure to meet you, Dr. Bailey. Thank you so much for taking such great care of my friend. He's very dear to me."

"It's my pleasure. Now that I know Mr. Rodriguez is one of your dearest mates I'll personally look after him regularly." He assured supportively.

Marisol overheard the conversation and was thrilled.

Blase shook Dr. Bailey's hand and proceeded down the corridor. He turned around and trotted to catch up to her. "Listen, would you mind having tea with me sometime? I'd love to chat it up with you a bit and get to know you."

Blase turned to face him. "How about this; if you take excellent care of my friend, once he's discharged and I know he's in the clear, we can absolutely have tea if you'd like."

Walter smiled. "All right then. I'll find you when Mr. Rodriguez is being discharged. Cheers!" He turned and walked back toward Mark's room.

Blase curiously watched him walk for a moment, and then turned to leave the hospital.

**BLASE** arrived at her hotel lobby to find Brielle and Fallon already having a drink at the bar and chatting. Brielle was speaking. "Fallon, I know I drive my husband crazy sometimes with my mania and screwy schedule, but if I ever found he had cheated on me, I don't know that I would just leave him. I mean I'd have to find out the circumstances of why he did it."

Fallon listened without judgment although she didn't agree. Cheating was just not tolerable under any circumstances as far as she was concerned.

When Blase walked closer to them, they stopped the conversation. They both turned and looked at her with empathetic expressions.

"Hey, girl." Fallon broke the silence.

Blase let out an exaggerated sigh as she sat in the seat to the left of them.

"What are you drinking?" Brielle asked.

"I'll take a glass of Chardonnay," she responded.

Brielle motioned for the bartender as Fallon started rubbing Blase's right arm. "Oh, honey, it will be okay. You know I know what you are going through."

Blase nodded and reminded herself to keep her composure. She refused to break down and cry, again.

The bartender asked, "Would you like the house Chardonnay or would you like a wine menu?"

Blase quickly responded, "House is fine."

As the bartender fetched Blase's glass of wine, the ladies turned and looked at her and in unison asked, "Are you alright?" They looked at each other and back at Blase after they realized what they'd done.

She stared back at her friends. "I'm managing. There is just so much going on right now. I can't believe it is all happening at the same time."

"If you don't want to talk about it, you don't have to. We can just have some drinks and talk about something else," Brielle said.

Fallon didn't quite feel the same. She wanted to know what was going on.

Blase took a sip of her wine and started, "Well, the other night I was paged to go to the hospital..."

As Blase described in detail everything that had happened to her in the past couple of days, the ladies listened intently. Offering words of encouragement and support here and there. They both couldn't believe what their friend was going through all while trying to stay focused on her career.

Brielle asked, "So how long do you plan on staying in this hotel? I mean that apartment is yours even though Miller bought it for you."

Blase took a sip of her second glass of wine. "Honestly, my intentions were to come here and stay a day or two until I could have a locksmith go and change the locks so that Miller won't just show up. Now I'm feeling like being here is kind of therapeutic and breaking the monotony of the mania. Or I could just move back in to my co-op downtown. My renters just moved out."

Fallon understood.

Brielle wasn't sure it was the right thing to do. She thought she should handle her issues head on and maybe Blase and Miller could work it out. "Have you talked with Miller?" Brielle inquired.

Fallon looked at Brielle and responded for her friend. "What the hell is there to talk about? She walked in on the man getting his dick sucked, Brielle!" She lowered her tone as she realized she'd begun to raise her voice.

Brielle was appalled at Fallon's response. "Yes, Fallon, I am aware of that but everyone deserves a chance to explain themselves no matter the circumstance."

"Explain what? That he'll never do it again? The trust is broken. You can't recover once trust is broken, and Miller doesn't deserve a second chance. I'm sorry, I just don't believe in the two-strike rule. Once a cheater, always a cheater," she sparred.

Brielle ignored Fallon and looked at Blase. "Listen, misery sometimes loves company. I say listen to your man and if you decide after the conversation to walk away, then walk and don't look back, but at least give him a chance to tell you what lead to what he did."

Fallon, incensed by Brielle's dig at her, sat in a silent simmer. Blase knew the position that both of her friends took on the subject of cheating and didn't want Brielle and Fallon to be angry with one another because they had a difference of opinion.

Blase said, "I am leaving Miller and that's it, but I will sit down with him and talk. We do have other loose ends to tie up anyway." She hoped this would appease both of her friends. "And Brielle, I don't think Fallon is at all miserable, I just think, like you, she believes that I deserve the best."

Fallon was happy her friend spoke up for her.

Brielle turned to Fallon. "I apologize, I didn't mean to insult you, Fal. I just want her to be objective about it. I respect what you went through with Melvin and I'm sorry for it. I just think each relationship is different."

Fallon peered at Brielle, accepted her apology but was still miffed. The ladies continued on with their drinks switching their orders to bottles of wine instead of glasses. After their second bottle, Brielle said, "Okay, I'm the only one who has to drive home, so I'm going to switch to water."

Blase offered, "Well, I am an elevator ride to my temporary home and if you guys want to stay, you are welcome."

"My husband wouldn't even understand it girl, so I'll have to head home soon," Brielle countered.

Fallon said, "I'm in for as many bottles as you are and we'll play it by ear. I can take a car service home or stay here." She looked at Blase with her glass held high for a toast. "You will get through this, girl and come out on the other side stronger than ever. Here is to strength, faith, and friendship. Love you, girl."

Blase clinked her wine glass to Fallon's and Brielle's water bottle.

"Yes, we love you, girl, and we are here for you," Brielle added.

THE next morning, Blase and Fallon decided to have breakfast together before Fallon headed back to New Jersey. After their breakfast, Blase went back to her condo to pick up a few forgotten toiletries that she needed for the week. When she arrived at the condo, Miller was sitting on the sofa watching television.

"Chocolate, baby, where have you been? I've been calling all over the place looking for you."

"Miller, first please cut the terms of endearment, they are completely inappropriate right now. I need some time to think without you in my head trying to give me some bullshit reason for your duplicitous lifestyle."

Miller stood up and started toward Blase. With all of his calling and searching, he still didn't know how to explain away what he'd done. "Blase, I'm sorry. I didn't mean to hurt you. Honestly, there is no reason. The opportunity presented itself and I did it. It doesn't mean that I don't love you."

Blase looked at Miller as if he was some sort of extraterrestrial. "Yes, Miller, that's precisely what it means. Is that it? Is that all you came up with since I saw you last?" she yelled.

Miller was prepared for her anger. "Baby, sit down and calm down."

Blase ignored his request and stood. "No, this is not a sit down type of conversation. I wish you would've told me you felt neglected or second to my work. I wish you would've told me you weren't attracted to me anymore. I wish you would've told me something that would make your indiscretion plausible, but opportunity Miller? I've had plenty of opportunities to sleep with other men, but I chose not to because I love and respect what we had." Blase, despite her best efforts, finally showed him her tears and at the sight of them, Miller's face and posture deflated.

Knowing his fiancée, he knew it was over. Blase and Miller argued for another hour before she finally told him to leave and not to come back. As Miller was leaving, he took his keys out of his pocket and put them on the coffee table. He apologized again and told her he would be there if she ever changed her mind. When Miller walked out of the door, he walked out of Blase's life forever as far as she was concerned. She stood in the silence listening to the palpitations of her heart until the space between each beat steadied enough for her to collect her thoughts. As she walked to her bedroom her anger transitioned to sadness and then to exhaustion. She lost all energy and motivation to do anything that day, so she climbed into bed and watched movies until she drifted to sleep.

After going back to the hotel and checking the next day, Blase got off the elevator in the hospital and immediately ran into Dr. Bailey.

"Good morning, Dr. Morgan. How are you today?"

"Good morning, Dr. Bailey. I'm good today. How about yourself?"

"I'm doing a lot better now that I've seen you."

Blase realized he was flirting so she managed a weak smile.

"I'm glad we've run into each other actually. I just left Mr. Rodriguez's room and he's doing very well. He won't be discharged for another few weeks because his speech is still slow so we want to do some more brain x-rays as he progresses and his leg still needs more x-rays as well, but he is doing well overall. When I mentioned your name he seemed anxious to know whether you were coming to see him today, so I'm sure he'll be pleased to see you."

This news made Blase smile genuinely and she responded, "Thank you for taking care of him. I'm on my way in to see him now. Enjoy the rest of your day, Dr. Bailey."

"Please call me Walter," he insisted.

"Enjoy your day, Walter," she surrendered.

"Very well then. You enjoy yours as well, Blase." He nodded and looked back down at the chart in his hand.

Blase continued down the corridor to Mark's room. When she entered, he was watching television. The blinds were wide open and he seemed in great spirits. When he saw Blase, he attempted to sit further up in his bed.

"Let me help you," she said as she rushed to his bedside.

Mark let Blase help him up. He could've done it on his own, but he wanted to feel her touch and smell her perfume. "Thank you," he responded after he was settled.

She looked at him with adoration. "So, Dr. Bailey tells me you are doing well. I'm glad to hear that. I told him to take the utmost care of you and to make sure you walk out of this hospital better than ever."

At this, Mark beamed and said slowly, "I don't know about better than ever, Belleza, but I will be happy just to walk out of here. The other doctor showed me the x-rays of my leg and it looks really bad."

"I've seen all of your x-rays and I have even seen the doctor's private notes. You will be just fine. You can trust me," she assured him.

Mark grasped Blase's hand. "You are making me feel loved." This was his attempt to find out if Blase still had feelings for him.

"You are loved, Mark," she confirmed with a slight tilt of her head.

This was his chance. "I still love you, Belleza. I've never stopped loving you. When I saw you with that Miller guy, I wasn't angry with you. That's the type of guy I figured you would want. Not me, but I just couldn't stop loving you."

Blase was dumbfounded. She'd left him, broken her promise to him, and he's telling her, after all of that time, he still loves her. "I'm sorry, Mark, for what I did to you. I never meant to hurt you. It was selfish and inexcusable. You deserve better than me, that's for sure."

Mark turned his head away. "But I only want you, Belleza,"

Blase squeezed his hand tighter as they both sat in silence watching game shows for the next hour. When Marisol walked in, Blase decided to leave and continue on with her work schedule.

# LUCKY NO. 5

**MARK** was discharged three weeks later. When he was wheeled out of his room and out of the hospital, he saw Blase standing in front of her car talking with another doctor waiting for him. Marisol had agreed to allow her to take care of him while he was doing his outpatient rehabilitation to strengthen his leg and learn to walk properly again.

Mark looked confused. "Where is Marisol?" he asked.

"She is at my apartment making sure everything that you love is there. I hope you don't mind staying with me while you recover."

Mark was speechless. They wheeled him to her car. She helped him in, closed the door, and walked around to the driver's side. She looked over and saw Walter standing in the doorway and mouthed to him, "Thank you!"

He mouthed back, "You owe me a date!"

She nodded and got in her car. When they reached her condo, Blase helped Mark out of her car and held his arm as they walked gingerly towards the elevator. When they reached the elevator, Mark grabbed both of Blase's arms and brought her into him for a kiss. The kiss was well received. After weeks without affection, Blase needed the attention and the passion. When they got to her condo Blase helped Mark in to the guest bedroom. She undressed him down to his bareness and gently laid him in the queen-sized bed. She then undressed herself in front of him and got in bed with him. Mark asked her to get on top of him and Blase indulged by tenderly straddling him. As she kissed his face, his scars, and then his lips, Mark grew to attention. They made love as if time had stood still and Miller never existed.

**AFTER** close to six months, Mark was back to his full health. He had a slight limp because of his leg injury, but his speech was fully recovered and his scars were starting to fade. Blase arrived home one evening to a wonderful surprise. She got off the elevator and smelled a very familiar smell. Not aware of where it was coming from, she opened her apartment door and it hit her. "Arroz con Pollo?" she said.

Mark smiled. "Tostones and flan also. I made it all, even the flan."

Blase laughed. "No you didn't. Is Marisol hiding in the closet or a cabinet or something?"

He laughed. "Belleza, I have never lied to you and I wouldn't start now."

Blase continued laughing. "Let me wash my hands."

"Would you like fruit punch or wine?"

"Fruit punch in a wine glass, please."

He smiled even harder because he didn't drink alcohol. When Blase sat down at the table, she toasted Mark's full recovery and he toasted his love for her. She was still uneasy at how much he still loved her but she toasted back nonetheless.

"Belleza, I want to thank you for all that you have done for me over these past several months, but I think it is time for me to go home now. I have interrupted your life enough and based upon all of the phone calls from your ex-boyfriend I know you have a lot of things you need to get in order. I am fine now and can take care of myself."

Blase listened.

"So I will be moving out at the end of this week, but I do hope that we can still see each other. I have enjoyed having you back in my life." Mark was still afraid to impose his love on Blase.

Blase responded, "I've enjoyed being with you, and honestly Mark it has been my pleasure to doctor you back to health. You don't know that having you here has been therapeutic for me as well. I appreciate your affection and your friendship."

Mark heard the word friendship and cringed but continued to listen.

"We will certainly still see each other. You are my heart."

After Mark moved out, Blase sat in her condo and listened to the quiet. She didn't like it, but it was the first time in years she realized she was alone. She called Fallon and Brielle and asked if they wanted to meet her for dinner. She hadn't had a chance to sit down with her friends in months while she was helping Mark recover. She wanted to catch up with their lives in person instead of the ten to twenty minutes conversations that she'd been relegated to over the past few months. They both agreed and she met them at The Motown Café on 57th street. She heard it may soon be closing and wanted to try it out before they shut their doors.

Brielle arrived looking pleasantly plump after announcing a few months before that she was pregnant. They shared a long hug and were escorted to their table. Fallon arrived shortly after. She sauntered in with a huge smile and a blinding tennis necklace on.

"Hi ladies." Blase got up and hugged Fallon the same way she'd hugged Brielle.

Brielle and Fallon kissed on the cheek and Fallon sat down.

"This place is so cute, Blase. I've never been here," Fallon said.

"Neither have I," Brielle added.

"Neither have I," Blase said. "I heard a bunch of celebrities own it," she added.

Fallon looked around some more and said, "Cute!"

As they caught up on each other's lives Fallon finally asked, "So what's the story with you and Mark? Are you guys an item again?"

"You know, I know Mark wants us to be together again, but I feel like it's too soon after Miller. Miller still sends me emails, so he's not really giving me a chance to get over him. Mark was great every time I received a flower delivery from Miller and he even talked with me about the whole relationship."

They listened in silence.

"So he provided a great cushion and friendship for me."

"Is that all you want from him?" Brielle asked.

"For now, yes. I know Mark wants more but I also know he won't push me. He's never been the pushy or aggressive type so he'll just go with the flow. He has told me he's just happy I'm back in his life." Blase started eating her sweet potato fries.

"Well I assure you darling, Mark wants more than just friendship with you. From the few times we've spoken, that man sounds like he's in love, and now that you've nursed his leg and his dick back to good health he's in it for the long haul," Fallon said.

They all laughed.

"Girl you are crazy, but damnit if he isn't the best lay that I've ever had. One hundred years could go by and that man would just put it on me." Blase sighed with her eyes closed.

They laughed and continued their jovial conversation well into the night.

Fallon told them the necklace was a gift from her new boyfriend Sergio. He played outfield for the New York Mets. She met him at one of her father's new hotel openings. Everyone knew Fallon liked athletes, so it was no surprise she was dating Sergio.

Brielle told them she was feeling a lot better in her second trimester than she was in her first. They talked about future plans, baby names, and career goals. Blase shared with them her intentions to go into private practice after she finished her residency and Fallon told them of her plans to start her own travel company. It was a great night for the Sister Circle.

Blase noticed Fallon and Brielle had gotten closer because they were making inside jokes she wasn't aware of. She assumed they became closer while she was busy tending to Mark. She was pleased about it because after the last time they'd all gotten together, she thought they were going to have a strained relationship.

On the Monday after Mark moved out, Blase got an email from Walter that read: *I have waited patiently for my tea date, so now I'm going to put my foot down, Dr. Morgan. Meet me at noon today at the Brown Cafe on Hester Street. See you there. Cheers!*

Blase thought the right thing to do was make good on her promise. She showed up to the cafe at exactly noon to see Walter sitting at a booth reading documents.

When he noticed Blase, he eyed her as she walked toward him. "Good afternoon, Blase, I'm glad you decided to join me. I was hoping you wouldn't stand me up," Walter said as he stood.

"Now do I look like the type of woman who would stand you up?" she asked through a cheerful smile.

"No, but you do look like a woman who makes a bloke wait," he remarked sarcastically as he pulled out her chair.

"Thank you." She ignored his sarcasm.

"What kind of tea would you like?" he asked.

"Actually I am more of a coffee drinker, so if you don't mind I'll have a regular coffee instead."

He nodded. "Of course I don't mind. You can have whatever you'd like."

"Great, then I'll also have a Portobello mushroom and arugula sandwich on Focaccia bread as well because I am starved."

"Then I'll have the same."

Blase and Walter sat and talked as lunch hour became dinnertime. She learned she had a lot in common with him aside from them both being doctors. Although he grew up and studied medicine in London, after medical school, he moved to Ethiopia for two years to do missionary work. He'd even stayed at a house in the town where her Sayt Ayat and Wund Ayat lived. He told Blase his sister was currently in Kenya doing missionary work. They talked about his time in Ethiopia, her family, and his family. By the end of their date, she was drawn to Walter for his humanitarianism and his love of his family. It helped that he was attractive in a quirky kind of way. Tall enough at 6'4", Walter wore his dark, curly hair messy and somewhat unkempt. With eyebrows the same color as his hair and intensely dark eyes, he almost looked Greek or Armenian rather than British. His smile was vast and sprawling. Although his teeth weren't perfectly straight, they fit his face. Even with what appeared to be a scruffy exterior, you could tell Walter was well manicured in a without airs kind of way, which was comforting to Blase. She agreed to see him again on Thursday evening, which coincidentally was a day off for both of them.

On their second date, Blase learned Walter had come from a very wealthy family in London. This shocked her because he didn't act or dress pretentiously. In fact, he didn't even dress as if he was one of the highest paid physicians in their hospital; which he was. She liked it. It was very different from the flashy life she had been living with Miller. Before she knew it, Blase and Walter were an item, and again, without thinking, Blase phased Mark out of her life. By the end of her residency a year later, Walter and Blase were successfully in an active love affair.

# Private Practice

**BLASE** stayed at Walter's Lower West Side townhouse most of the time. It was easier for her while she was finishing her residency at the hospital. When she completed her residency, Walter surprised Blase with a trip to London to meet his family. Her nerves were overloaded because she wasn't sure if she was ready to meet his parents. They had an incredibly comfortable and impulsively romantic relationship. Walter was thoughtful and worldly and they would do small gestures to show their affection for each other. Both taught each other a lot about their cultures and whenever a barrier of any kind presented itself, they broke it with little to no concentration at all.

He was the first European man she dated and Blase had confirmation that the rumors weren't true. White men were indeed good in bed and as far as she was concerned, his phallus was the perfect size for her with little to spare. Her friend's liked him and liked the way he treated her, and her parents adored him. But still, she was apprehensive.

As they packed for their trip, Walter asked, "Darling, what do you think of flying from London to France once we've finished visiting my parents?"

Blase's eyes lit up. "Is that a serious question, or are you kidding me?"

Walter laughed. "No, I'm quite serious. For whatever reason, I've never been and would love to take some time to go."

After hearing this, Blase picked up her suitcase and walked to the closet. She returned struggling to pull her large designer trunk behind her. Walter laughed at the sight and went to help her with her trunk. "My love,

I don't think we'll be gone quite this long, but I'm glad the news excites you."

"I just want to be prepared for anything," she said exuberantly as she collapsed on the bed. Walter lay beside her, took her hand into his, and began kissing it.

Blase turned to her side to face Walter and said, "I love you, Dr. Bailey."

Walter turned to face her and said, "I appreciate your love, Dr. Morgan."

Blase didn't like this answer, but she didn't split hairs about it. She didn't tell him she loved him expecting him to say the same in return. She believed when someone loved you, they would tell you without baiting.

Walter saw Blase's facial expression and climbed on top of her and began to tickle her. She tried to tickle him back, but because he was stronger, she couldn't get the better of him. Walter tickled her until she laughed so hard she passed gas right there underneath him. Mortified by it, Blase froze, but this made Walter laugh so hard that now he was in tears.

After he stopped laughing he said, "Alright then, I think we've hit a milestone in our relationship, my love."

She responded, "If you say so. If I were your complexion, you'd see how red I was right now."

Walter laughed again. "There's nothing to be embarrassed about. At some point during the rest of our lives, you'll pass wind in front of me and I you."

Blase took this statement to mean Walter intended to spend the rest of his life with her and this made her humiliation turn to delight so she climbed on top of him this time, but her intentions weren't to make him laugh, but to make him happy.

**UPON** their arrival at London Heathrow airport, there was a gentleman in a black suit with a sign that read DR BAILEY & DR MORGAN on it. Walter walked over to the chauffeur and told him he was Dr. Bailey and she was Dr. Morgan. The driver greeted them with a smile and went to retrieve their bags. Once they were settled into their car, Blase became a bit unnerved. She asked him something that until then never crossed her mind. "Walter, have you ever dated a black woman before?"

Walter was surprised by the question and he looked at her. "Yes, my love. I dated a young woman that I'd met in Ethiopia. She was from South Africa originally though."

"Did your parents meet her?" she asked.

"No," he answered. "We dated only briefly while I was in Africa. In fact, my parents don't know of her."

Blase became panic stricken. "Do you think they'll mind that I'm African-American?"

"Oh heavens no, my love. My parents are not at all daunted by color. Are you worried?" he asked as he locked his fingers with hers.

"Well, yes. You are the first white man that I've dated, but I knew my parents wouldn't have a problem with it because they themselves have traveled the world and dated outside of our race. But you've never talked to me much about your parents so I'm not sure how they'll take to me being African American."

"You've nothing to concern yourself with. They'll adore you, just as I do," he responded nonchalantly.

After his reply, Blase eased her mind and felt a bit less taut so she eased back in her seat.

As they pulled up to Walter's family's estate, Blase was floored. The gates to get into the estate were enormous. While driving down the stretch of driveway, the property was breathtaking. The landscape looked like it could've been in a magazine with its large statues, beautiful trees, and unique water features. "This is a joke, right? Your parents don't actually live here, do they?" Blase asked.

"Of course they do," he answered without looking up from the document he was reading. Walter never disclosed the details of his family's wealth after their first lunch together. When he mentioned them he would tell Blase they were hard working chaps who were enjoying their retirement years. As the driver came around to open their door, Blase stepped out first, and then Walter. Blase stood taking it all in for a moment, and then Walter grabbed her hand and led her towards the door.

She fixed herself a bit and wished she didn't have on the travel sweat-suit she'd worn to be comfortable for the long flight. Walter wore relaxed jeans, brown leather slide on loafers, and a plain white button down shirt. When the housekeeper opened the door, Walter greeted her as if she were an old friend. "Cheers, Pen. It's wonderful to see you again. How have you been?"

"I'm well, Master Walter. Your father is in his office tending to a phone call," Penelope, their housekeeper of 25 years, responded.

"And Mother?" he asked.

"She is in the garden in the back. Did they know you were coming?" Pen asked.

"No," Walter responded.

Blase jerked her head towards Walter and looked at him as if he'd just broken into a bank. Walter looked back at Blase and said, "Alright then, let's say hello to Mother first."

Blase was visibly upset. She thought Walter made the formal arrangements for her to meet his parents. She didn't realize this was an unexpected visit and for her to be the first black woman he was bringing home, suddenly she felt nauseous. Her grip on his hand became dank and weak.

"Are you alright my love?" he asked as they were making their way through the house to the back of the house.

"No I'm not, Walter. I can't believe you brought me here and you didn't even talk with your parents about this. Do they even know we are dating?"

"In fact they don't. I haven't made it a habit of calling my parents to discuss my romantic affairs since I was, well a young chap," he responded with a bit of annoyance in his voice. "Relax my love. We are together and no matter how my parents receive you, we will still be together. But I'm certain they will love you, so please trust me."

She looked at Walter and lessened the tension in her eyebrows but tightened her grip on his hand again.

"Alright then," he said and they proceeded to find his mother.

Walter's mother was elated to see him. She was less happy to meet his girlfriend while she was in her gardening clothes. "Walter, I really wish you would've told me you were bringing your beautiful girlfriend here to visit. You know I would never greet guests this way."

"Mother, Blase is not a guest so you've nothing to worry about." Walter seemed very apathetic about the entire occasion. It wasn't until then that Blase realized everything Walter did outside of his work as a doctor was languid. When she introduced him to her parents there was dinner and preparation. They'd dressed up and bought a bottle of expensive wine. She'd even invited her brother, Benny, to dinner, and here he was flying her all the way around the world and Walter hadn't even bothered to call his mother to tell them they were coming.

"Hello, Mrs. Bailey, it's a pleasure to meet you."

Walter's mother took her gardening gloves off and stretched her elderly hand to meet Blase's and said a breathy, "No my darling, it is a pleasure to meet you. Please come and sit down." She motioned for one of the house attendants to come over. "Una, please be a dear and get us some tea."

"Mother, Blase doesn't drink—"

Blase interrupted Walter. "That sounds perfect, thank you very much for your hospitality, Mrs. Bailey."

Walter's mother brushed the comment off. Of course she would be hospitable. They sat in the garden talking for the next thirty minutes until they heard, "Who are all of these voices I hear out here, darling? Have you taken to talking with yourself again?" Walter's father said with a chuckle.

When he noticed Walter, he smiled. "It's Walter! To what do we owe the pleasure of your visit?"

Walter got up to hug his father and said, "We were stopping through on our way to Paris."

Blase looked confused again. The entire situation was becoming increasingly unsettling to her but she herself came from a well-mannered family so she kept her composure and played along.

Walter's father looked over at Blase and said, "And who is this beautiful woman?"

Walter responded, "Father this is Blase, she's a doctor in the hospital where I work."

This is the same way he introduced her to his mother. Blase was fuming inside. She thought, *Woman that you work with? Is that what the hell you think of me? Have we not basically been living together for over a year? Does everyone back in the United States not recognize us as a couple? What the hell is going on here?*

Walter's father walked over to Blase and said, "Well cheers, Blase. It's a pleasure to meet you."

As Blase stood Walter's father continued. "I'll tell you this, Walter, if you haven't asked this woman to be your girlfriend, then you certainly should. I don't think I've seen a woman this stunning since I met your mother."

Blase smiled and said a gracious, "Thank you very much."

Walter smiled, ignored the comment, and said, "Is Ingrid still in Africa?"

Just then, Una brought their tea and sat it down on the garden table they were sitting at. "Thank you, Una. Please tell Penelope that Blase and Walter will be staying for a few days and to prepare…" she stopped in mid-sentence and turned to her son and asked, "Two rooms or one dear?"

He said, "One will be sufficient, Mother." He looked over at his father, who smiled.

"Please tell Penelope to prepare the Martineau suite for them. Also tell her to set four places for supper instead of two. That'll be all."

Una took in the information and turned and left. The four of them continued to talk for the next hour until they were told that dinner would soon be ready. They all retreated to their rooms to prepare. When they reached their suite Blase turned to Walter and said, "Walter, please help me understand what is going on. You didn't alert your parents that we were coming, you're giving them the impression that we are breezing through on our way to Paris, and you've introduced me as if I'm simply a work colleague. Is there something I'm missing here?"

Walter said coldly, "No my love, there is nothing that you're missing. Your accounting of everything is accurate."

Blase's feet felt like cement. She couldn't move and she couldn't believe his response. "What the hell are you talking about, everything is accurate? Have I been the only one in this relationship for the past year and four months?" she said, her voice level escalating.

"No my love, you haven't but I don't see the need to put titles on us just yet, and we are in fact breezing through on our way to Paris. We are staying here for five days and staying in France for four weeks."

This was the first time Blase had heard about them staying in London for five days. As matter of fact, this was the first time she'd heard they were staying in France for four weeks. Blase felt nauseous again and this time she felt faint. "Walter, I'm at a loss for words. I feel like I don't even know who you are right now," she said softly.

Walter walked over and sat down next to her on the bedroom sofa. My love, you took a leave of absence from work to travel, so we are doing just that, traveling. I was going to surprise you, but since you seem so up in arms about things, I was going to end our trip in the South of France. I figured you'd enjoy sunbathing on the French Riviera."

Blase looked at Walter and couldn't even muster a joyful grin. "Walter you are not seeing the bigger picture here. I'm feeling like a fish out of water. I've always enjoyed your spontaneity, but I'm talking about your description, or lack thereof, of our relationship to your parents. I feel like you're giving me mixed messages. One minute you are insinuating that we'll spend the rest of our lives together and the next you whisk me three thousand miles away to meet your parents and introduce me as if I'm simply someone you consult with for advice on your patients," she said.

Walter couldn't understand why everything puzzled her. "Blase, I think you over think things. Carpe Diem my love and enjoy these times."

Blase was even more perplexed than she was before he spoke, but at that moment she made a decision to do just that. Seize the day and enjoy her trip and not think about it. But she also made the decision that when they returned to the United States she would move all of her things out of his townhouse and return home, until he made a formal verbal commitment.

**WALTER** and Blase enjoyed their time with his parents. Blase found them to be a charming and witty couple. Through them, Blase learned so much more about Walter and his childhood. She was fascinated because there was so much more to him that she never knew about and could have never guessed, including how he fell in love with and married a young Chinese woman when he went to China for a month. He brought her back to London and she lived with him and his family for a year before she became pregnant and decided to move back to China. Walter let her go back to China without questions, he divorced her, and seemed to have never asked her if she ended up having the baby or not. According to Mrs.

Bailey, he has never spoken to her again. Walter's mother seemed to be very chatty after her afternoon Scotch. So, as it seems Walter could also be a father and no one seemed to know or care about it.

Their trip to the South of France was mind blowing. They dined at the best restaurants and Walter had even rented a yacht for them to sail on for two days while they were there. Blase had to admit, until then she'd never truly had first class treatment. It was what she read about in books and she loved every minute of it. As their trip drew to an end Blase felt that nauseous feeling again. On the flight back to New York they both read their respective periodicals and hardly said any words to each other.

**BLASE** reflected on the entire trip and couldn't help but let her mind drift back to catching Miller with his pants at his ankles. Here was a man who she thought she knew inside and out and she walked in on him cheating on her and had no idea how long he'd been doing it and he offered her no logical explanation as to why he did it. And here she was flying back across the world sitting next to a man who she had been falling in love with. He not only appeared not to feel the same, but was far more nonchalant about everything, including their relationship and what seemed to be life in general then she was comfortable with. That thought led to her original thought in London, to pack her things and formally move back to her condo.

In the car ride back to Walter's townhouse, Blase told him of her plans. Walter asked, "Did you not enjoy yourself in France, my love?"

She told him, "Our time in France will never be forgotten, Walter, but I can't continue to act like I wasn't affected by our time in London. In addition to what I perceived as your irreverence for our relationship, there was an entire chapter of your life that you never told me about, including your baby who could be roaming around China somewhere. Add to that your complete lack of concern for it is beyond unsettling. I'm sorry, Walter, but I cannot continue to live with you knowing that and wondering about the unknown, mostly your feelings for me."

Walter was astounded. The car pulled up to his townhouse and the driver came around to open the door. Blase got out and Walter followed close behind her. He told the chauffeur to bring the bags into the foyer of his townhouse. Once inside, Walter tipped the driver and sent him on his way.

By then, Blase had made her way upstairs and into the bathroom. Walter knocked on the door. "Blase, please come out and talk to me. What can I do to make you change your mind?"

Blase spoke through the door. "Honestly, Walter, nothing. I have no idea who you are and I certainly don't plan to stick around to haphazardly find out other information about you. I don't believe that you've been forthright with me and I don't believe that you love me. I don't know if you even have the capacity to love."

Walter leaned against the wall outside of the bathroom door. He really didn't understand what the problem was. He was blindsided. Until then, Blase hadn't said a word about any of this. He finally said, "Well alright then. If you want to move back to your condo, very well then do it, but surely you're not ending this relationship because I didn't tell my parents we were coming?"

Blase sat on the edge of the bathroom tub shaking her head thinking, *Did he not hear me mention his baby? What kind of man marries a woman and when she gets pregnant ships her back to her country without another word?*

Blase spoke, "So now we're in a relationship?"

"Of course we're in a relationship, my love. Why would you think I think otherwise?"

Blase opened the door and stood firm in front of Walter. "Because of the way you introduced me to your parents."

Walter sighed. "Is that all? Darling you must understand that I'm painfully private with things like that with my parents after my marriage—"

Blase cut him off. "Yeah and the marriage thing. I mean come on, Walter. How do you sleep with a woman for over a year, basically move her into your place, and not tell her that you were married? We've had countless conversations and not once did you mention your ex-wife."

Walter said, "Well in fact I have three ex-wives and I've never mentioned any of them because I didn't think they mattered in our relationship."

Blase's mouth dropped open. She stood there for a few seconds, turned, walked to the closet, and came out with her suitcase. "Walter, I'm leaving."

Walter stood there, still not understanding her anger or decision. He watched Blase pack her things and then leave. He didn't say a word and neither did Blase. Walter figured he would give her time to cool down.

**BACK** at her condo, Blase felt out of place. She hadn't acknowledged her condo as home in over a year. It was clean and neat the way she'd left it. Her brother had lived there for eight months before he moved to

California. The cleaning lady would come once a week to dust and make sure it was clean after he moved out. She settled onto her sofa and decided to call Brielle.

Brielle answered and Blase heard the baby screaming in the background. "Hey, B. Can I call you right back? This boy is throwing a fit right now because I won't give him ice cream. He is just like his father."

Blase responded, "Of course."

"Okay, I want to hear all about your trip. Call you back shortly," she said.

"Okay, girl." She hung up and dialed Fallon's cell phone number.

Fallon answered on the first ring. "Okay, I'm mad as hell that you're just calling me after four weeks, but tell me all about it. When you called me from London I could hardly hear you and trying to decode your emails after you'd clearly had a bottle of wine was like trying to translate Chinese."

Blase thought it ironic that she said Chinese. "What are you doing? Are you in the city?" she asked.

"Yes, I'm at my office. What's up?" Fallon sounded concerned.

"Can you come over? I'm at my condo." Blase's voice started trembling.

"Give me twenty minutes," Fallon was wondering why Blase was at her condo. In exactly 20 minutes, Fallon was ringing Blase's doorbell.

Blase answered the door with a glass of red wine in her hand. "Hey, girl. Thank you so much for coming over so fast."

"Your voice scared me a little bit, girl. Are you okay?" Fallon asked as she hugged her friend.

They walked over to the dining room table and Blase poured a glass of wine for Fallon while she dropped her briefcase. They sat down and Blase broke down and started crying. Fallon was confused but she sat muted while her friend purged whatever was troubling her though her tears. Blase cried and drank and drank and cried. Fallon drank with her not saying a word other than, "Let's go sit on the couch, honey."

They both went to sit on the sofa and Blase continued to cry. Fallon, though steady, was really starting to worry. She really hadn't talked to her friend in detail in over a month and she was afraid to find out what caused the floodgates to open. After 23 minutes of non-stop crying, Blase finally spoke. "Girl, Walter brought me all the way to London and introduced me to his parents like I was his assistant or something, and then I found out he has a Chinese baby and three ex-wives."

"What?" Fallon screamed. Blase sounded like she was babbling and not making sense.

Blase blew her nose and tried to calm herself. "Walter didn't even tell his parents that he was bringing me there let alone that we were a couple. While we were there his mother told me when he was out horseback riding with his father that Walter had been married to a Chinese girl he met in China and the girl got pregnant and they shipped her back to China."

Fallon spoke again. "What?"

"I know. That's exactly how I was feeling during the entire trip," Blase said, noticing her friend's sheer confusion.

"Hold on one minute. You have to explain this to me so that I understand it because right now it sounds crazy, girl."

Blase went on to detail every bit of their trip—the good and the bad. She told her how she felt when Miller had cheated on her and she felt the same kind of betrayal. She told her she moved back home because she couldn't live with a man who she believed to be disingenuous.

Fallon took it all in and said, "Well, I think you did the right thing. That man sounds crazy. I know my mama is Greek but I told you about messing with white men."

Blase shot Fallon a dirty look. "Don't go there, girl. This has nothing to do with Walter being white."

Fallon said, "Maybe it doesn't but girl with all of the crazy shit you just told me, he sounds like he's liable to do anything. Stay away from him."

Blase sat quiet, sipping her wine. Fallon sat with her. Finally Blase's home phone rang. She looked at her caller ID and saw it was Brielle.

"Hello," Blase answered.

"Girl, I've been calling your cell phone back for fifteen minutes."

"Oh, I'm sorry. It is in my bedroom and I have it on vibrate," Blase said.

"What's wrong? I can hear in your voice that something is up," Brielle countered.

"Ughhhh, it's too much to go into…hold on, I'll let you talk to Fallon." Blase handed the phone to Fallon.

"Girl, that motherfuckin' Walter…" and Fallon began to tell Brielle the entire story as Blase told it to her.

Brielle asked Fallon to hand the phone back to Blase. "So are you and Walter broken up, or did you just move out, B?" Brielle asked her.

"I just moved out for now, but I'm not going back, Brie. I just can't," she said.

"Well you know my belief girl, at least talk with him in detail one last time and see if he has anything sensible to submit to you. And don't listen to Fallon. The chic is irrational and unreasonable. But don't tell her I said that," Brielle said with a laugh.

Blase laughed with her. "Okay, girl. Thank you for listening. I love you!" Blase said.

"I love you too, and I'm coming into the city tomorrow. We'll have lunch so I can give you a big ole hug."

"Okay, girl, thanks again." They hung up.

Fallon was opening their second bottle of wine when her cell phone rang. "Girl that is Sergio. Let me take this call real quick," she said as she walked into Blase's kitchen to talk with her boyfriend.

While Fallon was in the kitchen, Blase got her cell phone from the bedroom and listened to her messages. There was a message from her parents asking her if she'd gotten back into the country. A message from her brother asking if he'd left his blue pinstriped suit in the master bedroom closet, and a message from Walter, and finally a message from Paul Graham, a Dermatologist who wanted to hire Blase in his private practice. She listened to this message again to retrieve the phone number from it.

"*Hi, Dr. Morgan. This is Dr. Paul Graham. I received your resume from Dr. Batiste who referred you to me. He said you were an enterprising young doctor who was looking to go in to the private sector of Dermatology. I have an opening in my practice in Brooklyn and would love to meet with you to discuss it. Please give me a call. I understand that you are out of the country so please call me when you return. My number is 718-555-2323.*"

Blase wrote the number down and looked in the closet for her brother's suit. When she didn't see it, she dialed his number. He answered on the third ring. "What it is, lil' sis?" he said cheerfully.

She didn't want her brother to sense her emotions so she perked up. "Hey big brother, I don't see your suit, but you do have a few pairs of shoes and some jeans in the closet. Do you want me to ship them to you?" she asked.

"Damn, it's not there? I don't know what I did with that suit. Naw, don't ship it. I wanted to wear it for my boys wedding next weekend. I'm flying to New York for the wedding, so I'll pick my stuff up then. Speaking of which, I'll be staying at your spot while I'm there."

"Oh, okay. Well I've moved back in, so you can stay in the guest room," she told him.

"Moved back in? Did something happen with you and the Brit?"

"No, I just missed my place." She tried to cover up.

"B, your spot is like 1200 square feet and it's nice and all but dude's townhouse is the shit!" His tone was animated.

Blase laughed. "Yes, it's nice. But this is my spot, so I'm back home."

Blase's brother didn't push the subject. He figured he'd talk to her when he got to town the next weekend. "Okay. Well I'll be there Friday morning. We'll catch up about your world tour then. I'm out," he said.

"Okay, I love you," Blase responded.

"I love you too," Benny responded and hung up.

Fallon came out of the kitchen while Blase was on the phone with her brother. She asked, "What is your brother up to now?"

"Oh what isn't Benjamin up to? You know he never tells me what is really going on, he just tells my mother. So, last I heard from Mom, he was out there trying to hustle up some clients. She said that as soon as he got out there he hooked up with some other guy and they decided to try and start their own practice together. That was the latest that I heard right before I left. So you know I'm going to get the entire scoop when he comes here next week. I'll let you know," Blase informed her.

"Good for him. I hope he does well with it," Fallon said.

Fallon and Blase sat drinking the second bottle of wine. Fallon filled Blase in on everything that had been going on in her life since she left for Europe. Fallon and Sergio were still going strong. She admitted to Blase that he was great and very different. She told her she wasn't sure if it was his Dominican roots or what but he was the most giving and caring man she'd ever dated. And he was insatiable sexually. Fallon laughed when she said that. She never normally discussed her sex life with anyone. Not even her closest friends. She told Blase she started the paperwork to incorporate her business Flynn Destinations. She had to expedite it because she immediately had ten clients as soon as she decided to make her hobby a business. She was still helping her father with building his hotel chains. They were working on his fifth hotel in Jamaica and she was excited to go and oversee that project.

"Hey, do you want to come and hang with me for a few weeks?" she asked Blase.

Blase was so exhausted from her flight and trip to Europe she couldn't even think about getting on another plane yet. "When are you leaving?"

"Not for another week. I have to tie up some loose ends with Flynn Destinations and make sure I'm all set up to be able to work remotely from Jamaica."

"Let me see what is going on with this Paul guy and I'll let you know," Blase answered.

"What Paul guy?"

"Oh there is a Dermatologist who has a private practice I'm considering joining."

"Oh that sounds nice. Let me know how it works out. Do you have a meeting date set with him yet?"

"Not yet. I'll call him tomorrow to set it up. He told me to call him as soon as I got back into the country, but I don't think it's appropriate to call him on a Sunday evening. "

THE next day, Blase called Paul Graham to set up the appointment to meet with him. The meeting was scheduled for the Wednesday of that week. Blase spent all day Monday and Tuesday unpacking and thinking about her relationship with Walter. He had called her several times since she left him, but she just wasn't ready to talk with him. On Tuesday, she received a delivery. Her doorman called up and told her to come down and get it. He told her it was from a Dr. Walter Bailey, so she assumed it was flowers. When she reached the lobby, she saw a cardboard box that was in the shape of a house. She walked toward the box and noticed it moving. She removed the roof off the house and when she looked inside she saw the cutest Pomeranian puppy. There was a note tied to the dog's neck that read: *Just so I'm not the only one in the doghouse. I hope you like her. I'm sorry, Blase. Please don't be upset with me, my love.*

Blase looked at the dog and gushed. She picked it up, and the dog licked her face. She couldn't help but hug the tiny and overly fluffy baby. She looked to confirm if it was a boy or a girl. When she determined it was a girl, she immediately thought of a name.

"You are the cutest little thing. I'm going to call you Sugar," she said in a baby voice to the dog as she put her back in the box to take upstairs.

The doorman said, "Wait, there is more."

Blase stood there for a moment, thinking there'd better not be more animals.

"He left another box," he said.

"Can you open it please?"

The doorman opened the box and inside was a few bags of dog food and every kind of dog accessory, including wee wee pads, a pink collar, clothes, and toys. Blase smiled again. "Okay, I'll have to come back down to get that one."

"No problem, Dr. Morgan. Take your time."

Blase turned and headed back upstairs to her apartment. She took the dog out of the box and Sugar looked around trembling for a few minutes. Blase picked her back up and asked her if she was hungry. She ran back downstairs to get the other box. When she returned, she fixed Sugar some food and put it in a bowl on the floor in front of the sofa where she was sitting. Sugar ate the food so fast Blase wondered if she should fill the bowl again. She decided against it and to just get her some water. She went to the accessory box because she wanted to immediately put the wee wee pads down; she knew she had to call Walter, too, at the very least, thank him for Sugar.

Blase dialed Walter's cell phone number. He answered on the first ring. "Cheers, my love. I suspect that you've received my little friend?"

"Thank you very much, Walter. She is adorable. I've named her Sugar."

"Sugar. Alright then, sounds like a fitting name. If I recall the little bugger was quite the adorable one," he said.

"Walter, I do enjoy the dog but I still have issues with how you handled me in London and your past."

"I understand, my love. Have dinner with me tonight and we can talk about anything you wish to talk about and as they say, I'll be an open book, yeah?" Blase agreed.

That night at dinner she and Walter talked for hours. They talked so long that the waitress had to remind them the restaurant would soon close. They headed to an after-hours bar to continue their conversation. Walter didn't go into details about his wives, but rather explained how he met the women and how they came to divorce. He also wouldn't go into details about why his first wife moved back to China. For the most part, though, Blase was satisfied with all that he'd told her but she still wanted to live at her condo. They agreed to continue seeing one another, but Blase thought maybe she moved in with him too soon and living apart would allow them to get to know one another better. She was also still apprehensive about what he'd told her and what he hadn't. That night, Walter went back to Blase's condo and they made love—intense love. For the last week in France, Blase was rejecting Walter's affection when thoughts of London clouded her mind, so their passion was for the loss in time. When they woke the next morning, they slipped into their usually routine of coffee, tea, and reading the newspaper until it was time for Blase to meet Brielle for lunch.

AFTER Brielle received Blase's email telling her she would be fifteen minutes late, she decided to sit at a table outside to people watch until her dearest friend arrived. Her mind was circling with thoughts of what could be wrong with Blase and at the same time she knew she needed some friendly advice herself.

Blase arrived with a gift bag in her hand. "Hey," she said to Brielle cheerfully.

"Oh hey, girl," Brielle responded as she turned around from her seat and saw Blase walking towards her.

They hugged rocking back and forth. When they finally released, Blase handed Brielle the bag. "Here, I brought you something back from France. I hope you like it." She had already given Fallon her gift the night Fallon came over to her house earlier that week.

Brielle sat the bag in the chair with her pocketbook and both ladies eased into the wicker chairs. They decided to order two ice teas without sugar and two starter salads. "So how was your trip aside from the rest of the craziness that Fallon told me?" Brielle asked.

"Oh my God, Brielle, had we not have gone to London and just went straight on to France, I would be floating above cloud nine right now. Walter spared no expense, even renting a 150-foot yacht for two days for us to sail around and tour some of the Islands off of the South of France. We swam, ate, drank, and made love on the yacht. There is something about making love while sailing on the French Riviera on the top of a beautiful yacht. It was very voyeuristic with the crew being on board and all, but Walter didn't care, so neither did I." She shrugged as she was putting her sugar substitute into her iced tea.

Brielle listened fascinated. She wasn't as well traveled at all and certainly had never done anything as daring as that.

"Oh and I took your advice and I met with Walter. He bought me a dog so we had dinner last night and *he* is the reason I'm late this afternoon." Blase gave Brielle a devilish smile.

Brielle commented, "Good, I'm glad you guys were able to work it out. A dog?"

"For now anyway, and yes a dog. He had it delivered to me. A little Pomeranian puppy. She's so cute. I named her Sugar. But I'm still going to stay in my condo."

Brielle agreed, "That's fine. Take your time and see where it goes. Despite that crazy stuff, you've told me nothing but good things about Walter. He seems like a nice guy. And I have to see this dog."

"She's right here; I brought her in the carrier he gave me."

Brielle hadn't even noticed the carrier sitting on the ground near Blase's feet. "Oh my goodness, she's so adorable. How could anyone resist a face like that?" Brielle said as she reached down to pet Sugar.

"I'm actually so glad he bought her for me. I don't feel as lonely in my condo as I would have without her."

As they continued to coo over Sugar, the waitress brought their salads to the table and Blase put Sugar back in her carrier so she could eat.

"So, I think Dwight is having an affair," Brielle blurted out.

Blase put her fork down and looked at Brielle. "Are you serious? What makes you think that?"

"Well it started right before I had the baby. He was working late, which initially I didn't think it was bizarre. We wanted to make extra money for when the baby arrived since we decided I wouldn't go back to work until the baby was six months old."

Blase nodded.

"My six months off you know ended up being a year off after I decided to transition into the financial industry. He was still working late. But strangely the more I did our personal banking and started taking over

120

control of handling our finances I realized we hadn't saved as much money as we should have given the amount of time he had been working overtime at that point."

The waitress came over and asked them if they were ready to put in their entrée orders. They were and they did.

Brielle continued. "I didn't ask Dwight about the money. I checked our credit reports to see if he had any other accounts I didn't know about. He did have a credit card that I didn't know about but the balance was paid off. So with no money going into any other accounts, I thought, well is he really working late? I mean it had been a year, B. We should've had a considerable amount of money. So I asked Dwight after he came home late again one night if he had started some type of account or CD for our son I may have overlooked. Dwight was caught off guard with the question and immediately said no. He thought I was going to set that up. So I told him that based upon my calculations of the overtime he worked, we should have at least $25,000 more in our money market account or some other account. He looked at me as if I was speaking some other language to him. I asked him again if there was an account somewhere that he didn't tell me about. He said no."

Blase looked at her friend as she began to get choked up.

Brielle went on. "So I asked him if he was having an affair. He said quickly and firmly, no. Now, I don't have any proof that he is having an affair other than my calculations for how much money we should have in our account, and I don't know what to do."

"Is he acting different? Are you guys still making love regularly?" Blase decided not to ask if he was doing things differently to change his physical appearance because the two of them were avid fitness enthusiasts. "Is he wearing different cologne or dressing differently?" Blase added.

Brielle answered all of her questions. "He is acting the same; we still make love three to four times a week, just in the mornings now. Dwight has always dressed great and tried different colognes so I can't put my finger on anything."

Blase looked at Brielle with no answers. She would've given Brielle the same advice that Brielle gives her all of the time. To sit down and talk with him, but it seems Brielle has tried that and hit a brick wall. Blase offered, "Hire a private investigator."

Brielle thought her friend was joking, but quickly realized she wasn't. "A private investigator?" she asked.

"Yes. I see it all of the time. In fact a woman in my hospital did it and she found out her husband had a gambling habit."

Brielle digested what her friend had recommended, "That's a good idea. I'll do some research."

Blase and Brielle's food arrived. They ate and changed the discussion to work, the baby, and fashion for the remainder of their lunch. Blase thought of how her friend had been going through this and she didn't even realize it.

THE next day Blase met with Paul Graham in Park Slope Brooklyn at his private practice. She liked his practice and she liked him; mostly because she wasn't at all attracted to him. Paul was a small, lumpy, slightly balding, middle-aged Dermatologist whose bedside manner needed a serious attitude adjustment. Blase did like the compensation package that he was offering and the flexibility he gave her to bring on new clients as her own. After their meeting, she asked him if she could think about it overnight and get back to him in the morning. Dr. Graham was happy to allow her that time.

The next morning Blase called Dr. Graham and accepted his offer and asked if she could use one of the assistants he already had on payroll. Paul agreed and they discussed her starting in the next two weeks. She told him she would have all of the documents signed and back to him that afternoon via messenger. After Blase signed all of the documents, she called Walter to tell him the good news. Walter wasn't as happy about the news. Somehow he'd forgotten that she wasn't coming back to the hospital. They quarreled for a while and after sometime, Walter hung up on Blase. She held the phone in disbelief. Walter had never hung up on her before.

*Why wouldn't he be happy for me?*

Before she could continue deliberating over his reaction, Blase's brother came through her door.

"Who are you in here yelling at? When I heard the shouts, I decided to wait in the hallway until you were finished with your conversation," he told her.

"Walter. He's not happy about me taking on a job at a Dermatology practice in Brooklyn."

"Oh, he'll be alright. That's some dumb shit," he said, brushing off the silly argument. "Congratulations on the new gig. How much are they paying you?" he asked being nosy.

"None of your business," she quickly retorted.

"Why the hell is there a furry rodent running around here?" he said, laughing.

"That's Sugar. She's my new baby. Isn't she cute? Walter got her for me to apologize for his insane behavior in London." Blase picked Sugar up to pet her.

"Insane behavior? What are you talking about? Do I need to go and pay the Brit a visit?" Benny's expression walked to concern.

"No, Benny, but you do need to take those dirty shoes off on my white carpet. Where the heck have you been?" she shrieked, looking at his shoes.

"Oh it's raining. My fault." He smirked as he took his shoes off and put them outside her door.

Blase and Benny sat on the sofa and talked about his new firm in L.A. and how they are looking to take on only celebrity clients and maybe try their hands in the sports agent industry. He told her he loved L.A. and was in the process of buying a house there for him and his long-time girlfriend. He planned on popping the question to her during the winter holiday at their parents' annual holiday party. It wasn't until then that Blase realized how long it had been since she actually sat down and had a conversation with her only sibling. They both had been so busy with school and life that neither took the time to talk with one another. They kept up with each other through their parents and had light conversation during holiday visits. Blase listened to her older brother and felt proud of him and proud of her parents for the way they raised them both. Her brother was a bit more of a challenge than she was, but he made it through it all.

WITHIN three weeks, Blase was settled in to her new position as a Dermatologist at Dr. P. Graham Dermatology & Associates. Sheridan was the assistant Paul had chosen to work with Blase. Sheridan knew the patients that Blase was to take over from Paul and would be able to handle the load of new patients Blase's advertising was bringing in. Blase had taken out an ad in the local newspaper introducing herself as a new doctor to the practice. She also placed an ad on the local cable television network with a 30-second commercial explaining the practice and what she planned to bring to it.

Dr. Graham enjoyed her enthusiasm and new innovative ways to market his practice. A few months after Blase's 32nd birthday, she was growing tired of her situation with Walter. His passive behavior hadn't changed. They were comfortable but she still felt like there were missing pieces. She still had a lot of unanswered questions about his past and just wasn't sure he was someone who she could see herself spending the rest of her life with.

She was busy with a patient when her nurse Helen knocked on the door. "Hi, Dr. Morgan, your next patient is waiting in patient room number three."

"Thank you, Helen. Tell him I'll be there in five minutes," she said as she finished up with her current patient. "So, I'm going to write you a prescription for a topical anesthetic for the acne on your forehead. Use this for four weeks. If your acne persists, we may have to switch you to an oral medication."

"Thank you, Dr. Morgan. Enjoy the rest of your day," the patient responded.

"You do the same and don't forget to see Sheridan on your way out to make a follow-up appointment," Blase reminded her.

Before Blase walked into the next patient's room, Helen walked over to her and exclaimed, "Ay dios Mio, Blase. You will never believe who is in that room. I didn't want to say anything while you were with your other patient, but I can't believe he is in there."

Blase looked at Helen who was now saying something in Spanish and fanning herself. Blase laughed, "Well who is it?"

Helen whispered, "Cup!"

Blase looked puzzled. "Pardon me?" she said as she smiled, noticing Helen was actually sweating.

Helen grabbed Blase's arm. "Cup...ummm Corey Cup Ponce. Ay dios Mio, he plays baseball for the New York Mets!"

Blase was still looking befuddled. The most she knew about baseball was what Fallon had told her since she'd started dating Sergio. Blase jokingly said, "What does he look like?"

When Helen started to answer her Blase said, "I was kidding, Helen. I'm about to see what he looks like right now," she said as she laughed. "Now calm down, he is still a patient after all."

As Blase looked over his paperwork before she walked in, she wondered how he'd come to know her practice. She opened the door while looking at his information and before looking at him she said, "Hello, Mr. Ponce."

"Hello, Dr. Graham. You're even more beautiful than Fallon said you would be."

At this Blase looked up at him and replied, "Thank you very much. I'll have to call Fallon and thank her for the referral."

"No, I'll have to call Fallon and thank her for the referral," he said brazenly. Cup stood up to shake Blase's hand. He was enormous. The ceilings in the patient room were seven-foot ceilings and Cup was six inches shorter than the ceiling. As they shook hands, his engulfed hers. Blase was visibly taken aback.

Cup smiled and sat back down on the patient bed.

"So, Mr. Ponce, what seems to be the problem?" Blase was making her best attempt at remaining professional, but she had to admit, he was a striking man.

"Well, Dr. Morgan, I think I'm allergic to my new uniforms."

"Why do you think that?"

"May I take off my shirt?"

Blase stood firm. "Of course. Let's see what's going on."

Cup took his shirt off to reveal red welts all over his russet colored chest, stomach, and back. Blase went to the drawer and took out a pair of microscopic glasses and rubber gloves. She put them on, walked back over to Cup, turned the magnifying lamp on, and pointed it towards his chest. Blase began examining his welts. While she was examining his chest and back, she asked him, "How long have you been wearing your new uniform?"

"About three months now."

Blase stopped and looked up at him. "Three months? How long have you had this rash?"

"For about a month now. At first it was just isolated to the left side of my neck and shoulder and then it started to spread to the rest of my upper body," he answered.

"Has it spread to any of the lower portion of your body?"

"Not that I know of." He smirked. "But I'd be happy to drop my pants so you can check."

Blase ignored the crude comment and kept examining him. "Have you started eating anything different?"

"No."

She noted that he smelled of citrus and leather. "Have you changed colognes recently?"

"Yes! My teammate launched a new cologne and asked a few of us to go around and promote it for him."

"Well, I'd suggest you start there and stop using the cologne. Because you don't have the rash below your waste, it leads me to believe that it isn't your uniform because your pants are made of the same thing that your jersey is made from, correct?"

"Correct."

"Do you wear anything different underneath it?" She took her goggles and gloves off.

"No, I wear the same t-shirts I've been wearing since I was in high school."

"Well then, we can probably rule those out also. I'm going to give you a prescription for an oral medication that will make the bumps subside. It looks to me like you have Contact Dermatitis. Take two of the pills immediately, and then follow the dosage instructions after that."

Cup sat bare chested. Not eager to put his shirt back on.

"I will also write you a prescription for a topical Cortisone cream to stop the itching. You can put your shirt back on, Mr. Ponce."

"Please call me Cup or Corey," he insisted.

"Here are your prescriptions, Corey. Please stop and see Sheridan before you leave. Thank you again."

Cup stood up, put his shirt back on, and smiled. Blase felt a bit wicked when she noticed the dimple in his left cheek and the cleft in his chin behind his low cut beard, but she kept her composure.

*Now I see why Helen was going crazy. He's adorable.*

As Blase turned to leave, Cup said, "No, thank you. I hope to see you again soon."

She turned back to him. "You will. Please make an appointment with Sheridan for a follow up visit in a few weeks. I want to check on you to make sure the medication is working. In the meantime, please apologize to your friend, but tell him that you cannot be his spokesmodel anymore."

"Do we have to do the follow up visit here, or do you make house calls?"

Blase looked up from the paperwork she was filling out, closed his patient folder, and was slightly offended by his request for her to come to his house. "I don't make house calls. I will see you in a few weeks, Mr. Ponce," she countered as she opened the door to leave.

Helen was standing right outside of the room waiting for Blase to come out. Blase looked at her, pursed her lips, and handed her Cup's file. "He's adorable," Blase said and walked into her next patient's room.

**LATER** that evening, as Blase was preparing to leave, she listened to her messages. There was one from Walter asking her to meet him for dinner at 8:00 p.m. She deleted the message and called him back on his home phone. After the third ring a woman answered with a heavy Asian accent.

"Hello," Blase said through her speakerphone. "I'm sorry, I must have the wrong number." She hung up and picked up the receiver and dialed Walter's number again. The woman with the accent answered again.

"Hello." Blase looked at her phone to make sure she'd dialed the correct number. "Hello, I'm trying to reach the residence of Dr. Walter Bailey."

"Yes, Walta hee-ah, one mini," the woman replied.

Blase frowned.

*Did Walter get a new housekeeper?* She thought of the missing Chinese wife. "Couldn't be," she said to herself out loud.

"Cheers my love. Are we meeting this evening for dinner?" Walter asked nonchalantly.

"Walter, who is the woman that answered your phone?"

"I'd much prefer to explain to you at dinner," he suggested.

"Absolutely not. Who is the woman, and why is she answering your phone?" she argued.

"Darling, please let's talk about this face to face."

"Is that the woman from China, Walter? Is she at your house? I'm not meeting you for any damn dinner for you to tell me that your long lost Chinese wife and your child have returned to your life." Blase was beginning to lose her composure.

"Alright then, my love. Yes, Liang is here. She contacted me two days ago and told me she was in New York and she wanted me to meet my son."

"She contacted you? Son? How did she contact you? You said you haven't seen or spoken to her since she went back to China almost two decades ago. How does one just come to New York and know that you're here living and breathing and call your house and then answer your phone two days later, Walter?"

He remained silent, allowing Blase to finish her tirade, then finally spoke, "I will explain it all to you in detail if you would just meet me for dinner, my love. This conversation is getting hostile."

"This conversation is exactly how it should be given the circumstances. I don't want to have dinner with you, and I don't want to hear the explanation of how…Liang is it? …is in your house. I'm pretty fed up with it all, Walter," she said before she hung up on him.

# Melesse Wellness Spa

**A FEW** days after finally meeting Walter for lunch and hearing him out about his now live in Chinese ex-wife and their 17-year-old son, Blase sat in her office in Park Slope and felt bushed. Sheridan walked in and asked her if she was feeling okay, and she faintly responded with, "For some reason, I've been feeling fatigued all day. I know I got more than eight hours of sleep last night, so I don't know what it could be."

Sheridan spied Helen walking passed and waved her into Blase's office. She told Helen Blase seemed unusually tired and her cheeks felt hot. Helen wanted to take Blase's temperature but Blase didn't want all of the fuss, so she attempted to wave them off, but they both insisted. When they took the thermometer out of her mouth it read 103.5 degrees.

"Aye yae yae mamita, your temperature is too high. I think you might have the flu."

Blase leaned forward in her chair, looked at Helen, and asked to see the thermometer. "I can't have the flu right now, I have way too much on my plate, and Paul has a vacation scheduled in the next few weeks," Blase spewed as she caved back into her slouched position.

"Well, Paul is just going to have to postpone that vacation or you guys won't be able to see patients because you are definitely coming down with the flu, mami."

Blase took the thermometer and took her own temperature. It read the same. She cursed and asked Sheridan how many patients she had for the next day. Sheridan confirmed she had six patients to see the next day. Fortunately for her, the next day was Friday. She told Sheridan to reschedule her Monday and Tuesday patients. Blase dragged to work the next day feeling worse than the day before. She saw all of her patients and barely made it back to her office. Sheridan noticed how flushed her face was and offered to drive Blase home. She agreed.

Once Sheridan dropped Blase off and got her all situated at home, she called a cab. As she was leaving, Blase said, "Remind me to give you a raise. You're the best."

Sheridan laughed. "Now I know you're sick, but I will remind you the moment you are back to full health, but for now I'll settle for cab fare."

Blase gladly accommodated her with extra money to get dinner.

When Sheridan left, Blase picked up the phone to call Fallon.

She answered on the second ring. "Hey girl, what's new?"

"The flu is new," Blase said softly.

"Who has the flu, you?"

"Apparently so."

"I'm sorry to hear that, girl. Is there anything that I can do?"

"Yes," Blase said. "You can tell me why you didn't warn me that Mr. Cup was coming to my office."

Fallon howled. "Girl, isn't he adorable? He's one of Sergio's good friends. When he told us he was single, I told him I had the perfect person for him. When I described you he started licking his lips."

Blase shook her head.

"So I told him you were a doctor. He asked me what kind, and when I told him, his eyes lit up. He asked if I had your office number and told us he was going to make an appointment," Fallon admitted.

"Well he did," Blase confirmed.

"What? We thought he was joking about the appointment. Was he a jerk or something? Did he waste your time?"

"No, actually he had a legitimate problem. He was nice enough though. He tried to get little flirts in here and there, but Fal, I'm so outdone with the whole Walter situation that I can't even think about Cup or Corey or whatever his name is right now." Blase thought for a second and continued, "Well, actually I could *think* about him." She laughed faintly. "But my love life is a mess. I need to take a break." Blase sounded worn out.

"Girl, you don't have to fall in love with him, but he'll take your mind off Walter. From what Sergio tells me, he's really a sweet guy. He's the relief pitcher for their team."

"I'm sure he's nice, but I don't know, girl. I think the reason I'm sick is from internalizing all of my stress. I've never really dealt with all of Walter's antics. I think my body is telling me I need to take some time to myself," Blase resisted.

"I understand. I don't want to force him on you. You guys have met, what happens after that is up to the two of you. But otherwise, is there anything that I can bring you?"

"All the way from New Jersey? No, but I appreciate it. I think Paul is going to have a conniption because I'm sick. I took Monday and Tuesday off to try and shake this bug. He's such a damn work horse."

"That little meatball will just have to deal with it. Your health comes first."

"Yes it does. I've only been there for a year and he and I seem to be butting heads regularly," Blase said.

"Really, about what?"

"Everything. From the way we advertise, to how we see and treat patients, answer the phone, file our records, and the overall aesthetic of the office. I know it's his baby and he was doing well before he hired me, but if it weren't for my marketing efforts he wouldn't be thriving the way he is now. His profits have quadrupled since taking me on." Blase paused to take a sip of her water. "I don't know, girl, I think my days are numbered with the meatball."

They both laughed.

"Well, do what is best for you. You know I have your back whatever you decide. Now, get some rest and we'll catch up when you're feeling better. I'll check on you tomorrow, but if you need anything in the meantime call me. No matter what time it is."

"Thank you. I should be fine. I probably just need some rest and fluids, and maybe a big cup of something." Blase laughed at her own joke.

Fallon joined the laughter. "You do. In fact, make it a big ole pitcher."

Blase laughed so hard she coughed. "Alright, I'll talk to you tomorrow." They hung up.

THE next morning Blase received a call from her doorman telling her she had a delivery. She told him to let the delivery man upstairs. When he arrived at the door, he was holding an enormous pink gift basket filled with medicinal products and a huge pink and yellow bow at the top. She signed for the basket and tipped the delivery guy. When she sat the basket on her dining room table, she read the card: *Belleza, I hope these products make you feel better. Call me if you need anything. Also, tune in to 99.1 FM today between noon and 4pm. I love you.*

Blase read the card, surprised to learn it was from Mark. She wondered how he knew she wasn't feeling well. It was already close to 1:00 p.m. when Blase received the delivery, so she walked over to her media cabinet, opened it, and turned on the radio. As soon as the station tuned in clearly, she heard Mark's voice. He was speaking in Spanish and sounded very energetic. Blase only understood a few of the things he was saying, but she heard Belleza a few times throughout his entire broadcast. As soon as he signed off the air, she called him.

Mark answered his cell phone immediately. "Hola, Belleza. Como estas, mi amor?"

Blase blushed. She hadn't spoken to Mark in almost six months. "I'm better now. Thank you so much for my gift basket. I needed everything inside of it. Even the tampons buried at the bottom." She laughed.

"Hey, you never know. I just wanted to be thorough. It's good to hear your voice."

"Yours also. How did you know that I was sick?"

"I called your office and spoke to one of your assistants. It turns out she used to work at the health clinic in Spanish Harlem with Marisol."

"Oh my, what a small world. Which one?"

"Helena"

"Helen?"

"Yes."

"Okay, yes she's very sweet. She's a hard worker too. I just heard your show. Of course you know I have no idea what you were saying, and I think that is the most Spanish language music I've ever listened to in my life, but it was exciting hearing you on the radio," Blase breathlessly told him as she climbed back into bed and pulled the covers up.

"Gracias, Belleza. I started a week ago. I interned here for a few months, and then when someone was out, they asked me if I would fill in, and I did, and so far I haven't gotten off the air."

136

"I'm very proud of you, Mark. I have to tell Fallon and Brielle to tune in. They both speak more Spanish than I do."

"Great. How are they doing?"

"They are great. Brielle has her hands full with her son and starting her new career. She's going into the financial services industry, and Fallon is still busy helping her father with his chain of hotels, but she did just have a launch party for her new travel business."

"Nice. Tell them to call me. Maybe I can arrange some advertising spots for them on the show," he offered.

"Oh, that's a great idea. I certainly will."

"Is she still dating Sergio?" he asked.

"Yes, they are still together. I think he may propose soon. He's been emailing me about ring suggestions, so my fingers are crossed for her."

"Oh yeah, well don't spend all of his money, Belleza. I know you have expensive taste." He paused for a reaction, but only heard Blase coughing in the background. He hoped she didn't hear that last part. "So what about you, Belleza. Are you still with that doctor?"

Blase sighed. "Actually no. Walter and I have hit a brick wall."

"I can't say that I'm sorry to hear that"

"I'm sure you're not, Mr. Rodriguez."

"I'd love to see you sometime. Do you think you can make time?"

"Of course I can. I always have time for you," she flirted.

"Great. As soon as you are feeling better. I want you all to myself for a night," he said.

"Then I'm all yours."

Mark always had a way of making Blase feel like she was the most important woman in the world. Nothing else seemed to matter to him but Blase, when she allowed him the opportunity.

**TWO** weeks later, Blase was sitting in her office in Park Slope after office hours checking her emails. She was exceedingly swamped the past week because Paul had left for his vacation to Egypt. After answering all of her business emails, she decided to check her personal email account. She had 386 emails. A few of them were from her brother and his fiancée about their forthcoming nuptials. She immediately switched to her schedule and typed in a reminder to send her measurements to Benny's fiancée for her bridesmaid's gown and to talk with Fallon about arranging their honeymoon gift package. She went back to her emails and saw a few from Brielle and Fallon with events they said she should attend. And then, she reached two that were weirdly one right after the other. She read the first email:

*Hello, Lace. I hope when you receive this email you are in good health and spirits. It's been a long time. We took on a new client in my firm the other day by the name of Miller Jones and in conversations over drinks one night, we realized that we had more than football in common. After talking briefly about you, I couldn't help but look you up on our college Alumni website and send an email. I haven't seen you at any of our homecomings and I'm hoping it isn't because you are trying to avoid me. ;) Anyway, I hope you are doing well. Based upon your company's website, it looks like you are doing great and you look beautiful as always. Let's catch up. I hope to hear from you. Warmest Regards, Adrian*

Blase hadn't talked with Adrian since he left her apartment all of those years ago. She often wondered how he was doing and if he was married with a family. She decided to answer his email after she read the second:

*Hello, Dr. Morgan. I hope you weren't turned off by any of my comments when I was there. I was with Sergio and Fallon the other day and they told me you weren't feeling well. I wanted to send you something but wasn't sure if it was appropriate. I hope you are feeling better! I really would like the chance to get to know you. I'm having a benefit for my non-profit organization, and I would like for you to be my date. If you don't have any other plans, the benefit is on July 2nd. The attire is formal and I would be proud to have you on my arm. Email me back or call me. I hope you can make it.*

*-Cup*

Blase clicked reply with her mouse to answer Cup's email first.

*Hello, Corey. Thank you for the invitation. I would love to attend your benefit. The second works for me. Please forward me more information and I'll be black tie ready.*

*Best Regards, Blase*

She clicked Send and then went on to reply to Adrian's message.

*Miller Jones?! What a small world. I would've never imagined that you two would connect. I hope the conversation didn't get too detailed. Overall, I have no complaints. Life is well. As you saw, I am in private practice right now specializing in Dermatology in Brooklyn. I absolutely love what I do. At the risk of being assumptive, I imagine that you went on to get your law degree; if so, congratulations. I hope you are well also. Please stay in touch.*

*Best Regards, Blase*

After Blase sent the two messages, she shut her computer down and headed out the door. As she walked toward her car, she noticed an SUV parked next to it. She knew no one was in the building, so she wondered whose car it was. As she approached her car, a man stepped out of the SUV holding a large bouquet of flowers. She immediately knew who it was before she saw his face by the way he was dressed, and she relaxed and smiled.

"Hello, Belleza, I'm glad you are feeling better, but I think I've waited long enough," Mark said.

Blase giggled. "I'm sorry. I've been meaning to call you."

He said, "Well, as luck would have it, I was in the neighborhood and you don't need to. Climb in. You're mine for the night."

Blase thought about it for a second and decided that if she didn't make it back to get her car she would take a car service to work the next day. Mark opened the back door of his SUV first to rest Blase's flowers on the back seat. He took her briefcase and put it on the floor. Always the gentleman, he opened the passenger door and helped her in.

When she eased into the seat, she shook her head and grinned. Mark climbed into the driver's seat and put the car in reverse to pull off. Their first stop was a quaint Cuban restaurant in Greenwich Village. Mark and Blase sat in amorous bliss, talking, catching up, and shamelessly flirting with each other. Mark was in heaven. He decided during dinner that he didn't want the evening to end. He actually didn't want the evening to ever end. He asked, "Are you tired?"

"Not yet," she answered. Blase wasn't ready for the evening to end either.

"Great!"

They got back in his car and ventured to midtown. When they pulled in front of a Latin club, Mark was greeted by the valet as if he was a celebrity. As they walked inside, Blase heard Spanish language music blaring from the speakers. She looked over and saw a live band on the stage and dozens of people on the dance floor. Mark grabbed her hand and ushered her to the dance floor. Blase's nerves and excitement were tangled. They reached the dance floor and Mark lead Blase into two hours of Salsa dancing. By the time they finished dancing, Blase was exhausted and sweating like she'd just finished a four mile run.

"Oh my goodness, I've never had so much fun dancing," she said to Mark.

"I'm glad you are having a good time, Belleza. What do you want to drink?"

"I'll take some water. I have to see a few patients tomorrow." She played it safe even though she really wanted a martini.

"Agua it is!" Mark guided Blase over to one of the love seats and went to the bar. As Blase looked around the club, she started feeling warm and romantic inside. She realized every time she was with Mark, she felt at peace and protected. He returned with two waters and napkins for them both to wipe their sweat. "So Belleza, what would you like to do now?" Blase wiped her forehead and put her hand on Mark's thigh. "What do you want to do?" she asked with a suggestive expression.

Mark took the hint and reached for her hand to lead her out of the club. As they drove, Blase observed that they were driving back to Brooklyn. She thought, *Oh no, I hope he didn't take that as me wanting to go to my car to go home.*

They drove down Flatbush Avenue and made a left onto Fulton Street. She realized they weren't going towards her practice, but couldn't figure out where they were going. As they continued on with a few more left and right turns, Mark finally stopped in front of a brownstone. She looked at him perplexed. He parked his car, got out, went around and took the flowers and briefcase out of the back seat, and then opened Blase's door. Blase climbed out and followed in silence.

Hand in hand, Mark and Blase walked up the steps of this brownstone, and Mark used his key to open the door.

"Do you live here?" she finally asked.

"Yes, Belleza. I bought this three months ago," he said as he opened the door to the foyer.

Blase immediately noticed a painting hanging in the entry she had given Mark when they dated years ago. "I can't believe you still have this painting."

"I've kept everything you've given me," he said as he took her purse and put it on the entry table along with the flowers and briefcase. He walked her into his minimalistic living room.

"Still decorating?" she teased.

"Yes I am. Will you help me?"

"Of course I will."

"Gracias," he whispered as he turned toward her and pulled her close to him. "Belleza, I want you to come to Puerto Rico with me. I want you to see my country and meet my family."

Blase's eyes met his and she said, "Okay," without a thought.

"I will take care of all of the details. We'll go for the 4th of July weekend. Is that okay?"

# LUCKY NO. 5

"Yes."

Mark looked down at Blase, grabbed her face into his hands, and kissed her. As she kissed him back, she felt that familiar sensation waft through her body. She closed her eyes, inhaled his scent, and lost herself in the comfort of his smell, the way he tasted, and the way he touched her. His touch was decided and reassuring, he never forgot how to make her feel...perfect.

Mark led Blase upstairs to his room, which was the only room in his brownstone that had been fully decorated and housed a massive flat screen TV. He also had a huge Puerto Rican flag hanging on one wall. She liked it. Mark turned on romantic Latin music and walked over towards Blase. She decided that she would take the lead. She sat Mark down on the edge of his king sized bed and let him watch her undress. She took off her pale pink blouse first exposing a deep magenta bra. She unzipped her grey skirt and as she slid it to the floor, matching deep magenta panties balanced her lingerie attire. When she stepped out of everything, she took off her black heels and straddled herself on top of him.

Mark gripped Blase by her waist and waited for her next move. At the feel of his massive hands, she began kissing his forehead, then his nose, his cheeks, then his lips. Mark parted his lips to take all of Blase in and she pulled back teasing him. She reached down and pulled his shirt over his head brandishing a scar on his left shoulder from his accident to which she softly kissed. Blase gently leaned him back onto his back and started unbuttoning his pants. She slid herself off him to pull his pants off by the legs and while she did this Mark folded his hands behind his head. After Blase removed his pants, she followed with his boxers. When she touched the waistband of his boxers, Mark's heart began to dash. He was already grown with excitement, but he was beginning to get nervous. She slid herself on top of him and he leaned up to unite his chest with her luscious breasts. Mark started kissing Blase with a hunger. He unhooked her bra and in one movement laid Blase on her back underneath him. They were close enough for Blase to feel his brisk heartbeat, so she reached up and kissed his heart. When Mark felt this, he couldn't hold in his lust any longer, every inch of Blase's body was his and he intended to make love to and satisfy her in the best way he knew how until the sun came up.

When she woke up an hour after she'd gone to sleep, Blase recognized she had to hurry to get to her office. Her first patient was at 9:00 a.m. She jumped up to find the bathroom while Mark was sound asleep. As she was walking down the hall, she saw another bedroom door open with a bunch of opened boxes in it. She tiptoed into the room and went to the first box she saw open. Inside were a bunch of loose photos and two photo albums. The first one she picked up was filled with photos of them throughout the years, his hospital band, as well as the press release article she placed in the newspaper introducing herself as a new doctor in the Park Slope practice. Blase began to tear up. She put the album to the side and picked up the second album, which was of family photos of Mark, his sister, Marisol, and their parents back in Puerto Rico. She sat down on the chair in the room and began looking through the photos. She thought about how painful it must be for him without his parents and how she didn't know what she would do without her parents. She noticed how happy they looked back in Puerto Rico and how much Mark looked like his father. As she was putting the book back in the box, she felt a presence, looked up, and saw Mark standing in the doorway with his navy blue boxers on.

"That is where I want to take you, Belleza. Back to where I grew up. I want you to see where I came from."

Blase got up, walked over to Mark, and kissed him on the lips. "I can't wait," she said kindly. They hugged for a few moments and then she went to take a shower.

Blase arrived at the practice that morning walking in to hustle and bustle. Helen and Paul's nurses were talking about something and Sheridan was sitting at the front desk with Paul's assistant standing up on the other side of the desk. Sheridan looked at Blase and said, "Paul left a mass message to everyone telling them he was staying in Egypt for an additional week, but when he returns to the United States, he wants to have a meeting with us all to discuss changes that he will make effective immediately upon his return."

Blase looked at Sheridan puzzled. She immediately walked around, sat down next to her at the front desk, checked her voicemail messages, and heard the message Sheridan was referring to. What she didn't hear was a private message to her about what these discussions would be about or letting her know he wanted to have this meeting with their staff. She went on to check her cell phone messages and email messages and nothing. Blase was irritated. She fired off an email to Paul asking what the meeting was all about and after two days with no response, she grew outraged. She made a decision to leave the practice. In the few months prior they had been disagreeing on everything and the differences were leading Blase right out the door.

Between patients one afternoon, Blase called her bank and inquired about obtaining a business loan to start her own practice. She made an appointment with her banker and made the arrangements to secure a loan.

A few days after she secured her loan, she contacted a commercial real estate agent and had a meeting to discuss possible locations. She settled on looking in Harlem. A few days before Paul was scheduled to return, Blase went out looking at possible locations for her practice. She knew she wanted something that was at least two thousand square feet to allow room to incorporate spa services, which Paul was opposed to doing. She found two locations that could suffice on her first visit. One was on Lenox Avenue close to Central Park and the other was on 125th street between Fifth and Madison. The next day she brought her father and Fallon with her to check out both locations. They both liked the Lenox Avenue location the best. Blase told her real estate agent to make an offer on the lease for twenty dollars per square foot instead of their thirty dollar asking price because it had been vacant for four years.

"I want this to include property taxes, common area maintenance, and garbage collection. I will pay utilities and insurance and all the costs associated with the construction and build out," Blase said.

Her realtor wrote it all down and nodded. After she said her goodbyes to her realtor, Blase took her father and her best friend to lunch. Blase asked her father if he was enjoying his recent retirement.

"I'm enjoying it so far. I think your mother is enjoying it more than I am. She hasn't stopped asking me to do things around the house since the morning after my retirement party."

Blase and Fallon laughed.

"She's driving me bananas trying to get the house perfect for your grand-parents arrival in a few weeks," he said.

"That's right. Sayt Ayat and Wund Ayat are coming in for Benny's wedding, right?" she asked.

"Yes. They are staying until the beginning of next year. So they'll be here for your 33rd birthday. We'd like to have a dinner party then. Is that okay?"

"Of course that's okay, Daddy. I don't have any plans for my birthday and I won't make any."

"Neither will me and Sergio," Fallon added.

"So tell me about this Sergio, Fallon. Is he treating you better than that football player fellow you were dating?" her father asked.

"Yes, Dad. He's a dream. I tell you, I don't know what it is, but there's something about Latin men. They just seem to take care of their women better than a lot of Black men these days."

Blase shot Fallon an annoyed look. She couldn't believe she'd said that to her father.

"What are you talking about? What does race have to do with it, Fallon?" Blase countered.

Fallon looked back at Blase with a smirk. "Well at my tender age of thirty-three, I've found that Sergio has treated me better than any black man I've ever dated."

"As far as I'm concerned, I don't care what color the young man is, as long as he treats you right. I certainly can't add value to this conversation because I don't date black or Latin men," Blase's father said, noticing his daughter's annoyance.

Blase smiled. She decided to switch the subject and talk about Benny's wedding. For the next hour and a half they talked about wedding details, Blase's ideas for her new practice, and how she would handle Paul when he returned with this mysterious news. Blase's father beamed as he offered Blase his and her mother's help for the opening of her new practice and then turned his smile and attention to Fallon to inquire about her parents and the success of the Flynn hotels. Fallon delighted in announcing the opening of their sixth hotel in Greece in the coming spring season. Mr. Morgan's expression grew to that of adulation with the mention of the sixth hotel. Last he spoke with Fallon's father he was going between Jamaica and Africa building his fourth and fifth hotels.

She laughed. "Yeah, Dad won't quit building hotels until there is one in every city of every country in the world."

Mr. Morgan laughed. "I'll give him a call. Maybe I can slow him down a bit."

"Speaking of slowing down. Blase, you missed out on a great vacation by passing up the Jamaica trip," Fallon teased.

'I'm sure," Blase responded.

"My mother is particularly excited about the Crete, Greece hotel. She wants to buy a house there as well so she can reconnect with her distant relatives."

Blase, her father, and Fallon continued their conversation well after they finished their lunches until finally Mr. Morgan had to run for an appointment.

After lunch Blase's father drove the ladies back to Blase's condo and continued back to New Rochelle.

Fallon asked Blase if she wanted to do some shopping.

"Yes. I have to buy a dress. I told Cup I would go with him to his benefit."

"Oh did you now?" Fallon asked with a grin.

Blase's cell phone rang. "It's Brielle, I'm going to see if she can meet us to shop."

Brielle agreed to meet them since she'd started working in the city and she was close by. They all met on Fifth Avenue and decided to make Saks Fifth Avenue their first stop. The ladies shopped until close to nine that night. They decided to go back to Blase's apartment to relax and finish their conversations, and since Brielle's son was with his father, she was able to join them.

When they arrived back at Blase's condo, Blase fed her dog, checked her messages, and then got three white wine glasses out of her cabinet. She arranged a platter of cheese, crackers and olives, and put the wine on ice in an ice bucket and brought it all into the living room. The ladies sat around updating each other on their lives. Brielle told them that after the private investigator found the apartment her husband and his mistress shared, she confronted him and he decided to go and live with his mistress. Blase and Fallon couldn't believe the news. Brielle didn't mention a word of it. The few times they would inquire, she would tell them she hadn't heard anything. As far as they knew Brielle and her husband were still together and the investigator was still investigating.

"Brielle, are you okay?" Blase asked.

"Why the hell are you just telling us this?" Fallon fired right after.

"You guys know I don't deal with things openly," she answered.

"Openly is one thing, Brielle, but to hold all of that to yourself. You must be going insane. I know I would be," Blase said.

"Actually so far so good. I love Dwight, and this is troubling me, but I love me more and I have to be strong for my son. I don't have time to break down." Brielle took a sip of her wine.

Blase and Fallon looked at their friend like she was crazy. They went back and forth with Brielle about it for another thirty minutes and then decided to switch the subject. Fallon told them her new travel company was getting off to a great start thanks to Sergio's teammates and some of her father's clients from the hotel. She said she would be looking for her own office space soon.

"You should open your office in Harlem next to my practice," Blase suggested.

"No dear. My location has to be reflective of the clientele that I have and intend to get," Fallon said.

"Oh!" Blase reacted. Both she and Brielle raised their eyebrows.

"So where are you thinking of opening?" Brielle asked.

"I'm considering a location in midtown, close to the theater district. I like the busyness of that location," she said.

"Just keep in mind as busy as it is, it may be difficult for your clients to get to you," Blase said.

"True," Brielle concurred.

"Well, I guess I'll put a little more thought into it. But in the meantime, Sergio is taking me to Fiji for vacation," Fallon said.

"Girl I want your life. You travel all over the world," Brielle said.

"Girl this trip is purely pleasure, but I plan on staying after Sergio leaves to visit and critique some hotels for Flynn Destinations. I also want to see if there is need for a Flynn hotel presence there."

"Well enjoy and take lots of pictures," Brielle said.

Blase agreed.

"So tell us about this benefit you are going to with Cup who you said you didn't want to start anything with?" Fallon asked both sarcastically and comically.

150

"Oh, right, I didn't finish telling you…" Blase went on to tell them both about the emails, the benefit, and the evening she'd spent with Mark.

"Alright, so what's the deal with you and Mark? Clearly he loves you and you always seem to make your way back to him," Brielle asked.

"Mark is so sweet, but I don't know. Maybe he's not aggressive enough, but for me it's just not clicking like that. I mean I thoroughly enjoy the time we spend together. Oh, he has a radio show now by the way. I told him I would tell you guys about it since you understand Spanish better than I do. It's on 99.1 from noon to four. You should check it out."

Fallon and Brielle both agreed to tune in.

"Anyway, honestly I don't know what the disconnection is with Mark and I, but there is one so we just take it for what it is," Blase said.

"You both take it for what it is, or he takes what he can get?" Fallon asked.

Blase contemplated Fallon's remark and then shook her head, she was at a loss for a response. She took a sip of her wine and continued to talk about Cup and Paul Graham. A few hours later, Brielle lay sleeping on Blase's sofa while Blase and Fallon continued to giggle about Cup and Sergio. Fallon made a note of how brilliant the moon was which made both ladies check the time. Just after midnight Fallon walked over to the sofa and woke Brielle up so the ladies could leave together.

**BLASE** arrived at the practice the Monday after Paul returned to see that everyone seemed to be on edge. Paul was in his office browsing through stacks of files piled on his desk. Blase knocked on the doorframe and said, "Welcome back, Paul. How was your trip?"

"Please come in and shut the door, Dr. Morgan."

Blase instantly became vexed by not only his tone, but the formal way in which he addressed her.

"What's going on Paul, why so formal?" she griped.

"Dr. Morgan, I've been looking through many of the files since we acquired you and I noticed in many of your patient files you initially suggest alternative medicines rather than writing prescriptions."

Baffled, Blase replied, "First, I want to address your going through my patient files. It was clearly defined when I signed on here that my patients are my patients. I'm not sure why you're going behind my back and checking my patient files, Paul."

"I don't necessarily have to explain anything I do here, Dr. Morgan. Contrary to what you believe, this is my practice and everything that goes on here is my business."

Blase could hardly contain herself. She couldn't believe what she was hearing. P. Graham & Associates Dermatology had tripled its patients and revenues since Blase came on board and it was through the marketing and advertising efforts that she paid for as well as the patient's satisfaction with her alternative solutions.

"I know you are new to private practice, but I didn't bring you on to change the direction of my practice to an alternative medicine practice. I've been in business for fifteen years and am not prepared to move in a different direction. That said, either you discontinue the practice of suggesting alternative Dermatology solutions or we'll have to discuss other arrangements."

Blase looked at Dr. Graham and thought, *This will certainly be his loss.* She said, "Other arrangements sound most appropriate. I'll talk with my attorney about drawing up separation documents today."

Paul was shocked. He didn't expect her to decide to leave that quickly.

For the rest of that day and the remainder of the week, Blase and Paul worked in virtual silence with one another, only discussing minor patient issues. After Blase met with her attorney she had her send all of the separation documents to Paul's attorney to finalize her departure. Blase had a meeting with Sheridan and Helen to see if either wanted to join her new practice. While Helen felt it was best for her and her family to stay with Dr. Graham, Sheridan liked Blase's ideas and decided to move on with her. Having begun the construction of her location in Harlem, Blase was excited about the progress.

Fallon, Brielle, and Mark would be her closest advisors on aesthetics and layout. Everything was coming together nicely. Blase's final day in the Park Slope practice came two weeks before the completion of her Harlem practice so she took the time to relax and spend it with Mark preparing for their trip to Puerto Rico. Mark had even surprised Blase and hired an interior designer to design her personal office space. He knew with everything else that she hadn't taken the time to design her own space.

The morning of the benefit Cup asked Blase to attend was the morning that Mark revealed the office space to her. With tear-filled eyes, Blase thanked him for his generosity, his love, and mostly, his patience with her throughout the years. He truly was one of her best friends.

Later that evening, as Blase returned from the hair salon she listened to Mark on the radio. His time slot was changed from lunch to rush hour. She hung her dress in the doorway of her closet and put her shoes underneath to get a visual of the ensemble together. Just as she was about to jump in the shower, her cell phone rang. She looked at the number and recognized it to be Cup's number.

"Hello."

"Hello, this is Cup, I mean Corey."

Blase chuckled. "Yes I know it's you, Corey. Are we still on for this evening?"

"Of course we are," he assured her. "I was calling to make sure you were still on. Since you are, then I will be there to pick you up by six o'clock."

Blase glanced at the clock and saw it was 4:45 p.m. "That's perfect, I'll be ready."

"Great. I look forward to seeing you and getting to know you better tonight, Dr. Morgan."

Blase smiled. "And you as well, Mr. Ponce. Okay, let me go so I can make myself beautiful."

"In that case, we can talk until I get there because you're already beautiful without putting any effort into it."

Blase blushed. "I'll see you at six, Corey, and don't be late."

"Oh, I won't be, trust me," he said before they hung up the phone.

At 5:58 p.m., Blase's doorman called up and told her she had a visitor. She told him to tell Cup she would be right down. She finished putting her lipstick on, threw it in her clutch, and headed towards the door. About to leave, she heard her name on the radio: "I want to send a shout out to the love of my life, Blase. My Belleza is opening her dermatology practice in Harlem, and I want you all to check her out online at..." Blase couldn't believe her ears. Not only had Mark told everyone about her practice on the radio, but he had professed his love, in English for God knows how many listeners.

Within minutes Blase's blackberry was buzzing with text messages from colleagues and friends. Helen texted her to congratulate her on her new practice, and her new man. Most of the texts messages were the same. As she was heading out of the building towards the limo waiting outside, Fallon called. Blase answered and quickly said, "I can't talk, getting in the car with Corey. I know you heard Mark. I'll call you later."

Fallon understood. "Okay, call me later."

They hung up and she walked up to Cup who was standing outside the car door waiting with one red rose.

"I'm speechless, Dr. Morgan."

"Please don't call me Dr. Morgan; Blase is fine. Is that for me?" she said, pointing to the rose.

"Oh, yes it is," he replied, forgetting it was in his hand.

"Thank you."

"It's my pleasure." He smiled as the driver opened the door to let them in. Cup held Blase's hand as she got into the limo and he followed. "So, I know I don't know too many women named Blase with a Dermatology practice in Harlem, but if my ears weren't deceiving me, you are a popular woman."

Blase looked at Cup with alarm and angst.

"The driver was listening to 99.1 so while I was waiting for you, I heard that Mark Rodriguez dude give who I think is you a shout out on the radio. I assume you two are dating?" he asked as he reached in to open a bottle of champagne.

Blase saw what he was doing and was happy he was doing it because she could use a drink. "Mark and I are very good friends. We dated many years ago, but I'm not quite sure what prompted him to make that announcement."

As Cup poured them both glasses of champagne he smiled.

"I don't want to get in your business, and I didn't expect a woman as beautiful as you to be completely single." He handed Blase her glass. "But unfortunately for your love struck disk jockey, as far as I'm concerned, he's been replaced." That said, Cup clinked his flute glass with Blase's and turned his head towards the front of the limo. "Andre, can you please change the radio station to R&B music and put the divider up?"

"Sure, Mr. Ponce," he said, following Cup's orders.

Blase had a tight smirk on her face.

"Take a sip. We won't talk about the radio show at all tonight. This evening is all about us and my benefit," Cup instructed.

Blase smiled and took a sip of her champagne. For the rest of the ride to the venue, Blase and Cup talked and got to know one another. As popular as he was and as crazy as his celebrity life was, he was old-fashioned and quite regular.

The limo pulled up to the venue and Cup and Blase exited onto a red carpet. Blase dated a professional athlete before but he wasn't nearly as famous as Cup appeared to be. There were news crews waiting and cameras flashing. Blase couldn't help but feel like she was headed to the Oscars. Cup took Blase by the hand and directed her in front of him. He put his hand on the small of her back while she led them both into the benefit. The evening for Cup was a complete success. He raised close to a million dollars for his charity. Even being pulled and tugged every way possible by people wanting to meet him or talk with him, he never left Blase's side. As soon as he saw it was getting to be overwhelming for her, he would wave people off and take Blase out onto the quiet patio for some alone time. During their patio visits Blase discovered amidst it all, he still had her best interest in mind. She was flattered. By midnight the event was winding down and Cup turned to Blase and asked her if she was ready to leave.

"Well, I certainly wouldn't mind taking these shoes off. As sexy as you've said they are, they obviously weren't meant for five hours of standing and dancing."

"Say no more." Cup motioned for his publicist and manager. "We're leaving; please make sure everything wraps up without any problems. I'm taking Blase home and we'll talk sometime tomorrow."

"No problem, Cup. You put on a wonderful event tonight. I think this is going to be great for your foundation and your career." Cup nodded as he and Blase turned to leave.

Once back in the limo, Cup leaned down and took Blase's right shoe off and began to massage her foot while she leaned her head back on the headrest and closed her eyes. Within a few moments of her eyes being closed, Cup took the opportunity to lean in for a kiss and without opening her eyes, Blase kissed him back.

"You're an amazing kisser," she said.

"Thank you. You're a great kisser yourself."

"Thank you." She blushed as she closed her eyes again.

"Ah'ight well can I have another?"

"Why Mr. Ponce, are you being greedy?" she asked coyly.

"Yes, if you can't tell already, I'm used to getting what I want."

"Oh, I can tell. Well don't let me be the first to turn you down." She leaned in to kiss him again.

After kissing for several uninterrupted minutes, they came up for air and decided to open another bottle of champagne.

"Do you mind?" Cup asked.

"Not at all," Blase responded.

They drank champagne, talked, and kissed for the remainder of the ride back to Blase's condo. When the driver pulled up, Cup said, "Thank you for joining me this evening, Dr. Morgan. You not only made a stunning escort but you made my night."

Blase smiled at him and realized she felt loopy from all of the champagne she'd had that night. "Well, the night doesn't have to be over. You're welcome to come up," she said, feeling extremely aroused.

"Really?" he said.

"Absolutely," she confirmed.

Cup tapped on the window for the driver to open the door and he stepped out. He held his hand out for Blase to step out and she did. Cup turned to the driver and said, "Thank you. I'll call when I need you."

The driver took the hint, winked, and said, "Okay, Mr. Ponce. Enjoy the rest of your evening."

The moment Cup walked into Blase's condo he smiled at her dog's excitement. He bent down and started petting her. He looked around at the walls.

"You like art?" he asked.

"Yes, I purchased my first piece when I graduated from medical school and have collected some throughout the years. My friends always pick pieces up for me on their travels as well," she said as she took her shoes off and went to the kitchen to get a bottle of champagne and two flute glasses.

Cup sat on her sofa and took in Blase's eclectic taste. He noticed an African drum and a few other African sculptures and ethnic paintings around and asked when she was last in Africa. She told him while she was in the kitchen that her grandparents were coming to the United States soon for her brother's wedding and they would probably bring something for her when they arrived, but she hadn't been since she graduated from medical school.

Blase sat next to Cup and handed the bottle to him to open it. He popped open the cork and poured the two glasses. Blase took a few raspberries from a dish and dropped them in both glasses. They toasted to a successful benefit and stared at one another for the next few minutes before Blase asked, "May I have another one of your great kisses?"

"You never have to ask for one of those." Cup leaned in to give her a kiss. They continued kissing and drinking champagne for the next few hours until Cup felt it was time to go. At the door before leaving, he told her he enjoyed the evening they shared and hoped to see her again. As Blase was walking back to her bedroom, she decided to take a few Tylenol so she wouldn't have a headache in the morning. She lay down and felt the room spinning when she remembered Mark would be there to pick her up in four hours for their trip to Puerto Rico.

BLASE and Mark arrived in Puerto Rico at 11:00 a.m. to a searing 89-degree hotness. Much to Mark's displeasure Blase slept the entire flight. When they exited the airport, Blase immediately put her sunglasses on and stood in a zombie-like trance while Mark and his uncle Jose put their luggage into Jose's car. Jose was their transportation to Mark's hometown on the northwestern coastline of Puerto Rico called Isabela. Blase slipped in and out of sleep for the entire hour and forty-five minute drive. Mark asked her why she was so exhausted and she told him she went to an impromptu event the night before. Not one to pry, Mark left it at that and continued to make sure she had water and anything else she asked for. Blase didn't take the time to check out the view during the drive to Isabela and Mark noticed she seemed very distant and aloof.

Blase did take mental note of the beautiful flowers along the way, but not much else. Within ten minutes of their arrival at Jose's house Blase told Mark she was feeling worse and that she needed a few moments in the bathroom.

"Are you sure you're okay, Belleza? I've been worried about you for our entire trip here."

"I'm fine. I really just think I had too many glasses of champagne last night. I think if I have something to eat and a nap, I should be fully recovered by this evening."

Mark was disappointed to hear she wanted to sleep because he had a big day planned for them. "Oh no problem, mi amore. What would you like to eat?"

"A sandwich or something like that will be fine."

"Okay, I'll go and get you a sandwich, babe."

When Mark left to get Blase's food, she took a shower to freshen up and then climbed into bed for her nap. Mark returned to find Blase fast asleep. He put the sandwich in the refrigerator and sat down in the living room to catch up with his Uncle Jose and Aunt Yolanda. They discussed all that was new in Puerto Rico since he last visited, and Mark talked with their 12-year-old twins about how much they liked school. He asked them if they wanted to come to New York to visit him. They beamed with excitement about the thought of going to New York. By close to midnight, Blase hadn't woken from her nap. Mark decided to go in the room and check on her.

He nudged her lightly. "Belleza, are you okay?"

Blase was sleeping so soundly Mark had to put his hand under her nose to make sure she was alive. He laughed to himself but thought, *Coño, how much did this woman have to drink last night?*

Blase finally shifted her body to acknowledge his nudging. In an irritated tone, she whispered, "Yes?"

"Are you okay? It's almost midnight."

"Is it?" she asked.

"Yes, do you want to eat something?" he asked.

"No, I just want to sleep. I'm sorry, we'll have lots of fun tomorrow, Mark, but tonight I have to sleep." She rolled over.

Mark sat on the edge of the bed staring. Bringing Blase to Puerto Rico was important to him so he was a little insulted she'd partied so hard the night before that she couldn't manage to enjoy their first day in Isabela together.

The next morning, Blase was awake by 5:00 a.m. She rolled over to see if Mark was awake. He wasn't, so she decided to brush her teeth, wash her face, throw on a sundress, and go for a walk. She walked around Jose's grounds and took in the fresh air and vivid views.

Jose's house was positioned right across the street from a private beach, which was too rocky to enjoy, but it had picturesque views of the sea. If you climbed to the top of the rocks on the left side of the beach, it looked like you could see the entire city of Isabela. Blase sat down on one of the massive rocks. She gazed out into the ocean and reflected on her evening with Cup. She really did enjoy her time with him. Cup seemed to have many traditional ideas about relationships and she liked that. She thought he kind of reminded her of Adrian in many ways. She thought about her practice and the direction she wanted to take it. She was excited about the possibilities of the future. Between the beautiful weather and equally amazing view, time got away from Blase. She looked at her watch and an hour and half had passed. Her stomach was telling her she should head back and get some breakfast.

When she reached the house, Yolanda was cooking breakfast. Blase offered, "Is there anything that I can do?"

Yolanda kept slicing the fruit. "No. I hab it all under control." Yolanda looked at Blase out of the corner of her eye and then back down at the fruit. "Would ju like sonting to drink?" Yolanda proceeded in best efforts at English.

"I would love something, thank you," Blase said.

Yolanda walked over to the refrigerator and pulled out mango juice. "Would ju like mango, orange, or pineapple juice?"

"Mango sounds delicious."

As Yolanda walked to the cabinet to get a glass, she said, "Ju know, Mark was really upset that ju went to sleep last nigh."

Blase could sense Yolanda's agitation with it as well. "I can imagine. I certainly didn't intend to fall asleep for so long, but I wouldn't have been much company if I would've stayed awake. I do apologize if I insulted you or Jose in any way."

Yolanda poured the juice and put the glass in front of Blase. "No, Jose and I are fine. I don like to see Mark's face looking a sad. I haben't seen him in many jears, so to see him for de first time looking a so sad was not a good thing…"

Blase continued listening.

Yolanda went on. "…Ju know. Blase, I don't know ju bery well, but Jose tells me that Mark loves ju and talks about ju all de time…"

Blase started to feel uncomfortable. She felt as though Yolanda's lecture had more behind it than her sleeping. She interrupted her. "Yolanda, again I truly apologize if I offended you or Jose in any way. I will apologize and discuss Mark's feeling with him when—"

Mark interrupted them. "What about Mark's feelings?" he asked.

Blase and Yolanda turned and looked at him at the same time. Blase spoke first. "Yolanda was telling me you were concerned about me sleeping so long last night."

Yolanda looked at Blase. Blase smiled back at her.

"Yes, are you okay, Belleza?" Mark asked.

"Yes I am, baby. Thank you so much for your patience and understanding." Blase got up and walked over to Mark to give him a hug.

Mark smiled and embraced her back.

Blase moaned because he squeezed her so tightly.

"Do ju want sonting to drink, Mark?" Yolanda asked.

Mark didn't look away from Blase. "Do you want something to drink, Belleza?" he asked.

Yolanda was visibly annoyed. "She is drinking mango juice, Mark. Do ju want sonting to drink?" She thought Mark catering to Blase was in vain. She didn't see love in Blase's eyes when she looked at her nephew.

"Yes," Mark said, continuing to look at Blase.

Blase whispered to him while Yolanda's back was turned. "I don't think Yolanda likes me."

Mark looked at her and whispered back, "We'll talk about it later." He said out loud, "Belleza, have you showered yet?"

"No, do I stink?" she answered with a giggle.

Yolanda sucked her teeth.

They both ignored her.

"Okay, go freshen up before breakfast. We have a long day ahead of us," he insisted.

"Okay," she said. Blase grabbed her juice and walked toward their guest bedroom.

When Blase was out of earshot, Mark turned toward Yolanda. "Yolanda, quiero darle las gracias por su hospitalidad, pero quizas Blase y voy en un hotel."

Yolanda looked at Mark as if he'd cursed at her. She knew Jose would be angry with her if he thought his nephew left and went to a hotel because of her. Mark went on, "Sé que están preocupados por lo que su tío José le ha hablado de Blase y yo en el pasado, pero no importa qué, yo sólo quiero hacer Este viaje especial de nosotros."

Yolanda looked at Mark reassuringly. "Nephew, I don wan to ruin jour trip an I don wan ju to go. Ju hab a lot of lub to gib and I just thing ju chould be with a woman who lubs ju as much as ju lub her. Now, that's all I'n going to say on the matter," she said as she scrambled the eggs.

"Gracias," Mark said as he kissed his aunt on the cheek.

Mark's Aunt and Uncle were just a decade older than him, but they had what people call old souls, so everyone tended to think they were older than they really were. Mark, Blase, Jose, Yolanda, and their twins ate breakfast in the kitchen. Jose and Yolanda told Blase old stories about Mark and Marisol growing up with his parents. Some of the stories choked Mark up because he didn't remember them. Blase enjoyed every minute of the breakfast, including Yolanda who despite her best effort was still a little chilly towards Blase.

After breakfast, Mark drove Blase around Isabela showing her all of the sites his hometown had to offer. He couldn't fit everything in because they had a huge Fourth of July party to go to at his cousin's house.

By the time they reached the party, Jose, Yolanda, and dozens of Mark's extended cousins were already there. Blase was surprised; she didn't have a large family, so everyone doting on her and Mark was a bit overwhelming, but she did enjoy it. Everyone was friendly and welcoming, offering food and drinks while telling her how beautiful she was. Very different from the reception she received from Aunt Yolanda. Blase hadn't laughed, danced, and eaten so much in one day, ever. By the wee hours of the morning, she was again exhausted.

"Are you alright, baby?" Mark asked her as he massaged her hands.

"Yes, I'm wonderful."

Her response made Mark smile. "Are you ready to go home?" he asked.

"Oh yes," she said with a sigh and a smile.

"Come on," he said as he helped her up from her lounge chair.

Just as they were about to walk out the backyard, one of Mark's cousins said, "Good night Mr. and Mrs. Rodriguez."

Blase looked confused. Mark laughed and ushered Blase out the door. He told Yolanda they were leaving. Yolanda told him the key was hidden in a rock behind the fourth shrub on the right side of the house. Mark laughed because he knew Yolanda probably bought the rock from one of the many catalogs he saw sitting on the kitchen counter the night before.

"Okay, see you in the morning," he said.

Blase said her good-byes as well. They arrived at Yolanda's house almost two hours later. It would've only taken one hour, but Mark took the scenic route showing Blase some of the sights that he didn't show her earlier in the day. He and Blase searched for the rock for fifteen minutes before Blase found it behind the second shrub on the left side of the house.

"Yolanda probably forgot that she moved it," Mark said.

"Or, she didn't want me back in her house," Blase said insecurely.

"Belleza, my aunt likes you; she is just worried because we have such a long history. In her mind we should already be married with kids by now," he said as he opened the door.

"I guess," Blase said not wanting to make a huge issue of it, or get into a conversation about marriage.

Though Mark and Blase were exhausted after the party, Mark wanted to take advantage of having an empty house. As Blase was showering, Mark opened the bathroom door and decided to join her. When he opened the shower curtain and saw Blase standing there glowing from the night's sun shining through the window, he smiled.

"You look beautiful," he said.

"Thank you. Will you wash my back?" she asked.

"Of course."

Mark picked up the soap as Blase handed him her washcloth. He re-lathered the washcloth and began washing Blase's back. "You know, Belleza, we've been on and off several years now and I've never asked you what your thoughts are on marriage and children."

Blase didn't want to get into the conversation. "I've never really thought about it," she said.

"Yeah, I haven't either until recently, but being here with my family has really made me think about it more. Okay, I'm finished. You can rinse off now," he said.

Blase turned around to face him while she was rinsing off her back. "Turn around, let me wash your back," she said.

"So what do you think about it?" Mark asked.

"What?" Blase said.

"About marriage and kids," he said.

"I just told you, I've never really thought about it."

"Blase," Mark said as he stopped her from washing and turned to face her. "You have to have thought about it. You were engaged before. Did you forget I know that?" His tone grew tense.

"No, Mark. I didn't forget, but I didn't think about it when I was with him. When he asked, it just seemed like the right thing to do since we had been together for so long," she said while she washed her legs.

"So we've been together for a long time if you add up all of the years. Don't you think it would be natural for us to get married and have children?" he asked.

"I hadn't thought about it, Mark. I mean we aren't in a monogamous relationship, so it wasn't something that crossed my mind."

"We aren't?" Mark asked surprised.

Blase looked at him with puzzlement. "What do you mean we aren't?" she asked.

"I just assumed that since we were seeing each other, we weren't seeing other people. I didn't know I had to spell it out," Mark said riled at the notion that Blase was seeing someone else. He finished rinsing off and opened the curtain. Instead of grabbing a towel, he walked to the bedroom dripping wet.

"Don't you want a towel?" Blase asked.

Mark ignored her and kept walking.

Blase sighed, rinsed off, turned off the water, and got out. She grabbed a towel and patted herself dry a little before she wrapped it around herself and headed for the bedroom. Mark was lying on the bed still wet with his arms folded behind his head.

Blase walked into the bedroom, closed the door, and looked at him.

Mark continued to look at the ceiling as he spoke. "You know, Belleza, I've never questioned you, forced you to make a decision or a commitment to me. I've always simply enjoyed our time together."

Blase stood silent with her arms folded around her towel.

He continued. "For years I thought I wasn't good enough for you. You were becoming a doctor and I was only a delivery guy. I couldn't believe that you would want to be with someone like me. But I'm not stupid. Do you think I don't know that I was always your fall back guy? The guy you would go to when some big time football guy or doctor guy didn't work out. I was okay with that time because I just wanted to be with you. I went to school and got my degree because I figured it would give me a better chance with you."

Mark sat up. "I can take care of us now, I have a career." Mark's face was honest and encouraging. "I'm not the guy I was when we met."

"I know that, Mark—"

"Let me finish." Mark got up to go to his carry-on bag. "I can't keep being that guy because I'm no longer that guy. I have a lot to offer and I need to know the woman I am with appreciates it." He pulled out a small felt bag from the side pocket of his bag and walked over to Blase. He sat down on the bed and as he was taking the box out of the bag he got down on both knees and said, "I invited you here because it meant a lot to me to do this in my country near my family. I wanted to do it tomorrow, but why wait."

Blase's heart thumped so hard she was sure Mark could see it. Her hands were shaking and her mind was racing.

Mark lifted one knee and opened the purple velvet box. "Will you marry me, Belleza?" he asked, displaying a glowing two-carat emerald shaped solitaire diamond set in white gold.

Blase was wordless as tears began to drape her cheeks.

Mark smiled and took the sight of her tears as a good thing. He took the ring out of the box and placed it on her finger, and pulled himself up onto the edge of the bed to sit directly in front of her. He pulled her in between his legs.

Blase looked at the ring, leaned down, and kissed Mark on the lips. She sat down next to him and looked at the ring again.

Mark was proud of his accomplishment. He didn't ask anyone for help with picking out the ring.

While Blase was still looking at the jewelry, her tears became waterfalls. "I can't marry you, Mark."

Mark turned to face Blase.

She continued. "I know we've been through a lot together and I know you've always been there for me when I've needed you, but I don't think the love that I have for you is the type of love you are looking for."

"What kind of love do you have for me?" Mark's tone became frustrated.

"I enjoy being with you, but I've never thought about *being* with you,"

"What?" Mark said as he got up and put his shorts on, feeling silly. He sat back down next to Blase.

Blase finally turned to look Mark in the eyes. "What I mean is we've been together for so long and it has never dawned on me to make a serious commitment to you. That says a lot. You deserve someone who will reciprocate your feelings. I am certain, even now, that I am not that woman. I love you enough to tell you that you don't want to marry me, Mark. And I don't want to marry you."

Mark kneeled down on both knees in front of Blase again. He put his hands around her waist and spoke. "Blase, maybe not right this minute you don't feel that way because this is all a shock to you, but I know you love me, and I know we belong together. I've always seen it in us, even when you didn't."

Blase continued to cry.

"Don't cry, Belleza. I know you are confused. You don't have to answer me right now. Think about it and let me know after you have had some time to process everything. I'm sure once you clear your mind, you will see what I see," Mark said as he wiped her tears and kissed her face.

Blase listened, but she knew for sure she didn't want to marry him. Blase kissed Mark back and decided to make love to him one last time.

The next morning when Blase woke, she saw a note from Mark that read: *Good morning to the future Mrs. Rodriguez. I had to go back to my cousin's house to pick up the twins by 9:00 a.m. Yolanda and Jose went to church. I will see you soon. Love, Mark*

Blase looked at the clock and saw it was just 8:30 a.m. She figured Mark would be gone for at least another hour talking with family. She got up, gathered the few items of clothes that were laying on the chair, put them in the carry on suitcase, and called the airline. She booked a flight back to New York and called a taxi.

Mark and the twins were laughing and joking when they walked back in the house. He'd had a great morning with them so far. He told them to go to their rooms to get their bathing suits so they all could go to the beach. When he walked into the guest bedroom, he saw the bed made and a note at the foot.

*I love you, Mark, but I don't deserve you. I can't continue to face your family knowing this. I'm sorry. ~Belleza*

Next to the note was the purple ring box with the ring inside. Mark picked up the box and stared at the ring. He was angry with himself for giving her the ring. He whispered, "I pushed her away." As the thought came out of his mouth, he felt a lump form in the middle of his throat and his heart began to sting.

The twins opened the door. "Marcos, estamos listos. ¿Dónde está la señora Blase?" the slightly taller one asked.

"She had to go back to New York to work unexpectedly," he said in English. "You guys ready to go to the beach?"

"Si," they yelled.

"Let's go," he said as he got up and put the ring box back in his carry-on bag.

# Center Hall Colonial

**BLASE** arrived back in New York after what seemed like a flight around the world. When she returned to her apartment, she sat on the edge of her bed and wept. She was overwhelmingly down. Still, in her sadness she believed she made the right decision. The morning after crying herself to sleep, Blase called her mother and told her what happened. Her mother made her feel a bit better by agreeing with her decision. She believed when Blase knew, she would know and so did Blase.

Blase had dinner with Brielle and Fallon and told them what happened as well. They weren't surprised. They both told Blase they had a feeling that he was going to propose. Fallon added that it was a matter of time before he did, and Brielle agreed telling her she should've seen it coming. Through all of their reality, they comforted their friend and told her to move on and she did what was the right thing to do.

Almost four weeks after Blase arrived back in New York, she finally decided to return the messages Cup left her. She picked up the phone to dial his number when Beth spoke into the intercom, "Blase, you have a call from a Mr. Ponce."

"Oh wow, I was just calling him. Put him through," Blase said. "Hello, Cup. How are you?"

"Hello, Dr. Morgan. I thought I was going to have to send a search party for you. How have you been?" he asked.

"I know you left me a few messages. I'm sorry I haven't been able to return your call. I was so busy with opening my practice. I didn't realize how busy I would be. My website is generating a lot of business. I'm very excited about it," she said.

"I'm happy to hear that. I'll be happier when you agree to go out with me again. You can tell me more when I see you." Cup got right to the point.

Blase laughed. She did think about Cup frequently since returning to New York, but wanted to focus on her practice. "Well I have a few patients to see in the morning tomorrow, but after that, I am free until Monday," she said.

"You have to work on Saturdays?" he asked.

Blase sighed. "Honestly if I thought I would actually have business and my staff wouldn't start sending me death threats, I would open on Sundays as well. I have to work as often as possible since the practice is new."

"I can understand that. I like a woman who knows how to hustle. Well, I have a game tomorrow afternoon. Can I send a car to pick you up tomorrow evening?"

"Absolutely!" Blase smiled.

"I will have the car at your place by six o'clock,"

"Sounds good. I can be ready by then."

"So tomorrow then."

"Tomorrow," she agreed.

When they hung up, Blase felt butterflies in her stomach. She didn't know what it was, but she liked Cup. He was different than Miller. After Miller, she assumed that all athletes were the same.

The next day, Blase breezed through her patients. Sheridan was wondering why she was suddenly so cheery when the past few weeks, she seemed melancholy and preoccupied.

"Who put that smile on your face?" Sheridan asked.

"My relief pitcher," she said.

"Oh, Cup. I didn't know you were seeing him. You haven't mentioned him since before you left for Puerto Rico. Speaking of Puerto Rico, you also haven't told me what happened there. Did you have a good time?"

Blase had begun to get closer to Sheridan and was sharing more of her personal life with her, but she wasn't ready to talk about Mark with her yet. "Puerto Rico was beautiful. Did you connect with the IT guy on the new Intranet system yet?" she asked, changing the subject.

Sheridan didn't hesitate to move on. "Yes, he's doing a great job. He is set to finish by the end of this month. I should have a soft launch for you by Wednesday of next week."

"Great, I'm excited to see the results. And he was able to design and program with all of the components that I want?"

"Yes, and I added a few additional administrative functionalities that I thought would help you and the staff," she said.

"These additions, were they within the budget?" Blase asked.

"Yes, of course. I wouldn't have added them if they weren't. Or I would've asked for your permission first," Sheridan said.

"Okay, great!" Blase walked into the room to see her last patient.

Sheridan turned and walked back toward the front desk. She was serving as both the receptionist and Blase's assistant until they hired someone who could work the front desk and phone lines.

Blase walked her last client out to the front desk and told Sheridan to make a follow up appointment for him for two weeks. She walked back to her office, shut her computer down, and took off her white coat. She shut the lights off and sped out the door. "Make sure all of the lights, machines, and the coffee pots are off when you leave," she said to Sheridan as she was walking out the door.

"Sure thing. Enjoy the rest of your weekend," Sheridan said.

"You too," Blase yelled as the door closed behind her.

At five minutes to six, Blase was sitting in her living room waiting for the call from the doorman. She sent Brielle a text to remind her about Fallon's birthday and asked her if she was joining them for dinner that week. Brielle responded yes, but asked why it would be during the week. She told her that Fallon was going away with Sergio after today's game until Tuesday. By thirty minutes after six, Blase decided to walk down to the lobby to see if the car was downstairs waiting and the driver just neglected to tell the doorman he was there. When she reached the street, she didn't see a town car or a limo anywhere. She thought to call Cup, but figured since he'd asked her out, she wouldn't call. As she turned to walk back to her lobby she looked over her right shoulder and saw the nose of a white stretch limo peeking around the corner. She continued walking, but slowly. The limo stopped in front of her, and the driver scurried out of the car and toward her building. She let him pass her as she entered and heard him telling her doorman he was there to pick up Dr. Blase Morgan.

"I'm Blase Morgan," she said to the bulky butter colored driver.

"Hello, Dr. Morgan. I am so sorry that I am late. I was waiting for Mr. Ponce at the stadium and I got the call that I was to come here and pick you up, and I came immediately," he wheezed as a few trickles of sweat ran down the sides of his face.

"No problem. Please just let me go and get my things," she said.

"Okay. I will be right here waiting for you, ma'am," the driver said.

Blase went back upstairs and grabbed her handbag off the dining room table and her Pashmina wrap off the back of one of the chairs. She double checked to make sure Sugar had enough water and food and then went back downstairs. When she reached the lobby, the driver said, "Right this way, Dr. Morgan. Mr. Ponce is still playing right now. His game is in extra innings so I was instructed to bring you back to the stadium."

Blase was surprised, but willing to go with the flow. She didn't really have any expectations so this was fine especially considering she had never been to a professional baseball game in her life. With all of the traffic, they arrived at the stadium at twenty minutes to eight. The driver received word that the game had ended and Mr. Ponce was going to shower and come out to the car to meet Blase.

As soon as Cup was in his locker room, he picked up his cell phone and called Blase.

"Did you win?" she immediately asked upon answering.

Cup laughed. "Yeah babe, we won. So tonight is going to be a great night."

"Would it have been a bad night if you hadn't won?" she asked.

"Nah it would've been a great night either way, but it'll be even greater now," he said through all of the noise in the background. "I'll be out in forty-five minutes. Do you think you can wait that long?"

"Sure, I'll just open one of these bottles of champagne and get the celebration started without you," she said.

Cup laughed. "Ah'ight, you go right ahead and do that. I'll see you in a little while."

"Okay," Blase responded as she scooted herself off the seat towards the champagne chilling in the ice bucket. She poured herself a glass of champagne and turned the radio to a smooth grooves R&B station. As she was turning the stations, she passed a few Spanish language stations and thought of Mark. "Blase, don't do that tonight. You've made your decision," she said out loud. When the R&B station tuned in, Earth, Wind and Fire's song *Reasons* was playing. She turned the volume up. Blase leaned back in her seat, crossed her legs, rested her head on the back of the seat, and enjoyed the music. She was feeling tingly inside and she hadn't even seen Cup yet. Maybe it was the atmosphere or the mystery, or maybe she just felt comfortable with herself and her life. She was content.

Blase was down to her last few sips of her glass of champagne when she heard the driver open his door and close it. A few seconds later the right passenger door opened and Cup was talking to the driver. She saw his tan soft leather slip on shoes, bare ankles, and cream slacks step one foot into the limo. She smiled. As the rest of him entered she immediately smelled his peppery cologne. When he got in, Usher's song *Burn* was playing on the radio.

With a smile he said, "You really did get the party started without me." He leaned in to give her a kiss on the cheek.

"Yes, I did. Would you like to join me?" she asked.

"Of course."

"Let me pour you a glass."

"Ah'ight thanks. You look sexy tonight," he said.

Blase had put on a mustard colored spaghetti strap mini dress that had a loose drop neck front to show off her slender arms and long defined legs. Her three and three quarter inch designer mules were adorned with a gold heel, mustard colored fabric, and gold hardware at the toe with a tiny gold D initial that dangled to the sides of each shoe. She admired them a few times herself that night because they were a last minute purchase. Her long, silky hair was down in soft curls which was a great contrast from the ponytail she wore at work every day. She completed her outfit with her gold and diamond cluster earrings and her designer gold watch she received as a graduation gifts from medical school years before.

"Thank you," she answered as she poured his glass. The driver drove off and Blase didn't ask Cup where they were going. She sat back next to him and allowed him to put his arm around her shoulders.

"Congratulations on your win today." She clinked her glass with his.

"Thank you."

"For a moment I thought I was going to be able to see my first baseball game."

"You've never been to a baseball game?" he asked.

"Never."

"Ah'ight, we are gonna change that."

"Okay," she said.

Just about thirty-five minutes later, the limo began to slow down and eventually stopped. The driver hopped out, came around, and opened their door. Cup got out of the car first and then held his hand to help Blase out of the car. When she emerged, it took her a few minutes to realize they were at a pier on the lower east side of Manhattan.

"My friend is having a private party tonight. Are you up for it?"

"I sure am. Where's the party?" she asked.

"Right there." He pointed with one hand as he interlocked his fingers with her in his other. Blase looked over and saw a mid-sized yacht with lights that looked dreamy against the sunset. She smiled and felt a surge of excitement. She'd been on a yacht before, but for some reason, she really had a good feeling this night. They reached the yacht and one of the deck hands stood at the top holding champagne flutes filled with Kir Royales for the arriving guests. Cup walked behind Blase. She passed on the Kir

Royale opting to feel out the party before she continued drinking. Noticing that she didn't get a glass, Cup passed on the champagne as well. They walked hand in hand and Cup immediately saw one of his good friends and teammates, Sergio. Blase smiled because she hadn't seen Sergio in a few months and since had only communicated via email about Fallon's engagement ring. Sergio came over, hugged Blase, and gave Cup a combination handshake-hug.

"Is this your party?" she asked Sergio.

"Actually it's a surprise party for Fallon," he said.

"Pardon me?" Blase said, knowing she wasn't invited or asked to help with the planning.

"Don't pardon me. I couldn't tell you, Blase. You and Fallon talk about too much so I couldn't risk you telling her," he said.

"Did you know this was Fallon's birthday party, Cup?"

"Of course he did," Sergio said.

"Yeah I did. He told me he was going to call you and tell you about it, but I asked him to let me take you out and bring you," Cup said.

"Okay, so that explains why I never received an invitation," she said, shaking her head.

"You know you were going to be invited. Fallon is not here yet. I told her my sister was having a party here so she is on her way with my cousin Judy. Go inside, the parents are sitting at our table. There is a place for you and Cup there."

Blase and Cup hurried inside. She couldn't believe Sergio did all of that himself yet had been emailing her for months to decide on one diamond ring. When she walked in there must have been close to one hundred people on the yacht. Blase spotted her parents sitting right next to Fallon's parents Frank and Raquelle and who she assumed where Sergio's parents given the remarkable resemblance the older woman had to Sergio.

"Mom, Dad, you knew about this party too?" she asked as she gave her parents and Fallon's parent's a hug and kiss.

"Yes, we did and we know how you can't keep a secret from Fallon so Frank and Raquelle swore us to secrecy," her mother said.

Blase introduced the parents to Cup.

"Great game today," Frank said.

"Thank you, sir. Everything came together for us today."

"I'll say. You did a heck of a job in those last few innings," Blase's father added.

Blase looked at her father not realizing he watched baseball. "Dad, you like baseball?"

"I watch every now and then," he said.

Cup asked Blase if she was ready for a Kir Royale. She was ready.

Fallon walked in with Judy thirty minutes later and everyone yelled, "Surprise!"

Fallon stopped in her tracks. As always she looked as if she were put together by a team of beauty experts. She put her hands to her mouth and tears formed in her eyes. Sergio walked in front of her with a bouquet of three dozen three-inch white roses tied together by an oversized silver bow. She took the roses, handed them to Judy, and hugged Sergio around his neck. Sergio lifted Fallon off her feet and kissed her.

"Feliz Complanos mi amor," Sergio said.

"I love you," Fallon responded squeezing him tighter.

Sergio put Fallon down and while he had everyone's attention, he immediately kneeled on one knee, "I love you too, so marry me, Fallita."

Sergio opened a white leather box with a silver lock on the front and exposed a seven-carat diamond shaped ring with a diamond eternity band attached.

"Finally," Fallon whispered.

Sergio laughed. "Is that a yes?"

"That's a hell yes," Fallon said as everyone laughed and clapped.

Sergio took the ring out of the box and put it on Fallon's finger. She held it up to the light then turned it around so everyone could see it. Sergio got up and hugged and kissed her again. He grabbed two glasses of champagne and gave one to Fallon as everyone yelled for them to toast. Sergio spoke first in his thick accent. "I want to thank everybody for coming out tonight. You know it was no small task keeping this a secret from Fallon. It helped that not one of you told Blase, so I thank you for that also." Some people turned to look at Blase as she stood close to Cup with her champagne glass in her hand and smiled.

Fallon waved to Blase and showed her the ring.

Blase laughed again and blew Fallon a kiss.

Sergio continued. "Tonight we celebrate Fallita's birthday and our love—"

"And that big ass rock," one of the onlookers yelled as others laughed at the outburst.

Sergio smiled. "Yes, I thought I said our love already. Thank you all for coming." He turned to Fallon so she could speak, but Fallon was still crying and speechless.

"What he said."

Everyone laughed again, clapped, and shouted congratulations as they all toasted.

They celebrated that night. They ate a delicious four course meal, danced to great music, and sailed around Manhattan until 3:00 a.m. When they docked back at the Pier, Blase said good-bye to everyone. She asked her parents if they were okay to get home and they said they were staying in the city at Fallon's parent's townhouse.

Blase and Cup left everyone to retreat to the quiet of their limo. "You and Fallon have great sets of parents. They remind me a lot of my parents," he said.

"Oh yeah, thank you. Tell me about your parents," Blase said.

"Okay, I'll tell you on the way. Would you like me to take you home?"

"Yes." As Cup was calling to tell the driver where to go, she continued. "Your house."

Cup turned and looked at Blase. She nodded yes again.

"Dominguez, we are going to my house."

"Okay, Mr. Ponce."

The driver started the limo and pulled out of their parked position. "So you wanted to know about my parents? Cool." Cup turned to face Blase and handed her the bottle of water he picked up. "My father owns two funeral homes in Richmond, Virginia where I'm from. He's owned them since I was born. My mother took care of me and my brothers and sisters. Now she sometimes helps my father with his businesses, but most of the time she is splitting her time between babysitting my nieces and nephews."

"How many brothers and sisters and nieces and nephews do you have?"

"I have six brothers and four sisters. I'm the third youngest. I have two younger sisters. I also have, last I heard, twenty-one nieces and nephews. My sisters and I are the only ones without kids."

"Oh wow! Nine brothers and sisters and twenty-one nieces and nephews. You have a huge family."

"Yes, I do. Three of my older brothers played in the minor leagues. I'm the only one who made it to the majors," he boasted.

"So you come from a baseball family?"

"Yes, my father was a big time baseball fan and that's what we did growing up, played baseball to stay outta trouble."

"Well you seem to be good at it, so it paid off."

"For me it did, yeah. My parents have been married for fifty-five years."

"Wow, that's a long time. How old are you?"

"I just turned thirty," he said. "I know I'm a little younger than you. I hope you don't mind."

"How do you know that?" she asked.

"Fallon told me you two graduated from college together and I know how old she is, so I assumed you are around the same age. Am I wrong?"

"No, you're not and I don't mind it at all," Blase said. She and Cup talked more about their families until they reached a tall building in Westchester County, New York. The driver opened their door and when Blase stepped out she saw they were no longer in New York City. Cup took her hand and escorted her into his building. The doorman said his hello and congratulated Cup on his win earlier.

"I moved here earlier this year when I was traded to New York. My agent has a realtor in this area and he told me Trump is where everyone is living right now."

"Okay. Do you like it up here?"

"It's nice. I've been considering buying a house not too far from here. We'll see what happens after this season."

"I grew up not far from here. My parents still live up this way."

When they walked into Cup's apartment, Blase noticed how monochromatic the apartment looked. Everything was white. "Is white your favorite color?"

Cup chuckled. "No, my realtor had an interior decorator come in and buy and set this all up. I couldn't care less what color it is, just as long as it was furnished. I'm hardly ever home anyway."

"Oh okay."

They chose to sit in the living room and continue their conversation. When Blase woke the next morning, she realized she was fully clothed and laying on top of the covers of Cup's bed with a blanket over her with Cup lying next to her. She got up and wandered into the bathroom. She washed her face and brushed her teeth with a washcloth she found in the linen closet. She fixed her hair with her hands and then applied a little makeup. She finished and went to the kitchen and found the fancy espresso and coffee maker. She found some unopened espresso coffee in the cabinet and decided to make a mug. With the mug in her hand, Blase suddenly heard music blasting throughout the apartment. The sound startled her so much that she almost dropped her mug. Cup came from the bedroom rapping along to the lyrics of Fat Joe's song *Lean Back*. He walked into the kitchen doing a little dance. When he stopped in front of Blase, he danced to the hook of the song.

Blase giggled. "You are crazy and that music scared the mess out of me."

"This song is the shit!" He kept dancing and rapping. Blase liked the song, so she started rapping along with him. She danced with him too.

Cup raised his eyebrows. "You know this song?" he asked.

"Of course I do."

Cup didn't think Blase listened to hip-hop music. "I thought you only liked jazz and opera and that type of sophisticated stuff," he said as he took an individual sized bottle of orange juice out of the refrigerator.

"I like all music."

"Good because I listen to hip-hop music most of the time."

"That's fine," she said as she took her coffee from the coffee maker. "So do you want to spend the day with me, or do you have plans?" she asked.

"I'm all yours," he said.

"Okay. We have to go back to my place so I can change."

"I'm with it. I'm gonna jump in the shower," he said.

"Okay."

After Blase dressed casually in white shorts, multi-colored sandals, and a purple top, she put the things from her clutch purse she carried the night before into her oversized white leather shoulder bag and told Cup she was ready to go.

"Cool, let's roll."

"Oh, you have a place in mind?" she asked.

"Yeah, my boy is having a little BBQ at his spot in New Jersey."

"Okay."

"Do you mind?"

"Not at all," she said.

They arrived in New Jersey an hour and fifteen minutes after they walked out of Blase's front door. Cup got out of the driver's side of his black Mercedes Benz CLK-500, walked around, and opened Blase's door for her. When she got out, she heard Snoop Dog's *Drop it Like It's Hot* song blaring from the backyard. A valet came and took Cup's keys and gave him a ticket for his car. Cup told Blase to follow him into the house. They walked in and Blase couldn't help but notice that every woman in the house looked like she could've been in a rap music video. She immediately felt out of place. Many of the women gave her dirty looks when they saw Cup holding her hand.

"I didn't know this was a BBQ where you had to dress up," she said.

"Don't worry about it, baby. These chics in here are diamond miners. They are here for show and to get the fellas to come out."

"Is that right?"

"Yeah, don't trip. You ah'ight, and you are finer than any of these women in here."

Blase never questioned her attractiveness, she just felt out of place. "I know," she said as she elbowed him in his side.

"Good, let's go in the back then."

"Okay."

They reached the backyard and there were more women, only these women barely had any clothes on. Some of them yelled Cup's name and a few even walked over and said seductive hellos as if Blase wasn't even standing there. Blase shook her head and thanked God she went to medical school.

Cup noticed the look on her face. "I'm sorry, baby. This might be how it is every time we go out. Is that a problem for you?"

Blase looked at him. "I'm not sure yet, we'll see."

Cup smirked at her answer.

Blase shrugged her shoulders back. *What did he expect me to say? I'm not a groupie.* Blase could tell Cup loved the attention. He was a different person then he was when they went out for his benefit gala. Cup noticed a few of his close friends and started walking towards them. Blase followed. For the remainder of the BBQ, Cup socialized and laughed with his friends. He introduced Blase to everyone he knew as well as their girlfriend's or wives.

Eventually the ladies all gathered at one table poolside and swapped stories. She was surprised to learn that many of the wives had good professional careers before they became Baseball wives. One was an attorney, one was in law school when she met her husband, but didn't finish, two others had their MBA's, and the last was a top level real estate agent in New Jersey. She realized then why Fallon wanted to keep her own identity.

Despite all of the women having their own lives and careers when they met their husbands, they all were presently housewives. Blase had never thought about being simply a housewife.

As the party dwindled down, some of the scantily dressed women were still haunting around, hoping to be chosen. Blase was having such a good time talking with the wives, she lost track of time, and Cup. She said her good-byes and walked around the party to look for him. After 15 minutes, she found him in the enormous basement playing poker.

"Hey, sweetie. Are you winning?" she asked.

"I'm doing okay," he said.

"Okay?" one of the other players said. "Man, this dude got me for ten thousand so far."

"Dollars?" Blase squeaked.

All of the men laughed at her.

"Let me just finish this hand, baby, and we're out. I'm quitting while I'm ahead."

Blase sat down next to him and watched. She'd never gambled and always wondered who could sit down at a table and throw away thousands of dollars. She watched, listened, and saw Cup win another five grand. She was amazed. Cup bounced up from the table after winning his hand and said his good-byes. He shook everyone's hand before he took Blase's hand to walk back upstairs. Cup found his friend who was a popular basketball player and thanked him.

"Aye man, thanks for coming out. Were you downstairs playing poker?" his friend asked.

"Yeah man, those dudes don't know how to play poker. I took them for fifteen and I was only down there for thirty minutes."

"Word? Where's the houses cut?"

"In my pocket."

They both laughed and gave each other a combination handshake-hug, and then Cup turned to leave. The valet brought Cup's car around and Cup tipped him fifty dollars.

They drove back to New York grooving to one of Cup's rap compilation CDs. While driving over the George Washington Bridge, Blase stared out the window at the moon and lights rebounding off of the Hudson River. She told Cup she was in the mood for ice cream.

"Do you know where to get some from?" Cup asked, not knowing his way around the area yet.

"Yes, I do," she said. Blase directed Cup to an ice cream parlor in the Washington Heights area of Manhattan. They pulled in, and when they walked into the ice cream parlor two of the employees stargazed over Cup. Blase found it amusing. Both employees asked Cup for his autograph. He was signing the papers for the autograph when a few teenage boys walked in. They immediately recognized him.

"Oh shit man, that's Cup from the Mets. Aye Cup man, how you doin'?"

"I'm alright. How y'all doing?"

A lanky, fair skin young man with long black curly hair pulled into a ponytail continued to speak in a heavy Bronx accent. "Oh we good! What y'all doin' in the hood?"

Cup laughed because Blase had her cup of ice cream in her hand. Blase was eating her ice cream, watching. One of the other young men hit his friend on the arm and pointed to Blase with her ice cream and whispered, "Damn you stupid or somethin'? Don't you see his lady wit da ice cream?"

The young spokesman didn't give him a chance to answer. "Oh I see y'all gettin' some ice cream. That's what's up. Aye yo, what's up with hookin' us up with tickets to your next game?" he asked boldly.

All of his friends collectively sucked their teeth and told their friend he was stupid for asking that question.

"Oh young homie, I tell you what. What are y'all doing on Tuesday afternoon?" Cup asked.

"We ain't doin' nothin'," one of the other boys answered visibly excited at the thought of getting tickets to a baseball game.

"Well I need some volunteers for an event that my foundation is putting together. I need some young brothers like yourselves to come out and pass out t-shirts, pamphlets, that kinda thing. Y'all interested?" Cup asked.

"Hell yeah," they all said except for one.

"Oh you're not interested, young homie?" he asked the silent one.

"I don't know, man. It's gonna be hot as hell outside."

"Okay, well you don't have to come. I don't want to force you." Cup directed his attention to the other young men and gave them the phone number of the organizer of the event. All of the young men, except for the one, were putting the information in their cell phones.

"You tell Lonnie that I asked you to volunteer on the Public Relations team."

"That's what's up, Cup. Aye but before you leave, can we get your autograph?" the spokesman said.

Cup and Blase were walking out of the ice cream parlor. He opened the door for Blase to walk out. He turned and said, "I'll give you an autograph when you show up on Tuesday."

Cup heard them all saying, "I'll be there," and saw them all giving each other handshakes.

"Does it ever get exhausting?" Blase asked, enjoying her ice cream.

"Sometimes," Cup said as he started the car and pulled out of the parking lot.

"I can imagine. I'm exhausted just watching it all."

"For the most part though, I like the attention. It makes me feel like what I'm doing means something more than just throwing a ball into a glove."

Blase looked affectionately at Cup.

"How is that ice cream?" he asked.

"Delicious, would you like some?"

"If you'll feed it to me, then yeah."

Blase took a big scoop of her chocolate and vanilla soft serve twist ice cream with caramel and chocolate sprinkles and slowly fed it to Cup, gazing in his eyes. With the ice cream in his mouth Cup said, "Girl, you gonna make me get into an accident."

Blase laughed. "Are we going to my place or yours?" Cup asked.

"I have patients to see in the morning, but I don't want the night to end, so if you don't mind I'd like for us to go back to my place."

"Lead me to it," Cup said as he put his hand on Blase's thigh.

They walked into Blase's apartment. As always, Sugar was excited to see her. She taught her to use wee wee pads in the house if she had to pee, but walked her for all of her other business. "I have to take Sugar for a walk; she hasn't been out since this afternoon."

"How long have you owned, Sugar?" Cup asked.

"A few years now. She was a gift."

"You know I've given a lot of gifts, but I never thought about giving an animal."

"Do you like animals?" Blase asked.

"Not really. I just think they are meant to entertain kids. If you don't have kids, what's the point?" Cup said as he sat on the sofa.

Blase shook her head. "Do you want to walk her with me?"

"Sure. I can't let you walk out there all by yourself."

"I don't want you to get bombarded, so if we'll be met with all of the fanfare then you can wait here for me," she said while she put Sugar in her leash.

Forty-five minutes later at 1:37 a.m., Blase and Cup plopped down on Blase's sofa.

"I really enjoyed myself with you this weekend," Blase said.

"I did too. You are a trooper I see."

"Most times, sometimes I like peace and quiet though. Do you like to hang out a lot?"

"I work so much, I like to enjoy myself when I can."

Blase shook her head in acknowledgement. "Well let me get you a towel and washcloth," she said as she was hoisting herself up from the sofa.

Cup grabbed her hand and pulled her back down on his lap. "Don't move so fast. Suppose I was enjoying you here next to me," he said as he hugged her around her waist.

"You have my deepest apologies," she flirted.

Cup reached up for a kiss and Blase met him half way. Three minutes into their kisses, Cup scooted himself and Blase forward on the edge of the sofa. He grabbed her legs and lifted them both up and carried Blase into her bedroom.

"It's the second door on your right," she said.

"You spoiled the fun of finding it," he teased. Cup laid Blase on her bed and pulled his shirt over his head. He leaned over Blase and took her top off for her.

"I see the medicine worked," she said and she ran her hand across his chest and shoulders.

"Yes, Dr. Morgan. I'm straight now, thanks to you." He kissed her neck. While he was taking off his shorts, Blase decided to take hers off as well. Standing next to Cup's substantial frame made her feel protected. By three o'clock in the morning, she was exhausted. She realized that while Cup wasn't as endowed as Walter, he certainly had more stamina and tricks.

Cup took a shower and Blase went to sleep. The next morning, Blase was busying herself with getting ready while Cup was sleeping. She woke him up just before she was leaving. "I have to run. The door locks when you leave, just call down to the doorman and he will have your car brought around and waiting in the front for you when you go downstairs."

"Okay, baby. Have a good day," he said and kissed her lips. "Brush your teeth before you leave too because your breath could kill someone right now." She laughed.

Cup laughed along with her as he put his head back down on the pillow. "There are tooth brushes in the linen closet in my bathroom," she added as she pinched his butt and walked out the bedroom door.

"Aye, what about that dog?" he yelled.

"I walked her already. Go back to sleep," she yelled while walking towards her door.

BLASE and Cup had intensely busy schedules, but every moment they could steal to spend time together they did. Cup's season ended and he was frustrated that his team didn't make it to the playoffs. Blase blazed through the first six months of her new practice with ease. She was working so hard and was pleased with the work of her new employees. She first acquired Marta Jones by calling her old hospital to see if she wanted to work for her as her Physician's Assistant. Marta joined in the second month. Blase hired Fumiko Tanaka to be the practice's Esthetician and Nail Technician from an ad she placed on the internet. She stumbled upon Juliette Dixon, who had recently relocated from Ocho Rios, Jamaica and was looking for work. She called the two resorts in Jamaica that Juliette had on her resume to obtain references, and when she received stellar reviews she hired her to start the next day as their Masseuse. Her last hire was Darshana Vijaykrishna, She asked everyone to call her Shana for short. Shana had her own beauty salon, but after three of her four employees left to go to larger salons and months of trying to find replacements, she was forced to sell her business. Blase had been to Shana's salon for a waxing so she decided to hire her to do facials, waxing, threading, and Botox injections when Blase wasn't available to do them herself.

By the next baseball season, Cup and Blase were an item. Blase took Cup to her brother's wedding where he met her entire family, including her grandparents and cousins from Ethiopia and South Africa. He also met many of her extended family from down south. Cup enjoyed Blase's family and how close she was to all of them. Until Blase, his adult dating life consisted of beautiful women who only seem to want to be with him for his celebrity status and his money. Blase didn't need Cup's money and made it clear by offering to pay for things any time she could. He loved that she listened to him—his dreams and his views—and didn't judge him or dismiss the conversations for more superficial talks.

Cup decided on a way for them to see one another more often. After his fifth game of the regular season, he asked Blase if she would move in with him. "I think it makes more sense, and we can see each other more often," he said.

Blase immediately agreed. "But baby, I'm not moving from my two bedroom apartment into your one. Wouldn't it make more sense for you to move in with me?" she asked.

Cup had no desire to live in the city and after she told him that her ex-boyfriend bought the condo for her, he didn't want to live in an apartment that another man bought.

"I think it would make more sense for us to buy a house up this way," he suggested.

Blase sat for a moment contemplating the thought of a house and living outside of the city. She had never lived outside of the city since moving back to New York for medical school. But she knew she was falling in love with Cup.

"Okay. Where would you want to live up your way?"

"A few of my teammates live in Purchase. They have nice houses, so we can start looking there."

"Purchase may be too far of a commute, Cup."

"Well I said we can start there. I'll call my real estate agent and see what we can get."

"What's our budget? We haven't even discussed that."

"Baby, look, I know you are an independent woman and all of that," he said with a smile, "but I'm going to take the lead on this."

Blase didn't disagree.

"So we'll go out when I get back from out West and look for some cribs. I want my shit to be on MTV cribs," he said.

Blase frowned.

"Come on now, babe. This comes with the package. Love me or leave me alone," he said, stroking his own chin.

"That's not a choice," she said. "There will be no leaving. This house is a huge commitment, Cup. I mean I guess I would have to rent out my condo. I don't want to sell it just yet."

"Nah, baby. Don't sell it, keep that. We can start buying a bunch of properties in fact and get our Donald Trump mogul on," he said, laughing.

"You are so crazy." Blase laughed with him.

**TWO** weeks later, Blase and Cup were out looking at homes in Purchase, New York. Fallon wanted them to move to New Jersey, but Cup didn't like New Jersey. The first house they looked at was a 5,200 square foot five bedroom, six bathroom colonial with a post-modern feel. It had a stone pool with an attached whirlpool spa listed for $3.8 million. Blase never discussed price with their realtor, just what she wanted the house to have. At least four bedrooms, a formal dining room, a master bedroom suite, and a level yard. The second home was a 6,100 square foot five bedroom, five bathroom Dutch colonial on over five acres of beautifully landscaped property. It had a rose garden, in-ground pool with a guest house with a perennial garden. Blase loved it but thought $72,000 in taxes was outlandish. Cup told her not to worry about that, but she couldn't help but worry. She thought the taxes were too high for the $4.1 million asking price. They went to see four more homes similar to the first two.

"These are all beautiful, Cup, but I think the commute to the city is a little long for me and it just seems too quiet up here," she said.

"The realtor told me about an area called Scarsdale. Do you know where that is?" he asked.

"Yes. The commute is a lot better from Scarsdale. We should look there."

They turned to their realtor and asked to have some properties set up for Scarsdale for the next day. The realtor agreed and they went their separate ways.

The next day they met at the first Scarsdale home. The realtor told them they wouldn't get as much land in Scarsdale, but the homes and school system were great. The first home they met at was new construction in a gated community. Cup immediately disliked the fact that their neighbors would be so close so he ruled that one out before even going inside to look at it. They continued on to the next house which was on a private road and sat on almost two acres of land. A serene looking 6,300 square foot bleached brick colonial waited as they drove up the horseshoe driveway. They walked through the oversized cherry wood front door and saw the custom chef's kitchen, formal dining room with a table that could sit sixteen people, a generous living room with fifteen-foot ceilings, and a large wood burning fireplace. Blase loved the finished family room with a complete bar, the media room, and the steam/sauna room, and was completely sold with the master suite with a fireplace that had his and hers bathrooms and one large custom closet with a dressing area. The pool in the backyard was paisley shaped with an outdoor kitchen and entertainment area. Blase wanted the house. She thought the $52,000 in taxes was reasonable and the $3.5 million asking price was within their budget. She contained herself while they viewed the next four homes, but was set on the bleached brick house. Cup liked that house as well, so they told their realtor they would sleep on it and call the next day. That night, they decided to offer $3.3 million on the house that was quickly accepted.

**CUP** and Blase threw a two hundred guest housewarming party. Both of their families flew in from out of town, except for Blase's grandparents and extended family from Africa. Blase stood in the kitchen and couldn't believe they owned a house. Her name wasn't on the mortgage, but she and Cup decided to put her name on the deed. Cup didn't want Blase to worry about paying bills.

Blase stood with a glass of iced tea in her hand talking with Fallon, Brielle, and Sheridan. "I still wish you guys would've moved to Jersey. You could've been right next to us and I bet you your taxes would've been cheaper," Fallon said.

"Cup said that wasn't an option. He really just doesn't like New Jersey," Blase said. "But enough about that. So did you decide on a wedding dress? The two choices we saw were beautiful," she asked Fallon.

"Yes, I chose the white strapless Vera Wang. The silk one with the fitted bodice and four-inch beige ribbon at the waist. I am going with a burgundy ribbon instead of beige. I thought it was simple and elegant."

"The one from her spring collection?"

"Yes that one," Fallon said.

"That was my favorite," Blase said.

"I thought you liked the Monique Lhuillier dress," Brielle said to Blase.

Blase laughed and said, "I liked them all. But I think that Vera Wang dress will look stunning on Fallon."

"Me too," Brielle added.

Fallon said, "I hope so. So you guys have to meet me and all of the ladies this weekend for the first fitting of your dresses." Fallon asked both Blase and Brielle to be in her wedding.

"How many of us are there?" Brielle asked.

"I have nine other bridesmaids you make ten. Blase as the maid of honor, my sister as the matron of honor, two flower girls, five junior bridesmaids, and Sergio's nephew is going to be the ring bearer."

"Geeesh! How many people do you have on the guest list?" Sheridan asked.

"We've invited three hundred and fifty people. And I had to cut if off there. Between my parents and Sergio's parents, they wanted everyone from the United States and the Dominican Republic at our wedding," Fallon said, shaking her head and sipping her iced tea.

Cup walked in on them talking and when he realized they were talking wedding talk, he quickly turned around and left.

Blase smirked. "I think Cup is allergic to weddings." She laughed.

"So are you apparently. So you're a match made in heaven," Brielle said sarcastically.

Everyone looked at Brielle with scowls. Brielle had become so bitter and cynical since her problems with her husband became apparent.

"Whatever," Blase said. They all decided to go outside in the backyard to continue the party. By 3:00 a.m., Blase and Cup were virtually kicking the last of the attendees out. After the last person left, Cup turned to Blase and asked her if she was happy with their new home.

Blase took off her sundress, bra, and panties, and began dancing around the living room naked while she sang, "Does this look happy?"

Cup laughed and turned the music up even louder and said, "I guess it does. I know it's making me happy." He got undressed and danced with her to the Pussy Cat Dolls hit song Don't Cha. Before the song could end, Blase and Cup were introducing their living room to their sex life.

AS winter approached, Blase and Cup were completely settled into their new home. Blase was able to find tenants who paid top dollar to rent her condo. The rent more than doubled what her monthly expenses were for it, so she was pleased with the profit. Five months after their first fittings, Blase was so busy with her practice and finalizing all of her responsibilities for Fallon's wedding that she hadn't noticed that Cup was flying out of town almost every week after his season ended. His team didn't make it to the playoffs again.

"Are you going away again?" she asked the Saturday after their Thanksgiving dinner party while they were shopping for Christmas decorations.

"I have to go out to Seattle for a few days."

"Is this for the foundation?" she asked as she picked up oversized silver Christmas tree ornaments and put them in their cart.

Cup stopped walking and started looking at other decorations. Without looking at Blase, he said, "Ah'ight, babe. I probably should've told you this a few weeks ago, but I got cut from my team."

"What? Baby, oh my God. Why didn't you tell me?" she said as she walked toward him. Blase couldn't believe she didn't hear about it from Fallon.

"Nah, babe. I didn't want to tell anyone. I asked Sergio not to mention it to Fallon. I've been flying out to meet with teams."

"I'm so sorry, baby. Are you okay?" she asked.

"I'm Ah'ight, I just didn't expect it. They got this other kid to come in and replace me, so I've been taking meetings with other teams."

"What other teams?"

"As many that will look at me. It's looking more like I'm going to end up out west though."

"Out west?"

"I like the Padres franchise a lot."

"Padres? Where is that?"

"In San Diego."

"So what will that mean? Will you have to relocate out there?"

"You mean will WE have to relocate out there, right?"

Blase was quiet.

Cup took that as her answer. "Ah'ight, well it doesn't mean we would have to relocate. It would just mean I would be away during the season and here during the off season," he said.

Blase wasn't liking the sound of it all. They just purchased their home together. She was just getting comfortable in their relationship and now he may be going to work two thousand miles away. "Baby, I imagine you want to go and play for a team that has a good record and a good chance of going to the playoffs because that's what I've heard you saying over the past few seasons, but aren't there any teams that you like on the east coast?" she asked.

"Yeah, but none of them are looking at me, babe." Cup's voice grew cross.

"Okay, let's finish this conversation at home. I don't want to upset you," she said. They stayed in the store for another hour picking out all of the holiday decorations for their first Christmas in their new home, and talking about Christmas gifts for different family members.

The day of Fallon and Sergio's rehearsal dinner, Blase and Cup were getting ready in their room with a house full of guests who was in for the holidays and for the wedding. Blase and Cup never continued their conversation after their Christmas shopping. He didn't think it was that big of a deal since it came with the business he was in and he told Blase he had already played for three teams when he met her.

"So, I decided to sign with the Padres," he said as he was standing in their closet deciding what to wear.

"What did you say, babe?" Blase said back from their bathroom.

Cup walked into the bathroom and repeated himself.

Blase stopped putting her makeup on and looked at him. "That's the team in California?" she asked.

"Yeah."

"That's wonderful news, baby. Congratulations. Are you happy?"

Cup was leery of her question. "What do you mean, am I happy?"

"Are you happy with your decision?" she asked again.

"Yeah I'm happy. I told you I liked their franchise."

"Okay, as long as you're happy." She continued putting her makeup on.

Cup was thrown off by Blase's acceptance of his decision. Blase decided after their conversation that she would support whatever decision he made. She thought about if she were in a profession where she had to make such choices, she would want a partner to support her decisions. Cup walked back in the closet and decided to wear his black slacks, with his black suede shoes, an off-white button up shirt, silver cuff links with Onyx and diamonds as well as an Indigo dinner jacket. He thought it would be a great compliment to Blase's dark blue off the shoulder cashmere sweater dress with her black leather belt and her blue and black crocodile skin leather pumps.

They arrived at the restaurant in the meat packing district of New York City twenty minutes before the dinner was to start. Fallon was talking with both the restaurant owner and her wedding coordinator. A photographer walked over and asked if he could take a photo of the two of them. After the photo, they made small talk with each other for a few minutes until Fallon made her way over to them and said, "Hey guys. Don't you two look cute all color coordinated." Blase hadn't even noticed until she mentioned it. She looked at Cup then herself and smiled.

"Where's Sergio?" Cup asked.

"He's upstairs with our parents. Let's go up there," Fallon said.

Blase and Cup followed Fallon upstairs to a private dining room. They walked through the door and aside from the generous size of the room; they saw three long tables with at least twenty place settings at each table. Blase noticed each table had three centerpieces that were made of a variety of white and burgundy flowers in clear and dark grey colored hand blown vases. The color scheme of the dinner appeared to be silver, dark grey, and white. The tables were decorated with dark grey tablecloths with all white dishes and small white votive candles in mini clear and dark grey hand blown candleholders to match the vases. The dark grey cloth napkins were inside of the wine glasses at each place setting and on the plates rested mini antique silver picture frames with dark grey backgrounds and the guest's names written in silver with the date on it.

Sergio and Fallon decided to have authentic Dominican food for the rehearsal dinner. As guests arrived, each were asked to take a photo and then given a glass of champagne as they walked upstairs to the dining room where Spanish language love ballads played in the background. Blase and Cup talked with the parents while everyone arrived and ate hors d'oeuvres the waitresses were bringing around on trays. "Would you like some chicken, ma'am?" one waitress asked.

Blase looked at the small piece of perfectly round roasted chicken sitting on top of a Tostone. "Sure," she responded.

"So how are you two enjoying your new house?" Fallon's mother asked them.

"We love it," Cup answered.

"Yes, we love it. It's a lot of house," Blase added.

"A lot of rooms to clean," Blase's mother added.

"We just hired a cleaning service for that," Cup responded.

Blase's mother looked surprised.

"Blase doesn't have to worry about that," Cup added.

"Have you used that huge kitchen yet?" Blase's mother asked.

"Yes, Mom. I actually made our first meal in it a week after we moved in," she answered.

"Yeah, I didn't know my baby could cook that well. It was delicious," Cup added.

"I didn't know you could cook either," Blase's father said.

Blase laughed. "I didn't either, but I guess if you can read you can cook. Let's just say I follow directions very well."

They all laughed.

Everyone seemed to have arrived and were mingling and talking when the wedding coordinator announced for them to all be seated at their places at the table. Once seated, the waitstaff came around to take everyone's orders as the photographer continued to snap pictures. Sergio and Fallon stood next to each other and Sergio spoke first. "I want to thank you all for coming to our dinner. You all are very special to us and we appreciate you for being a part of this occasion. As you can see, Fallon and her crew did a wonderful job putting this dinner together, so I hope you enjoy it. All I know is there better be some pork on the menu somewhere."

Everyone laughed.

"Yes, thank you so much for being here with us. All who were chosen to be in our wedding, we love you for putting up with the craziness of the planning over the past year. I especially want to thank my parents, as well as Mr. and Mrs. Garcia for their support and Blase and Brielle for putting up with me. I know I was probably a challenge to deal with, but I just wanted this time to be perfect." Fallon turned to face Sergio and continued. "I also want to thank my incredibly handsome husband to be because if you guys think you had it hard, can you imagine what he had to go through!"

Everyone laughed.

"We have bats in the house, and he didn't use them!"

They laughed again.

"I love you, baby. You have always made me feel like Mrs. Garcia, so I can't wait to make it official." As she finished talking, their wedding coordinator brought out two gifts and set them down on the table in front of them. Fallon picked her gift up first. "This is a token of my love and appreciation for you," she said to Sergio.

He opened his gift and saw a toy sized replica fishing boat. As he held it up, he heard something jingling, so he fidgeted with it until he understood that he could open the top. Inside were a set of keys with a silver key chain with the inscription Moca. "There is a life sized one waiting for you at a slip in Long Island. We can go see it whenever you are ready," she said.

Sergio responded with a smile. "You bought me a fishing boat?"

"I hope you like it. I had Moca written on the side." Moca is Sergio's hometown in the Dominican Republic.

Sergio picked Fallon up and kissed her. He said to everyone, "I've been wanting a fishing boat for a few months now. Thank you, Fallita, I love you."

"I love you, too."

"Open yours, Fallon," one of the anxious guests said.

"Okay, okay," she said with a giggle. Fallon opened her gift, and inside was a twelve- carat Asscher cut diamond tennis bracelet—two carats for every year they had been together—with a wide key chain dangling from it and one key that had a diamond encrusted Mercedes emblem. She looked at the bracelet, as did everyone in their seats and she gushed.

"Oh my, Sergio. This is beautiful. Thank you so much," she said.

"Baby, that key is not for show. You will see your car after dinner."

Everyone oooh'd and ahhh'd.

"You bought me a new car?" she said excitedly.

Cup leaned in to Blase and said, "Damn they are making this hard to top."

Blase looked at Cup and laughed. "Well, they have been together for six years so this is a long time coming," she said.

For the rest of dinner, everyone laughed, ate, drank, and had a wonderful time. At the end of dinner as dessert was being served Fallon's father made a speech welcoming Sergio into the Flynn family and telling them both how proud he and her mother were of their impending nuptials and life together. After dinner, Fallon and Sergio went and spent one last night as a single couple in a hotel in midtown.

Blase and Cup decided to go listen to Jazz music at a place called Smoke on Broadway in Manhattan. After they were seated, Cup ordered a bottle of champagne for their table.

"Have you ever thought of marriage?" he asked, realizing that he'd never discussed the topic with her before.

"Not really."

"Why? None of those other dudes ever popped the question?"

"I was asked once or twice," she said not wanting to go much further than that with the topic.

Cup looked surprised and continued. "So what happened?"

"Different things."

"Oh. Ah'ight. I can tell you don't want to talk about it, so we can move on."

"Okay."

Cup was a little bothered, but he continued. "So you're really okay with going to California?"

"Sure, I'm okay with you playing in California. I understand the nature of your business, baby."

"Good, I will be away a lot this year. I will have my schedule soon so when I get out there, you can set it up to come out there for a few months."

"Months? Baby, I can't come for a few months. I was thinking more weekends or maybe I can try and take a week off, but I can't leave my practice for that long."

"Why not? Just tell your patients that you have to go see your man play," he said with a smile.

"I can see my man play from New York, baby."

"Ah'ight, well let's just see how the season goes," he said.

"That sounds like a plan to me. You and Sergio don't get crazy at the bachelor party tomorrow night. I don't want to see anything in the papers," she said as she was leaning in to kiss him.

Cup kissed her back but didn't respond. They sat and listened to music, drinking champagne for the next few hours until they decided to head home.

The next afternoon, Blase kissed Cup goodbye and headed back to the city to meet Fallon, Brielle, and the other bridesmaids to check into their hotel. Fallon had lunch set up for all of the ladies in the hotel's restaurant. When the ladies checked in, they were given their room keys, a gift bag with beauty products, and a gift certificate to Saks Fifth Avenue. The ladies lunched on salads with both grilled chicken and seared scallops and sipped white wine spritzers before they all went to get manicures, pedicures, and massages at the Saks Fifth Avenue spa. Fallon arranged for Blase and Brielle to be in a private area with her while they were getting their pedicures.

"Are you nervous?" Brielle asked.

"Not at all. I've been waiting for Sergio to propose for about four years now. I thought I was going to have to do it for him." She chuckled.

"How are you doing?" Fallon asked Brielle.

"I'm fine. There really isn't any other way that I can be. I mean, being sad or angry isn't going to change things and it certainly won't make Dwight a different man," she said as she sipped her ice water.

"But if you have emotions you need to get out Brie, you shouldn't keep them bottled up. It's okay to be something else other than okay," Blase said.

"She's right," Fallon added.

"Well I can only be what I am, y'all, and right now that is okay."

"Good because there are going to be a lot of eligible bachelors at the wedding," Fallon said.

"Girl please. You know I don't date athletes." Brielle looked visibly disgusted.

"Excuse the hell out of us," Fallon said visibly offended.

"There will be other men there who aren't athletes," Blase added somewhat offended herself.

"No disrespect to you both, it just seems they are all the same."

"As opposed to your soon to be banker ex-husband, right?" Fallon said, rolling her eyes.

The pedicurists were busy working on their feet but all looked at Fallon when she made her last statement.

"Okay, let's not go there," Blase said. "If you aren't ready to start meeting people and dating Brie, that's your prerogative." She looked over at Fallon with a smirk.

"She's right, but lay off the athlete comments. Sergio has been very good to me," Fallon said.

"He sure has and so far, Cup has been great to me," Blase added.

Brielle remained quiet listening to the ladies praise their men. She was a bit jealous of their relationships but didn't want to admit her faith in love and marriage had faded after she found out about Dwight's mistress.

Just before they were headed in for their massages, Fallon handed them little white gift boxes with burgundy ribbons. They looked at Fallon and opened the top of the boxes to reveal their gifts. Blase's gift was a gold Gucci horse link bracelet with a diamond signature charm that she had specially made for it. Brielle's was a white gold Gucci bamboo bangle bracelet.

"Thank you so much for being patient with me, for being wonderful friends, and beautiful sisters. I love you!" Fallon said as they opened their gifts.

"Oh my God, girl, this is beautiful. It must've cost you a fortune. Thank you so much," Blase said as she hugged Fallon.

"Yeah, girl, this is too much," Brielle said, feeling even guiltier for making the comment earlier. "I really am happy for you and Sergio. And I'm blessed to have you both as friends," Brielle added.

"Awwww," Fallon and Blase said at the same time as they all hugged.

"I have something for you as well," Blase added. She walked on her heels towards her locker so she wouldn't mess up her pedicure, took out a small bag, and removed a box wrapped in pink parchment paper with a burgundy butterfly ornament attached to the top.

"For me?" Fallon asked, smiling. "As if you haven't done enough," she continued as she opened the box. Inside was a Tiffany framed photo of the first photo they had ever taken together at their college's orientation where they met.

"Where did you get this? I've never seen it," Fallon asked.

"My mom had it in her archives. I had never seen it until about a year ago. It was the day we met. I knew you hadn't seen it so I figured I would wait and give it to you today," Blase said.

"Oh my goodness, girl. We look so young. Look at our hair and outfits," Fallon said, laughing.

Brielle looked over Fallon's shoulder at the picture. "Aren't those my earrings?" she asked Blase, laughing.

"Probably, I think you went to college with half of my wardrobe and I think I went with half of yours."

The photo was in a tiny blue crystal frame with an inscription FRIENDSHIP IS LOVE. "This is beautiful, thank you."

The morning of Fallon's wedding, the hotel room doors of the 33rd floor where all of the women were staying were busy opening and closing with photographers in and out, hairstylists, makeup artists, and the bridal party. Some of the men were staying in the same hotel as well a few floors down. Fallon was finally ready to leave for the church ten minutes after the wedding was to have begun. They arrived at the church thirty minutes late and all of the ladies exited the stretch limousine perfectly put together in their burgundy bridesmaid's gowns with their white flowers.

The wedding and reception were impeccable. Fallon, Sergio, and all of their friends and family celebrated and danced until late in the evening. Right after the reception, Fallon and Sergio went straight to the airport for a flight to Bora Bora for their two week honeymoon.

**CUP** and Blase celebrated their first Christmas in their home five days after the wedding. They decided to have a select few family and friends over since they had been so busy with Fallon's wedding that month. For New Year's Eve they went to a cabin in Vermont to ski and take some down time. They spent New Year's Eve night quiet, alone, and making love into the New Year.

By the time Pitchers and Catchers started, Cup was already immersed in travels back and forth to California to secure his residence and meet more of the team's back office staff. Blase had fallen back into her work routine as well. The first few weeks of the season were great, Blase managed to make it to California twice, but with business booming, she couldn't seem to fit in many more visits for the remainder of the season.

Cup was growing frustrated with what he considered her lack of effort to try and see him. The Padres move proved to be a better opportunity for him because, while they didn't make it to the World Series, the Padres did make it to the play-offs, but were eliminated by the Cardinals in a game four loss. This sent Cup back to New York in October. By the time he got back they not only had a lot of catching up to do, but a lot of talking to do about their future. Though they spoke regularly on the phone and via email, it wasn't the same as having face time. Blase figured because Cup had been gone since February that she would go ahead and surprise him and have the house set up like a complete home when he returned. She knew he would be upset because they didn't make it to the World Series, so when he arrived, she had a surprise party waiting for him. Cup ended up coming home the day before his birthday. All of his friends and family members from Virginia and even some of his new Padres friends were there waiting for him at the house.

Cup saw some of the changes Blase made to the house and liked most of them, but thought she was going to wait for his input on some of the others. He was happy to see all of his friends and family, but most of all, he was happy to see Blase. She looked fit and beautiful just like she did the last time he saw her. "I miss you so much, baby," he said as he grabbed her and kissed her in front of everyone.

"I missed you too. Now go upstairs and get dressed so we can party." Cup was happy about the party but really wanted the evening alone to make love to his love the night he came home. After the party, Blase and Cup went upstairs and devoured each other, as if it were their first night ever making love.

The next morning Cup rolled over to talk to Blase. "If I asked you, would you sell your practice and move to California?"

Blase opened her eyes and blinked a few times. "Happy Birthday, baby. Asked me what?" she said.

"To sell your practice. Would you?"

Blase became more alert at the reality of what he was saying. "You want me to sell my practice?" she asked.

"I'm asking, would you? I'm not gonna lie babe, this year was hard. There were times when I needed to see you and you couldn't make it out or I couldn't make it home. I mean I am a man."

"So what are you saying? Did you cheat on me, Corey?" She got serious.

"Nah, baby, I didn't cheat on you, I'm not that kind of dude. I'm just saying it was hard."

"Well it was hard for me too, but I figure since you made the decision to play out there that we would just deal with it."

"Yeah but when you said you supported my decision, I figured you would be down for making an effort to come and spend time with me out there. I mean time, not just a day or two here and there."

"I understand, but I've worked so hard for this business. My whole adult life has been dedicated to this practice, so to just sell it because you want to see me more often sounds unfair," she contended.

"How is that unfair? We are together? What? You need something more concrete to make a move? Marry me then," he demanded.

"Cup, I'm not going to marry you just because you want me to come out to California more often. That's not a compromise."

"Well what will happen when we do get married? You will be my wife then. Will your practice come before me?"

"I didn't even know we were thinking of marriage."

"Of course we are. I may be younger than you but I want a family. Don't you?"

"I've never really thought about it," Blase said as she got out of the bed to walk to the bathroom.

"Is that your default answer for everything? I'm sayin', babe, we've been together for a few years now, and we bought this house. What did you think would be the next step?"

"Not you asking me to marry you so that I could come to California to see you more often."

"Come on now. You know that's not really why I said that. I didn't technically ask you. I was just saying that to see if that is what you need for you to make that commitment. I'm saying babe, damn you are acting like this is a chore. You don't want to see me?" He got out of the bed to go into the bathroom with her.

"Of course I do." She turned to face him, discovering where the conversation could go. "Don't be foolish, Corey. I guess because I was immersed in the practice and we do talk every day that everything else would just work itself out."

"Nah, everything else can't work itself out. A man needs his woman, not over a computer, not over the phone, but right next to him, in his arms and in his bed," he said as he pulled her naked body closer to him.

Blase sighed. "Okay, well I don't want marriage to be on the table just for me to come see you more often. I will come see you more often next season. I promise."

"That's my baby. That's what I wanted to hear. I bought a house out there."

"You did? When did you manage to have time to do that?"

"When I was home alone with nothing to do," he said sarcastically as he turned to get ready to walk back into the room.

"Whatever!" she said as she kissed him on his back. "So can you show me that thing you showed me last night?" she said flirtatiously.

"What thing? This thing?" he said as he turned around to display his erectness.

"That's the thing," Blase said.

Cup lifted Blase onto the bathroom counter and they made up for lost time. She gave him what he wished for on his birthday—her.


THE next season was no different than the first. Blase went out to California to see Cup's new home and she liked it, in fact, she loved it, but not enough to visit more often. Her patients were increasing monthly and she was starting to feel overwhelmed as if she needed to take on a partner. Cup's feelings went from frustrated to uninterested. He stopped calling as much and returning Blase's correspondences.

When Blase finally realized what was going on, she booked a flight to California to surprise him. She opened the door to his house, walked upstairs to the bedroom, and noticed the few things she had there were packed in a suitcase. Cup walked in the door an hour after Blase arrived and saw her sitting in the living room with the bag next to her.

"What up, babe?" he asked nonchalantly.

"You tell me," she responded coldly.

"Ah'ight well I was going to bring that suitcase back with me the next time I came back to New York. This just isn't working, babe. I told you last year what the deal was. I need you here. You decided to choose your career again. I can't live like that. I'm a man and I'm not a cheater. I don't want a woman who I can't see and who doesn't seem to want to see me. I'd rather be single."

"Are you serious? Are you breaking up with me?"

"Will you move here with me?" he asked.

"I can't move with you right now, Corey. You know that."

"Then yes, I'm breaking up with you," he said flatly.

Blase was stunned. She didn't expect this reception at all. "This was your decision to move out here. It wasn't OUR decision. We met in New York. I had a thriving business then. What did you expect me to do?"

"I expected you to do what a thousand other women would give anything to do in your position. Play your position as my woman first."

"So that's what this is about? Do you have some other woman who you are interested in?" she asked.

"Nah I don't, but I want to." He walked in the kitchen as he spoke. Cup was angry and he couldn't hide it.

"You want to?"

"Yep, I want to." He turned and looked Blase directly in the eyes. Blase began to silently cry and the sight of this tore Cup up inside, but he was tired of taking second place to her career. "Listen, I don't mean to hurt you, but I've told you what I want you to do. If that is not what you want to do then there is no sense in us continuing to front like we are a couple when we aren't," he said as he handed her a tissue.

Blase took the tissue and wiped her tears. "Corey, that's why I came here. I realized we hadn't seen each other and I wanted to come and visit you. To be with you," she pleaded.

Cup was immune. "It's August, B. I've been here since February. You've been here three times, this time included, since then. Come on, babe. It's done. I can't do it anymore," he said.

"So do you want me to leave?" she asked.

"I think its best."

Blase cried harder, but still quietly. She took her bags and left. She cried in the cab to the airport, on the flight back to New York, in the car to Scarsdale, and in the house. She sat Indian style on the kitchen floor and cried with Sugar in her arms. A week later, she called a realtor and looked for an apartment closer to her practice. Her realtor told her about a new condominium building in Harlem, and on her first visit, she made a full price offer.

When Cup returned to New York in October, the house was empty. He called Sergio who told him she bought a place in Harlem, but Fallon wouldn't tell him where because she knew he would tell Cup. Cup decided that if Blase didn't want to be found, he wasn't going to go looking for her. He called his realtor a week later and put their house on the market.

# BUZZ

# The Vacations

**THE** morning after her dinner with Sheridan and Fallon, Blase decided to do her research from her home office. She had everyone's contact information except for Millers. She heard from friends that he had been traded a few times since being with the New Orleans Saints. She didn't want to contact Adrian to get Miller's information because it would be awkward and obvious, so she checked to see if he had a website and of course, he did. Miller Jones had gone from rookie to rock star with a website boasting all of the Hollywood bells and whistles which made Blase a bit apprehensive about contacting him. Would he be over the top arrogant and obnoxious now that he has secured his position as one of the NFL's top players? She opted not to send him a message through his website, but instead, look him up on Facebook. Surely if he had this elaborate website, he had a presence on Facebook. After calling Sheridan for the log in information, Blase logged on to her Melesse Wellness Facebook account and located Miller's page. She sent him a message that simply read:

*Miller?!*

*"Chocolate" – Blase@melessewellness.com*

Within fifteen minutes of sending the message, Blase's cell phone buzzed with an incoming email message. She picked up her phone, typed in the password to unlock it, and saw the message was from Miller.

*Word…Chocolate?! Is that really you? You look good baby. Call me. I'm in Chicago. I play for the Bears now. I want to see you. Holla!!- 312-555-1212.*

Blase smiled thinking this might be easier than she thought it would be. She decided to hold off on giving him a buzz until she had all of the plans set and ready. She picked up the phone and dialed Fallon's number.

She answered on the first ring. "So have you rethought this crazy idea of yours?"

Blase laughed. "No, actually I just got Miller's information. He looks so good, Fal. I mean really good," she emphasized.

"I can imagine. He wasn't bad looking back in the day."

"Okay! So what are you doing tomorrow? I want to come to your office and check on some packages. You got my email with the budget parameters, right?"

"Oh wow, girl, you're really doing this! Okay, come by around three o'clock," Fallon said.

"Great! The locations I'm considering are Jamaica, The Seychelles Islands, Hawaii, The Cayman Islands, Aruba, and Addis Ababa." Blase wrote them down as she said them to confirm to herself those were her choices.

"Wait, that's six vacations, B. What happened to Lucky number five?" Fallon asked.

"I know. I want to go to see my grandparents. My Wund Ayat is turning ninety-five in June and I want to be there for his birthday."

"Oh that's nice. Now there is a place that I've never been. Would you mind some company on that trip?"

"I would love some," Blase sang back.

"Okay, so for that one you just need a flight and maybe some recommendations on restaurants?" Fallon asked.

"More or less," Blase said.

As she was talking with Fallon, her second line beeped in. She looked at her cellphone and said, "Hey Fal, I have to take this call. I'll see you tomorrow."

"Okay honey, see you then."

Blase answered the second line. "Hello."

"Baby, what's going on? Are you still mad at me? I called and texted you all day yesterday."

Blase paused to prepare herself for the conversation. "Randy, this is not working for me. I know you told me about your situation from the start, but I just don't want to do this with you anymore."

Randy hung up.

Puzzled, she thought, *Oh no this fool didn't hang up on me.* Then she felt relieved because that was it. She had no intentions of ever calling him again, and then her phone buzzed. She laughed and answered, "So was that a tantrum, or are you really just crazy?"

Randy lied, "No, baby, our call was dropped. My cell phone carrier sucks. But baby, I'm really sorry about the other night. If I could've gotten out of it, you know I would've."

"Randy it's bigger than the other night. First of all it isn't the first time that you'd done it and I'm sure it wouldn't be the last, but more importantly, this relationship just isn't going anywhere so I see no point in continuing it if I'm not happy and Randy, I'm not happy."

"Baby, I promise you I won't do it again. Please just let me see you so we can talk about it in person."

"No, Randy. My decision is final. This is one decision that you cannot contribute to. I have a lot of traveling that I'll be doing over the next few months anyway so there's no need for further discussions."

They sat in silence for a few moments. Randy, with his voice faint and deflated said, "Baby, I don't want this, but I will respect your feelings. I'll miss you. Can I still call you from time to time?" he asked.

"Sure, Randy as long as you don't get upset if I can't take your call or call you back immediately."

"Okay, well where are you going, if you don't mind me asking?"

"I do mind actually. I have to go now, but you take care of yourself and much success to you."

"You as well, baby. I love you," Randy said.

Blase hung up.

The next day Blase arrived at Flynn Destinations at 2:45 p.m. Fallon was in with a young couple who sounded as if they were planning their honeymoon. The couple exited, one holding a brochure that said Fiji in one hand and a hurricane glass filled with a pink frozen drink in the other. The other holding a folder that said Bali in one hand and a box with what looked like a custom designed golf ball in the other. By the way they were dressed, Blase pegged them for either attorneys or bankers.

Fallon's assistant told Blase that Fallon was just on a quick call with her father and to go into her office.

"Daddy, I'm not sure if I can make it out there in the next two weeks, I have so much to do here, and Sergio and I have a few events planned. I'm going to call you back a little later after I talk with my assistant to see what my next month looks like, okay?" Fallon paused and listened to her father for a few moments. "Okay, Daddy. I have to call you back. Is Mom there with you in Australia or is she still in Greece?" After Fallon's father said a few more things, they ended their call with a promise to discuss her going to Australia later.

"Hey," Fallon said to Blase and she reached over the top of her desk for a hug.

"Hey, Miss Busy. How could you turn down an offer to go to Australia?" Blase asked as she put her briefcase on the floor next to her chair and hung her pocketbook on the arm of her chair.

"B, you know I would love nothing more than to go to Australia, but I really can't keep helping my father any longer. I have my own business that I'm running and thank Heavens it is booming. I keep telling him to hire someone who is willing to travel with him, but he refuses."

"Why?"

"Probably because he wouldn't know what their title would be, how much to pay them, or how to define their job description because I do everything. I pick up all of the slack of his entire staff. It's like a cross between an assistant and the President," Fallon said, sounding exasperated.

"Oh wow. Yeah it sounds like you are cheap labor," Blase agreed.

"Well he'll just have to manage. I can't keep dropping everything I'm doing to come and cross all of his T's and dot all of his I's. Plus Sergio doesn't want me away that much. It's bad enough that our schedules are so crazy. Hell, he doesn't even want me to work."

Fallon dialed her assistant's extension. "Diane, are Blase's vacation packages on the network? Great, thank you. Can you also bring in the hard copies of the package folders? Thank you."

Fallon located the files for Blase's vacation packages on her computer. As she pulled them up, the first one popped up on the 50" flat screen TV that hung on her wall to the right of her desk.

Blase was impressed. Not only by Fallon's one woman operation, but how professional and upscale her office looked and how well prepared she was.

"Okay, so all of these packages are within the budget breakdown you emailed me last night. The first package I'm going to show you is Aruba."

On the screen was a photo of a beige ranch style villa with a pink slate roof. It had palm trees strategically scattered throughout the front and sides of the home. "I know you wanted to do all hotels for your trips, but there are no Flynn or Ritz hotels in Aruba as of yet. So I decided to try something different for this package. I thought a full service house rental would be equally as romantic, including maid and butler service, private chef, and your own private masseuse, and it falls within your budget."

"Really? I can get all of that for 10 days?" Blase asked.

"Yes. The house is located in the exclusive Gold Coast beach area of Aruba." Fallon began using her remote to change the photo slides of the property and areas in Aruba. "The house has three bedroom suites, each with their own private baths and a Master suite with its own balcony. It has central air conditioner; each bedroom has a television and telephone. There is a formal dining room and an eat-in-kitchen, as well as an outdoor dining room on the patio. The rear yard has a hot and cold Jacuzzi with a waterfall in its 32 inch in-ground pool and encased in a lush tropical garden. I think it will be perfect. You can tailor your menu for the week to what you and your guest would like. I can have your alcoholic beverages of choice stocked in the bar. Your chef will also know how to pair your wines with your meals and he or your butler can make any mixed cocktails you might want."

Blase was amazed. Fallon leaned over and handed her a folder with a photo of Aruba on the front. "Inside that folder will be all of the forms that will help you tailor your menu and set up each meal time and arrangement. There is also a form to schedule your spa services.

"Just fill them out and send them to me along with your agreement on the contract page and I will have this and all of the packages I show you today finalized. Do you like it, or would you prefer something different?"

"I love it. Did you have something else to show me in Aruba?"

"Good because I sure didn't." Fallon laughed. "Oh, another thing, we can arrange a limo to and from the airport, but if you want to get around the Island, you will need a rental car. I can arrange that for you also. There are luxury car rentals available as well. Just fill out the car rental form in the folder with your preference."

Blase took the folder and put it in her designer briefcase.

"Your next package is your Cayman Island package. As requested, there is a Ritz Carlton in the Caymans."

On the screen was a photo of a cream colored cross between a Spanish style and Greek style building sitting atop an off-white sandy beach that had diamond flecks sparkling throughout and translucent turquoise water serenely resting on the edges of the beach. As the photos went on, Blase saw the grounds, spa, guest suites, and all of the other hotel amenities. She was sold.

Fallon explained in detail what the hotel had to offer and what activities she and her guest could partake in. "In your Cayman folder are forms with choices of activities, spa services, and dinner venues. Make your selections on those and I will have it all set up for you."

Blase put the Cayman folder in the briefcase next to the Aruba folder.

"Aloha! Welcome to Maui," Fallon said as she walked over to Blase and put a Lei around her neck.

Blase laughed senselessly. "Go ahead on, Fal, sell these packages!"

Fallon laughed with her and said, "I present to you The Ritz Carlton in Kapalua, Maui."

Hawaiian music was playing in the background. "Oh wow, Fallon, that photo is amazing."

She was viewing a photo of a tropical sand castle abut a three tiered cascading pool, surrounded by endless palm trees with white cloth cabanas. Fallon explained her Maui package much like the Cayman Island package and gave her a Maui folder. Blase left the Maui folder in her lap as she waited for her next destination description. After seeing the destinations so far, she was super excited about her decision to take the vacations and couldn't wait to sit down and go through all of the folders and assign them to her ex-boyfriends. *Who am I going to take where?*

"Everyting Irie in Jamaica mon," Fallon said in her best Caribbean accent. Next on the screen was a photo Blase recognized. It was Flynn Negril, Fallon's father's hotel in Negril, Jamaica. As the sounds of Bob Marley floated through the air, Fallon's assistant brought in a green coconut with a pink and blue umbrella and a white straw in it. Blase smiled and thanked her before turning to Fallon and asking, "Do you really do this for all of your potential clients?"

"Absolutely," she responded. "I told you we are not just a travel agency, we are a destination boutique."

Blase sipped her Pina Colada and realized it had rum in it. When Fallon noticed her facial expression she said, "My other potential clients all get virgin drinks, but I know how you like to sip on a lil' sump'm sump'm." Fallon picked up her glass of ice water and took a sip. "I would have one with you but I have a full day of appointments after you," she added.

Swaying back and forth to Bob Marley's hit tune *One Love*, Blase sipped and looked at the expansive 144-acre resort. Flynn Negril looked like a little village of private huts surrounded by tropical coconut trees and flowers, mini pool enclaves with one long continuous pool spanning the length of the resort. Each hut had its own private Jacuzzi built in to its deck. There were also bars and restaurants scattered throughout the property that were made to look like square stucco boxes painted muted yellow and white to distinguish them from the huts. The beach looked like perfectly raked wheat flour and in the front of the resort sitting on top of a man-made hill was a large square building which was the same color as the bars and restaurants. Once you made it up the oval shaped driveway to the front of the resort past the huge glass sign that had Flynn, Negril etched in script in it you noticed the mirrored glass up close was actually see through.

"I gave you this coconut because all guests arriving at Flynn Negril are greeted with a similar Pina Colada. You are offered your choice of alcoholic or non-alcoholic. Because you will have already given your name to a Flynn representative at the airport, once you arrive, you will not need to check-in; you will simply be escorted to your hut by one of the Flynn shuttle cars. You will be designated your own personal hut keeper who will be the only person taking care of your quarters for your entire stay, no matter how long or short your stay is. If you chose to stay for thirty days that same hut keeper will be with you for thirty days," Fallon said.

"You mean you wouldn't give the person a day off?" Blase asked with worry.

"No, but trust me they will be well compensated if they had to stay that long. You will be given a phone number to dial your personal hut keeper for anything, including in hut meals, cocktails, towels, toiletries, or anything else you may need." Fallon continued the virtual tour. "All of our huts are air conditioned with thirty-two inch flat screen TVs and landline phones. They have private Jacuzzi's on the deck and steps from the deck down into the continuous pool. There are huts that have beach views. One side of the hut is the poolside and the other has a French style shutter doors with steps onto the beach and private outdoor shower. The beach view huts have their decks and Jacuzzi's facing the beach. All of the decks and Jacuzzis are enclosed by nine foot shutters for privacy."

"I want one of those," Blase said.

"I knew you would so your package includes a beach front hut. There are a few other perks in your Negril package compliments of Daddy that you'll find out once you get there," Fallon said as she winked at her friend.

"Thanks, Dad," Blase said as she touched her coconut with Fallon's water.

"Girl this is fun. I am sending everyone I know to Flynn Destinations. Hell coming here is like a vacation!"

Fallon burst out laughing. "That's my goal girl! Last but certainly not least, Bienvenue sur Flynn, Mahe." Fallon spoke it in French.

"Excuse me?" Blase said not even knowing her friend could speak French. "You speak French? Can you speak it fluently?"

"Yes, I can. So now I know Greek, Spanish, French, Italian, and Portuguese. I am learning Japanese now, but I don't see me mastering it, it's a hard language to learn. They do speak Seychelles Creole in Mahe more than French, but I know you speak French, so you'll do just fine."

"I'm impressed that you can speak all of those languages. And I'm excited to be able to speak French."

Anchored comfortably in the Indian Ocean, Mahe is a part of the Seychelles Islands which is off the coast of East Africa. Flynn Mahe appeared to be nestled on the Southern most coast of the Island in Anse Cachee. It was designed similar to Flynn Negril, but with 20 oversized Villas replete with authentic looking African mud and thatch huts. These huts were made of brick and tin, but the exterior appearance was that of the traditional African huts and each had its own view of the Indian Ocean. The fronts of each African hut had two hand carved wooden pole sculptures, oversized Coco De Mar trees, fragrant vanilla orchids and bright orange Watsonia Irises. The Jacuzzis in the patios of the huts looked as if they were an accident because they were made to look like a tiny hot spring made of mud and the huts sat on the top of a cliff looking as if it was tilting into the Indian Ocean.

Blase was excited about going to East Africa because she had never been. The package was the same for Mahe as it was for Negril with the same surprise perks from Fallon's father.

"You will have a traditional African attire clad hut keeper in Mahe, but if you are assigned a male hut keeper and would prefer that he wear a t-shirt, we can arrange that."

Blase raised her eyebrows at the photo on the screen of the perfectly chiseled espresso man wearing nothing but animal hide flaps held together by two intertwined pieces of animal skin straps holding a serving tray.

"In each package you will also find frequent flyer forms for the possible airlines. Just fill in all of your frequent flyer numbers and let me know if you would like priority club level service at the airports when you go." She handed Blase her Flynn Mahe folder and a business card.

"This card has your log in name and password to your account with us. All of the virtual tours I showed you today are on your personal FDA, which is your Flynn Destinations account. You can check all information on this account including flight status and the arrival and pick up times of your limos for your flights. You can also upload photos of your trips and share them with your family on your account. If you do not wish to fill out the paper forms that are in the folders and fax them to us, you can log in and fill out the forms for your package online. They will auto populate into our database so when we finalize all of the purchases and plans for your vacations, you will get all of the necessary credits." Fallon sat down in her chair as she finished her presentation and was impressed. She had never had to do a presentation for multiple trips before so it was great practice to be able to do it with her friend.

"I'm so impressed by all of this, Fal. I can't believe you had the time to do all of this."

"Honestly, Diane is the best. She's responsible for putting together the folders, the virtual tours, and she does an amazing job maintaining the client database in the website. I had the website customized to my company. It took me two months and fifteen thousand dollars to get it perfect," she boasted.

"Well it was money well spent. Any person looking for luxury should come to you."

"I hope so. So who are you taking—" Just as Fallon was about to ask her who she was taking where, Diane buzzed in and told her that her four o'clock client had arrived.

Blase looked at her watch and saw it was ten minutes to four. "Okay, I'll let you get ready for your next performance," Blase said with a chuckle. "Good luck, and I'll be online later to begin filling out the forms and assigning names to the trips."

"Okay, can't wait to see who gets to go where."

They hugged and Blase went on her way.

When Blase left Fallon's office, she dialed Brielle's number from her cell phone and got her voice mail.

"Brie, its B. You have to call me back sooner than possible. I just left Fallon's office and I am so excited about my vacations. I want you to come over tonight so I can show you. Call me back." She hung up and text Brielle a condensed version of the same message.

She dialed Sheridan's number.

"Hello jet setter," Sheridan answered on the first ring.

"Sheridan, are you home yet?"

"No, I just finished passing out the payroll checks. I'm about to close the system out for the night and double-check the appointments for tomorrow. I'm so glad I don't work on Saturdays. Oops, did I say that out loud?" she said sarcastically.

"Don't get too glad, you might have to work them soon. New position; new responsibilities."

"Well, I won't mind then. But what's up?"

"Meet me at my apartment. I just left Fallon's office and I'm so excited about my trips. I want to show them to you and Brielle."

"Nice. Yes, I'll be there. I just want to stop and grab something to eat. I'm starved."

"No, don't eat. I'm ordering Indian food. You do like Indian, right?"

"Sure do."

"Okay, I just don't have that sweet wine you like, so you might want to pick up a bottle of it for yourself."

"I'll do that."

When Blase hung up the phone, her cellphone buzzed with a text from Brielle that read: *I'm working late tonight. How late will you be up?*

Blase responded back and told her to come whenever she finished and she would have Indian food and wine waiting for her when she got there.

Brielle texted back: *You sold me with the Indian food and wine. LOL*

Blase laughed as she got in her car to head back to Harlem.

# The Assignments

**SHERIDAN** and Blase moved Blase's coffee table to the side and made a picnic on her multi colored area rug in her living room. There were two glass buckets of ice chilling two different kinds of white wines. Blase opened her laptop and hooked it up so you could see what was on the screen of her large 62" flat screen TV. She grabbed her glass of wine and touched hers with Sheridan's.

"Here's to fun in the sun," Blase said.

"And tramping in the tropics," Sheridan added as they laughed and took sips of their wine and then exchanged glasses realizing they each picked up the wrong glass. After they finished laughing, Blase showed Sheridan all the packages and described how Fallon had presented them to her.

"Oh I have to use Fallon as soon as I get my promotion," Sheridan said half joking, half serious.

"Yes you do. She works with all budgets, but isn't our new boyfriend a hedge funder?" Blase asked.

"Yes. I didn't think about his money. I guess I'll be alright." Sheridan sighed at the thought of finally having a man who was financially secure.

"Yes you will, Sher. It will all fall in to place, trust me."

Blase and Sheridan went through the virtual tours again and the printed brochures with a fine tooth comb, noting all of the perks and beautiful amenities of each destination.

"So, who goes where?" Sheridan asked anxiously.

"Honestly I don't know. I guess it will depend on their schedules."

"What do you mean it will depend on their schedules? You haven't called to see if they are available yet?"

"No."

"Well, what the hell are you waiting for? Call," Sheridan said and she picked up Blase's house phone and handed it to her.

"I guess I should do that, shouldn't I?"

"Yes you should and it's a good thing I am here. I can write all of the names and dates down so you don't get confused."

"Oh perfect!"

Blase grabbed her cell phone, unlocked the phone, and scrolled to the address book. She called Mark first. He answered on the first ring. With loud noise in the background he said, "Hola Belleza. Uno momento."

Blase waited until she heard silence on the other end.

"Are you there?" he asked.

"Yes, I'm here, Mark. How are you?"

"I'm wonderful now that I'm hearing from you. It's been what, five years now?"

"Yes, at least."

"How are you?" he asked.

"I'm wonderful. How are you?" she asked again clearly nervous.

Sheridan tapped her on the leg and mouthed to her to relax. Blase took a big gulp of her wine.

Mark laughed. "I'm good. Are you all right? Is everything okay?" he asked.

"Yes, I was wondering what you were doing in May?"

"May?"

"Yes, May."

"Belleza it's December. I have no idea what I'll be doing in May," he said, sounding confused.

"Okay, well let me ask you this, are you seeing someone?"

Mark was silent for a few moments. Blase took that opportunity to sip some more of her wine. His silence indicated to her that he was indeed seeing someone.

"Yes," he said shortly.

"Is it serious?"

"What is this all about? Why do you want to know if I am seeing someone or doing something in May?"

"I guess I'll just come right out with it then. I am taking vacation in May and I would love for you to accompany me to…" she picked up the first folder she saw "…the Cayman Islands."

Even though Mark had been with his current girlfriend for just under two years, he didn't hesitate. "I would love to go."

"Wonderful. Do you still live in Brooklyn?"

"Yes, I do."

"Okay, I will have all of the details sent to you. All you have to do is pack and show up with that beautiful smile of yours."

Mark smiled at the compliment. "It's a plan."

"Are you sure you will be able to go? I don't want to make the arrangements and you cancel on me."

"As long as I am healthy and breathing, nothing will keep me from seeing you, Belleza. I miss your smile."

Blase's heart jumped.

Sheridan heard the last part because Blase was leaning next to her to grab more wine.

"I'm looking at the third week in May for ten days," she told him.

"Sounds good. I will plug it into my phone when we hang up."

"Perfect."

"I have to get back inside now. Thank you, Belleza, I will speak to you soon."

"No, thank you, Mark. We'll talk soon," she said and they hung up.

"See, that wasn't nearly as painful as you thought," Sheridan said. "So, that's Mark for the Caymans. Got it," Sheridan wrote it on her notebook paper.

"So it is," Blase confirmed.

The next call was to Walter. She'd spoken with him a few times throughout the years and saw him at a few medical events. She knew he was still living with his Chinese ex-wife, but she also knew he wasn't happy with the arrangement. She dialed his home number and Liang answered. "Hello."

"Hello, may I speak with Walter?" Blase asked.

"Walta no heeya," Liang responded.

"Okay, thank you," Blase said as she hung up. She dialed his cell phone number.

He answered on the first ring. "Cheers! To what do I owe the pleasure of this call?"

"Hi, Walter. How are you?"

"I'm well, my darling. How have you been?" he asked.

"I've been wonderful. I am calling because I was wondering if you had any vacation time available in the next few months."

"In fact, I do. I was planning on taking two weeks off at the end of January. Why do you ask?"

"Because I have some vacation time I'd like to take in January also and I was hoping we could go away together."

"Really?"

"Yes really. Why do you sound so surprised?"

"Because you all but told me to go to bloody hell the last time we had a conversation about us, so I'm just taken aback is all."

"So is that a yes, or is that a no?" she asked.

"Where would you like to go? It's an absolute yes. I'll have my travel agent make the arrangements," he said.

"That won't be necessary. I'll have mine do it, all you have to do is show up and be on time for when the limo picks you up. Is Jamaica good for you?"

"Jamaica is perfect." Truthfully she could've told Walter anywhere and he would've given her the same answer.

"Wonderful, but I can't do two whole weeks Walter. Is ten days good for you?"

"Yes, ten days is lovely, darling."

"Great. I'll have my travel agent send you all of the details. I'm going to schedule it from January 15th to the 24th, so pen in those days on your calendar. I'll have my assistant send you an outlook invitation for the dates also because I know you'll forget the moment we hang up."

Walter laughed. "Very well then, Blase. It seems that you have it all ironed out. I'll be Jamaica ready on the 15th. I can't wait to see you."

"You as well, Walter," she said, and with that they hung up.

"Two down, three to go," Sheridan said.

As Blase was scrolling through her phone for Cup's number, her doorman called up to tell her their food delivery was there. She told him to let the delivery man up. As they set up the food in the picnic area, the doorman called up again to tell her she had a visitor. Blase asked who it was because Randy had continued to text her nonstop since their telephone conversation and she didn't want him just showing up at her apartment. When she confirmed it was Brielle, she gave him permission to send her up.

The doorbell rang and Sheridan answered it. "You're just in time. The food just arrived," she said as she cheek kissed Brielle.

"Great because I am famished. So what did I miss so far?" she asked Sheridan while Blase was in the kitchen getting plates and utensils.

"Blase has already called Mark and Walter and invited them on their vacations."

"Wow. I still can't believe this woman is doing this. Where is she going?"

"I'm going to Negril, Mahe in the Seychelles Islands, Maui, Aruba, and the Caymans," Blase sang as she was entering the living room.

"Sheridan, show her the virtual tours while I fix the plates please. We are having a living room picnic Brielle, so shoes off and join us. The vodka is in the freezer and the olives are on the door of the fridge."

"Oh, I'll just have some wine. I want to keep it light tonight. I have to take my son to soccer practice in the morning."

"Okay, here's a glass," Sheridan responded while she was pouring her some wine.

Sheridan gave the quick version of the virtual tours because she didn't want Blase to lose her courage to call the other three exes.

"Blase, who's next?"

"I'm going to call Cup," she said as she dialed his number while her friends dug into the Chicken Tikka and Tandoori.

Cup's answering machine came on. While his outgoing message was playing Blase's other line rang. She looked at her phone and saw it was Cup calling her back so she answered.

"Hello."

"Dr. Morgan. It's been a while," he said somewhat dryly.

"Yes it has, Corey. How are you?" she said, her voice cracking.

"I'm good, just taking it easy."

"Are you in New York?" she asked.

"No, I'm in Virginia for the holidays with my family. What are you up to?"

"I'm here in New York with my family and friends."

"Ah'ight, how are your mom and dad doing?"

"They are doing well, thank you for asking.

"And your grandparents and Benny and his wife?"

"Oh, everyone is great. Benny and his wife are expecting twins."

"Ah'ight, that's nice. I didn't know twins ran in your family."

"No, they don't. They run in his wife's family."

"Oh ah'ight, that's nice. Boys or girls?" he asked.

"They don't want to find out until they have the babies so we are planning a big ole beige and purple shower."

"Oh okay," he said, chuckling.

The small talk was making it a bit awkward. It had been a few years since their break up, but Blase thought time would heal all wounds.

"The purpose of my call is to see if you had any free time before you go to Pitchers and Catchers training?"

"Time for what?"

"For a vacation."

"A vacation?'

"Yes, Cup, a vacation. With me. For ten days. I have vacation time coming up, and I was wondering if you would go away with me."

"Go away with you? I haven't even seen you in, what, about three years now?"

"All the more reason for us to get reacquainted." She felt his rejection coming on. She knew he may have still been bitter, but she took the risk anyway.

"When do want to take this vacation and to where?" he asked, softening up.

"I was hoping you could do it the middle of February like the 12th to the 22nd. It's for about ten days."

"Ten days. Can I get back to you?"

"Well, I would actually like an answer tonight, if possible. I saw a great deal on the flights and I want to book it."

"Wow. You call me out of the blue after three years and ask me to go away with you for almost two weeks and you want an answer on the spot. You have not changed, Dr. Morgan."

"Corey, I don't mean to sound demanding. Please don't get upset. I'm just excited about this trip and want to put the plans in motion tonight."

"Okay. Where are you planning to take me?" he asked.

"To Aruba! I have a great deal on a beautiful private house there with our own butler, maid, and masseuse. We'll have fun."

Cup laughed at Blase's excitement. He still cared for her very much. "Ah'ight, hold on one second." Cup put the call on hold. Blase sat in silence, watching Sheridan and Brielle hold their own conversation but didn't hear anything they said. She sipped her wine and ate a few pieces of chicken before he came back to the line.

"Okay, I called my agent and my assistant, and I can definitely do those dates. You'd better not flake out on me."

"Oh trust me I won't. I just clicked to purchase the tickets."

"You don't play around."

"You know I don't. You do still live in the same house in San Diego, right?"

"Yes."

"Okay, let me get the rest of it squared away. I will have the details sent to you and a limo outside of your house to take you to the airport on the twelfth."

"Ah'ight," Cup said with a smile on his face. "I'll talk to you before then though, right?"

"Of course you will," she assured him.

"Cool. I have to go. Talk to you soon," he said.

"Soon," she confirmed and they hung up.

"Whew!" Blase said. "I knew Cup was going to make me work."

"He should've," Brielle said.

Blase gave Brielle a friendly scowl.

"Who's next? You have two more to go and we are running out of wine," Sheridan said.

Blase got up from her Indian style sitting position and scrolled through her email messages for Miller's phone number. She grabbed another bottle of white wine and gave it to Brielle to open.

"I'm calling Miller next."

They all kind of sat there looking at one another for a few moments before Blase finally found and dialed his number.

He answered sounding half asleep. "Yeah who's this?"

"Hello, Miller?"

"Yeah, this is Miller. Who's this?"

"This is Blase Morgan. Did I catch you at a bad time?"

"Oh shit, nah. What's up, Chocolate?"

Blase heard an angry female voice in the background say, "Chocolate! Who the hell is Chocolate, Mill…" the voice trailed off as it sounded as though he was walking away from the woman.

"Miller, if I've caught you at a bad time, I can call you back another day," she said, feeling awkward.

"Nah, I told you right now is fine. What's up, baby? How you doin'?" he asked, sounding wide awake now.

"Oh not much, just figured I'd give you a call and catch up. So, you're with Chicago now? How do you like it in Chi-town?" she asked.

"It's cold as a motherfucker out here but I get more play here than on any other team, so I'm doing my thang. You'd like it out here. It's nice. You wanna come and visit me?"

Blase smiled because Miller was never one to beat around the bush. "Well it's funny you mention that. I have some vacation ti—"

Before she could finish he said, "Yeah, that's what I'm talking about. I'll book the tickets. When can you come?"

"No, no Miller, slow down. What I wanted to say was I have some vacation time in March. I just opened my second practice, so I won't be able to take any time off until then. I'm juggling patients in both locations—"

He cut her off again. "That's what's up, baby. I see you are doing what I knew you would be doing."

"So, I wanted to see if you could take some time then, since your season would be over and you will be rested. I want to go to Maui for ten days in March. Does that sound doable for you?"

"First, Chocolate, my season is over right now, but March is cool, baby. Whatever works for you, I just want to see you. I miss you."

"I miss you too, Miller. So I will have Fallon book it all for us. She owns a travel agency. Well actually she calls it a destination boutique." They shared a laugh.

"Sounds like something Fal would call it. So she did it, huh? I heard she married that dude Sergio. Hey, I met your college sweetheart a few years back."

"Yes, I know. He told me. He reached out to me to let me know that. I hope you guys kept it clean," she said.

"Oh nah baby, you don't have to worry about that. You were an off limits conversation for both of us. It was strictly business with me and dude."

"Good. So I'll have Fallon send all of the information to your house. I'll even have her arrange a limo to take you to the airport. Just give me your address so I can have it sent to you."

Miller gave Blase his address. She wrote it down on the notepad Sheridan was writing on.

"Will we talk before March?" he asked.

"Of course we will."

"Great."

"I'm about to go out, and it sounds like you have an angry friend you have to make up with," she said.

"Oh nah, she was just something to do."

*Sounds familiar,* she thought.

"Well go handle your business," she said.

He laughed and hung up.

"Miller, check," Sheridan said.

Brielle shook her head. "I am so amazed you are doing all of this. How much is all of this costing you?" Brielle asked.

Sheridan was curious about this also.

The only person who knew was Fallon, and Blase planned on keeping it that way.

"Hopefully in the end, no matter what the cost, it will have been worth every penny. You can't beat five vacations with five attractive men, in five months time, all to find my prince charming," she said.

"Listen, you know all of these men. I still say they are exes for a reason, but girl do what makes you happy," Brielle said.

"Here we go with Brie's cynicism," Blase said.

Sheridan listened.

"I'm not cynical, Blase, I'm real. If you break up with a man then obviously he either didn't do right by you or he wasn't someone you felt you could spend the rest of your life with. Three of the five of your exes proposed to you and you chose not to marry them. That didn't happen by accident, B."

"No, it didn't, but maybe at those times in my life I wasn't focused on family and sacrificing for love and a family."

"If you say so. I think you did it the right way. Look, I sacrificed and it got me a lying cheating ass husband so I say you did the absolute right thing."

"You do sound cynical though, Brie and bitter also, honey," Sheridan said gently as she poured Brielle more wine.

"Whatever!" Brielle said as she got up and headed towards the bathroom.

"But we love you either way," Blase said with a laugh. She knew that Brielle was still angry at her ex-husband for cheating on her. She felt her pain all too familiarly, but Blase didn't have a child or a marriage when it happened to her.

"Anyway, last call. I'm getting tired," Sheridan said.

"Well, stay here," Blase said.

"I guess I could," Sheridan responded.

Blase dialed Adrian's number. She was nervous about his call because someone mentioned that he had gotten married, and it was close to 1:00 a.m. The phone rang twice before it went to voicemail. Blase thought about hanging up and dialing the emergency number mentioned on his voicemail but opted to leave a message.

"Hi, Adrian, this is Blase. I know it's late and I'm sorry for calling so late. This isn't an emergency so take your time in calling me back, but I hope to hear from you soon."

She disconnected the call.

"Well four out of five isn't bad," Sheridan said.

Blase got up to go to her linen closet and get a towel and washcloth for Sheridan. "Here you go. There is cotton underwear in a brand new pack in the drawer in the guest room as well as an unopened toothbrush," she said.

Sheridan looked fascinated. "You wouldn't happen to have a brand new dress and heels in there I can wear tomorrow, would you?"

Blase smiled "No, I don't but you can borrow one of mine if you want."

"No, I'm going to head home in the morning to change. I'm turning in," Sheridan said.

"Okay. Thank you for your support tonight. I really appreciated it."

"No problem. That's what friends and assistants are for, right?"

"Yes, you're right. Sleep well, Sher," Blase said.

"Thank you."

Brielle and Blase sat up for the next hour talking more about Brielle's business and how she was coping and moving on since her divorce. She didn't want to ask her the other day at breakfast. Brielle told her she wasn't really focusing on her ex-husband, but keeping sane for her son. Her regular workouts kept her mind clear and focused.

"You've been divorced for several years, Brielle. Don't you think it's time for you to start dating again?"

"Blase, with this new business and my son in every little sport imaginable, I don't have the time to think about a man right now," Brielle barked.

"Okay, Brie, I don't want to upset you. I just want you to be happy."

"I know you do and I'm happy seeing my son happy."

"Okay."

"Speaking of son, I think it's time for me to head on back to the suburbs. Dwight is dropping him off in the morning so I can take him to his soccer game. You would think his trifling ass would just take him to his soccer game, but that's another story."

Blase empathized with her friend. Brielle got up and straightened her clothes.

"Do you need help cleaning up?" Brielle asked.

"No, I'm fine. Thank you for coming over, Brie. You know if you ever want or need to talk I'm here. You don't always have to be so controlled and quiet with your emotions," Blase said as she hugged her.

"Thank you, B. I'm fine, really," she said as she kissed her on the cheek. "Love you, girl. I'll be living vicariously through you with those vacations. The packages look amazing. I'm impressed with Fallon's work. I may refer some of my clients to her," Brielle said.

"You should. It was even better when she did it in person."

Brielle grabbed her purse and walked out the door and down the hall to the elevator. Blase watched her get in the elevator before she closed her door. She walked over to the picnic area and sat on the sofa to take the whole night in. Deciding that she'd had enough wine, she put the remaining wine in the refrigerator. She took the plates into the kitchen, rinsed them off, and put them along with the utensils and wine glasses in the dishwasher. She also threw the empty take out containers in the garbage and picked up the used cloth napkins and the throw blanket she'd laid on the carpet and threw them all in the laundry basket in the guest bathroom. Struggling to move the heavy marble coffee table, Blase opted to leave that for the morning when she could ask for Sheridan's help. She shut all of the lights off and went in the kitchen to make sure Sugar's water bowl was full before she headed to her bedroom. She was closing her bedroom doors behind her when her phone rang. She looked at it and saw it was Adrian's number. *Wow, he's calling me back at 2:20 a.m.*

She answered, "Hi, Adrian. I didn't expect to hear from you tonight."

"I didn't expect to hear from you either, so we are even."

"What are you doing up at this hour?"

"I was about to ask you the same thing. I was prepared to leave you a message."

The tone of both of their voices slipped into a sultry after midnight nature. "Well, I was having dinner and wine with Brielle and my friend Sheridan, but I called you to ask you something."

"Ask away."

"Will you be up for another fifteen minutes? I just want to take a quick shower. I will call you right back."

Adrian agreed as his mind drifted to the visual of Blase's naked body. Exactly fifteen minutes later, Blase climbed into her bed, snuggled under the covers, and called Adrian back. They talked about everything—their current lives, professions, college days, and family. Adrian confirmed he wasn't married and still had no children. Before Blase new it, the sun was rising and she still hadn't asked Adrian to go on the vacation.

"I can't believe I've talked to you for almost four hours," she said.

"I know. I missed talking with you, Lace."

"You too," she said through a yawn.

"So, before we go, what was it you wanted to ask me?"

"Now you know how much I have on my plate with these practices, but I'm planning on taking a much needed vacation in April, and since I've been thinking a lot about you, I was wondering if you would be interested in going with me?"

"On vacation?"

"Yes, on vacation."

"I don't see that being an issue. It will be great to spend some time with you after all of these years. Hell, I need a vacation myself. I'm always busy with my clients, but I'll make the time. When exactly are you thinking of?"

"Ten days in April; around the end of the month."

"That can work. Do you have a location in mind?"

"Yes, the Seychelles Islands off the coast of East Africa. Mahe to be exact."

"Okay, Dr. Morgan. I see how you are doing it up there in New York. I like the way you operate. That sounds nice. Just tell me how much—"

Blase cut him off. "I invited you, so I don't need anything from you. I need you to email me your address and I'll have Fallon send you all of the details. All you need to do is pack your bags and meet me in New York so we can fly together, unless you'd prefer to meet me in Mahe."

"No, no, I'll come to New York to pick you up," he said, laughing.

Blase was deliriously tired, but she managed to squeak out a laugh. "We will talk before then, but right now I'm about to pass out," she said.

"Okay, babe. I will email you as soon as we hang up and we will talk sooner rather than later, right?"

"Yes, baby."

"I like the sound of that. Can you say it again?"

Blase smiled. "Yes, baby."

They both said goodnight at the same time and laughed as they were hanging up. Blase was asleep within three minutes of hanging up the phone.

# Happy New Year

**TWO** weeks after Blase met with Fallon and made the phone calls to all of her ex-boyfriends, she found herself home alone on New Year's Eve. She and all of her exes had been exchanging phone calls, emails, and text messages, but to avoid any kind of confusion and deviation from her plan, Blase made it a point not to see any of them before their designated vacation dates.

After coming home early from one of the most pretentious New Year's Eve parties she had been to in a long time, she sat in her apartment on the sofa next to her black Swarovski crystal adorned evening clutch, fully dressed in a soft metallic pewter mini dress with black strappy heels with Swarovski crystals up the front and large beaded crystals on each end of the wrap around straps. Blase turned on her television to Dick Clark's New Year's Eve special and saw the time was 9:59 p.m. *Two hours. Hmm, maybe I'll just go to sleep and call this New Year's Eve a wash. No, I'll pour myself a glass of champagne first.*

She untied her shoes and kicked them to the side of her sofa, walked into her kitchen, and pulled a bottle of champagne out of her refrigerator. As she was reaching for her flute glass, her cellphone buzzed on her coffee table. She ran into the living room to grab the phone. It was an unknown number. Instead of her usual response of ignoring unknown callers, she answered cheerfully, "Happy New Year."

"Happy New Year, Dr. Morgan," the respondent said.

Blase couldn't recognize the voice. "Who's speaking?"

"This is Bryant Monroe. We met at the W Hotel a few weeks ago."

Blase thought for a moment before she remembered. While she was waiting for Randy, Bryant had a drink sent over to her. *Ahh, the shadow colored stranger who sold Jaguars at a Jaguar dealership in Manhattan.* She'd forgotten they exchanged business cards.

"Yes, I do remember you now. The Jaguar salesman, right?"

"Yes. I'm glad to know I left an impression on you," he said as Blase sensed a smile in his tone.

*Not really but I am still considering trading in my BMW.*

"So what does a Jaguar salesman do on New Year's Eve?" she asked as she sat at the breakfast bar in her kitchen.

"Well, I was calling to ask you the same thing. I know this is very impromptu but I just left a party and was going to go home, but you ran across my mind so I pulled out your business card and called the cell number you wrote on the back. I hope I'm not catching you at a bad time."

"Not at all actually. I just walked in the door myself from a party I couldn't manage to stay at. Way too many business cards being exchanged for a holiday party as far as I was concerned."

Bryant laughed. "Too stuffy for you, huh?"

"Yes."

"Well, if you're not doing anything, would you like to get together for a glass of New Year's Eve champagne?"

Blase thought about it. She knew any place they went would be overcrowded and over-priced. She decided to invite him to her rooftop lounge. Her building had a roof top pool as well as an indoor and outdoor lounge both with a fireplace. She knew there were people up there because she'd just come down from checking it out.

"You know what. My friend lives not far away from me in Harlem. She has an awesome rooftop lounge area. I'm sure we can go over there and it would be a lot more fun than fighting to get into a bar or restaurant at this hour," she suggested.

"Sounds perfect to me. What's the address? I can be there in fifteen minutes."

Blase gave him the address. "Oh and I have champagne, so you can just bring yourself."

"Great! Although, I do have a bottle also so I'll bring mine just in case."

"Okay, I'll see you soon."

Blase hung up and picked up her house phone. She dialed down to Max, but remembered she had a New Year's Eve gift for him so she decided to put her slippers on and go down and talk with him in person. When she reached the lobby, Max flashed his reassuring smile and said, "Good evening, Ms. Blase. Going back out?"

"No, Max. I'm actually having a guest, but I wanted to talk with you in person. Before I do all of that, I have something for you."

Max looked thrilled. Blase handed him a box wrapped in jet black wrapping paper with a silver bow around it. He took the box and thanked her.

She said, "No need to thank me. You do an excellent job here, Max. I really enjoy seeing your face every day." Blase went on to explain to Max that a man was going to come for her. She told Max his name. She explained that she didn't want the man to know she lived in the building, so she asked Max to take his business card and driver's license as ID for her and write his license number down on the back of the business card. Once he verified who he was, send him right up to the rooftop. Max wrote it all down and happily obliged. "And Happy New Year to you, Ms. Blase. Thank you again for the gift."

"You're welcome, Max. Happy New Year to you," she said as she kissed him on the cheek.

Blase went back upstairs and grabbed two cylinder shaped flute glasses. She also grabbed a basket and filled it with fruit and cheese, a cheese cutting knife, napkins, and two small plates from her cabinets and the bottle of champagne. Blase snatched a blanket and two seat pillows out of the hall closet just in case and headed for the roof. When she reached the roof, it wasn't as crowded as it was when she got home so she was a bit worried. She hoped Max would remember her instructions. She was glad she hadn't changed out of her party attire yet because she felt especially sexy in her outfit.

Blase looked at her watch; it was almost 10:30 p.m.. The elevator opened, and out stepped Bryant clad in a long black coat. He immediately noticed Blase and she motioned for him to take his coat off and hang it in the closet before he came through the glass doors to the lounge area. As he walked toward her she checked out his charcoal grey tailored suit and black button up shirt underneath with its top button undone. He opened the doors and smiled. Blase gave him the once over and saw his black lace up shoes, silver cuff links, and oversized watch.

*Nice!*

"Hello, Ms. Blase," he said as he hugged her. "You look even more beautiful than I remember."

"Hello, Bryant. Thank you very much. You look quite handsome yourself."

Bryant was about an inch taller than Blase with her heels on. His skin was a fraction lighter than the color of his button up shirt and his hair was silky and curly, similar in texture as Blase's. As she took him in for the second time, she realized not only was he quite handsome, but he reminded her very much of her father in complexion, hair texture, stature, and smile. Bryant's smile was crowded and chalk white in contrast to his skin, though fitting for his chiseled features. His nose was sharp, almost European, and his eyes looked confident and mysterious.

"The doorman here is very cautious. You said this was your friend's building?" he asked.

"Yes, it is. Max is great. My friend loves him."

"Well I can't blame him. There are a lot of crazy people in the world."

"You've got that right!" Blase said a little too accusatory for Bryant.

"Oh don't worry, baby. I'm not a criminal, just a salesman," he retorted.

Blase realized how what she said came out. "Oh, I'm so sorry, I wasn't insinuating that you might be crazy, I was just agreeing with you." She touched his arm in an effort to ease the tension she caused.

It worked. Bryant eased up and nodded. "No problem. This is unexpected after all."

"Since it is unseasonably warm out, would you like to sit outside near the fireplace. There are two chairs right there. I have snacks for us," she said with a smile as she held up her picnic basket as if it were a peace offering.

"Sure, outside looks nice. In fact, this entire roof is pretty hot. Is this a new building?"

"Yes it is. It's about two years old."

"Are they condos?"

"Yes they are."

"What's the make-up of the building?"

"What do you mean?"

"Are there any three bedroom units in here?"

"As far as I know there are six three bedroom units that make up the top four floors and there is only one left for sale according to my friend."

"I might have to look into this building. I like what they've done over here."

"Where do you live now?"

"I live in Riverdale right now in a rental, but I'm looking to buy a condo."

"Well, this is great area and very close to everything."

"Do you live close?" he asked.

"Yes, I do."

"Nice."

Blase set the seat cushions down on top of the iron chairs and the picnic basket on the table in front of the fireplace. She pulled out all of the contents and set the table with the plates, flute glasses, cheese, and fruit. She pulled out two cloth napkins and handed one to Bryant. He was impressed. "Wow, you brought all of this from your place, for me?"

"I thought we'd be out here talking for a while. Do you think it's too much?" She looked embarrassed.

"Too much? Hell no, I think this is sexy, baby. Here, let me open that champagne for you," he responded as he took the champagne bottle out of Blase's hands.

The pop from the champagne cork made a few of the other people on the roof turn and look. They yelled, "Happy New Year!"

Blase and Bryant, responded, "Happy New Year!"

One of the people inside noticed their party duet and brought them out two extra black and silver party hats. Bryant laughed. "I'm not putting this on," he said.

"Well I am," Blase said as she put on her black top hat.

Bryant leaned in and tilted it to the side. "Beautiful Gangsta," he said. Blase giggled.

He poured the champagne in the glasses and handed Blase her glass.

"To new beginnings," Bryant said as they toasted.

*Perfect toast!* she thought.

She tilted her head to the side and smiled. "Yes, to new beginnings." She was thinking about her forthcoming vacations and he was thinking about his recent divorce.

After an hour and fifteen minutes of laughing and talking about life, Blase and Bryant heard everyone start yelling, "Ten, Nine..."

Bryant quickly grabbed Blase's glass and filled it with champagne and did the same for his. He stood up and extended his hand to help Blase up from her seat. Blase had her shoes off and was sitting under one of the blankets in the chair. She took Bryant's hand to stand up. They both looked at each other and whispered, "Four, three, two, one... HAPPY NEW YEAR!" They touched glasses for the second time that night and both took sips of their champagne. Because it just seemed like the right thing to do, Bryant gently pulled Blase into him and kissed her on the lips. Blase didn't resist, and even parted her lips and wrapped her arms around him for a full all inclusive embrace.

They stood there kissing and hugging for longer than they expected because the people around them started clapping and wooing them. When they disassembled they looked at everyone clapping and felt embarrassed.

"Happy New Year love birds," someone yelled.

Bryant smiled and took his right hand and whipped his mouth with one of his finger. Blase dabbed her mouth with her left hand and took a sip of her champagne. Bryant admired Blase for a few seconds before sipping his champagne and suggesting they sit and continue their conversation.

"You're a wonderful kisser." He broke the silence.

"So are you."

"I liked that."

"Me too."

Bryant cleared his throat. "Ahhh so you were saying you plan on taking some vacations soon. Where do you plan on going?" He decided to keep the conversation going rather than make the obvious physical attraction between them awkward.

Blase appreciated his perception. "Yes, actually..." Blase went on to explain the places where she was going and who she was going with. She felt like she had nothing to hide from Bryant, so she told him the absolute truth about the ex-boyfriends, the trips, and why she wanted to do it.

"Do you feel like you can't meet anyone new?" he asked.

"Not at all. I just want to make sure I didn't miss anything with any of them, that's all." It wasn't until then she had the notion that the entire idea may have sounded illogical to a stranger. Bryant thought it was an interesting concept and respected that she was footing the bill for the entire thing.

"Does that mean I'll never get to see you again?" he asked.

"Of course not, but it does mean you'll have to respect what I am going to do, if and when we do see one another again."

"That's cool with me, baby, as long as I can see you again. I'm really enjoying myself tonight." Truth was Bryant wasn't ready to rush into anything anyway because he was four months divorced. He did think Blase was sexy and her independence was an aphrodisiac, so someone to spend some time with was all he was seeking.

"I'm enjoying myself also. Who would've known? I was fully prepared to get into my jammies and watch Carson Daly all night," she said.

"Everything happens for a reason," he said as he instinctually leaned in for another kiss.

Blase allowed him to embrace her face for another kiss. They kissed and talked and talked and kissed until 2:30 a.m. They finished both bottles of champagne, all of the fruit, and a good portion of the cheese. Blase took the other blanket and wrapped it around her upper body. "You're getting cold. Maybe it's time to call it a night?" Bryant asked.

"Or we can go to my place," Blase said.

Bryant looked uncertain.

"Or maybe not," Blase said.

"Or maybe so," he corrected her. "I would love to, and I promise to be a perfect gentleman," he added.

"Good!" They both packed everything, including the empty bottles back into the picnic basket. Blase folded one blanket while Bryant folded the other. She grabbed Bryant's hand as she bent down to pick up her shoes.

"Do you want to put these on?" he asked.

"Not yet. Will you carry them for me?"

"Of course!"

He assumed she would put them on while he was grabbing his coat before they headed for the elevator.

He asked, "Do you have a coat?"

"No."

When they got in the elevator and Blase still didn't have her shoes on, he figured she wanted to put them on in the lobby. Blase pressed the twenty-two button. "You live in this building?" he asked.

"Yes," she said.

"Now I see why you had the doorman take my information." He laughed.

"That's correct." She blushed as she interlocked her arm with his.

Bryant had to smile at her caution. "I understand," he said as he took the picnic basket from her hand.

When they opened Blase's door, Bryant was immediately impressed by her décor and the size of her condominium. "These units are big. What's the square footage here?" he asked.

"Let me show you around," Blase said. Once they put his coat in the closet and sat the basket down, she asked him to take off his shoes because she didn't want scuffmarks on her mahogany hardwood floors. She took his hand and led him down a hallway towards her spacious room. She showed off the meticulously decorated rooms, including her favorite pieces like her office desk that was once a barn door, her diverse art collection and she pointed out her dining room table that was repurposed from her old sliding glass doors that once led to her five hundred square foot balcony. She led him through her barely used custom kitchen and down the hallway to French doors that led to her master bedroom. "My apartment is the shape of a capital t actually."

"Very nice," he said as his eyes peered around Blase's simply decorated yellow, black, beige, and white master suite. After finishing the tour of Blase's house, Bryant wished he would've gone to some type of post-secondary school. He lived a comfortable life and provided for his family fine, but since his divorce, he was truly starting over. He started to feel a bit intimidated by Blase's success and lifestyle. He thought, *Chill out B, you don't want to marry her; you just want to hang out with her from time to time.*

He said, "You have a beautiful home. I like your taste."

Blase thought, *Am I crazy? I have this strange man in my house. I hope he doesn't get psycho.*

She said, "Thank you. Let's go back into the living room. Can I get you something to drink?"

"Sure, water would be great," he said.

"I've got that. Please have a seat in the living room, unless you want to go back outside. I don't have a fireplace out there, but I do have a fire pit. It's wood burning and there is fresh wood under the cover outside next to the doors."

"Alright, we can take it back outside for a while." Bryant went and prepared the fire pit and lit the fire.

Blase got a water out of the refrigerator and took it to Bryant. She went back in the kitchen and got a mug out of her cabinet to make herself a cup of tea. She took her tea and two large, heavy blankets out to her balcony. She gave Bryant a blanket and she kept one for herself. Bryant had located the lounge chair cushions and put them on two of her lounge chairs. He made sure the lounge chairs were close enough to the fire to feel the warmth but far enough away so they wouldn't catch on fire. "How about we try and snuggle up on one chair together," Blase suggested.

"Are you sure? I told you I would be a gentleman and I will honor that."

"If you don't want to, that's fine also," she said.

"No, I'd love to." Bryant put one of the blankets on the lounge chair and put the other on top of it. He climbed in and opened the cover and patted the space next to him. "Climb in."

"I'd love to." She chuckled. When she climbed in, she felt the warmth of Bryant's body and it gave her a chill. "Are you that cold?" he asked.

"No, I'm that comfortable," she said as she turned her body around to face his. "I'm glad you came over today. Spending New Year's Eve with you has been great," she said. Before he could respond, she reached in for a kiss. A passionate one.

Bryant pulled away. "You're making this gentleman thing very hard."

"I give you permission to be slightly ungentlemanly," she said with an inviting smile and soft, sexy voice.

He moaned back as he hugged her closer and kissed her deeper. Twenty minutes into their adolescent like make out session, Blase made her mind up that she wanted a one-night stand. It had been almost two months since she was intimate with Randy, so she was feeling a bit frisky. She positioned herself below his body and spread her legs open to allow his lower body to feel the warmth of her inner thighs.

This feeling made Bryant's enjoyment be known. He stopped and asked, "How far do you want this to go?"

Blase kept her eyes closed, arched her back, and said "As far as you'll take me."

Bryant took the hint and lifted Blase's dress over her head. They continued kissing as Blase unbuttoned his shirt, slid it off, and dropped it on the ground next to the lounge chair. After she unbuttoned his pants and pulled them down as far as she could get them, Bryant used his legs to take them entirely off. They continued kissing and moaning and caressing each other's bodies. Before Blase could ask, Bryant reached into the inside pocket of his suit jacket hanging on the back of the lounge chair and pulled out a gold condom wrapper. Blase moaned a sigh of relief and kept kissing him as he proceeded to adjust the back of the lounge chair so they were completely horizontal. In one cadenced motion, Blase scooted her body up while Bryant slid her panties down and then positioned his body directly over hers. Like a graceful dance routine, he slid her right breast out from the binds of her bra while she twirled her hips.

Blase took Bryant's arousal in her hands and bit the bottom of her lip. "Nice," she said as she looked at him.

"I'm glad you're happy with it," he said.

She pulled his boxer briefs off for him as she kissed his chest. Before he took it further, Bryant wanted to completely enjoy every bit of Blase possible. The fire, blanket, and their body heat kept them warm. Bryant explored Blase's body and Blase discovered his. They both felt the rapture. Blase had never had sex on her balcony and Bryant had never done anything like that before, so they were open.

After an hour of mixing fantasy with reality, Blase spooned in Bryant's arms and they both watched the fire. He leaned down over Blase and took two more pieces of wood and put them on the fire. They lay there and drifted into their first dreams of the New Year.

When the sun began to rise, Blase woke from both the light and the chill in the air. She opened her eyes and realized the fire was reduced to smoldering ashes. Bryant was still soundly asleep. She turned her body to face him and started kissing his nose.

He smiled. "Hey, baby."

"Good morning," she said back. "Let's go to my room."

He nodded. Bryant lifted his body and Blase's at the same time and wrapped them both in the blanket. They stepped in unison to the bedroom. Blase closed all of the curtains and climbed into bed with Bryant. She turned to spoon with him again, but he stopped her, "Oh, we're up now. We have to make use of this awake time."

"Well, how do you think we should do that?"

"I have some ideas," he said as he began to lick her breasts. They enjoyed each other again and again until Blase collapsed and fell asleep right on top of Bryant. He loved it and fell asleep along with her.

When Blase finally woke up, Bryant was gone. She thought for a moment that it was all a dream, until she saw the condom wrappers on the nightstand. She smiled and thought, *What a wonderfully unexpected New Year's Eve.* She sat in her glory and then a wave of panic set in. "What if he robbed me," she said out loud. She jumped up and walked out of her room naked. She walked throughout her apartment and everything seemed to be intact. Bryant had even put the firewood and cushions for the lounge chairs back in their storage spaces and cleaned the fire pit out. She looked around and didn't see a note, so she began to get offended. "No note?" she said out loud. *Oh well, you did only want a one night stand, Blase.*

She picked up her cellphone and unlocked it to see 33 emails and 21 text messages. She scrolled through the text messages and saw nothing from Bryant. She scrolled through her emails and saw the last one was from him. She breathed a sigh of gladness.

*Blase, you didn't think I was going to leave without saying goodbye? Well, I guess I did actually leave before saying goodbye, but after all of the work you put in last night, I didn't want to wake you. (smile) Last night was the best New Year's Eve I've ever had. In fact, it was one of the best nights of my life. I have never met a woman like you and I want to know more. I had to run because I have to pick up my kids to spend time with them. The next time we get together, I will tell you more about them. Crazy enough, I miss you already and I'm just downstairs in my car typing this message to you. Call me, text me, or email me when you wake up. Your voice is preferred, but any communication is gladly accepted. Happy New Year Beautiful Gangsta...talk to you soon!*

*XO – The Gentleman*

Blase read the message again before she ran back into her room and jumped back in her bed. She had never had a one night stand before and it was spontaneously perfect; a perfect way to start her year and her journey.

# 14 Days Until

**BLASE** stood in her living room staring out onto her patio, reminiscing about her evening with Bryant. She looked out and thought her patio needed a makeover. She decided to have a professional come in the summer and give her decorating advice on her outdoor living space. Melesse Wellness Spas were closed until the Monday after New Year's Eve so Blase used that time to have meetings and sign contracts with Tracey Steele, her new Partner. Tracey's contract was exclusive to Blase's White Plains practice, with a per diem sub-contractor agreement for her Harlem location. Blase liked Tracey's work, but didn't want to forfeit everything she'd built. Because the White Plains practice was new, it was easier to merge Tracey into that practice.

Blase sat across from Tracey on Saturday with the contract her attorney had drawn up. All of the details were ironed out including the separation proviso in case it didn't work out. After what Blase went through with Paul Graham, she made sure to include that portion. Tracey looked over the contract again. Her attorney had already reviewed it with her and gave her the green light to sign, but Tracey and Blase agreed to meet for dinner for the final signatures. They both signed and Blase put her copy of the contact in her briefcase and Tracey did the same.

"I look forward to getting started," Tracey said.

"Yes, we're excited you are joining the practice. The White Plains office is already set up for you. Feel free to make any decorating changes you'd like. You have carte blanche for that office," Blase said.

"Thank you. I really liked the marketing plan you have set out for the White Plains office. You and Sheridan did a great job with that," Tracey said as she tore three packets of no calorie sweetener open to pour in her iced tea.

"Sheridan is really great with understanding my…our vision. When I told her you and I had the same professional goals in mind, she agreed that the marketing would be easy."

Tracey nodded.

"So she'll be training your assistant for the next two weeks in our Harlem location until I leave. Are you sure you don't want to wait to start when I come back from Jamaica?" Blase asked.

Tracey wasn't starting for another two weeks. Her start date fell on the fourth day after Blase left for her trip. "No, I will be fine. Remember I did this for a long time in Washington, D.C. I also have to get my daughters set and ready for school. Plus I'll be coming in periodically for the next few weeks to meet the staff and get myself trained on the office software and operating system, so it seems like I'm starting on Monday anyway."

"No problem. Have you spoken to your ex at all?" Blase asked.

"You would think he would be calling me daily to check on his daughters, but he hasn't called once. The girls are too busy getting settled in to notice it just yet, but I'm sure they'll mention it to me at some point."

"Is it hard?"

"Is what hard?"

"The transition to being a single mother?"

Tracey looked a bit uncomfortable with the question but decided she wanted to talk about it. She needed to. Finally. "Yes. I mean, Blase, I can understand him maybe not being attracted to me anymore, hell I've gained over sixty pounds. I can even understand if he just fell out of love with me, but these girls are my life and I thought they were his. When I married him, and formally adopted them, I made the decision that while I didn't give birth to them that I would raise them as if they were my own."

Blase looked empathetically at her new partner.

"I know his first wife is turning over in her grave at him just abandoning their daughters. So I have no choice but to stay strong, no matter how hard the whole transition is. Losing their mother to cancer was hard for them and now with their father disconnecting for his younger wife and plastic surgery practice I'm sure at some point, I'll have to explain the whys and how comes, but for now I'll just keep them active and remind them how much I love them."

Blase touched Tracey's hand, "Wow. What a piece of work he is. Of course, if you need anything outside of work—babysitters, tutors, recommendations on pediatricians, hair salons, anything—you let me know!"

Tracey smiled. "Enough about that idiot, I don't want to lose my appetite. The waiter has come over here four times already. I think we should order before they throw us out."

Blase agreed and changed the subject. They ate dinner and discussed more about the practice and their visions for it. Blase told Tracey just a little about her vacations, but didn't want to go into detail about taking all of the ex-boyfriends, so as far as Tracey knew, Blase was just taking some much needed downtime, while still keeping the business going.

As Blase was getting into her car after dinner her phone rang. She saw Bryant's number and quickly answered. "Hello."

"Hey, beautiful gangsta. How are you tonight?"

"I'm wonderful and yourself?"

"I'm wonderful also. Are you busy?"

"No, I'm headed home. I just had a dinner meeting with my new partner."

"The Dr. Steele woman you told me about?"

"Yes, her. She starts a few days after I leave for Jamaica."

"Cool."

"What are you up to tonight?"

"I was calling you to ask you the same thing," he said with a dip in his tone.

Blase responded, "Well, you know where I live."

"I'm on my way."

After Blase and Bryant hung up, her phone rang again. She looked at the phone and saw it was Randy. She pressed ignore and thought, *From time to time, doesn't mean every day, Randy. My goodness.* She parked her car in her buildings garage and got in the elevator to go up to meet Bryant in the lobby. He'd texted Blase and told her he was there.

*So maybe it'll be a two-night stand,* she thought as a chill needled through to the nape of her neck. When she reached the lobby, the doors opened and there stood Bryant and Randy. She stood in the elevator and tried to figure out what to say. The doors closed again and she pressed the button to open them. Blase walked towards them and saw Bryant was holding a bottle of wine. He smiled as she approached but noticed the wound up look on her face. Blase walked past Bryant and directly up to Randy.

"What are you doing here?" she said.

"I've been calling and texting you. I told you I wanted to see you."

"And I told you no. I thought agreeing to speak from time to time was generous enough, Randy. This is crossing the line."

Randy noticed Bryant standing there watching them argue. "Is this guy here for you?"

"Leave!" she demanded.

"So this is why you broke up with me?" he said louder.

Bryant's stance became defensive. Blase looked at the temporary doorman and thought, *Where is Max when you need him?* She said, "Call the police!"

"What? You're going to have me arrested for trying to see you?"

Blase remained silent.

Bryant contemplated stepping in, but opted to stay quiet until and unless she needed him.

"Leave," Blase said calmly.

"No problem. You won't ever have to worry 'bout hearing from me again." Randy walked out of the building and threw the bouquet of flowers he had in the street.

Blase was embarrassed, and still fuming. She turned to face Bryant. "I apologize for that."

"Now I see why you have the doorman frisking and checking driver's licenses around here. You got brothers stalking you," he said with a smirk.

"Honestly nothing like that has ever happened to me before; well, not when I didn't want to see him," she corrected.

"So what you're saying is I can surprise you as long as I'm on your good side?" he asked now smiling.

"Makes sense, doesn't it?" she responded with a smile. "Is that wine for me? If not, I'll buy it off of you," she joked, but was still a bit shaken.

Bryant put his arm around her, "This is for us if you're still up for the company."

"Of course I am." She wrapped her arm around his torso and they headed to the elevator.

Bryant didn't leave until 6:00 a.m. Monday morning. While he was driving home, he and Blase talked on the phone. She told him she wouldn't be able to see him again until after her Jamaica trip because she was going to be busy seeing patients and helping her new partner assimilate. Bryant understood.

The Wednesday morning of that week, Blase received a flood of email confirmations from Flynn destinations. She had Sheridan print everything out and put the confirmations in their respective folders. Blase sent emails to all of her ex-boyfriends with the limousine pick up times and reminders to pack at least two outfits for a night out on the town.

Since she didn't have any more clients that afternoon, she drove over to the White Plains office to make sure Tracey was getting settled. When she arrived, she saw Tracey had changed a few things around. It looked nice. Tracey opted to go with simple, minimalist, contemporary furniture with just her degrees hanging on the walls as decoration for her office.

Tracey and Blase talked for a while and Blase told Tracey she liked her assistant and she was picking up their system very quickly.

Tracey also informed Blase that she had a full calendar of clients until May.

Blase was happy. "Where did the clients come from?" she asked.

"Many of them are clients of mine who are traveling up from Washington to continue to work with me. Others are leads generated from updating your website. So I guess I have you to thank. It seems some of your patients were waiting for plastic surgery services."

"Yes, that is true. I've referred a lot of my patients to a plastic surgeon downtown, so it makes sense that now that we have an in-house surgeon they would book with us. It's funny because Sheridan hasn't even mentioned it."

Blase thought to call Sheridan to have a conversation with her about it after she left the office.

"Well, I'm glad you are transitioning nicely. I'm here for another week so let me know if you need anything. Are you happy with the current staff?" Blase asked.

"Yes, I am. They seem to fit in well here. I do want to consider a different cleaning company though. I'm not happy with them."

"Go for it. Okay, I won't hold you up anymore. I'll talk with you before I leave," Blase said.

When she left, she went to the mall to do some shopping for her trip to Jamaica. She picked up a few bikinis, cover-ups, two straw hats, sandals, and Ray Ban sunglasses. She decided to do her toiletry shopping closer to her departure date.

While she was browsing through Bloomingdale's she called Sheridan.

"Melesse Wellness Spa," Beth answered, sounding sprightly.

"Hi, Beth. It's Blase. May I speak with Sheridan?"

"Hi, Blase. Yes I'll transfer you to her."

"Melesse Wellness, Sheridan speaking," she said, sounding rushed.

"Hi, Sheridan. Are you training right now?" Blase asked.

"No, just trying to feel my way around the new website interface."

"Interesting that you mention that. That is exactly why I'm calling. Tracey told me she is basically booked until May. I don't remember you mentioning that to me."

"I'm sorry, B. I've been so busy with training and rearranging your calendar and maintaining the overall operations of both offices that I forgot," Sheridan said.

Blase wondered if she had given Sheridan too many responsibilities too soon. At dinner she discussed and got approval from Tracey for Sheridan's promotion to manager, but never thought it would impede on her being able to do her assistant duties as well.

"Sher, I think we should hire another assistant for me on a temporary basis until you get situated in your new position."

Sheridan stopped what she was doing. "No, Blase I can handle it."

"I know you can handle it, and if you can't I know you will work harder, but I don't want you to be overworked. I would rather the offices be run efficiently then you scheduling my appointments and arranging my calendar. Call a temp agency and find a temp. You can start the temp after you finish training Tracey's assistant. I don't want to pay more than fifteen dollars an hour."

"If you insist," Sheridan said, feeling a bit relieved.

"No problem. I want someone in by Monday."

"Okay. Actually, I have a cousin who is looking for work. She is a college student at night and needs a day job," Sheridan said.

"Is she okay with fifteen dollars an hour?" Blase asked.

"Are you kidding? She would love it. She is waiting tables for peanuts right now. She's a business major so she would love this, and she's a quick learner," Sheridan added.

274

"Hire her. And if she can start tomorrow, bring her in."

"She can and will do."

"I can't offer her benefits right now though."

"No problem, she still gets them through her parents."

"Great."

When Blase got in her car to drive home, she dialed Fallon's number.

Fallon answered by saying, "Are you excited?"

"Yes. Can you have dinner tonight?"

"For you, of course. When and where?"

"I am in White Plains now, headed to the city. How is seven at The Red Eye Grill?"

"See you then," Fallon said.

"Okay." They hung up.

After Blase stopped home to feed and walk Sugar, she headed downtown to meet Fallon. Her phone rang. She couldn't believe it was Randy. She ignored the call and decided to call her mother.

"Morgan residence," her father answered.

"Hi, Dad. How are you?"

"Who is this?" her father asked facetiously.

"This is your daughter." She smiled.

"What? I have a daughter?" he said still teasing.

"One and only."

"Hey, baby. How are you?"

"I'm good, Daddy. How are you?"

"I'm doing fine. Your mother was just asking me about you. She said she hadn't spoken to you since you took her and your Aunt Bernice to see that FELA play."

"I know. That's why I'm calling. I've been so busy with getting Tracey situated in White Plains I haven't had a minute to breathe. You and Mom should go by and see Tracey. You haven't seen her since I was in college. She looks so different now."

"I'll drive up and take a look at the place and talk with her. By the way, did Fallon tell you? Your mother and I are going to Australia to visit her parents."

"No, she didn't mention it. I know her father is trying to get her to come out there to do some work, so maybe he forgot to mention that to her."

"Well we are going the middle of February."

"Oh, I will be in Aruba in the middle of February, Daddy."

"Aruba. That sounds nice. Okay, here's your mother." Her father handed the phone to Blase's mother, figuring that whatever she told her mother, he would find out anyway.

"Hi, Mom!"

"Hi, Melesse. Where have you been?" Blase's mother always used her middle name.

"I've been busy with work. The new location is coming along nicely. I told Dad you guys have to go over and see Tracey. She looks different."

"You mean she gained weight," her mother said, knowing exactly what different meant.

Blase laughed. "Well yes, she's gained weight, but she cut her hair and she's not at all as flashy as she used to be. I don't really know what happened in her marriage, but I know she has two adopted daughters she is taking care of."

"Well, I'm sure you'll find out in due time. Did you get your Sayt Ayat's invitation to the party?" she asked.

"Yes, I booked my flight already. Fallon and Sergio may come as well."

"And are you bringing someone?" her mother asked, attempting to see if her daughter was dating someone new.

"I am not sure yet, Mom. I want to tell you what I'm about to do, but I want you to promise me you won't tell Daddy. I know he won't approve," she insisted.

"I don't tell your father everything, Melesse," she said shallowly.

Blase remained silent. Her mother said, "Okay, I promise."

"Thank you. I know you know I'm going to Jamaica in a few weeks."

"Yes, I know. Be sure to bring me back some of that jerk seasoning I like. I haven't made jerk chicken for your father in quite some time."

"Okay. Well, what you don't know is..." Blase went on to tell her mother about her plan to take all of her ex-boyfriend's away.

Blase's mother was quiet.

"Mom?"

"Yes."

"Well?"

"Well what?"

"So what do you think?"

"Melesse, you've already purchased the tickets, asked them to go with you, so does it matter what I think?"

"Well, yes. I mean I know I am still going but I would like your insight on it."

"Well, you girls do things differently nowadays, so maybe this is normal, but to me it just sounds crazy. Melesse you are a beautiful and smart woman with a doctorate degree and a successful business. I am sure you can find a man who will treat you right without going to such lengths."

"Mom, I understand where you are coming from. I guess I just feel like there are pieces that are missing from my life that I didn't allow to come together."

"Again, your mind is made up, so I don't see where there is anything to discuss. I do want you to let your father and I know you are okay."

"Of course I will. But Mom, don't tell Daddy about the exes. He won't understand," she said as she pulled up to the garage around the corner from the restaurant.

"Yes, I know honey."

"Okay, Mom, I have to run. I am meeting Fallon for dinner."

"I do want to say this. As far as I'm concerned, anything is better than you dating someone else's husband. Call me before you leave," her mother said and hung up.

Blase's mouth flew open. She never told her mother that Randy, Frank, or Brady was married. She was curious where she got her information.

Blase walked in the restaurant and started to ask the hostess for a table for two when she saw Fallon waiving at her. She was pleasantly surprised because Fallon was always late.

"Hi," Blase said to her friend as they hugged.

"Hi. I know you're surprised to see me here already, but I was done early today."

"I'm glad you're on time because I am hungry."

"Good, I ordered us some crab cakes and two glasses of Chardonnay. I just ordered them as you walked in the door."

"Great. So, I was just having a conversation with my mother about my trips and needless to say she doesn't get it, much like the rest of you."

Fallon raised her eyebrows at Blase as she put her napkin in her lap.

"She didn't disapprove but she didn't approve of it either. But honestly, my mother knows if I have my mind set to do something, I'm going to do it regardless of what others think."

Fallon nodded. "We all do."

Blase took a sip of her water. "What was unusual though, Fal. Mommy knows about the married men I've dated."

Fallon's face turned Fuchsia. Fallon realized her mother must have mentioned it to Blase's mother. The two had become best friends over the years.

"B, I mentioned it to my mom. She must've gotten the information from her."

"You did?"

"Yes, I'm sorry, girl. It was purely innocent. My mother always asks me who you are dating and I tell her and you know my mother is nosy, so she asks endless amounts of questions. Eventually I always give in."

The waitress came over with their glasses of wine and bread.

"Well, what's done is done," Blase said. "I know my mother doesn't judge me, I just think she'd like to see me settled, and she definitely wants grandchildren from me with Benny and his family living all the way in California."

They both sipped their wine.

"Oh yes, our mothers are one in the same. It's even worse for me since Sergio and I have been together for so long. Actually, Sergio wants to have children."

Blase's expression broadened "Really? Do you?" she asked.

"I do, but I'm nervous, B. I mean me, a mother?" she said panicky.

"Fal, are you kidding? You will be a great mother, and I can't wait to be an auntie."

Blase and Fallon ordered their food and talked about their businesses, Blase's vacations, and Blase told Fallon about Bryant.

"He's young though, Fal. Bryant is only thirty-three."

"And?" Fallon asked.

"Well, I'm just telling you."

"Girl, who cares how old he is. As long as he keeps making you feel the way he does. And he sounds level headed to be younger considering he didn't say anything when Randy pulled his stunt—"

"Oh, do you know he called me today?"

"I believe you. He's special, B. He needs medication and a reality check."

They both laughed.

"His reality check will come when he dates a woman who is equally as unraveled as he is and she turns his world upside down."

"True indeed," Fallon agreed.

The waitress brought their food to the table and for the rest of their dinner they ate, laughed, and talked.

# BON VOYAGE

# Jamaica

**THE** day before Blase was set to meet Walter at the airport for their trip to Jamaica, she made sure Sheridan was comfortable in the Harlem practice running things with the staff. Blase's calendar was cleared for the next ten days and all of the clients knew that she would be out of town. The only appointments at the Harlem practice would be for Fumiko, Shana, or Juliette.

Tracey was working nicely in the White Plains practice and her assistant had caught on to the system quickly, so everything was running smoothly.

Blase dropped Sugar off at her parents' house to dog-sit while she was away. After Blase had Sugar for a few months, Blase's mother fell in love with her and went out and bought a Pomeranian of her own. Sugar and Shea would often have doggie play dates. Everything was all set. As she was driving down Interstate 95 South toward the city, her cell phone rang. She looked down and saw it was Walter.

"Hi, Walter. Are you ready? We will be there to pick you up at 5:30 in the morning."

"All right. There's been a slight change in plans. I have to be at the hospital for the better part of the evening, so if you can pick me up from there, it would be a lot better for me. Is that doable, love?"

"No problem. I was afraid you were going to tell me you couldn't make it."

"Heavens no. You've never taken me for the dodgy kind before. I wouldn't miss this trip for the world."

"That's good to hear. So I'll see you at 5:30. Remember, our flight leaves at seven, so we can't be late."

"All right then, no problem. Cheers until tomorrow."

"Yes."

The next morning, Blase arrived at the hospital where Walter worked at 5:15 a.m. She waited outside in the car for him to come out while she went over their travel itinerary. She was excited about relaxing in Jamaica and was hoping to enjoy being with Walter. He insinuated in one of their recent phone conversations that his situation at home had changed. She heard the driver open his door and the trunk pop open. When she looked up, she saw Walter opening the door to get into the car.

"Good Morning," she said.

"Good morning, darling."

"You look exhausted," Blase said as she kissed him on the cheek.

"It was a long and emotional night. There was an incident in midtown where some scaffolding fell on a group of teenagers from Germany here on holiday."

"Oh my goodness, were there any losses?"

"Thank heavens no. All of the children survived, but some were banged up pretty terribly and the hospital was in an uproar with worried parents and frenzied chaperones."

"I can imagine."

"Needless to say, going to Jamaica is a great way to end this day, love," he said with a smile.

"Of course." They talked more about the scaffolding incident and some of the injured children as well as Walter's level of exhaustion with working in the hospital. He never thought of going into private practice until recently.

They arrived at John F. Kennedy airport and after checking their bags and securing their seat assignments, they decided to go and have coffee. Blase really wanted breakfast, but because it was so early the only thing open was McDonalds. They settled on Starbucks and scones. She figured they would get some type of breakfast in their first class seats on the plane. They went to the club room of their airline, sat down, and Blase showed Walter some of their package information. He was impressed with Fallon's work.

"She's doing very well in the business then, yes?"

"She's doing a great job. I wouldn't be surprised if she didn't have to take on some additional travel consultants in the next few months."

"That's great news. And your business, how is it doing?"

"I've just taken on a partner. We are doing great. My partner does plastic surgeries, so we've broadened our client base."

"When did you take on a partner?" Walter asked as he sipped his Grande latte.

"Just recently," she said, breaking her scone apart.

"Really, and you're vacationing?"

"Well I took on my partner so I could vacation."

"I trust you have it all worked out, love."

"Yes, I do." She smiled.

Before they knew it, they heard the announcement to begin boarding their flight. Blase got up and threw the garbage from their scones away, walked back over to Walter, who was grabbing her carry-on bag, picked up her coffee, and they proceeded to their gate. Walter slept the entire flight, while Blase started reading the first book of five she planned on reading throughout her vacations. She ate a little of the food that was provided, but still didn't seem satisfied by it.

When they arrived in Jamaica, the weather was a dull 86 degrees. Blase looked in her Flynn Destinations billfold and saw the weather forecast was hazy in the morning, but clear skies by the afternoon for the first day and cloudy with a chance of rain for the last day and sunny for the remaining days.

"This isn't quite what I was hoping for," Walter remarked.

"Me either, but we'll make the best of it."

A Flynn representative approached them and asked if they would come in to the Flynn customer service office. They followed. In the office, they were checked in to their hotel by the representative and given a bottle of water, their activities itinerary for the week, along with two passes for their travels to the hotel.

"Mr. and Mrs. Morgan, Elvin will escort you to your transportation to your hotel," the representative said as they turned to see Elvin standing in the doorway.

Walter laughed at the representative calling them Mr. and Mrs. Morgan. "I guess I'll be Mr. Morgan for the week. Has a ring to it, love."

They both got up from their chairs and followed Elvin. They walked through a long hallway to glass doors. When Elvin opened the glass doors, they spotted three helicopters parked. "Mr. and Mrs. Morgan, your helicopter is right this way."

Blase was amped and excited. "This must be one of the perks Fallon was talking about."

"Nice perk. How far is the hotel from here?" Walter asked Elvin.

"It will be a fifteen minute ride in the helicopter, Mr. Morgan." Walter smiled again as he looked at Blase.

"Please call him Dr. Bailey, he's—"

Walter interrupted her. "Mr. Morgan is fine. Shall we proceed to our helicopter?" he said, looking at Blase while he placed his left hand in the small of her back to scoot her along.

Their helicopter ride was picturesque as Elvin pointed out all of the beautiful scenes while Blase took pictures. They landed on the Flynn grounds and were immediately offered a cocktail from the bartender who waited at the Tiki style bar stand, while a representative waited in a modified hummer style golf cart with Flynn written on the side to take them to their hut. The driver put their bags in the hummer while they told the bartender what they wanted to drink and they climbed in for their five minute ride to their beachfront hut.

Walter was impressed. "This is beautiful, Blase. I wasn't aware the Flynn hotel chains were this luxurious."

"You should see the one in Greece."

"Maybe we'll go there one day." His tone was filled with hope.

Blase ignored his comment by sipping her drink as they pulled up to a cluster of huts. By the time they reached the huts, the sun was shining and the temperature was heating up.

"Mr. and Mrs. Morgan, please follow me to your hut."

They walked through a few dwarf coconut palm and bottlebrush trees while Blase took more photos. They finally reached their hut. A short, sturdy, sepia colored woman dressed in a white front button dress with a nametag awaited them at the door. She wore her hair in a bright red afro.

"Good mornin'!" she said with a heart-warming smile and dense Caribbean accent.

"Good morning," both Blase and Walter said in unison and smiled at each other.

The driver introduced their hut keeper as Hyacinth.

"Hello, Hyacinth. My name is Walter and this Blase. It's a pleasure to meet you."

"Yes, you too. Please let me know if there is anyting you need. Your bags are in your hut and my numba is on deh desk. Call me anytime, okay?"

"Yes, thank you."

"Where yah from?" Hyacinth asked as she watched them walk into their hut.

"We are from New York," Blase said.

"New York?" Hyacinth asked. "It sounds to me like yah from London or someting like that." She looked at Walter.

"I am originally from London, but I've lived in New York for quite some time."

"Oh okay, well me won't boddar you. Call me if you need me, otherwise, I'll return to turn yah beds down at seven o'clock dis evenin'."

"Okay, thank you. Are there towels for the beach here?" Blase asked.

"Yes ma'am, dey are in deh batroom on deh shelf, I can get dem for you—"

"No, that won't be necessary. I appreciate your help, Hyacinth. No need to fuss. We are low maintenance, but we would like to order some lunch. Can we have it on the beach?" Blase asked.

"Of course you can," she said and she went to pick up the menu and handed to Blase. "Just look tru deh menu and call me, or you can call deh restaurant directly and place yah orda and it will be delivered to you on deh beach. Just give dem your location, okay?" she added.

"Perfect!" Blase said.

Hyacinth smiled and proceeded out of the hut. Blase and Walter looked around and as rustic as it looked, it was very modern and cozy.

"This is gorgeous. It feels like we are in a tree house, but with all of the modern amenities," Blase said.

"Yes, love. I agree."

Blase immediately walked to the bathroom and picked up two towels. "Let's go to the beach," she said as she grabbed the menu and cordless phone to take with her. They both stripped down and put their bathing suits on and preceded the 20 steps down to their private section of the beach. When they reached the beach, Hyacinth had two lounge chairs set up under an umbrella with yellow towels on them. On the table between the lounge chairs was an ice bucket with four bottles of water and a little Flynn note card that read: *I hope you enjoy your stay at Flynn. I look forward to servicing you. Hyacinth*

Walter and Blase went for an afternoon swim in the Tiffany blue colored ocean while they waited for their lunch to arrive. They played and laughed and forgot all about their lives in New York. They ate their lunch and both fell asleep on their lounge chairs for the next few hours. Finally, they were awakened by what sounded like thunder. They saw the sun had retreated behind the clouds.

Walter looked at his watch and saw it was six o'clock.

"I thought it was only going to be cloudy this morning," she commented.

"Well, love, weather is ever changing, so you never know. Do you want to dress and take a walk around the resort?" he asked.

"Yes," she responded. They went back to their hut, showered, and changed for their walk. They toured the grounds as if they were on a nature walk. Every hut looked pristine, every tree and shrub looked well cared for. The entire grounds looked perfectly manicured. By the time they reached the main building, the thunder turned into light showers. They walked in and went to the main bar in the lobby and sat down.

"What would you like to drink dear?" Walter asked.

"I'll have a pineapple margarita. Do you know how to make that?" she asked the bartender.

"Yes mon," he responded.

"I'll have a vodka and tonic with a lime, please," Walter said.

As they waited for their drinks, Walter began, "So, my darling, while I'm completely flattered you wanted to take this beautiful trip with me, I can't help but wonder what prompted you to want to go away with me."

Blase knew this conversation was coming. "I just feel like when your ex-wife showed up, it kind of forced our relationship to stop. I mean, I had my reservations before that, with your apathy about telling me about your past, but surely you didn't think I would continue our relationship while you lived with that woman," she said.

"I don't know that I didn't expect it. I expected you to be more understanding of the sudden circumstances and give me a chance."

"A chance for what? She lived with you until recently. It's been years, so the circumstances didn't change."

"They may have, had we have stayed together."

The bartender put two coasters in front of them and sat Blase's margarita glass down in front of her first and then Walter's drink followed. "Can I get you anyting else?" the bartender asked.

"No we are fine for now," Walter said. He picked up his glass to toast. "Cheers to Jamaica and a fresh start."

"Cheers."

Blase touched her glass with his as they both took their first sips. "Walter quite honestly, I was angry with you for not telling me about your past and for casually introducing me to your parents as if we weren't a serious couple. I couldn't believe you sold me on the trip as if it were a huge deal because I was meeting your parents, but didn't even tell them we were coming."

"Yes, I did think about that while we were in France and thought I may have offended you, but you have to understand love, my parents wouldn't take me seriously if I made a big to do about you coming. Now that you know about my past, clearly you see they don't take my level of commitment to relationships seriously."

"Do you?" she asked.

"Of course I do."

"I didn't think you did, Walter. You seemed to be very casual about everything. Of course the opposite wouldn't have been attractive either, but showing interest would've made me comfortable."

"I understand. So do you think there is a possibility for us to try again?" he asked.

"Where is your son and his mother?"

"Bai is in medical school, and Liang lives in her own apartment in Queens," he said.

"That certainly is good to hear." Blase sipped her margarita.

Walter leaned in a little closer at the sight of Blase's smile. They continued to talk and laugh before heading off to do dinner. By the time they reached their hut after dinner, the rain was torrential.

The next morning, they woke to more rain and unexciting weather. They decided to rent a movie in the hut and order in, hoping the rain would clear up by the afternoon. Unfortunately, not only did the rain not clear up for that afternoon, but it rained consistently for the entire remaining eight days of their vacation. For a moment Blase thought that might have been a sign, particularly since much of their time in the hut was not spent making love or even talking. She read her book as Walter caught up on some of the medical books and articles he had been meaning to read. They did manage to go to a few great restaurants and one club, but Walter not being much of a dancer made it difficult for Blase to let her hair down with him.

On the last day of their trip, they were packing their suitcases up to leave and Blase noticed sun peaking in through the hut. She opened the shutters and saw the sun dancing a vibrant dance in the sky. She sneered and shook her head.

"I can't believe the sun is coming out today," Walter said.

Blase replied, "For some reason, I can." She walked down to the damp beach to enjoy the last hour of the weather. Walter joined her on the lounge chairs with two Red Stripe beers he took from the hut refrigerator.

"Thank you," she said.

"So my darling, will I see you after this trip?" he asked wearily.

"Of course you'll see me. I'm glad we came on this trip, Walter. I had a great time with you despite the weather. I think being virtually confined to a room with you for ten days with no distractions really gave me more insight into who you are."

"I'm hoping that's a good thing. We'll just play it by ear when we get back to the states."

To that they toasted their beer bottles.

Their helicopter ride back to the airport was particularly beautiful because Blase was able to get a photo of a rainbow through the eyes of a bird. She felt like she was riding the rainbow back to the airport.

When they reached Walter's townhouse in New York, Blase gave Walter a hug, a kiss, and a promise to see him soon.

Once back home, Blase checked all of her messages. She had over four hundred emails though many of them were personal because she checked a lot of her work emails while she was in Jamaica. She picked up the phone to call Fallon first.

"How was your trip?" Fallon answered without saying hello.

Blase laughed. "Hey," she said with a sigh.

"Oh goodness, what happened?"

"Well other than the wonderful tropical rain storms the entire trip, absolutely nothing."

"Are you kidding me? Diane double and triple checked the forecast."

"Things like that can't be predicted. They said it was unseasonable weather, so you know I took it as a sign."

"Well I'm sure it allowed you and Walter to make your own thunder and lightning," Fallon said as she whispered for Sergio to make a left.

Blase laughed. "Not even a spark. It was as if we were business colleagues who took a vacation together to get work done without interruption."

"Ouch, that sounds very unsexy," Fallon said.

"Extremely!"

"I'm sorry, girl. Well, one down, four to go!"

"Hope for better weather all around for the next few," Blase said.

"I am too. Did you like Flynn?" she asked.

"Oh yes, that resort is beautiful. I would've had even more fun if the weather was better, but the service was outstanding. Our hut keeper's name was Hyacinth. She was adorable."

"I've met Hyacinth. She's the best one they have. That was one of the perks. Did you like the helicopter ride?"

"Yes! I was a little nervous at first, but once we were up in the air it was exhilarating. I have pictures, so I'll upload them to the website in the next few days."

"That'll be awesome. Also if you could write a review of Flynn for Dad, we would really appreciate it."

"Oh, I hadn't thought of that. Of course I will. Well, I just wanted to touch base with you to let you know I'm home. I'll connect with you later in the week."

"Okay. I'm sorry about the rain, but it sounds like even if it were sunny, Walter would've been too drab to have a good time with."

Blase laughed. "Yes, he was cloudy with a chance of rain himself."

They both laughed.

"Talk to you later," Fallon said.

They disconnected the call.

**FOR** the next few weeks, Blase met with clients and Tracey to make sure things were still running smoothly with the practice. Everything seemed to be fine. Sheridan was settling in to her new position nicely and enjoying the promotion. Blase spoke with all of her other exes on and off throughout the weeks over the phone and on email and decided to have a few dinner dates with Bryant.

A few days before her trip to Aruba with Cup, Brielle surprised Blase showing up at her practice and inviting her to lunch. They decided to go to Sylvia's in Harlem.

"So how was your trip?" Brielle asked.

Blase told her everything she mentioned to Fallon and Sheridan.

"No fire being reignited there, huh?" Brielle asked.

"I don't think so. Since we've been back, Walter has tried on numerous occasions to get together, but I've been blowing him off. He's sent me flowers and even had this cookbook delivered that we saw there and could only be purchased there."

"That was nice of him."

"Yes he can be very nice when he wants to, but what he can't be is my life partner."

"I'm glad you had to go all the way to Jamaica to figure out what I think you already knew," Brielle bite back.

Blase thought it wasn't an appropriate comment, but she knew Brielle's cynicism ran deep so she ignored it. "So what's going on with you?" Blase asked.

"Dwight and I are thinking of getting back together."

Blase almost choked on her iced tea. "Excuse me. Did I just hear correctly?"

"Yes you did. I didn't tell you, but we've been talking a lot over the past few months and he told me things aren't working out with him and that woman."

Blase was dumbfounded. "Are you kidding me, Brielle? Is this coming from the woman who has told me over and over again that they are your exes for a reason? A woman who thinks my trips are unreasonable? This man had an entire life with another woman and has now fathered another child with this woman and you are considering getting back together with him?"

Brielle held her head up and matter-of-factly retorted, "I still love him."

Blase just couldn't believe her ears. She was both disappointed and amazed. "Have you talked with Fallon about it?"

"No, because I don't want to hear what Fallon has to say. I am telling you because I know you'll understand."

"But I don't, honey. I really don't understand."

"Well, I'm sorry you don't. He's moving back in with us at the end of this month."

"So you're not thinking of getting back together, you are getting back together?"

"Yes. My son has been so excited about seeing him in the house lately and me seeing my son excited has made me happy."

Blase sat with her eyes raised, her back arched, and her mouth agape. She shook off her shock and continued. "Okay. If you're happy, then I'm happy."

"No you're not."

"Okay I'm not, but I respect your choices, Brie. We are grown women and we are not getting any younger. Hell, if you can respect my decision to travel halfway around the world with five different men, then I can respect your decision to get back together with your ex-husband."

"There is more."

Blase took a bite of her macaroni and cheese "Do tell," she said.

"His daughter is moving in with us, and—"

"And?" Blase said.

"And I think I'm pregnant."

Blase began chewing her macaroni and cheese fanatically. She picked up her tea and took a sip to swallow it down. "Pregnant!"

"Yes," Brielle said excitedly.

"Have you been to the doctor?" Blase asked.

"Not yet, but I've taken two pregnancy tests and they were both positive."

"Does Dwight know?"

"No, he doesn't know yet. I know he's going to be excited." Brielle sounded unconvincing.

Blase sat back in her chair with a look of apprehension on her face. She wasn't too sure Dwight would be as warm and fuzzy about it as Brielle. Dwight's pattern in his relationships was pretty muddy. He cheated on his high school girlfriend with Brielle, he cheated on Brielle with his current girlfriend, and cheated on his current girlfriend with another woman while she was pregnant with his daughter.

"I'm nervous, Brielle. I'm nervous for you. I trust that you are making the best decision for your family, but I'm nervous," Blase said, nodding her head up and down with her eyes bulging. "And you really are going to have his daughter move in with you guys? Are you sure you're ready to take on that responsibility?"

Brielle was growing frustrated with all of Blase's concerns and questions. "Yes," she said bluntly.

Blase took the hint and decided to lighten up the conversation. "Well here's to new beginnings," she said and she raised her glass.

Brielle smiled. "Here's to them. One more thing. Will you be in our wedding?"

*WEDDING!*

She responded, "Of course."

# Aruba

**THE** morning of her trip to Aruba, Blase was nervous. She wasn't sure how she would feel about seeing Cup again. She felt like of all of her relationships, they had left the door wide open and until then, neither would walk through it. She'd heard from Fallon he never ended up selling the Scarsdale house in case they got back together. Since Cup left her a message saying he would be in New York the week of their trip, Blase had Fallon change his flight to leave with her.

She was running late because she decided to have dinner with her parents the night before her trip and ended up staying there until late in the evening, so she didn't have time to drop Sugar off at Camp Canine. She dialed Sheridan's number on the way down to the car.

"Good morning," Sheridan answered, sounding as if she were still asleep.

"Good morning. Are you at Melesse?" Blase asked.

"Blase it's 6:30 in the morning. Of course I'm not at Melesse."

Blase was so stressed out she forgot it was the crack of dawn. "Oh right, I'm so sorry, Sher. I am running so late. I was supposed to be at Cup's hotel to pick him up forty-five minutes ago. We have an eight o'clock flight."

Sheridan sat up in her boyfriend's bed. "Oh wow. Do you think you'll make the flight?"

"I think I will if I hustle, but I need a favor," she said as she climbed into the town car.

"Sure, what's up?"

"Can you stop by my apartment and pick up Sugar and take her to Camp Canine for me? I've arranged for her to stay there for the next ten days."

"No problem. Are you sure you want to put her there? Has she ever been there before?"

Blase sighed. "No, I'm nervous about it. They said they have small dogs there and the facility looked nice and clean, but I'm still uneasy."

"How about I do this, I'll pick her up and keep her with me today and stay at your place and dog sit her for the next week or so."

"Oh that would be perfect. I didn't think that was an option."

"Are you kidding? I love your apartment and I'll be closer to work for ten days. You just can't be mad at me if you come home to an empty wine chiller," she said, laughing.

"If you dog sit Sugar for me for ten days, you can have all the wine you want, and if there is food there you don't like, just call Fresh Direct and have them deliver some groceries for you, on me."

"This is becoming a more attractive situation by the minute," Sheridan said.

"I'm sure it will be cheaper than Camp Canine either way."

Sheridan shook her head. "Sugar just doesn't realize how good her life is."

Blase laughed. She talked to Sheridan a little more until they pulled on the street where Cup's hotel was and she told her she had to call Cup to tell him to come down. Though, when Blase pulled up to the hotel, Cup was standing outside talking with the doorman. He looked at his watch as she got out of the car.

"I know. I'm so sorry. I had dinner with Mom and Dad last night."

Cup smiled as he hugged Blase. "It's ah'ight. You look beautiful."

Blase smiled. "So do you."

Both Cup and the doorman laughed. "Let's go. I don't want to miss this flight. That house sounds hot!" he said. Cup shook the doorman's hand and tipped him. He jumped in the car with Blase and they were off to the airport.

When Blase and Cup realized they were alone in first class, they used their four hour flight as an opportunity to talk. Blase was sipping her coffee when Cup put his paper down and asked, "Why didn't you want me to know where you moved to?"

Blase looked at Cup, turned her body to face him, and responded, "I think it was less of me not wanting you to know where I lived and more of me being hurt and needing time to get over you, Corey. I don't think my actions were unreasonable, considering," she said, acknowledging her bitterness over their breakup.

"Ah'ight, I understand that, but let me ask you, what did you expect me to do?"

"I expected you to give me a chance."

"I gave you a chance. In fact I gave you several chances and you didn't seem interested in making us work."

"But when I came out to San Diego, you didn't even want to talk, Corey. I can't believe you had my bags packed. There was no discussion. You completely shut me out."

"I didn't expect you to show up, babe. You know I'm not a dramatic dude. You caught me off guard when you showed up so there was no way to break it to you gently at that point." Cup signaled to the flight attendant to get him a glass of orange juice "Do you want another coffee?" he asked.

"Yes," Blase said, beginning to revisit the hurt she felt years before.

Cup could see the hurt in her face and didn't want to start the trip on a bad note. "Ah'ight well we are here now, so let's celebrate us being together now, but for the record I didn't mean to hurt you."

The flight attendant brought their drinks and quickly left sensing the tension between the two of them. Blase picked up her cup and drank a big gulp of it quickly.

"Come on, babe. I'm sorry. Let's just chill and enjoy our trip." He gently turned her face toward his and leaned in for their first kiss in almost three years.

Blase gave in and kissed him back. The kiss was familiar and soothing. The flight attendant witnessing their kiss took the opportunity to ask them if they were ready for their in-flight meal.

"What's on the menu?" Cup asked.

The flight attendant told them their breakfast choices, and Cup ordered eggs, sausages, and potatoes. Blase ordered eggs and potatoes with wheat bread. Before the flight attendant left to put their order in, she asked Cup for his autograph for her son. He gladly obliged. Blase looked at him, smiled, and said, "Just like old times."

Cup and Blase ate and after a mimosa they both fell asleep.

Once in Aruba, the weather was an arid 80 degrees. When they made it through baggage claim, a man in an all-white suit walked over and asked them if they were Mr. and Mrs. Ponce. Blase found it interesting that on this trip they used his last name.

"Yes," Cup answered.

A few people who de-boarded the plane noticed who he was and began to ask for his autograph. Cup signed a few autographs while the man in white waited. Once he finished, the escort called one of the porters to take their luggage. The porter loaded their luggage on to a cart and followed them to their waiting car. Fallon arranged for their luxury rental car. The man in white was a representative from the car rental company. He chauffeured them to their house where someone was waiting to pick him up. Cup was impressed by the house as they pulled up. The long driveway to the private residence was lined with Bougainvillea plants and two Divi-Divi trees on the front lawn.

"Thank you, Mr. and Mrs. Ponce. Enjoy your stay in Aruba," the man said as the butler took the bags out of their car and brought them into the house.

Once they finished talking with the rental car representative, they turned to walk into the house. They were greeted by the housekeeper. "Good afternoon Mr. and Mrs. Ponce."

"Good afternoon," they both replied.

"My name is Aubrey, and I will be your housekeeper for the week. Jack is your butler and resident mixologist. We have your food selections of the week, so we took the liberty of preparing some possible menus for you, so feel free to choose from the menus or give us your requests for food. Breakfast will be served every morning at eight unless you'd like it later." She continued talking as they all walked into the kitchen and sat down at the breakfast bar.

"Lunch will be prepared on demand or in advance if you just call my cell phone and tell me what time you would like it prepared. Jack will serve any cocktails you would like and deliver them to you anywhere on the premises. I generally check in at eleven to make the beds and clean the rooms. Of course if you wish for me to come later, just text me and let me know. Here is your cell phone to contact myself, Jack, or your masseuse who is off premises but will come with one hours notice."

Blase smiled at how thorough Aubrey was. "Thank you, Aubrey. We really appreciate your thoroughness."

"Of course," she responded. "Now let me take you on a tour of the house and property. Can I offer you something to drink before we go?"

"Yes," Cup said. "Do you have bottled water?"

"Sure, Mr. Ponce," Aubrey replied as she walked to the refrigerator.

"Would you like a bottle as well, Mrs. Ponce?"

"Sure," Blase answered.

Aubrey showed them their room first and then the rest of the house. She showed them the outdoor living area and even walked them to the beach. Blase thought the property was more beautiful than the photos. Once they returned to the house, Jack asked them if they were ready for a cocktail. They both said yes.

"Do you have a specific drink you would like?" Jack asked.

"You know what brother, we'll let you take the lead on our drinks. Just no brown liquor for Mrs. Ponce," Cup said with a smile on his face.

Blase laughed at him calling her his wife.

"No problem, sir. Will you need those drinks delivered to you at the pool, beach, or will you be in the house?"

"We'll be in the bedroom," Cup responded.

Blase's eyebrows rose. Cup walked over and grabbed Blase's hand and pulled her to the room. Once they walked in, Cup began to kiss Blase as if time hadn't escaped them. She kissed him back and it was then Blase realized she still very much loved Corey Ponce. Just as they were about to undress, Jack knocked on the door with their drinks. Cup opened the door and Jack sat the drinks on the table in the room.

"Will you need anything else at this time?" he asked.

"Yeah, where are the towels for the pool?" Cup asked.

"I believe they are in your linen closet in your bathroom, Mr. Ponce," Jack said.

Cup walked in to the bathroom and checked for the towels. "Ah'ight, they were in there. Thanks, my brother. That's all," Cup said as he walked back out.

Blase was sipping on her drink. "Mmm Jack, this is delicious. What is it?" Blase asked.

"It's called an Aruba Ariba, Mrs. Ponce. I'm glad you like it. It has Vodka, Rum, Crème de Bananas, Pineapple, Orange, and Cranberry juice and a local liquor called Coecoei," he responded.

"Well, keep these coming, Jack. I love them."

Cup picked up the beer Jack brought for him and took a swig. "This is pretty good too, Jack. Is this local?"

"Yes, sir. That is Balashi beer. Do you like it?"

"Yeah man, this is ah'ight."

"Great. I will be on my way then. Two satisfied customers," Jack said with a smile as he closed the door.

Blase took a long sip of her drink and walked back over to Cup to continue what they started. Cup undressed Blase. "Ah'ight, let's get this vacation started with a bang, or two."

Blase laughed and said, "Or ten."

They made love until it was time for dinner.

Cup called and told Aubrey they wanted dinner on the patio leading to the pool outside of their bedroom. Aubrey told them to come out in an hour. They decided to use half of that hour to make love again. Thirty minutes before their dinner was served they took a shower together. Cup suggested they put their bathing suits on under their clothes so they could swim in the pool after dinner. When Cup opened the French doors in the bedroom that led to the patio, Aubrey had the table made with candles and fresh flowers. A bucket on a stand sat next to the table with a bottle of champagne chilling, and Blase noticed all of the lit candles in the tall Candle stands tucked into the tropical flowers around the pool.

"Wow, Corey. This is beautiful," she said.

"You're beautiful," he responded.

Blase blushed.

She had on a white bikini underneath an orange sarong she wrapped around her body and tied at her neck. Her hair was pulled back into a loose bun. Cup wore simple swim trunks with a t-shirt and Addidas flip-flops. They sat at the table and their personal chef brought out each course of their meal, while Jack poured their champagne.

"Yo, this is fly, girl. I'm impressed," Cup said.

"I'm impressed too. Fallon put all of this together."

"I have to thank her the next time I see her," he said. Cup plugged his iPod into their outdoor stereo system and played jazz music for Blase.

She smiled. They ate, flirted, and laughed through dinner. An hour after they finished their dinner, Cup turned the music to hip-hop, walked over to Blase, and untied her sarong. "It's time to go swimming."

"I'm ready!" Blase said.

Cup took his t-shirt off and dove into the water. When he came up, Blase was standing their watching him.

"Come on in, the water is warm."

Blase didn't hesitate; she dove in. When she came up, she said, "You were right, the water is warm." They swam, played, and reacquainted until a little after midnight. Blase climbed out of the pool exhausted and told Cup she was going to bed and if he was smart, he should join her. Cup was right on her heels when she said it. They showered again and climbed into bed. As they were kissing and attempting to make love, they both were so exhausted they fell asleep in each other's arms.

The next day was as perfect as the day before. They spent it on the beach. After asking Aubrey and Jack to give them privacy, they decided to swim and sunbathe nude. The freedom of sunbathing nude made Cup horny and within a few minutes of ascending from the water, Cup had slid his body on top of an unsuspecting Blase and began kissing her neck. She smiled and turned her head to face his, took off her sunglasses, and kissed him back. Their bodies moved to the rhythm of the wind for the next hour. Before they fell asleep Cup moved their umbrella over them so they wouldn't get sunburned and they slept together on the beach until the sun went down. That evening they decided to drive around the island and take in some of the nightlife. They went to a local bar where Cup was met with some fanfare, but for the most part they were able to party and enjoy the night with everyone.

The next day, Cup wanted to lounge by the pool again. In fact for the rest of the vacation, they both decided to stay at the house and enjoy each other in romantic solitude. They had individual massages throughout the week and the day before they left, asked for an additional masseuse to get a couples massage.

By the time the rental car agent arrived to take them back to the airport, Blase and Cup were wishing for another day. "I wish we could stay for another week," Blase said.

"I do too. This trip was tight, baby. I enjoyed you and I'm glad we got a chance to talk."

Blase laughed. "Is that what you call it?"

Cup laughed with her. "Oh come on, babe. We talked."

She kept smiling. "Yes, we did talk. I'm just kidding you."

Jack was putting their bags in the car. After he finished Cup turned to him and said, "Jack my brother, you hooked us up this week. We really appreciate everything you did, man. Thanks." He shook Jacks hand and slipped in a tip. Jack smiled and thanked him and welcomed him back.

Cup already tipped Aubrey after their breakfast that morning. They got in the car and went to the airport. Though they tried to stay awake and talk during their flight back to New York, they were exhausted and fell asleep. Cup wasn't looking forward to the second leg of his trip. He decided to fly back to New York with Blase and then catch a flight to San Diego.

After de-boarding the plane, Cup asked Blase, "Where do we go from here?"

"We'll play it by ear," she said.

"Ah'ight, I have Pitchers and Catchers camp starting in a week. Once camp is over, I'll call you and maybe you can come to see me."

"That sounds great," Blase replied, realizing she would have to take additional time off for the trip.

"Ah'ight, my flight to San Diego leaves in two hours, so I'm going to head to the club room," he said.

Blase reached up to hug Cup. They hugged, kissed, and before Cup turned to leave, he reached in his carry-on bag and handed Blase a gift.

"What's this?"

"Just something I picked up while we were in town a few days ago." Cup kissed her on the cheek and walked away leaving Blase standing there euphoric.

When Blase opened the door to her condo, Sheridan was sitting out on the patio listening to music and talking on the phone.

"Oh honey, let me call you back, Blase just walked in the door." She hung up the phone and walked over to Blase to give her a hug.

Blase was busy petting Sugar, so they cheek kissed.

"Hi, how are you?" Sheridan asked.

"I'm good. How are you? How was your vacation?" Blase asked.

Sheridan laughed. "It was great, but I'm more curious about your vacation. I'm judging by that permanent smile on your face it went well," Sheridan suggested.

Blase sat with Sheridan and told her about her entire vacation. Sheridan was happy to hear she and Cup made up.

"Is there a need for you to go on the other vacations?" she asked.

"Of course there is," Blase said.

"Especially Africa, huh?" Sheridan laughed.

"Especially Africa," Blase said, laughing as she took her suitcases in to her room.

"You didn't practice making little hedge fund babies on my bed, did you?" she joked with Sheridan.

"Not your bed, but the rest of your apartment and your dining room, you might want to have sterilized," she joked back.

Blase laughed as her cell phone rang. She looked at her phone and right on queue, Fallon was calling to check on her trip.

"The temperature was hot and I was horny the entire trip," Blase answered.

Fallon burst out laughing. "Well that's good to hear, but did you like the house?" she asked through her continued laughter.

Blase sighed and sat down on her bed. "Fallon, it was beautiful. Corey was beautiful. Girl when I picked him up on the way to the airport I wanted to jump his bones."

"The house, girl. Was it nice? Was the staff efficient? I want a service review before we get to your legs touching the sun."

They both laughed.

"Aubrey, Jack, and our masseuses were great. We hardly left the house and they waited on us hand and foot. It was wonderful. Aubrey went above and beyond making every meal especially romantic with flowers and little candies. One day she even had a little fresh flower tiara made for me to wear on the beach. Cup took so many pictures of me that day. Oh and Jack and his Aruba Ariba drinks were smoking. I'll upload the photos this week."

"That's fantastic! I'm glad you enjoyed it. I will refer them for future house rentals. So now I take it that you guys caught up on old times?" She snickered.

"Yes, we talked a lot. He's been very successful with the Padres. He's single right now, but he did date someone after me. You know I didn't like hearing that."

"I know he dated someone. Sergio told me."

"You knew?"

"Of course I knew, B. He is one of Sergio's best friends. I just didn't think you would want to hear about it."

"You're right, I didn't want to hear about it."

"But he did ask about you a lot, but after a while he just stopped. Sergio didn't want to make it uncomfortable for me."

"It's good to know he thought of me after he ran me out of California," she said, walking back into the living area where Sheridan was. Blase noticed fresh flowers sitting on the dining room table.

"Who are these from?" she asked Sheridan with Fallon still on the phone.

"Those are from Walter. They arrived on Thursday," Sheridan said.

"They are beautiful."

"He's making an effort," Sheridan said.

"Walter sent you some flowers?" Fallon asked.

"Yes, but Walter is making efforts in vain. I know for sure there is no future for us," Blase said.

"Well then move on. Do you need to go away for the rest of the trips after such an amazing time with Cup?" Fallon asked.

"That's the same thing Sheridan asked."

Blase looked at Sheridan, who looked back wondering what she'd asked her.

"I'm going to Africa, Fal, and Hawaii, and the Caymans. Does that answer your question?"

"Yes ma'am. So I guess he didn't shift your twist too far to the left then?"

"Oh he did, but I'm sticking to the plan."

"Okay, good. So dinner before you go on your next trip?" Fallon asked.

"Yes, we should all get together," Blase suggested.

"Sounds good, put it together. I have to run. See you soon."

"Soon," Blase said before she disconnected.

The weeks before her next vacation crept along. Blase lived off of the euphoria from Aruba for the first week, but after the second week of long hours and meeting with Tracey, she was desperately looking forward to her next trip. She spoke with Cup every day and ignored most of Walter's correspondences until finally she decided to send him an email telling him she didn't want to pursue a relationship with him. Walter emailed back with a casual note wishing her well in life.

The week of her trip to Hawaii, Blase arranged for her friends to meet her for dinner. She decided on 8:00 p.m. at her favorite Sushi restaurant, Nobu Fifty Seven on 57th street. Blase and Sheridan arrived first after they closed the practice. They secured a table upstairs and informed the hostess two other women would be coming and gave them their names. Brielle walked in shortly after and told the hostess she was there to meet friends. After taking her name, the hostess escorted Brielle upstairs to meet them. Fallon arrived thirty minutes later with little gifts she received from one of her clients who recently opened an accessory boutique downtown.

"Hi, ladies. I'm sorry I'm late," Fallon said as she put gift bags in front of them.

Everyone, excited about their new gift, immediately forgave her for her tardiness, not to mention they knew Fallon would be late. They all looked in their bags and inside were beautiful ornate necklaces, earrings, bracelets, and a pair of sunglasses.

"These are lovely, Fal. What's the name of this new client's store?" Blase asked as she kissed Fallon on the cheek and watched her take her place at the table.

"Her name is Abigale Satin and her store is called Satin. It is downtown on Broome street right next to Calypso boutique."

"Oh, I know that place. I've walked past it a few times with my boyfriend. I'll just have to drag him in there with me the next time we happen upon it," Sheridan remarked.

"How are things with you and your boyfriend?" Fallon asked.

Brielle knew they would get on the topic of men, but not this fast. She wasn't sure if she was ready to tell everyone about her news.

"We are good. He's been really awesome, kind, and considerate. I think he's a keeper," Sheridan answered.

"How long has it been now?" Blase asked.

"We've been together for almost six months. In fact, he's taking me to the Adirondacks the weekend of our six month anniversary."

"Awww, that's nice. I wish you guys continued happiness. Where are our drinks? You guys didn't order anything yet?" Fallon asked, wanting to toast to Sheridan's love interest.

"No, we were waiting for you. We couldn't decide on Saki, wine, or martinis," Sheridan responded.

"I voted for a martini. All I drink is champagne and wine on vacation," Blase said.

"Martinis can work for me too," Fallon said.

Sheridan agreed as well and they waited for Brielle.

Blase, knowing Brielle's situation, waited to hear what she would say.

"I am not drinking tonight ladies, so I will stick with my juice," Brielle said.

"Ladies and gentleman welcome to the lame section of the table," Fallon said, laughing.

"Whatever!" Brielle said, laughing with her. They all ordered their martinis and appetizers and continued talking. Blase told them about the details of her trips so far and she was glad she'd made the decision not only for the thrill of seeing her exes but also because the vacation packages were turning out to be amazing. Sheridan asked Fallon if she and her boyfriend could meet with her because they wanted to plan a vacation for the summer.

After eating their appetizers and ordering their entrees, Fallon abruptly said, "Sergio and I are going to have a baby!"

"What?" Blase call out.

"Let me rephrase that, Sergio and I are going to begin to try and have a baby. I've stopped my birth control and we are going to try and have a baby or three as he put it. He wants four children. I want two."

"Congratulations Fal, that's wonderful news," Sheridan exclaimed.

"And it's about time," Brielle added.

Blase smiled. "So when are you putting this plan in motion?"

"I put it in motion about a month ago and we have an appointment with my doctor later this week. I'm afraid my age might affect the pregnancy so we're having some tests done to make sure everything is okay with my oven," Fallon said.

"Awesome!" Sheridan said.

"I don't care what part of the world I'm in, I still want to be on the top ten list of phone calls you make once you find out," Blase said.

"Top ten," Fallon said. "Girl, I'll probably call you before Sergio."

They all laughed.

"So Brielle, you're awfully quiet. What's been going on with you?" Sheridan asked excited to hear all of the great news from her new friends.

Brielle took another sip of her juice not really wanting to get into her personal life. "Not much, just working so hard and being a mommy. I'm so glad to hear you're joining me in mommy world, Fallon," She looked at Fallon.

Fallon replied, "I am nervous about it, but I'm sure I'll be fine. But what's going on with you? Are you dating anyone now? Have you stopped working out? You look like you're putting on a few pounds."

Blase smiled and thought, *Leave it to Fallon to come right out with it and tell Brielle she's gained weight.*

Brielle looked over at Blase who raised her eyebrows. Finally Brielle relented. "I'm pregnant."

"Pregnant? By who?" Fallon asked.

Brielle looked at Blase again for comfort. "Dwight," she answered, waiting for reactions.

Both Sheridan and Fallon looked at her as if they were waiting for a punch line. Fallon looked over at Blase and when she saw the expression on Blase's face didn't match hers, she realized Brielle was telling the truth and Blase already knew about it.

"I'm speechless, Brie. I didn't know you were even speaking to Dwight," Fallon said.

"We've been talking and we decided to get back together."

"You've obviously been doing more than talking," Fallon said.

"Well I'm happy for you," Sheridan interjected. "If this is what is going to, or has made you happy, then I'm happy for you."

"Thank you, Sheridan," Brielle responded.

"I just don't understand. We talk to you all the time and you sit around making these exes are exes for a reason comments and borderline judging us on our choices in men, shit, judging Blase on her decisions and you get back together with a lying, cheating snake?" Fallon said.

Before Brielle could bark back, Blase interrupted trying to avoid an explosion. She touched Fallon on the hand. "Despite her opinions, she and Dwight have reunited and we should all respect her decision and not chastise her for it." Blase looked at Fallon with scolding eyes as if to gesture to her to let it go.

Fallon rolled her eyes, shook her head, and took another sip of her martini. Sheridan sat quiet watching.

"Quite frankly, I don't have to explain myself to anyone. The decisions I make for me and my family are my business."

"Then don't judge anyone else for their decisions. It's hypocritical," Fallon spat.

"Look, Fallon, I'm not going to sit here and argue with you," Brielle said as she reached in her bag and took some money out for her portion of the bill. She put it on the table, grabbed her bag from the back of her chair, and got up to walk away.

Blase got up and followed Brielle to the stairs. "Don't leave, Brie. Come on, you had to know Fallon was going to react like that. I mean you have to admit you've been giving me a hard way to go about some of my decisions. Fallon was just defending me; she didn't mean to offend you."

"I don't need to be lectured."

"I agree. Just come back to the table and let's call a truce. This argument isn't necessary or worth any bitter feelings."

"I just don't have the energy to deal with Fallon and her opinions right now."

"Okay, but to play devil's advocate, that's how she was feeling when you made your comments in the past, but we never got angry with you and stormed out on you. Come on, come back to the table and let it go."

Brielle turned to Blase and gave in. "I'll come back, but I want an apology."

"Then you need to apologize for your previous comments. I mean really, Brielle, get off of the throne and join this judgment free friendship with us."

Fallon was at the table talking with Sheridan. Blase and Brielle walked back to the table and Brielle stood. She looked at Fallon and Fallon and Sheridan looked back. "I apologize for being judgmental in the past. I guess it never really clicked until Dwight and I started talking about reconciliation that sometimes there are unresolved feelings and things could possibly be worked out. I never expected to reconcile with Dwight..." Brielle started to tear up. "...but the truth is, I've only loved Dwight and as hard as I've tried, I couldn't stop loving him, so I guess I hid those feelings behind my remarks and ridicule. Truth is, I know how Dwight is and I'm terrified, but I'm miserable without him. I love you guys and I don't want to fight; especially not now when I need you the most."

Fallon softened up, sipped her martini, and said, "I apologize for calling Dwight a name. Now sit back down and tell us how you're feeling and give us the details on your reconciliation."

Brielle smiled as she sat back down and started telling them everything. For the first time, she let her guard down and shared everything. They all listened, laughed, and cried with her and she hugged all she was missing throughout the years—her friends and sister circle.

# Hawaii

THE weather was a blustery 50 degrees in New York the morning Blase was leaving for Hawaii. She spoke with Miller throughout the night before their trip and he was just as excited as she was. Her flight was scheduled to leave at 10:00 a.m. Blase woke up at 6:30 a.m. and walked Sugar. Sheridan decided to stay at her condo and dog sit since she had such a good time the month before and it was convenient for work. At 7:15 a.m. the car was downstairs ready to take Blase to the airport. She arrived at a few minutes before 8:00 a.m. She ordered breakfast and pulled out the book she started during her trip to Aruba to finish the last few chapters so she could move on to her new book. She figured, new vacation, new book.

Because of the weather, her flight was delayed two hours. She forgot to check her Flynn Destination account and when she looked at her phone, she realized one of her emails was an alert letting her know the flight was delayed. Blase called Miller in Chicago to see if his flight was delayed. He said his flight was on time. She told him to go ahead to the hotel and check in and she would meet him there. She called Fallon and asked her if she could change the time of their transportation from the airport to their hotel and arrange for two cars instead of one. Fallon checked online and realized Diane had already made the arrangement and sent an email to Blase. The extra time allowed Blase to finish her second book and respond to some emails. As soon as she opened her email account, she saw an email from Cup.

*Hey baby. I'm done with Pitchers and Catchers, but spring training has started. I know you said you would go out to San Diego to visit me, but guess what? I'm back in New York. I didn't want to tell you until it was official, but the reason I was in New York the week before our trip was because I was signing with the New York Yankees. I'm a Yankee now! I've been so busy meeting front and back office staff and studying that I am just now coming up for air to tell you. I'll be staying at our Scarsdale house, but I'm down in Florida now for spring training. I need to see you, and soon! I miss you and I love you! Call me!*

*Love, Corey*

Blase couldn't believe it. Cup was in New York. She picked up her cell phone and dialed Fallon's number again.

Fallon answered, "Hey, please tell me the flight is not canceled."

"No, it's still on the two hour delay. Fallon, tell me you didn't know Corey plays for the Yankees now."

"The Yankees? Since when?" Fallon turned over and slapped Sergio on the arm. "Cup plays for the Yankees now?" she asked him.

"Yeah," Sergio answered as he turned his body away from Fallon annoyed that she woke him up.

"Apparently he does. Sergio just said he does. I didn't know. How did you find out?"

"I just checked my email and he sent me one telling me so."

"Wow, so what are you going to do?"

"Right now, go to Hawaii."

"Well then call me when you get back. I should be back in town by then. Right now I have to kiss and make up with my husband since you made me wake him up after a long week of spring training."

Blase breathe out, "Sorry girl, I'll call you when I get back."

Fallon hung up.

# LUCKY NO. 5

Blase arrived in Maui exhausted after her two hour delay, hour layover in California, and all around 15 hour travel to Hawaii. When she walked into the hotel, she went to the front desk of the Ritz and told them her other party checked in already.

"Yes Dr. Morgan, Mr. Jones left word that he would be in the Alaloa Lounge," the front desk attendant told her.

Blase took her key and decided to go to the room and freshen up before she met him in the lounge. When she opened the doors to the room, the view was breathtaking. Miller must've gone out to the terrace because the terrace doors were open and there was an unfinished beer sitting on the table between the two balcony chairs. She opened her suitcase and took out a cream colored mini-sundress, grabbed her toiletry bag, and went into the bathroom to take a quick shower. Afterwards, she put on a little mascara, lip gloss, her bone colored mule stilettos, grabbed her bone colored bag, and headed to the lounge. When she walked through the doors, Miller looked bored surrounded by men talking about football. He was on his cell phone typing as she approached.

When he saw her, his face lit up. "Excuse me fellas, thank you for the conversation but my date just arrived," he said.

All of the men turned to see who he was talking about, and when they saw Blase they all smiled politely. Blase heard one of them say, "Hey, what happened to that actress you were dating?"

Miller gave him a fixed look and didn't respond, but instead just walked away from the men.

"Hey, Chocolate. You look sexy," he said.

"Thank you," she said as she hugged and kissed him. "So what did happen to that actress you were dating?" Blase asked with a smile.

"She's history," he quickly responded. "Can we get out of here? These dudes are getting on my nerves."

"Sure, where do want to go?" she asked.

"Well it's early; do you want to grab some dinner?"

"Sure. I'm hungry."

They walked to The Terrace and Banyan Tree restaurant. Blase and Miller talked for a few hours before Blase's exhaustion got the best of her and she wanted to get some sleep. She had to adjust her body to the time difference.

"I'm sorry, Mill, I'm so tired. I don't know if it was the long flight or the two Blue Hawaiian's I just drank, but I really need some rest."

Miller wasn't quite ready to go to the room, but he agreed. Blase couldn't help but notice at dinner and walking back to their room that Miller was texting on his cell phone quite a bit.

She asked, "Is everything okay?"

Miller didn't understand the question. "What do you mean?"

"I mean you've been on your phone since we walked in to the restaurant. Is everything good back home?"

"Oh yeah, everything is cool. Just talking with a few of the fellas."

*Hmmm.*

Blase didn't say anything else about it, though she thought it was rude considering they hadn't seen one another in years.

Miller continued to text. Blase had hoped that once they reached the room, they could talk more and maybe rekindle some of the romance, but Miller wouldn't put his cell phone down so she decided to change and climb into bed. Miller went to take a shower and when he emerged with a towel wrapped around him, he was still on his cell phone texting. At the site of this, Blase decided to go to sleep.

The next morning, Blase woke refreshed and ready to see what Maui had to offer. Miller was fast asleep. She shook him to wake him. "Mill, let's go to the beach."

"Nah, not right now, babe. Give me like an hour or two. Go without me and I'll meet you there."

Blase was confused. This wasn't what she had planned, but she wanted to see Maui, so she got up, showered, and put on her orange string bikini, beige gold and brown sheer cover up shirt, beige and gold flip-flips, beige hat, and brown sunglasses, and headed for the beach. She ordered breakfast and coffee from the restaurant on her way. When she reached the pool, she decided to rent a cabana. She had one of the staff members call and leave a message in their room letting Miller know which Cabana she was in.

The weather was a breezy and humid 72 degrees. Blase figured she would start her third book. By the time she got close to the middle of the book, she realized almost four hours had passed. She packed up her things and went back to the room to make sure Miller was okay. When she got back to the room, Miller had hooked up his video game and was sitting in front of the TV playing NFL Madden. She stopped in the doorway.

"Oh, hey babe. Where were you? I was here waiting for you," he said.

"I left you a message, Miller. I've been down by the pool at a cabana waiting for you. Did you check the room messages?"

"Oh, nah. I didn't even look at the phone."

"Maybe I should've sent you a text message," she replied sarcastically.

Miller didn't even stop playing his game. He laughed thinking she was just joking.

"Will I be able to pry you away from technology this week so we can enjoy our vacation?"

"Yeah, babe. Let me just finish this game and we are out. What do you want to do today?" he asked still playing the game.

"I'd like to go explore the hotel first, then maybe take in some water sports. What about you?"

"Nah, I'm not really into water sports. Did you forget I don't know how to swim?"

"I did forget. I'm sorry. Then let's go explore the island."

"Okay, give me a few more minutes to finish this game."

Blase maintained her patience. "I'm going to change."

"Cool," he said.

Blase picked out her next outfit. When she came out of the bathroom, Miller finished his game, but was back on his cell phone texting.

Blase was annoyed. "Miller, are you going to be on your cell phone for this entire trip?"

"Oh, my bad, Chocolate. Nah, I won't be on it for the entire trip," he responded as he continued texting.

Blase didn't know what to think. She thought Miller wanted to see her and spend time with her, but he was acting as if he had no interest in being there with her. He finally put his phone away and said, "Okay, where are we headed."

Blase said sarcastically, "You are headed back to the airport if you don't give that phone a break."

Miller walked up to Blase and grabbed her around her hips and said, "I'm sorry, Choc. You know how it is."

"No, I don't know how it is. Why don't you enlighten me while we look at the resort."

"Cool." They walked around the resort and Miller filled Blase in on everything that had happened in his life since their split. He told her the move to Chicago proved to be his best move because his stats shot through the roof and his endorsement deals were coming in left and right. People were paying him to show up at their parties and dating his ex-girlfriend was a good look because it increased his celebrity a little more.

Blase couldn't believe some of the things Miller was saying. He seemed a completely different man then he was when they dated. He was obnoxious and bloated with the facade of Hollywood. By the time they reached the beach again, Blase wasn't sure she could do an additional eight days with him. Miller kept making reference to himself in the third person and kept telling her about all of the models he'd dated since her. He went on and on about his ex-girlfriend, so Blase couldn't help herself and she asked him why they'd broken up. He said she wasn't on his level anymore and he needed to fire her and move on. His name dropping had become unbearable and even after she made the comment, Miller continued to text. Blase made a decision by the evening she didn't want to continue the trip with him. Miller wasn't the man she'd fallen in love with years ago.

"Miller. I don't really know how to tell you this, so I'll just come out and say it. I would honestly prefer we continue this trip in two separate rooms."

Miller didn't understand. "Why?"

"I came here because I wanted to see if there was any romance left between us and I know for sure there is nothing left for me, so I would prefer not to have to spend the next eight days listening to you name drop and watching you text your friends back in the States."

Miller became angry. "You flew me all the way out here to see if there was some romance left between us? I could've told you there was none. Listen, baby, you aren't my style anymore. I date models and actresses now. I thought we were just gonna kick it and have a good time as old friends—"

Blase listened to his tirade unfazed. "Porn stars and reality stars you mean," she interjected sarcastically.

"Man, fuck you. I don't need to listen to this shit. Who do you think you are?" he blared.

Blase responded, "The woman who is putting you out in Maui. I hope the hotel isn't booked, because you aren't staying here another day with me. Be gone when I get back." She turned and walked out of the room. She couldn't help but wonder what she was thinking. Since making the phone call at Christmas, she'd googled him and found countless articles and photos of him with different women and at different parties as well as some of the statements he'd made to the press. By the time she ate dinner and got back to the room, Miller was gone. Blase spent the next eight days, reading, taking tours, shopping, and relaxing. It was perfectly unpretentious.

As soon as she arrived back in New York, she called Sheridan to check on the practice. Sheridan told her everything was still going fine, but two of her patients couldn't wait until she returned, so they booked appointments with Tracey. Blase was upset hearing this, but she understood some people wouldn't want to schedule their medical conditions around her vacations.

"Is Tracey taking care of them?" she asked.

"Yes, Tracey told me they really didn't need to schedule appointments with her, but she didn't want to make them wait if they insisted."

"I understand that."

"Juliette said she is feeling overwhelmed and asked if we had intentions of hiring another masseuse."

"Really? How many clients is she booking per week?" Blase asked.

"In the last four weeks, she's had four clients a day almost."

"Are you serious? That's great, but I don't want her to get burned out. Call the placement agency and then ask Juliette if she would like to do the first phase of interviews for a new masseuse."

"Will do. So how was your trip?"

"It was relaxing, but I didn't spend it with Miller."

"Huh? What do you mean?"

Blase explained what happened and Sheridan was shocked. "Oh he sounds like he's a complete asshole now," Sheridan remarked.

"Completely. But I got you, Brielle, and Fallon something."

"Aww thank you very much. By the way I was wondering if you wanted to start ordering flowers for the front desk since Brady stopped sending them."

"Did he? When did he stop sending them?"

"About a month ago."

"That's strange. I talked with Brady via email two months ago and he asked if I was still getting them."

"Hmmm, let me do some research before I start ordering them."

"Okay. I'll see you tomorrow at nine," Blase said.

"See you then."

Blase arrived at Melesse at 8:00 a.m. the next day. She had an 8:15 conference call with Tracey to discuss new marketing ideas, her patients that booked with Tracey, and hiring a new masseuse. It was ten o'clock when Sheridan walked into Blase's office with two cups of coffee after noticing she was off the phone.

"Good morning," Sheridan said.

"Good morning, Sher. Is that for me or are you having a two cup at a time morning?" Blase attempted a joke.

Sheridan smiled. "One is for you. Do you have a minute to talk before your first patient?"

"Sure. Sit down."

"Thanks. First I think we need to start looking for your new assistant. Going back and forth between the practices and keeping up with your schedule is starting to exhaust me. My cousin is working out well with Tracey, but I think I need to let my assistant title go to focus on my new responsibilities as the Melesse Director of Operations."

"Nice title. You should keep that instead of office manager. You stuck it out for three months, so I imagine it is time to start interviewing candidates. I don't think I'll find anyone as good as you, but I'll leave it up to you to interview the candidate for that position. You know what I need and want out of an assistant. Tracey said she was happy with her new assistant."

"Yes, I love her too. She's young, but she's very smart and efficient."

"Great."

"So the second thing I want to talk to you about is Brady."

Blase looked away from her computer when Sheridan mentioned Brady's name. "What about him? Did you find out why he stopped sending flowers?"

"Yes, B. He had a heart attack five weeks ago while he was on business in Utah. After several surgeries, he passed away a week later."

Blase couldn't react. She looked at Sheridan. "He had a heart attack five weeks ago?" she finally said.

"Yes," Sheridan answered with a remorseful look on her face. "His funeral was a week later in Colorado. I'm so sorry, honey." Sheridan touched Blase's hand.

"I don't even know what to do. I mean Brady was only 53-years-old."

"I was told by his assistant he had suffered two minor heart attacks a few years before and was taking heart medication."

"Are you serious? He never mentioned any heart condition with me...ever."

"Well since it's been five weeks, I don't think it would be appropriate to send anything to his company, but I just wanted to let you know. Again, I'm so sorry, girl," Sheridan said.

"Thank you," Blase said as she sat back in her chair. "Okay, let me get ready for my first patient," Blase said, giving Sheridan the hint to leave her alone.

"Call my extension if you need me."

"Thanks."

When Sheridan left, Blase pulled up the last email she'd exchanged with Brady and her heart felt heavy. She couldn't cry, but she couldn't shake the sadness for the next few days.

The next few weeks went by with Blase still communicating with Cup. She met with him a few times when he flew to New York and those times really had her reconsidering her last two trips, but since the plans were made and the trips were paid for, she would go anyway. She also wouldn't tell Cup she was taking the trips because she knew he wouldn't understand. Even though they hadn't made any formal commitments to each other, they discussed often about reconciling and how they would handle it if they were to get back together.

Blase was also fending off Bryant, who was attempting to see her more often. She agreed to go out with him two days before she left for Africa and as usual, he was a perfect gentleman. Bryant still respected her decision to take her vacations but he didn't take them seriously. His confidence was attractive and as he was settling into his divorced life, he started to talk about him and Blase getting serious when she finished with her last vacation. She and Bryant were still very open and honest with each other, which Blase appreciated. He told her he met someone else and they were dating casually, but he didn't see himself settling down with her because she didn't want children. This was fine with Blase because he respected her wishes for no sexual contact while she was taking her vacations, so they were becoming great friends.

# The Seychelles

THE day before Blase's trip to The Seychelles, she was swamped with work. She was finalizing the hiring of the new masseuse and her personal assistant. She met with them both to offer them their positions and have them sign their contracts, non-compete, and confidentiality agreements. Blase left by noon to make sure her apartment was all set for Benny and his wife who arrived in New York that morning for a two week vacation. They agreed to take care of Sugar while she was away. Before she left, her family decided to have dinner since everyone was in town. Blase's parents pulled out all of the stops and there was enough food to feed a family of thirty rather than the seven of them.

Benny asked Blase what she was up to and when she told him, Benny thought she had completely lost her mind. He asked his parents if they agreed with what she was doing and they both told him they supported whatever decision Blase made. Blase knew her mother wouldn't be able to keep the information a secret. Benny's wife told her she thought it was a brave thing to do, while Benny thought it sounded desperate and pathetic. Even though they didn't agree, Benny told her to be careful and to call him if she needed anything.

As Blase drove home, she thought of how beautiful her niece and nephew were. Every time she saw babies or toddlers lately, she yearned to have a child. She arrived at her apartment while Benny and his family were right on her heels. She set them up in their rooms and headed off to bed without much conversation. She didn't want Benny to start asking her about her vacations again.

The next day, Blase was out of the house by 8:00 a.m. to meet Adrian at the airport. His flight was scheduled to arrive by 9:00 a.m. and their flight was scheduled to leave a few minutes after eleven so Blase and Adrian agreed to meet in the airline's club room.

When he arrived, Blase was sitting at the bar drinking coffee and talking with another dermatologist she'd met. Adrian beamed as he walked toward her thinking, *She looks stunning*. Her posture was confident and elegant and her hair was a lot longer than it was in college and the last time he'd seen her.

Blase noticed someone approaching in her peripheral so she turned her head in his direction. She smiled as he walked up. Adrian, though a little heavier seemed more chiseled and defined. His hair was longer but still cut low to match his beard and mustache. It was a dark contrast for his light skin and blue eyes. He was dressed in relaxed jeans, a button up shirt, and a sports jacket with hard bottom brown shoes.

"Hi." Adrian put his carry-on bag down next to her bar stool.

"Hi," she responded, promptly reminded by how easily she could get lost in the swell of his eyes.

"Oh, Adrian. This is Dr. Dennison. He practices Dermatology as well and is on his way to California."

Adrian turned to Dr. Dennison and shook his hand. "Good to meet you."

"Are you a physician?" Dr. Dennison asked.

"No, I'm an attorney," Adrian replied confidently.

"Ah, well I hope you two enjoy your trip to The Seychelles. Dr. Morgan, it was a pleasure meeting you and you also Adrian. That's my flight they are announcing."

"Pleasure to meet you also, Dr. Dennison. Enjoy your trip," Blase said.

"Thank you."

When Dr. Dennison left his seat, Adrian sat down in it and he and Blase admired each other for a few minutes.

"Wow, Lace. You look more beautiful now then you did when we were twenty-one."

"Thank you! Owning a spa helps. Juliette and her massages keep me relaxed and stress free," she said. "You look great too. Your eyes still take my breath away!"

Adrian blushed. The bartender walked over and asked Adrian if he wanted anything. He ordered a cup of coffee.

They talked as if the world didn't exist around them. So much so, the front desk agent of the club room had to come over and pat Adrian on his shoulder to tell him that their flight was boarding and they announced their names. They had talked through two boarding announcements and one of their names. They asked the agent to call to the gate and tell them they were on their way. When they reached the gate, they apologized for the delay. The entire flight and first class was booked, so their seats were the only ones empty when they boarded the plane. The flight attendant immediately asked them if they wanted a beverage before they took off. They both asked for coffee and water to begin their 22 hour travel time.

Their conversation continued with them either holding hands or Adrian having his hand on Blase's thigh. He told her he enjoyed working at his firm, but was ready for a change. He started working with entertainers and artists and found it to be financially rewarding, but there weren't a lot of those types of clients in New Orleans so he was considering relocating to Miami or California. Mainly somewhere he and his brother could acquire more clients.

They rushed in Athens to their connecting flight and before they knew it the crew announced their decent into the Sitia airport.

"Wow, this flight went by quickly," Adrian noted.

"I know," Blase agreed.

"Or was it just the company?" Adrian asked blithely.

Blase smiled. "I think that's what it was," she returned.

They de-boarded the plane and Adrian carried his and Blase's carry-on bags to the baggage claim area. There was someone there holding a sign that read DR. MORGAN. Adrian retrieved their bags and the Flynn representative escorted them to the Flynn Mahe customer service office where they checked into their hut, decided on a few activities, and were given the information of the perks Mr. Flynn arranged for them. He arranged to have another helicopter from the airport to Flynn Mahe as well as a Flynn Yacht for them for three of their days to sail to two other Islands.

Adrian was blown away. They arrived at Flynn Mahe a little under an hour after they left the airport. Most of the helicopter ride was an air tour of The Seychelles Islands. Blase took photos of the seascape and of her and Adrian. When they pulled up to the main building, they were offered Takamaka Petit Ponch cocktails by the Flynn waitress and shortly after were escorted to their hut in a similar looking custom cart as the one in Jamaica, but this one was styled like a Mercedes. They drove through the Coco de Mar trees, Rothmannia Annae plants, and an array of Watsonia flowers under the 84 degree morning warmth to meet their hut keeper whose name was Chike. Chike was a soaring, obsidian man with shoulders that bragged over his perfectly etched body.

Blase asked Adrian if he minded having a male hut keeper.

"Not as long as you keep your eyes on me for this vacation," he said, smiling.

"You don't have to worry about that." She did however tell Chike that she would prefer he wear a t-shirt for their stay and he agreed without hesitation.

When he spoke, his voice was thin and matronly for such a large man. At the sound of his voice, Adrian smiled. Chike had their bottle of champagne chilled and opened as they requested while they were at the airport. He gave them their personal cell phone and told them there was no one checking in to the neighboring huts until the last day of their trip and he winked.

Blase and Adrian laughed. Since it was early, they ordered their lunch in the hut.

"Thank you my man, that's all we'll be needing for now," Adrian said as he reached in for a handshake. Chike's handshake was much like his voice, delicate.

As soon as Chike walked out, Adrian turned to Blase, pulled her close to him and said, "I think waiting seventeen years for a kiss is long enough." The kiss was deep and consuming.

At the end of it, Adrian opened the double shutter doors leading to the patio where the Jacuzzi and shower were. He stood outside the doors and began taking his clothes off were he stood. Blase was sifting through her suitcase for her bathing suit when she turned and noticed what he was doing.

She asked through her laughter, "What are you doing?"

"I'm about to get in this Jacuzzi, that's what I'm doing. Are you coming in?"

"With no clothes on?" she asked.

"Yes. What do we need clothes for? There won't be anyone around us for the entire trip."

Blase thought about it and agreed. She walked out the doors and watched Adrian with his glass of champagne smiling and soaking in the sun. She smiled and began undressing in front of him. With each article of clothing that she peeled off, Adrian's smile grew and so did his nature.

"Damn, Lace. You are still so damn beautiful."

"Oh, I bet you say that to all the girls," she said, smiling as she slid into the Jacuzzi and grabbed her glass of champagne.

"Here's to a love everlasting," Adrian boasted.

Blase touched her glass, curious by the toast.

"Come on Lace, you know you will always be my number one. You can only have one first love."

"You know you're right. You never quite love anyone like you do your first love," she added.

"Exactly," he said as he slid closer to her. They sat in the Jacuzzi, naked and sun drunk for the next two hours talking and playing with each other. They picked right back up where they left off when they were happy together. They carried on as if they were still in college but their maturation while apart was obvious and well received. They both had lived life, fallen in and out of love again, and realized they had a respect for the friendship they shared in addition to their love affair when they were in college.

# LUCKY NO. 5

The knock on the door forced Adrian to get out of the Jacuzzi and put his towel on to allow Chike to enter with their room service order. Blase got out and wrapped herself in her towel before he walked their food to the patio table. Chike set an arrangement of Gardenia flowers down and set the table for them. They ate and laughed about some of the funny things that happened during their long travels. By the time they finished lunch it was almost dinner time, but they were exhausted. They were up for about twenty-four hours give a few hours of sleep time while they were in the air. They both showered on the outdoor patio shower and climbed into bed fully naked. They slept in each other's arms until the sun prowled in through the shutters the next morning.

Adrian woke first, got up, and opened the shutter doors. When the sun occupied the room, Blase's eyes opened instantly. She covered them with her hand and looked to see Adrian's bare naked butt standing with one hand leaning on the doorframe looking out at the beach.

"Great view," Blase commented, which startled Adrian. He jumped and turned around.

"Better view," she said, smiling.

Adrian laughed. "I'm sorry. Did the sun wake you?" he asked.

"Yes it did, but if you're up then I want to be up. What time is it?"

"Almost seven. I'm still a little tired and jet lagged, but I'm ready to see what there is to get into here. This place is so dope, Lace. It's like 82 degrees already."

"Really? That's great. I checked our itinerary and the weather should be great for the rest of our trip."

They had another ten full days in Mahe. Fallon told her of the long flight so she booked an extra two days to account for the travel time. They showered again and dressed and decided on having breakfast in the resort's main restaurant. After breakfast they went swimming in the beach where they acted like the college sweethearts they were. Adrian complimented Blase every available moment. He didn't realize just how much he'd missed her. After an hour in the sun, Blase was fatigued. She suggested they change and go in to Victoria, the capital of the Mahe Island, and do a little shopping. She wanted to get that out of the way so she wouldn't forget. She told Adrian her brother and his wife and children were in town and she wanted to get something for them, her parents, and her friends. He happily agreed. They walked around and sipped coconut water while taking photos of local sites and people.

A few hours after their trip into Victoria, they were standing in front of a small house with an old couple sitting next to one another talking. They stopped and asked the couple if they could take a photo of them and one with them. As they walked away from the couple Blase and Adrian made up a whole story about their lives, supposing they had been married since they were teenagers and lived modestly in that small house and all they needed were each other.

"That's how I felt about you when we were in college," Blase remarked.

Adrian stopped walking. "Lace, I honestly don't know what came over me when we lived together. I guess I let my boys get in my head. I was afraid time would go by and I would be an old man with kids who hadn't lived and experienced life. Neither of us really talked about what we wanted to do after graduation so the first thing that popped in my mind was getting a law degree since my father and brothers were lawyers."

Blase looked intensely into Adrian's eyes as he continued. "I really didn't want to become a lawyer. I wanted to do something different but I didn't know what. When you moved out I could tell you had emotionally checked out of the relationship but instead of swallowing my pride and admitting my mistake I just let us go through the motions and figured I'd clean it up with a ring. I didn't even think you may have been making plans for a future without me."

He stroked Blase's face. "When I came to New York and you rejected me, I was devastated. When I left you, I couldn't immediately go to back to New Orleans. I called your parents and told them what happened and asked them not to mention it to you, and then I flew back to Washington, D.C. for a week. I didn't want to face my family either. My intentions were to propose and stay in New York with you and figure out what I was going to do from there. When I got to D.C., it was then that I really decided to go to law school after hanging out with some of my boys. So, I flew back to New Orleans and started studying for the LSAT. I never meant to hurt you, and I never meant for us not to spend the rest of our lives together. I figured there would never be a chance again. Until now. Why did you really invite me here?" he asked.

Blase was so busy gazing into his eyes and listening to his heart she had to clear her throat before she spoke. "I…I guess I wanted to see if there was still love between us. Once I made the decision to go to medical school, I didn't turn back and wasn't going to let anyone or anything stop me from my goal. Now, having reached my goal and happily enjoying my business, I don't want to come home to an empty house. I want the dream I had so many years ago."

Adrian leaned in and kissed Blase. This kiss sent one long stirring message down her back into her toes. This was Adrian, her Adrian, the first man she'd ever fallen in love with. She was happy in his arms, she was home in his arms. They stopped kissing and started hugging and Adrian whispered, "I still love you, Lace." Blase wilted further into his arms. She didn't tell him she loved him back, but she felt like it was right if for nothing but nostalgia's sake.

The next day they set sail on their yacht. They cruised to Alphonse and Bird Island for three days. It was exquisite. Fallon's father arranged for Chike to wait on them on the yacht along with a Flynn personal chef on demand as well. Blase and Adrian marveled at the prettiness of the island of Alphonse. On the third evening on their way to Bird Island they enjoyed a delightful dinner under the stars. The perfection of the entire trip was starting to settle in by the end of dinner, they were feeling romantic. They lay under the stars on the front end of the yacht and made out, like they used to in college. Within twenty minutes they retired to their cabin for a romantic experience in the middle of the Indian Ocean.

The remaining days of their trip were like the first few. They met more old couples sprinkled through town, talked about old friends and who was doing what with their lives. Adrian seemed to have stayed in touch with a lot of their friends from college whereas Blase left that part of her life behind her when she moved to New York, choosing only to remain close with a select few.

On the flight back to New York, they talked, slept, kissed, and laughed until their sides split. Adrian had a way of making Blase laugh more than anyone she'd ever known. At the airport, he asked if she would come down and visit him soon. She agreed without hesitation. She didn't want to leave him then, but knew she had other obligations. He asked, "What if my brother and I decided to move our practice to New York?"

Blase couldn't contain her smile. "Would you be doing that because you want to live in New York? I mean, had you thought of New York as a location before this trip?"

"Honestly, Lace, I hadn't. This trip was unbelievable. It was like the honeymoon we should've taken after the wedding we should've had. I think now, just like I thought back then we are meant to be together."

The sound of Adrian's heart speaking made Blase feel mushy and emotional. She couldn't believe she had so many unresolved emotions for him.

"Can we settle back into our lives for a while and make sure we are not just flying because we had a great vacation together?" she asked.

"Yeah that's fair. You know what, I agree with you. It's been a long time and we don't want to make life long decisions based on twelve days," he said as he caressed her face. "I need to get to my gate for my flight. I had a great time with you, Lace. Thank you for inviting me. If we do end up married, you really set the bar high for our actual honeymoon." He laughed.

"Start saving now," she said flirtatiously.

"I will," he responded confidently. He kissed and hugged her one last time and they parted ways.

"Call me when you get to New Orleans," she said.

"Of course," he responded as he walked away. When Blase walked outside to get into her limo to go home, she turned her phone on and all of her messages popped up with rapid fire. She scrolled through her text messages and the most recent was from Adrian; *An amazing vacation with an amazing woman. I love you!*

She replied: *It was amazing because you were with me. I love you too. Travel safe!*

When Blase arrived home, her brother and his family had already left for California. She saw that Sugar was gone and called Sheridan.

Sheridan told her she came over and was out walking her which made Blase happy because she was so exhausted. She dropped her bags at the door and went straight to bed. She slept until her phone rang.

"You made it home safe?" she answered.

"Yes. You sound like you're sleeping," he replied.

"I was, but I set my phone to a special ringtone for your call."

Adrian smiled. "Go back to sleep. We'll talk tomorrow."

"Okay."

"Sleep well, baby."

Still half sleep she whispered, "You too."

Adrian chuckled and hung up.

Sheridan came back from walking Sugar and noticed Blase's bags but didn't see or hear her. She opened her bedroom door and saw she was sound asleep. Deciding not to wake her, she collected her things and left to go to her boyfriend's house.

**THE** next morning, Blase woke up still feeling lethargic and heavy headed. She decided to stay home since she didn't book any clients for that day either. She called Tracey for their morning conference call after she made herself a cup of coffee.

Tracey told her everything was fine, but they needed to discuss how busy the practice was getting and possibly expanding the practice's hours. Blase told her she only had one additional vacation and then she would be back in full swing. She explained to Tracey before taking her on that it might be hectic while she went on her vacations but she would take up the slack while she was in town and after the vacations. Blase spent the rest of the day catching up on emails and phone calls. She had a brief conversation with Sheridan about the new staff and some administrative issues. Sheridan asked her about the trip and she told her she would have to talk with her about it another time, but briefly told her it was beautiful. While Blase was walking Sugar, she dialed Fallon. Fallon answered, "Did you get my message?"

"No, when did you leave me a message?"

"While you were frolicking in Mahe."

"What did it say?"

"I'm pregnant, B!"

"WHAT? Congratulations, honey! How far along are you?"

"I'm about five weeks according to my Gynecologist."

"That is wonderful news. I'm going to be an Auntie! Are you excited?"

"I'm more nervous than excited. A Mom, B! Me?"

"What do you mean you? You'll be a great mother and if it's a girl, she'll be the best dressed little girl in town."

Fallon laughed. "I mean I'm nervous. That's another life, a tiny little life."

"Well I'm here and with Sergio's family, you'll be fine."

"I couldn't wait for you to call me so I could tell you. I haven't told anyone else. Only Sergio, his sisters and I know. I told him I didn't want to tell anyone else until I told you."

"Oh, honey, thank you. I love you, girl."

"So how was the trip? You know what I want to know first."

"The flight was long as hell, but Flynn Mahe was incredible, Fallon. Your father arranged a yacht for us for three days. Did you know he was doing that?"

"He didn't tell me what it was, but he told me it would blow your mind."

"It did. Mine and Adrian's."

"Great!"

"The staff was great and the resort was the most beautiful place that I've ever seen. It was so organic and peaceful."

"That's great to hear. I haven't been to Dad's Mahe resort, so you have a leg up on me there. Sergio and I were planning to go this winter, but now that I'm pregnant I'm sure he won't let me travel anywhere."

"We have to start shopping," Blase said.

Fallon abashedly replied, "I've already started."

"Of course you have, I know who I'm talking to."

"And Adrian? Was he better than Miller?"

"Fallon, he was perfect. Everything was perfect."

"More perfect than Cup?"

Blase sighed. "I guess because Adrian and I have such a long history it felt more perfect than Cup. I had a great time with Cup and my heart feels beautiful when I'm with him also. This is crazy, Fal. I really didn't expect Adrian and me to have such a good time since we hadn't seen or barely spoken to one another in so many years."

"My heart is breaking for you, B. You have two successful men who still seem to love you. What shall you do?" she said mockingly.

"Oh hush. Wasn't this the point of the trips?"

"Either this or to boost your ego through the roof."

344

Blase sucked her teeth. "Listen Miller and Walter certainly weren't ego boosters."

"True."

"Damn!" Blase exclaimed

"What?" Fallon said.

"Sugar just went to the bathroom on someone's bag while I wasn't watching. Let me go. I'll call you tomorrow. Lunch later this week?"

"As always."

"Okay. Congratulations again! Tell Sergio I said congratulations."

"I will."

As promised, Blase picked up a lot of the slack from her absence. So much so, she made Tracey take a few days off despite her resistance. Two weeks after returning from Mahe, Blase's body was just getting back to normal from her jet lag. She was talking with Cup and Adrian regularly, but made no formal arrangements to see either again as yet.

Bryant noticed her lack of responses to his correspondences and grew concerned that she may have fallen in love on her recent trip. He finally got her on the phone. "Did I lose you?" he asked.

Blase giggled. "No, I'm still here and I'm still single."

"How was your trip to The Seychelles? Was your college sweetheart better than the Hollywood Football player?"

"Much!"

"I don't know whether to be happy or worried."

"No need to worry. You've been a great friend, Bryant. I appreciate your friendship and would let you know if something major happened."

"That's good to hear. So can I see you before you fly off for your last vacation? The last one might be the charm. What did you say on New

Year's Eve, Lucky number five? I want to see you in case you come home married."

"I would never come home married. I have too many people who wouldn't let me live it down."

"So can I see you?"

"Sure. Are you free for dinner later this week?"

"I'm free anytime you're free," he said.

"Thursday night?"

"Thursday night," he confirmed.

"Okay, I'll cook," she said.

"You will?" his voice lifted.

"Oh please. I cook."

Bryant huffed. "But is it good?"

"Time will tell."

"Yes it will. I will see you Thursday. What time should I be there?"

"Eight works for me."

"See you Thursday at eight."

"See you then." They hung up.

Dinner with Bryant was entertaining as usual. He was easy to talk to and enjoyable to be around. As the Cayman Island trip drew near, Blase wasn't sure she wanted to go. She was exhausted with traveling and not sure she wanted to revisit her relationship with Mark, but she had to follow through with her plans so she would go.

Before she left she checked on Brielle to see how things were going. Brielle told her the pregnancy was going well and Dwight was new and improved. She was content. Her family was together again and she felt complete. Blase was still leery of Dwight but pleased to hear her friend was happy again after years of seeming to be in a veil of pessimism.

# The Cayman Islands

**SATURDAY** rolled around effortlessly after her dinner with Bryant. Blase sat at the Brooklyn Brewery in JFK airport waiting for Mark's arrival. Their flight was on time and Blase was early arriving at the airport. She sipped some of her diet soda and felt a tap on her shoulder. She turned around in her bar stool and saw Mark standing there with a backpack on his right shoulder, a smile, and what appeared to be twenty-five extra pounds on him. "Good afternoon, Belleza!"

"Good afternoon, Mark. Was your check-in okay?"

"Yes."

Blase stood up and gave him a hug. The extra pounds were solid, but not defined.

Mark thought Blase looked stunning as he always did.

"Sit down and join me," she said.

"Okay. What you are drinking?"

"Diet soda. Would you like one?"

Mark smirked. "Are you trying to tell me something already?" he asked, feeling insecure about his additional weight.

"No, I didn't mean it like that. I think the extra weight looks great on you," she said in an attempt to make him feel comfortable. "More of you to hold on too."

Mark smiled as he put his backpack on the stool next to him. "I'll have a club soda with lime," he told the bartender. "You look beautiful as always." He turned to get a good look at Blase.

"Thank you. Owning a wellness spa has its benefits," she said as she took a sip of her soda.

Mark looked good. Despite the weight, he looked like the same, fine, wholehearted, and welcoming man she always retreated to.

"We have about an hour before our flight. Do you want to get something to eat?" Blase asked.

"If you do, sure."

They ordered two sandwiches and talked. Mark told Blase he was really skeptical of coming on the trip given that the last time they saw one another she left him. Blase apologized for leaving him, but she really didn't want to hurt him any further. She didn't realize the conversation would come up so soon.

"Why did you leave?" Mark asked innocently between sips.

"Mark, you proposed. If I would've said no, it would've ruined our trip anyway and I couldn't face your family."

"Why did you say no?"

"Huh?" Blase was confused.

"Belleza, by you leaving you said no. So why did you say no? Why didn't you see me as someone who could be your husband? Why do you want me here with you if you didn't want me to be your husband?" Mark's tone hinted of resentment.

Blase knew she would have to deal with anger from him. "Mark, it was less about you and more about that time in my life. I probably should've been more decisive with you and us and I certainly should've been more forthright—"

He interrupted her. "Yes, I mean Blase you'd strung me along for so long. It wasn't until you left that I thought about all of the years of our relationship and I feel like you used me emotionally."

Blase was quiet as she sipped her soda. Just then the waitress brought their sandwiches to the table. Blase had no choice but to face reality and fess up. "You're right, I did. In hindsight I can see how I treated you. To me, you were always reliable, Mark and your love for me had always made me feel secure. But I took it and you for granted. I apologize."

"You're damn right you did," he said, taking a sip of his seltzer. "I was so angry with you, Belleza. I thought I could never forgive you or let go of the hurt. Our entire history was you walking out on me or choosing some athlete over me."

"Mark, it wasn't like that. It wasn't about me choosing anyone over you, honestly. It was about me just not appreciating you for who you are, and for that I sincerely apologize. I can't take back the past, but I can try and make it right between us now, no matter what the outcome. I know you're in a relationship, but I just felt like I owed you an apology."

"So we are going to the Cayman Islands as an 'I'm sorry' vacation?"

Blase's heart hurried. She thought Mark might curse her out and walk out on her right there. "No, not at all. Well it could be that, but it's more of a 'hey give me another chance' vacation."

Mark heard those words and every wonderful feeling he'd ever had for Blase jolted through him. He was overwhelmed. So much so, the middle of his throat swelled and his face reddened. All he'd ever wanted was for her to see him the way he saw her and her acknowledging that she wanted another chance packed his heart with elation and possibility. He swallowed the knot and turned to face Blase. "Is this really a trip for us to try again, or is this a 'let me see if Mark still has feelings for me because he's secure and gullible' trip?"

"Mark, please babe. I don't want us to start our trip angry. I really did ask you to come with me to see if there is any love between us—"

"Between us or if you could love me the way that I'd loved you?" he asked not letting up.

"Yes!" she exclaimed. "This trip is to see if I could possibly love you the way you've always loved me. I don't know what the outcome will be, but I wanted to give it a try. Are you still willing to go with me?" She was frustrated he wouldn't allow her to be her usual elusive self with him.

"Thank you. Finally you're being completely honest with me. I have one more question. Have you taken anyone else away on one of these vacations?"

Blase felt like she was on trial, but she understood why. She'd tested Mark's manhood more than once. She looked straight ahead and exhaustedly answered, "Yes. I have, Mark." She turned to look at him. "But it was only because I had unresolved issues with the others—"

Mark interrupted. "Others? Coño, Belleza! How many of these vacations have you taken?"

She laid it all on the line. "Four others."

Mark stood from his stool and looked at Blase as if she was out of her mind. He rubbed the back of his neck with his hand, shook his head, picked up his bag, and left.

"Mark, don't leave." Blase tried to call him as quietly as she could to avoid a scene, but Mark continued walking away.

Blase sat feeling exposed and idiotic. She wasn't prepared for that. She kept looking around, hoping Mark just needed to go for a walk, but by the time they called their flight for boarding she realized he wasn't coming back. She grabbed her carry-on bag and headed for the plane. She sat down in business class and started crying. She hadn't thought of how unfair her trips would be to the men until then, particularly to Mark.

The flight attendant offered her a box of tissues and asked her if she could get her something else. Blase declined. She texted Fallon and told her what happened. Fallon texted her back and told her not to go. Blase said she was going to go to really collect her thoughts and figure out what she'd been doing over the past few months. Fallon supported her decision and told her she loved her.

The flight crew made an announcement and as the flight attendants were walking to the front to close the doors, Mark walked through them and looked at Blase who was looking out the window. He sat next to her and put his hand on her thigh. She turned to see who it was and when she saw him she cried harder. As the plane pulled away from the gate, all she could say over and over again was she was so sorry. Mark leaned in, hugged Blase, and forgave her again.

They arrived in the Cayman Islands to flawless weather conditions. Mark was calm and relieved he decided to go back to the gate and take the trip. After their hug, Blase and Mark ordered drinks and talked. Their limo driver took them to the Ritz where they immediately went to lunch before even going to their hotel room.

"Belleza, I know I agreed to come on this trip to see if there is any love left between us but I don't want to lead you on. I don't want to cheat on my girlfriend, so I want to say this up front. I cannot make love to you on this trip."

352

Blase smiled. "Mark, I don't expect you to cheat on her and I certainly didn't assume we would make love. I just wanted to be here with you so we could talk and become friends again. That's all I want." Mark looked at Blase, stroked her face, and kissed her on her nose.

Their trip was just as Blase thought it was be—pleasant, peaceful, and caring. They didn't do anything but lay on the beach, eat, and drink. Mark got to know Blase, the Blase he never knew, the one who told him everything, the one who looked at him like he was worthy. Mark was happy; he was where he wanted to be. Respected.

When they arrived back in New York, Mark was honest with Blase and told her he had a wonderful time, but he didn't want to break his girlfriend's heart. He felt like he owed her a chance at the possibility of a life together. There was nothing wrong with their relationship, so he wasn't going to make any hasty decisions based on one vacation. Blase understood, although her ego wanted him to make the decision to leave her. Even though she wasn't sure what she wanted from him. They parted ways with a promise to stay in touch, but he asked Blase to respect his relationship. Blase wouldn't think of compromising his happiness for her selfishness anymore. She agreed.

**BLASE** was consumed. She spent the past five months on a mission of the heart and needed her friends. She walked in the house, sat on the sofa, and sent a mass text message to her girlfriends that read:

*Subject: SOS*

*I'm home and I need my girls. Dinner 2moro @ Shelly's NY @ 7. No is not an option. C U then!*

Everyone sent separate text messages back agreeing to meet her. The anticipation and curiosity must've gotten to all of her friends, because they all arrived at exactly seven. Blase, however, was late. She didn't walk in until ten minutes after seven. They were sitting at a table chatting waiting for her sipping on Perrier. Sheridan didn't want to be the only one drinking, so she started with Perrier water also. Blase smiled at the sight of her friends. They all smiled back as she approached.

"You look well rested." Brielle spoke first.

Blase laughed. "As well rested as I am, I feel exhausted."

"Why? Did you party that much alone in the Caymans?" Fallon asked.

Blase rolled her eyes. "Right. Last we spoke, I was alone. After I finished texting you, Mark made a quiet entrance onto the plane and we went together after all."

Brielle and Sheridan listened, not knowing what they were talking about. Blase turned to them and told them what happened at the airport.

Brielle had no comment, and Sheridan just said, "Wow!"

The waitress came over and asked Blase what she wanted to drink. She ordered a French martini. After she ordered, Sheridan took that as a permission slip and asked for the same thing.

"Thank you. I certainly don't want to drink alone," Blase said.

"You never have to worry about that as long as I'm around," Sheridan said, smiling.

Blase surveyed her friends. Though she had been seeing them between her trips, it was as if this was the first time she'd seen them in months. Brielle filled out nicely as her body embraced her pregnancy. Blase didn't know if it was the pregnancy that looked good on her or the contentment of being back with Dwight.

354

Fallon, though she still didn't look pregnant, glowed as bright as her diamonds. Sheridan, with her new responsibilities and new relationship, looked more at ease. She began seeing a personal shopper to dress accordingly for all of her boyfriend's corporate functions. She looked matured.

Blase looked down at her hand as she set her martini glass back on the table. "Is that a ring?" she asked Sheridan.

Sheridan was thrown off by the question still waiting to hear about Blase's trip to the Caymans. "Yes!" she said excitedly. "Greg proposed the day after you left!"

All of the women congratulated Sheridan and asked to see her ring. Sheridan's ring was a four-carat round diamond in a vintage 1920's halo setting. She showed it off and told everyone it was Greg's grandmother's ring.

"That's beautiful," Blase said. She looked at all of her friends again. Everyone at the table was in wedded or soon to be wedded bliss. She talked with them about all of the vacations and compared them all. Brielle said she wasn't surprised to hear that Miller was a jerk. Fallon concurred. She was glad she didn't like her trip with Walter because secretly Fallon didn't like Walter for Blase. They all gave their opinions, advice, and support over dinner. Blase was thankful to have such a devoted group of friends. She was happy she made the trips and reunited with all of the men, be it good or bad. It was an experience she would never forget. Before their dessert was brought to the table, Fallon gave Blase a gift. It was a scrapbook of her trips.

"How did you do this so fast? I just got back from the Cayman's last night?" Blase asked.

Fallon admitted, "I told you Diane was the best."

Blase reached in and kissed Fallon. She skimmed through the book and smiled. After it was all said and done, Blase decided whatever happens with Adrian, Mark, Cup, or even Bryant was meant to be and only God and time will decide the outcome.

# BLISS

# Addis Ababa

**THE** anticipation grew as Blase's plane landed in Ethiopia. She was excited about seeing her grandparents as well as her extended family. However, she was less thrilled about another twenty plus hour flight to Africa. This time she prepared herself a little better and spent the day before her trip drinking a gallon of water to make sure she was hydrated. Blase hadn't seen her grandparents since her brother's wedding almost five years ago. Her parents flew on the same flight as well spending most of their time awake reminiscing about Benny and Blase's adolescent years, her determination, her vacations, and what she'd hoped to achieve from them.

"I hope I achieved what I wanted, Mom, but we'll see," she said, smiling as she turned and looked in the seats behind them to see if their conversation could be heard.

Her father remained silent. Her mother said, "I hope so too," as she turned around in her seat and smiled at Blase's father. All of the smiling was too much for Mr. Morgan, so he nodded as he got up and went to walk around to stretch his legs. When he walked away, Blase's mother whispered, "Your father never said anything about your trips, so I'm not sure if he completely approved of them, but I know he wants you to be happy and I definitely know he wants you to have children." She flipped through the airline's magazine.

"Really, Mom? Did he tell you that?"

"Yes, he did. He said all of those brains and that beauty shouldn't go to waste," she said with a giggle. "And I agree with your father. You know, Melesse, you have danced to the beat of your own drums and we have always respected your decisions and believed that you were making the right choices for yourself. If I haven't told you before, I'm proud of you and you know I love you, sweetheart."

"Thank you, Mom. I love you too. You and Daddy set the bar high, so I really appreciate that." She reached in and gave her mother a kiss.

They were greeted at the airport by what seemed like dozens of extended Melesse family members. Benny's family's flight was scheduled to land fifteen minutes before theirs so they all planned on taking the same car to Blase's grandparent's house. Blase greeted her cousins with a hug and greetings in Amharic. Some of them, whom she hadn't met, were surprised at how well she spoke the language. Her mother greeted a few of her cousins she hadn't seen in years with tears and the site of this made Blase emotional as well. Mr. Morgan shared in these reactions, but for a different reason—Addis Ababa was where Blase's parents were married.

Within 30 minutes of the Melesse family standing and talking in the airport, Benny and his wife approached with children running amok. Everyone cheered and greeted them the way they greeted Blase and her parents. Benny was less fluent in Amharic so he spoke in English. They all left and traveled back to the grandparents' house and helped prepare for the big celebration.

ON the fifth day of Blase's visit, the day of her grandfather's party, she sat in the guest bathroom and stared at herself in the mirror. Her connection to Ethiopia was profounder on this trip than any other. To her, it felt almost unreal, with her family and the spirit of her ancestors around her, she was humbled. She finished getting dressed and decided to walk through her grandparents' house before she went to the backyard where the party was taking place.

Dr. Hagos Melesse and Mrs. Selam Melesse lived in a grand stucco contemporary style tri-level home that resembled an ornate church in many parts of the United States. It had a horseshoe driveway with a white stone three-tiered bird feeder on the lawn. There were four decorative wrought iron exterior terraces, one overlooking the generous tailored backyard lawn which was coupled with over 400 square feet of stone patio and another three tiered bird feeder.

Blase walked through the bathroom door and peered around the octagon hallway until she looked back into her guestroom, which now seemed so small in comparison to when she would come when she was a little girl. She walked down the hall and opened the second guest bedroom door and smiled because her grandmother was meticulous, and she made sure everything was the same when they stayed there. The artwork on the third level was all made by relatives. A painting signed by a cousin, another signed by a baby cousin, a drawing signed by an aunt, and a hand carved shield done by her grandfather. Blase made a mental note to see if her grandmother had any extra artwork in the house she could take back home with her.

The hardwood floors under the hallway rugs were spangled, and the floral wrought iron railing overlooking the second floor was custom designed according to her grandmother. Blase trailed her hand on the railing as she walked down the stairs to the second level. She strolled down the hallway looking at all of the family photos on the walls. Many of the family members on the wall she was reuniting with for the first time as an adult that day. Her grandmother had a knack for placing the photos in such a way that the frames, even if empty would've looked decorative on the walls.

*Maybe it's because Wund Ayat made each frame,* she thought.

She opened the two guest room doors on that level and walked in both of the bathrooms to smell the towels in each. Her grandmother would wash the towels with different perfumed soaps for each bathroom when she was a child and she told their housekeeper to continue the tradition. Blase inhaled them all. When she walked into the master bedroom, the air tasted like a fusion of her grandmother's gardenia soap and her grandfather's scent of timber. All the furniture in their bedroom was minimalistic wood hand carved and stained by her grandfather.

"What an amazing couple," she said out loud as she lay back on the bed.

"With an amazing granddaughter," she heard a voice say.

She looked over and saw Adrian standing in the doorway.

"Where did you come from?" she asked.

"I was out back talking with your grandmother and she insisted I come in and tell you to come outside, so I came looking for you. When I saw you looking at the photos, I didn't want to interrupt."

He walked over to the bed and lay down next to her. They both looked at the ceiling in silence breathing in the fragrance of part of Blase's history, her grandparents' loyalty, romance, and their seventy-five years of true love.

Without looking at her or saying a word, he took Blase's left hand into his and slipped a diamond ring on her ring finger. Blase didn't turn her head or say a word when she felt the ring, she just smiled.